Moving Targets

ALSO BY WILLIAM J. REYNOLDS

The Nebraska Quotient

MOVING TARGETS

William J. Reynolds

St. Martin's Press / *New York*

MOVING TARGETS.

 For information, address St. Martin's Press, 175 Fifth Avenue, New York, N.Y. 10010.

Design by Laura Hough

Library of Congress Cataloging in Publication Data

Reynolds, William J.
Moving targets.

I. Title.
PS3568.E93M6 1986 813'.54 86-3662
ISBN 0-312-55072-3

First Edition

10 9 8 7 6 5 4 3 2 1

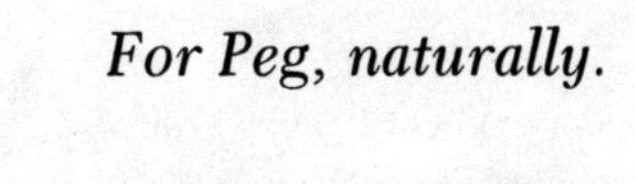

For Peg, naturally.

Moving Targets

Chapter One

A hard, gritty, sandy snow filled in the wrinkles and depressions of his clothing, half-hid one booted foot, and collected in his right ear. He didn't mind. He wouldn't mind anything, ever again. People get that way when they're dead.

And Jack Castelar was dead, all right. No question. Even from twenty, thirty feet away, even in the gray predawn, I could see he had that look, the look the dead take on almost immediately when life leaves them. Something—some indefinable *something*—abandons them. They change. It's a subtle thing. I can't describe it, but I can recognize it.

Less subtle was the black and evil-looking wound in Castelar's right temple, about an inch north-northwest of his eye, and the reddened snow in which he lay, face-down, his left ear pressed to the cold country backroad as if he were listening for the Wells Fargo wagon. You don't have to have read as many detective novels as I have to figure out the story.

I stood near the body, shivering, trying to burrow deeper into the fur lining of my coat. A parka, I'm afraid, not a trenchcoat. The latter is in keeping with the image of the private eye, but the former was better suited to the weather. It was going to be a cold one. Hell, it already was. The skies had cleared overnight and the wind was steady and the cold behind it was that dry, brittle cold that makes your fillings ache and cuts right through you like a scythe, no matter how warmly you dress. It was bad in the city; it was worse out here in the open, among these few lonely farm buildings scattered like forgotten toys on the outskirts of Omaha. It was, I reflected, the kind of weather that paralyzes cars, overtaxes furnaces, and kills people.

Jack Castelar wasn't among those people, though. He was dead before he dropped, in the middle of the road at the end of his own driveway, six or eight hundred feet from the privacy of his own home. He never knew what hit him.

I could empathize. There was a lot here I didn't get, either. Who killed Castelar, sure; but also more basic stuff like why *I* was there, why Mike Kennerly had called me out of a nice, warm bed and into the cold, dark world, saying only that something terrible had happened and that he wanted me there—here—in the middle of nowhere, ASAP.

Kennerly was right; something terrible *had* happened. But he didn't need me to tell him that. What he did need me for remained to be seen.

Some boys from the county came to remove the decedent. Since they had jobs to do and were probably no happier than I was to have been called out at that ridiculous hour, I moved away to let them work. But I moved slowly; the stuff underfoot was treacherous. The grainy snow that had fallen intermittently since midnight, whisked around by winds gusting to sixty miles an hour, acted like jeweler's rouge on the existing hard-pack, polishing it to a perilous sheen. On it I walked, we all walked, with the uncertain, jerky stiff-leggedness of a newborn colt.

Fortunately, once I had moved to the side of the narrow and unpaved road I had plenty of things to hang on to; the road was well lined with various county, state, and Omaha city vehicles—police, sheriff, medical—as well as several unmarked sedans, some with tax-exempt plates, some without. I understood then why the OPD uniform had made me leave my car at the intersection of the main road and hoof it the quarter-mile or so to what we trained detectives and late-night TV enthusiasts call the scene of the crime.

It takes a lot of people to investigate a homicide—more than you might think—but not, usually, this many. The number of cars plus the number of people, garishly colored by the flashing and blinking emergency lights as they moved in their various activities, added up to one answer: Jack Castelar had been a pretty important man, even if I had never heard of him until the previous afternoon. Having heard of him, I knew that he was—had been—the president of the West Omaha State Bank and Trust, a small but lucrative family-owned bank somewhere out in these parts, so far on the edge of town that it was in fact out of town, despite the name. If the pond was on the small side, Castelar was still a big enough frog. Now a big *dead* frog, and all the other frogs, small, medium, and large-economy-size, would want to know why.

And that, as they say, plus ten cents . . .

I spotted Mike Kennerly in a small knot of people perhaps twenty feet from where I stood casually clinging for dear life to a conveniently parked van. He was engaged in animated conversation with three other men and a woman. I couldn't hear them, but I didn't need to in order to get the gist of the discussion. I left the slight wind break afforded by the van and carefully slid toward the group. Barely three steps later a cop stopped me.

He was county, not OPD. The uniform was styled differently, the trousers were gray instead of blue, and the badge was a star, not a shield. If that wasn't enough, he wore a big patch on his shoulder that said DEPUTY SHERIFF in gold letters. Guys in my line of work know how to spot vital clues like that.

The deputy was big—tall—but kind of bony and angular. He wore a small blond mustache (frosting over), a thick down-filled jacket (regulation), and a cap with the visor pulled low over his eyes (even though the sun hadn't yet put in an appearance). The eyes beneath the visor were expressionless. His rectangular plastic name tag read G. KNUT. G. Knut carried a fourteen-inch Kel-Lite—one of those long black aluminum flashlights that traffic cops always tote—which came down in front of me like a barricade at a toll booth, and with much the same effect.

"Going somewhere?" Knut asked.

"Over there." Okay, not a brilliant riposte, but it was very early and I was very cold and, you have to admit, the question wasn't too bright either.

"I don't think so, pal," Knut drawled in the sort of voice you pick up watching too many cop shows. "No sightseers. If you're press, you wait up there with the rest of them." He used his long, wedge-shaped chin to point up the road, the way I'd just come. "If you're not, you just head back that way anyhow and keep going, okay?"

"Look, it's all right. I'm supposed to be here. Mike Kennerly sent for me—"

"Well, that's between you and him. What's between you and me is me telling you to take off—so *take off!*"

With that he gave me a shove. Not even a shove. A prod, just a little prod of his left hand against my right shoulder. Nothing to it. Except I was trying to catch Kennerly's eye, to get him to come explain to this bullet-head who I was and that I belonged there, so I didn't see it coming. I wasn't prepared for it. My boots slipped on the waxy surface. I grabbed for something to break my fall, and the nearest something was Knut's outstretched flashlight.

We took a quick turn on the dance floor and when the music stopped, one of us lay flat on his back gazing uncomprehendingly at the slowly lightening sky. And it wasn't me.

Knut was making some completely baseless speculations on my lineage as Kennerly and the woman he had been in conference with came over as quickly as they could. The woman was saying, "Jesus, Knut, we've already got *one* corpse," and Kennerly was saying, "Nebraska, where in hell have you been?" and the cop was saying, "Shit, lady, I thought *your* people were supposed to secure the scene," and I was saying, "Frozen battery, Mike, you know it *is* about 273 degrees below," and so on. We eventually decided that Knut wasn't permanently damaged and hauled him to his feet. He fixed me with a long, hard, Charles Bronson–type stare that I guess was supposed to set me to shivering in my boots—I *was* shivering, but I'm afraid it was because of the temperature, not his steely squint—turned, and stalked angrily, bruisedly away.

I said, "He should cut out that daredevil stuff before he winds up in traction."

"No sense, no feeling," Kennerly's friend said. Then, turning to me: "Okay, show's over; what *are* you doing here? Who are you?"

Kennerly answered. "This is the private investigator I was telling you about, Detective. Nebraska, this is Detective Kim Banner, OPD Homicide."

"Oh, yeah, wonderful," said Banner cynically. "That's just what I need—Philip Marlowe come to crack the case for me." Banner was a compact woman, perhaps thirty-five, thirty-six years old. Her voice had a hoarseness to it, and when she spoke I caught the heavy, sweet scent of throat lozenges on the cloud of her breath. She looked up at me speculatively. "Somehow, with a name like Nebraska, I expected you to gallop up on a white stallion."

"He's too hard to find in the snow," I said pleasantly. I could have told her the endlessly entertaining story of the origin of the surname: How my dad's old man, in patriotic fervor, named himself after the place fate and an empty wallet deposited him when he came over from the Old Country; how I, personally, was forever grateful that he hadn't ended up in Tallahassee; how—well, you get the idea. But I had discovered back in the sixth grade, which is so far the last time I punched somebody out for cracking wise about the name, that if people want to hear the story, they'll ask. If they don't, it's only wasted on them. Banner didn't ask, so I didn't volunteer it. Instead I kept quiet and studied her studying me.

There wasn't much of her to study, though there was plenty of knee-length black leather coat, long gray scarf and matching gloves, and black Russian-looking hat with pull-down earflaps. But I liked what little of her I could see—mainly, about three square inches of frostbite-courting face; a narrow, pointed nose; small, dark eyes; and a few stray wisps of dark blond or light brown hair. Kim Banner was small but seemed strong and projected an aura of easy competence like competence was something she possessed, not something she had read about in a self-help article.

She quickly worked her way from my Irish walking hat to my L. L. Bean Sub-Zero Pacs and back up to my face, taking it all in, filing it all away. I'd've bet she was damn good on the witness stand.

"You don't look like much of a Philip Marlowe to me, Nebraska." The throat disk clicked against her teeth.

"Pleased to meet you, too."

"Wow, what a sharp wit. Am I bleeding, Kennerly?" She snatched off the black hat and scrubbed a hand through her hair a couple of times. Blond. The hair was blond, but that deep shade we used to call dishwater-blond before, I guess, everyone got dishwashers and forgot what color dishwater was. Her hair was of medium length and she wore it in a nondescript noncut that I imagined was easy to take care of. She slapped the hat back over it, tugged down the earflaps, and said, "Okay, look, Nebraska, I'll give it to you the way I already gave it to Kennerly. I don't want to be a bitch, but I do have a homicide to investigate here. Jack Castelar was a pretty important guy with some pretty important friends, so that means I'm going to be dinking around with the media and my lieutenant and the brass downtown and Castelar's pin-striped Rotarian buddies and for all I know Mike Wallace, too. 'Why isn't the investigation proceeding faster?' 'Why haven't you made any arrests?' 'Why aren't there any new leads?' That's the sort of stuff they'll want to know, and it won't do me any good to tell them it's because I've been spending my time answering idiot questions from dildos like *them*.

"Then there's this doofus Knut, a real hot dog. He thinks he should have the case because *he* got here *first*, which I guess gives him dibs on it or something. Never mind that the sheriff doesn't have the manpower or the facilities to handle this kind of investigation—and, being a pretty smart fellow, wouldn't want the hassle of it even if he did. Knut, he doesn't care. He can smell the headlines from here. He thinks."

She paused, finally, for air. "So the upshot is," she resumed, "I don't have time to mess around with Castelar's lawyer and a small-time private eye on top of it. The law says you're entitled to poke around. Personally, I think you should wait and see if just maybe we can do the job before you go spending your time and money playing Holmes and Watson or Starsky and Hutch or Batman and Robin or whoever you are. But the law says you're entitled, and my boss says cooperate with Mr. Kennerly here. Fine. I don't have any trouble with that—*as long as* you stay out of my hair. If you don't, the law says *I'm* entitled to shut you down. And I will, gentlemen, believe me, in a minute. Do you follow me?"

"Like a trail of bread crumbs."

Banner looked bleakly at Kennerly, then back at me. "You know," she said, "I don't think I like your attitude."

"'Yeah, I've had complaints about it, but it just keeps getting worse.' Dick Powell to Douglas Walton in *Murder, My Sweet*."

"What?"

"Hey, you wanted Philip Marlowe."

She started to say something, stopped, frowned, then, finally, said quietly, "Nebraska, you really don't want to fuck with me."

I try to exercise my self-restraint once a day, just to keep it from getting fat. This looked like a good time for it. So I simply said, "Sorry."

Banner made a vague gesture with one gloved hand as she half walked, half skated to where Castelar had reposed only a couple of minutes ago, where warm blood leaking from the exit wound in his head had eroded a deep cavity in the soiled snow.

Kennerly, at my elbow, said, "Making friends wherever you go."

"Yeah, well, maybe if I just understood what I was doing here . . ."

"Hey, Sam Spade," Banner called. "The counselor asked me if I would fill you in, so if you could spare a minute . . ." Kennerly poked me and motioned me forward, but I stood my ground.

"Forget about it," I said stubbornly. "You wake me up at four in the morning—a bloody damn cold *January* morning, for Crissake—you don't tell me what in hell for, but that I should get dressed, get in my car, and get out here, about eight hundred million miles from civilization."

"Gentlemen," Banner called.

"Nebraska," said Kennerly.

I ignored them both. "So I get downstairs—haven't even had a crummy cup of coffee—and find I've got a battery-flavored Popsicle under the hood. Luckily I have a neighbor who starts work at six, and she was already up. I got her to drop me at an all-night truck stop, bought a new battery, conned a guy into giving me a lift back, installed the battery *in the dark*, and beat ass out here."

"Guys," Banner said.

"Nebraska," Kennerly repeated.

"And for what?" I said obstinately. "To freeze my tail off, get pushed around by crazy cops, and learn about cases that don't have anything to do with me? No, thanks, amigo. I'm not taking another step, except back to my car, unless I find out just what the hell I'm doing here."

"Well, if you'd shut up I'd be delighted to tell you," Kennerly said with quiet venom. "Just one minute, please, Detective," he called to Banner, who I swear had steam rising off her. Then he grabbed me by the elbow in a surprisingly strong grip—Kennerly's a pretty small and slight guy—spun me in the direction away from Banner, and said in low tones, "All right, listen closely. The man they just took away was not only my client, he was my friend. Okay? Know that up front. Now: Jack's flight back from Denver last night was delayed by bad weather. It didn't get in until after midnight. He cabbed it from the airport, probably because it was late and the weather was lousy and he didn't want to drag anyone out to come get him.

"As you can see, the driveway is blocked with snow, so the driver let him out here in the road and, presumably, drove off. The killer must have stood in those trees on the other side of the road"—I turned to look but he pulled me back—"and he must have called Jack's name or made some sort of noise, because the forensics people say Jack was turning in that direction when . . . when the bullet caught him in the temple and spun him back toward the house."

Kennerly paused, composing himself a minute, then plunged in again in the same hurried, breathless way. "The police estimate this must have been between one and one-thirty. The body was discovered at around four, when the family dog had to be let out. The family called me then. *I* called the sheriff—but first I called you. I wanted you here before the police. I waited as long as I dared, then I simply had to call them; I was running too great a risk."

"I guess I should be flattered, Mike, but like the woman said, we could let the cops have a couple hours on the job before we decided they aren't up to it."

"How long do you think you could go without pretending to be clever? I don't want you to investigate Castelar's murder. The police have a good idea who did it, and they've already inaugurated a search for him."

"Not Castelar? Then—"

"Not *that* Castelar. Not the father, but the daughter. Get it? It's Kate. She's turned up missing again. And as far as anyone knows, you're the last to have seen her."

Chapter Two

It so happens that I hadn't kidnaped Kate Castelar, or killed her, or even so much as lobbed a spitball at her. Yet I felt the blood rush to my head when Kennerly told me I may have been the last to have seen her yesterday. The result, no doubt, of having read too many mystery novels in which the noble detective is accused of a crime he didn't commit and can clear himself only by cracking the case himself while dodging cops who have orders to shoot first and ask questions never. Once I realized that I wasn't being accused, merely informed, I drifted earthward again.

But not before doing a mental fast-scan through the previous afternoon.

I was grappling with a box of corn flakes when Kennerly called. Though it was well past noon, I had been up only a few minutes—Jen and I had had a late night, and she, in fact, was still copping zees in the other room—and while I waited for water to boil for coffee, I did my morning calisthenics with the cereal box. I was trying to get the top up without tearing it in half and thus destroying its handy reclosing feature. About the time I was wondering whether anyone had ever thought of using cereal box-top glue, the strongest adhesive known to man, to fasten those heat-resistant tiles to the space shuttles, the telephone rang. Rather, it bleated. Jen had decided I needed one of those new one-piece jobs that trills or coos electronically instead of ringing.

Whatever it does, it did. I jumped. The box top ripped, and with it the waxed-paper lining it had been glued to. And little flakie-wakies flew everywhere. I estimated six months to track them all down.

I grabbed the phone on the second warble.

"All right, already, you don't have to take my whole head off," Kennerly said easily. "You literary giants are a temperamental lot, aren't you?"

"Who asked you?" I growled.

Kennerly laughed mildly, the way he seemed to do everything. I've seen this small, dapper, sixtyish man in court, grilling witnesses until they were nothing but cinders, and never raising his voice. In his quiet, understated, ever-so-proper way, Mike Kennerly was one of the twenty best lawyers in the country. One of the national lawyers' magazines had made it official about a year back. But some of us had suspected it all along.

Back in the not-so-old days, when I starved as a private investigator instead of as a free-lance writer, I did quite a little work for Kennerly. Tracking down eyewitnesses, finding experts—"hired guns"—to testify, tracing the occasional heir, that type thing. But I had retired from the sleuthing dodge, except for some infrequent lapses, and Kennerly and I almost never crossed paths anymore. Omaha's not all that big a city, but big enough, apparently. Kennerly and I made all the usual noises about how long it's been and how we should get together sometime.

"I'd like that, I really would," Kennerly said. "But right now I'm up to my Adam's apple in this asbestos thing, and I don't expect to have a spare moment before Memorial Day, if you can believe it. In fact, I'm due back in court in just a few minutes, and then that's going to eat the rest of the day."

"I guess somebody's got to stand up and defend those

blue-suit types. Get them off the hook and back into the executive suite."

"Michael M. Kennerly, defender of the rich, oppressor of the weak. Listen, I didn't call just to chat. I've got a little job for you, if you're not busy this afternoon. And if you can still bring yourself to sully your hands with honest labor. It'll take you a couple of hours, tops, and since it's such short notice, I'll double the going rate. Interested?"

I did a little mental arithmetic—a little was all it took—and decided I'd better *get* interested even if I weren't. My checking account was back on the critical list and needed a quick transfusion of cash to give it the will to live. I had a couple of magazine assignments to polish off and polish up, and a batch of query letters to type and mail. And I was supposed to be working on the sequel to The Book, my major opus, which a devil-may-care publisher was bringing out in the spring. The truth, however, was that I was expending the most energy on concocting reasons *not* to do any solid work on The Next Book—if you don't try, you can't fail—and that, plus everything else, prompted me to tell Kennerly to give me the story. "Not for my own sake," I assured him, "it's just that my landlord tends to get kind of edgy at about this time of the month, and liberal applications of cash seem to be the only thing that helps."

Kennerly chuckled again. "What a relief. I was afraid you'd be too busy with publishers, agents, and film producers to waste time on a runaway kid."

"Oddly enough, I find myself between literary luncheons at the moment, so I can just manage to squeeze you in." I didn't know where Kennerly was getting his information, but if he was even one-quarter serious, he had been badly misinformed. Sure, I had gotten a nice little dividend when I signed the contract for The Book. Six figures—if you count the right side of the decimal point. But life had changed in fewer ways than you might expect or I might have liked. I still scraped along six or eight inches above the poverty line. I still lived in the same cramped apartment in the same not-quite-bad neighborhood on Decatur Street. I still drove the same wheezing old Chevy. I still hadn't heard from Clint Eastwood, begging me to let him make a blockbuster movie based on my detective novel. And so I still routinely racked up ten- and twelve-hour days trying to make it as a free-lance writer.

And when that wasn't enough, I still took on the odd bit of investigative work.

Officially, I wasn't supposed to like doing it. The master plan was to get me out of that line and into the writing business. Anything that interfered with the latter or dragged me back to the former was to be shunned. Unofficially, however, my reluctance to give the PI permit a workout varied greatly in some kind of proportion to the number of checks I expected in the mail at any given time.

At this given time that number was exactly zero.

Besides, I didn't mind runaways that much—at one time, in fact, a large portion of my small business consisted of just that work—and if Kennerly was right I could punch this one out in no time and renew my flagging acquaintance with the typewriter.

And at double fee . . .

So I told him to lay it on me and he did. That's when I first heard the name Jack Castelar.

"I've known him forever," Kennerly told me. "We went to school together. He's the president of a bank you probably haven't heard of either, the West Omaha State Bank and Trust, out toward Bennington a ways." Bennington was, and is, north and west of Omaha. "Small, but profitable," Kennerly said of the bank. "It's mainly agricultural banking out there, of course, and you know how farming has its ups and downs, but somehow Jack does all right. It's a solid business, founded by an uncle or great-uncle, I think, back in the teens. Survived the Depression. Still owned almost entirely by the family."

Besides the bank, Castelar had a wife, Emily, and three kids, Kate, Vince, and Amy. The runaway was the oldest of them—well, after the wife—Kate, who was twenty-three. "I really don't know the details," Kennerly said in that muted tone of voice you automatically adopt when you call from one of those half-booth monstrosities they stick pay phones in now. "Kate has been spending quite a lot of time with a fellow that Jack and Emily—well, 'disapprove of' is the nice way to put it, but 'despise' is probably more accurate. Walt Jennings. He's ten, twelve years older than Kate, has a reputation as a roughneck, a drifter, has never held a job longer than six consecutive months. That type."

"I sympathize," I said sympathetically, "but if the girl's twenty-three then she's not a girl, she's a woman, and she can make her own choices. Like the men she wants to see, the hours she wants to keep, whether she wants to leave home . . ."

"Yes, but that's not how it is in this case. Let me back up.

"As you might guess, there have been quite a few arguments over the past few weeks about this . . . relationship. Mainly between Kate and her mother. Oh, Jack's not fond of this Jennings fellow—believe me, there's no love lost between those two—but he usually ends up as mediator between Kate and Emily, just to try and keep some peace in the house."

The two women had gone at it again that morning, with vigor. It seems that Kate had been out until past four with Walt Jennings, and Emily had had some problems with that. She shared her opinions with her daughter, who in turn had some opinions of her own to share. And this time there was no one to peel them apart and send them to separate corners: Castelar was in Denver on business, had been for a couple of days, and wouldn't be back in the Big O until later that evening.

"Evidently the argument escalated into a shouting match that ended only when Kate stormed out of the house, vowing never to return," said Kennerly. "And Emily, who is rather high-strung under the best of circumstances—"

"Which these were not."

"—got on the phone to Denver, got Jack pulled out of his conference, and demanded he do something."

"Uh-huh. A trifle difficult, all considered."

"Just a tad. Anyhow, I'm sure you get the picture by now . . ."

"Jack tried to calm Emily, failed, promised to get you to do the aforementioned 'something' . . ."

". . . called my office, which relayed the message here when we recessed for lunch, yes. Essentially, Jack wants me to make sure Kate doesn't do something crazy—you know, like run off with the guy—before he can talk to her. But I don't have time to go chase after her, and I've got all my regular people tied up on this case, too. So I'm asking you."

My head was fairly spinning with the number of calls that had shot back and forth in a short span of time. No one was wasting any minutes, that was for sure—and that's not always a good thing in situations like this. I said, "Far be it from me to argue myself out of a check, but it sounds like the kid just needs time to chill out. This happens all the time with runaways. They get mad, they leave, they swear they'll never darken the doorstep again—but leave them alone and they'll come home. Wagging their tails behind them."

"You're probably right." His voice said he thought I was probably wrong. "But Emily Castelar is, as I mentioned, an extremely nervous woman. She won't relax until her daughter is safely back."

"Mike, what's it been, a couple of *hours?*"

"I know, I know. Indulge me, will you? Go after her.

Talk to her. Get her to come home—or, failing that, get her set up someplace where we'll know she'll be all right until Jack gets home tonight. In fact, as I think about it, that might be the best bet all around. It'll pre-empt any more fights between Emily and Kate. Yes, do that. Find her, set her up in a hotel, bill it to my office, and have her stay put until her father can come talk to her. Then Emily can relax and Jack can relax and I can relax and just have a really nice afternoon in court. Will you do this for me?"

It sounded like a waste of time, but I suppose it's never a waste as long as someone else is picking up the tab.

"Okay," I sighed. "If that's how you want to spend your money. Give me the address so I can go talk to the bereaved mother, get a snapshot, find out where the kid might have gone—"

"No need for all that," Kennerly interrupted. "We know where she's gone. At least, we know where she said she was going: to the boyfriend's."

"Really rubbing Mama's nose in it." That, too, was fairly typical with these star-crossed lovers.

"Something like that." Kennerly gave me an address for Walt Jennings. I jotted it on a paper napkin, nearly bleeding my felt-tipped pen dry in the process. He also gave me a good description of Kate Castelar, the clothes she was wearing, and the car she was driving—make, model, and license number.

"What, you don't know which side of the street she parked on?—You know, since you know where she is and all, you could probably save your client some money if you just went and picked her up yourself."

"Are you kidding? I bill out at five times what you cost. And if your conscience really bothers you, just look on it as a belated Christmas present from your Uncle Mike: easy money."

Chapter Three

"Uncle Mike" was right: It was a gift, sure enough. Less than sixty minutes after I put down the phone I was standing alongside Kate Castelar's maroon Cutlass. Which, conveniently, contained Kate herself. Easy money.

I had made coffee in the infusion pot, using the good Kona beans that someone had given me, grabbed a quick shower, and jotted a note to Jen, who looked so warm and soft and peaceful cocooned in flannel sheets that I couldn't possibly bring myself to wake her. I estimated that my wife and I had spent two months together, total, in the past three years. And yet, every time she showed up—like this time, unannounced, blowing in on the Christmas snows—it immediately seemed *right*, as if everything fit, as if no time had passed, as if she had never been gone to who-knew-where with who-knew-who.

But I felt, I sensed, I knew that our idyll was again coming to an end. We were about to go on hiatus, as they say of television shows that may or may not be back in the fall. It would be the same as always: Jen would express her boredom with and contempt for Omaha, the Midwest, the continental United States, you name it. And I would express my unwillingness to spend my life leapfrogging the globe in a futile and never-ending attempt to be always at the *in* place. So she would go and I would stay. Neither of us liked the arrangement, but neither of us would budge. And neither of us would be the first to end, truly end it. At least, neither of us had so far.

I poured half the coffee into a large thermal mug, found my keys, and went out in search of distressed damsels.

The concrete stairs outside of my apartment building were snow-packed and slippery; when I grabbed the handrail I could feel the bitter coldness of the steel throbbing right through my glove. Steam roiled off the surface of the coffee mug like smoke from a burning building. I had my doubts about the Chevy but, while it didn't think much of the idea, it did crank eventually and we creakingly headed up the Decatur hill.

Southbound 480 was virtually deserted. I caught it at Hamilton Street and followed it down to the Kennedy Expressway, which took me to this little dilapidated neighborhood not far from the old stockyards.

There isn't much to the Omaha yards these days. Not like when I was a cowboy-crazy kid, and the place rivaled the Chicago yards. Its decline was sad in a way, although the people who had to live in the adjacent neighborhoods during the summer months might not have agreed. I found myself wondering what the Chicago stockyards were like now, but it was too damn cold for sentimental journeys. And I had work to do. Being a trained investigator and everything, I found Walt Jennings's street without undue trouble.

The street was gray and narrow and didn't go anywhere; the houses were gray and narrow and were occupied by people who weren't going anywhere, or had already been. I thought maybe on a warm and sunny day the block would look better. Maybe not. The Jennings place was no better or worse than any of its neighbors. It sat next to one of those funny bunker-style houses that people built during the Second World War, the kind you were supposed to put a real house on top of when you were sure Omaha wouldn't be a candidate for blitzkrieg. This was before they built SAC headquarters outside of town, putting us right up at the top of the list for the next Big One. When that one comes, the few unconverted underground houses you occasionally come across aren't going to fare any better than the average dwelling.

I put the car up against where the curb would have been if not for six inches of dirty snow, across the street from Jennings's place, across the street from Kate's, or Kate's dad's, Olds. I don't like to park my car too close to cars like that one; it aggravates the poor old thing's inferiority complex.

Reluctantly, for the heater had only just begun to thaw me out, I climbed out, letting the engine run to boost the battery. The wind was coming up good now, telling me that it was time to break out the parka—my trusty corduroy coat just wasn't up to this kind of assault. Too bad: It looked great, especially over my brown cord sport coat, tan chamois shirt, and new blue jeans with the cuffs rolled up to show off the flannel lining. My teeth may have started chattering before I got the car door closed behind me, but at least I had the satisfaction of knowing that I looked preppy as hell. Except my sport coat had no leather patches on the elbows, cuss it.

Mike Kennerly's description had been good. The young woman behind the wheel of the big car could have been no one but Kate Castelar. She was a pretty girl with dark brown hair, small, regular features, and a serious set to her narrow mouth. As I came across the street I could see she wore one of those short down-filled jackets with a ski-lift ticket dangling from the plastic zipper. It was green—the jacket, I mean, not the ticket, which was blue—and in it she looked like the Michelin man. She sat with her head back against the headrest, arms folded around her, eyes closed. You didn't have to be a detective to see she had been crying.

I tapped on the window and she jumped, looked at me accusatorily with red-rimmed eyes. I tried a winning smile. It didn't help. Blame it on the three-day-old beard I was sporting. It was coming in all right, but I still felt like a bum every time I caught my reflection in a shop window. In a couple of weeks, though, I figured I'd stop looking like a panhandler and start looking like the published author I was about to become.

Meanwhile, I could attest that a new beard affords almost no insulation whatever. I stamped my feet and clapped my arms around me once or twice. "Pretty cold," I said loudly, still smiling. The idea was for her to take the hint and unlock the door for me. I guess that was dumb to expect. But she did hit the electric switch on her armrest and let her window down two inches. She said nothing.

"My name's Nebraska." I leaned close to the window so as not to let the whole block in on our business. "I'm a private detective, hired by your father to make sure you're okay."

"You don't look like a private detective," she said uninterestedly.

"I know; the Acme Institute of Private Detection forgot to mail me that lesson, so I thought I'd try to get by looking like what I look like." I dragged out my wallet and flattened the laminated photostat (fabled in story and song) against her window. She didn't so much as glance at it. "That's the usual reaction," I said, and folded it away.

She said, "Look, I don't have to go with you. I don't even have to talk to you. So leave me alone. I don't want to have to call a *real* cop."

"The young can be so unfeeling, but I'll try to hide the

hurt. No, you don't have to do anything. Hell, no. You're an adult. They tell me." She looked up. I said, "I figure we're about even now. Want to quit sparring? Save a little for your mother?" She moved the toggle on the armrest and up went the window. I managed to get my nose out of the way just in time.

"Listen," I said loudly. "Your mother got upset and called your father. Your father called his lawyer. The lawyer called me. No one wants to make you do anything, but everyone wants to make sure you're okay. If you don't want to go home, fine. But you can't sit out here in a car for the rest of your days. Let me get you situated someplace safe until your father gets back and can talk to you."

The window buzzed down an inch. Kate made a face at me. "Someplace like *your* place?"

It was the beard, all right.

"Thanks for the offer," I said charmingly, "but I'll pass. The wife and I are pretty liberal, but that sort of stuff's never gone over real big around our place. She just can't sell me on the idea."

That almost produced a smile. And it did produce a little half-sigh of resignation, after which she unlocked the passenger door. I made a point of going around the front of the car—I had a similar situation once where a guy peeled out when I went around the back—and slid in. "Thanks," I said sincerely. "I was shivering so hard I was afraid something was going to shake loose."

A real smile this time, if a trifle sad. Yes, she was a pretty kid. If you're still a kid at twenty-three. She looked like a kid to me, that's for sure, although if her boyfriend was ten or twelve years older—well, hell, that was about *my* age. I didn't want to take her out or anything, but if I did I didn't think I'd feel like I'd be robbing the cradle. Much.

It didn't bear thinking about. So I said, "Well, what do

you say, want to get out of here? I'll take you home—your home—I'll put you in a hotel, we can go to the movies, whatever you want. Besides"—I cocked my head toward the house on our right—"it doesn't look like he's home anyway."

"No, he's not," Kate said, and her voice trembled a bit. "But someone is."

I looked at the dingy, sagging little house. It was the same color as the sky, which made it hard to see, but it looked empty, even deserted to me. I saw no movement behind the thin, faded curtains on the front windows.

"She wouldn't answer the door, but I know she's in there." Kate sighed heavily. "Now I know why he never had me over, or let me meet him here. He always said the neighborhood was bad, so we should meet somewhere else." I looked at her. She was looking at the house. I looked back at it, just to make sure it hadn't burst into flames under her stare. "I don't know what's worse," she said quietly, in eerie contrast to the violent look in her eyes, "having him think I was so stupid and naive that I wouldn't ever figure out why he never brought me home . . . or *being* that stupid and naive. It's what I deserve, I guess." She snuffled wetly and I steeled myself for the great flood, but it never came. Had enough of that, I guess. She yanked a handful of white tissues from a plastic caddy straddling the hump, blew her nose with the demureness of a bull elephant, and stuffed the wad into a litter bag dangling under the dash. "Well, screw them," she said bitterly, wiping her eyes with more Kleenexes. Then, suddenly: "I don't suppose you'd like to buy me lunch. I haven't eaten all day and I'm starving."

I mentally shook my head and ran to catch up with her. Wondering if I ever had that kind of resilience at her age, I patted her hand in what I hoped was an avuncular fashion. "Courtesy of the client," I said. "Just follow me."

We formed a little convoy back up the expressway,

picked up I-80 where it veers off from 480, and followed it west to the Seventy-second Street exit. There was still almost no traffic. People with more sense than yours truly try to stay indoors on cold, gray days like this, when the Midwestern sky closes in until you almost think you could stretch up and touch it, when the wind seeks out the smallest crack to whistle through and prod you with its icy fingers, when the very atmosphere seems alive with possibilities—and all of them are gloomy. A granulated snow snicked against the windshield, which did little to brighten up my day.

Kate followed me up Seventy-second to Grover and into the parking lot of a Perkins there. We could have eaten in any of a dozen places along the way, but I chose the pancake house because it was right next door to a Ramada that I hoped to get her settled into. There are better hotels in town, and worse, but if nothing else this one had easy access to the freeway. It also had a painfully trendy bar and satellite TV and little sparkly things imbedded in the ceilings.

I checked my watch while we waited for the hostess to seat us. Just past two-thirty. I figured out my hourly rate and decided that if I'd had more cases like this one, I'd've never dreamed of giving up the business. Easy money indeed.

The lunch crowd, if this miserable day had produced one, was long gone, so we got our table and our orders quickly. Kate tackled a club sandwich with chips, a side of fries, and a brownie à la mode. Me? Just coffee. Kate commented on it, and I said, "I once calculated that a full day at the typewriter consumes roughly point zero-zero-zero-zero-three calories, which, as middle age creeps up on me, becomes something to think about."

She wiped mayonnaise from a corner of her mouth. "Typewriter? I thought you guys spent your time tracking down crooks, seducing rich women—"

"—and cracking tough cases—tough cases, incidentally, always being 'cracked,' never merely 'solved'—by speeding around in low-slung sports cars? 'Fraid not. If this job was half as glamorous as its reputation has it, it'd be the growth field of the eighties. Believe me, it ain't. So I'm only a sort of part-time sleuth these days." I told her about The Book. The subject had become easier for me to discuss since the manuscript had been accepted. Writing a book's no big deal—who *isn't?*—but having one slated for publication makes people take notice, makes women cry and strong men faint, and, let's be honest, I got a kick out of it. Only problem was, people would inevitably ask if I was at work on another one, and that was an uncomfortable subject. Partly because I don't like discussing works in progress—less time talking and more time doing, that's my motto—and partly because I wasn't. Hard at work, that is. Not really. Despite my motto, despite what I told everyone. Including me.

Kate asked, of course. I trotted out the works-in-progress excuse, then deftly turned the conversation back to her. "So what do you think, kid—what are you going to do with the rest of the day?"

The waitress came and cleared away the debris. Kate ordered a cup of tea. When the woman was gone she said, "God, I don't know. I've never felt so stupid in my whole life. My big speech about going to live with Walt and then, guess what, he's already filled that position. God."

Our waitress returned with tea for Kate and a significant look for me. No telling what she thought about this dirty old man buying brownies for the sweet young thing in the fuzzy pink sweater and gray wool skirt. Oh, I had a rough idea. But I was feeling too much like a kid on a date to worry about it.

Kate surrounded the heavy ceramic mug with both hands. They were small and delicate and trim, like the rest of her. "I suppose the only thing to do is to go to a hotel. I could use the sleep, for one thing. I had kind of a rough night." I didn't know whether she was referring to her morning with her mother or her evening with Jennings, but in any case she gave me a sly look and her small pink tongue briefly touched her lower lip.

To take my mind off it, I said, "No point going home and trying to patch it up with your mother?"

"Well, let's see: By now"—she consulted the small gold watch on her left wrist—"Mommie Dearest should be about two-thirds looped. She eats those pills of hers like they were M&Ms. So I don't think so. Even if she were straight, I don't think it'd be worth it. We just keep going around and around, and we never get anywhere. The real problem is she's jealous." Kate smiled gently and shook her head. "I should have moved out years ago. I should have gone to a college out of town. Dad talked me out of it, and I guess I really didn't want to leave much, either, but . . ." She drained her mug. "Well, it's not too late. I'll wait for Dad to come home, and then I'll talk to him about my getting an apartment. It won't solve my mom's problem, but at least we won't have to go through this every day."

I looked at the check and left a tip on the table. "Of course, if you're through with Walt Jennings . . ." I had wondered about Kate and Jennings. If he was half as despicable as Kennerly had made him out to be, and as Kate's parents seemed to feel, then what was the attraction for her? I'd seen similar pairings over the years, and I never understood them, either—the fascination some women have with rough men, losers, even criminals. And that some men have with pretty unsavory women. Like the song says, love is strange. That ain't the half of it.

Kate unwadded her jacket from a corner of the booth. "That doesn't make any difference. Sure, they don't like

Walt, but I could be going with a priest and my mother would still object to it." She breathed a laugh. "Well, yeah, I *guess* she'd object to a priest. Make that an Eagle Scout, or a Nobel Prize winner. She'd find something wrong with him. Not Dad—well, Dad, he doesn't usually think much of my guys, either . . . but it's different. He always thinks I can do better." She smiled lopsidedly. "And he's usually right. Mom, she's jealous is all, and there's nothing I can do about that. I like guys and they like me. Sure, I manage to fall for some real winners, but I'm old enough to make my mistakes; I'm old enough to decide who I want to be with and whether I want to sleep with them—and *how* I want to sleep with them."

I felt the waitress giving me the evil eye from her station. I ignored her and directed Kate to the front counter, where I paid the bill. "Coincidentally enough," I said, "there seems to be a hotel right here." Kate laughed and helped me with my coat. "Let's get you situated, and then I'll let Kennerly know where you're at so he can tell your father."

There being no objection to the plan, we left the restaurant. The wind was even stronger now, colder, and the sky was dark and malevolent. The gritty snowfall had quit, but white boomerangs of it were collected in this or that corner on top of the old gray stuff. We climbed over a wall of hard snow that separated the restaurant's parking lot from the hotel's. Kate nearly slipped on the uneven surface and grabbed my hand. She kept it until we entered the hotel.

I got her checked in okay and arranged to have the bill sent to Kennerly. The elevators stood under circular awnings on the other end of the wide, carpeted lobby. We stopped before them.

If this were a Ross Macdonald novel, if I were Lew Archer, Kate would at this point invite me upstairs with her. If this were a Mickey Spillane novel and I were Mike Hammer, it would not have taken even this long. This being neither, Kate simply went up on tiptoes and kissed my cheek. "Thanks, Nebraska," she said when she finished. "Thanks for lunch. Thanks for everything."

When the closing elevator doors cut her from my view, I left the building and drove home. I needed the headlights before I got there. The afternoon seemed more claustrophobic, more ominous than ever. I tried to shake the feeling. I shouldn't have. Within twelve hours Jack Castelar would be murdered, Kate would have disappeared again, and the police would have begun a manhunt for Walt Jennings.

Chapter Four

"Why Jennings?"

We had joined Kim Banner, who eyed Kennerly impatiently as he took a lungful of refrigerated air and coughed it into his glove before answering. "For good reason," he finally pronounced. "Jennings frequently and publicly threatened Jack's life." He swallowed another breath and let it escape whitely into the atmosphere. "About three years ago, Jennings bought a small farm not too far from here, financed through Jack's bank. A nice little place, as I understand it. Well, I don't know much about farms—nothing, in fact—but I would be willing to guess that they're extremely tough to operate from a bar stool."

Apparently so. In short order Jennings ran the farm into the ground—so to speak—and, inevitably, was foreclosed. I made one of those wild from-the-gut guesses: "And Jennings blamed Castelar for his troubles."

Kennerly made a sour face. "Guys like Jennings—they never have anyone to blame but themselves, but they'll never face up to it. Yes, he blamed Jack. The actual foreclosure and sale—eighteen months ago, whenever it was—was handled by the feds, but Jack held a few of Jennings's notes. That made him a convenient scapegoat, and Jennings never missed an opportunity to tell anyone who'd listen that someday he was going to get even with him."

I said, "Why didn't you tell me this yesterday?"

Again he looked at Banner. She remained silent, her mouth downturned. "Yesterday it wasn't important," Kennerly said. "Today it's all-important."

"You see," Banner inserted, "it's possible—in fact, it's likely—that the girl is with Jennings, wherever he may be. What we don't know is what her involvement—"

"If any."

"—thank you, Counselor—if any, is. Assuming Jennings is our man, did he kidnap Kate, either before or after killing her father? Or did she go with him willingly, before or after the fact? Was she aware of what he had done? Was she in on it?"

"Absolutely not," Kennerly said—hotly, by his standards. I'm one hundred percent certain that Kate is an unwilling participant, a victim, a hostage. If indeed she's a participant at all. After all, she's run away before; perhaps she has again, and her disappearance is merely an unhappy coincidence . . ."

"Perhaps," said Banner slowly, in a tone of voice that indicated she was thinking the same thing I was, that the possibility belonged under the heading Wishful Thinking. Still, neither of us was willing to accept the challenge in Kennerly's eyes as they shot back and forth between us.

I said, "Okay, say Jennings did kill Castelar, and say that he did snatch Kate. The question is—why?"

"Why which?"

"Either. Both. Take the first first. Why did Jennings wait so long before killing Castelar? If I were going to kill somebody I'd do it right now, when I was good and mad. Not a year or two later."

"Unless you let it fester, fumed about it, drank over it, got hotter and hotter about it until finally you had to do something or bust," Banner said. "Which it looks like Jennings did. About six months ago the sheriff's department out here arrested him for lobbing rocks at the bank's sign. And since he moved into Omaha, I don't know how many times we've picked him up on drunk-and-disorderlies. His folder's full of them. And almost all of the officers' reports indicate he made repeated and explicit threats against Castelar."

"There's a big jump between throwing rocks at a sign and putting a bullet through somebody's brain. But even if he finally worked up to it, why did he grab Kate?—I'm assuming he kidnaped her, because I was with her yesterday, when she decided the, uh, relationship had come to an end, and she was quite definite on the subject."

"Well, there you have it, then. Maybe he tried to persuade her to come along, and when she wouldn't, he took her. Why? Unrequited love, spite, perverseness—or to use as a bargaining chip. I don't know. Tell you what. When we nail him, I'll let you ask that question yourself."

"You must be pretty sure he's your boy."

"I am," she said solidly. "Oh, there are one or two other names on the list—bankers make enemies like picnics make ants—but Jennings is right up at the very top."

"All of which is academic," Kennerly interposed before I could take my next shot. He faced me. "Let's let the police worry about Jennings." He made it more than a suggestion. "I told you, I'm not hiring you to look for Jennings. Your job is to find Kate."

"That's a very fine distinction, under the circumstances."

"That's what I say," Banner told him. "Why not back off and give us room to do our job before you go pulling in PIs? Even if Jennings is using the girl as an insurance policy, she's in bad trouble the minute he decides she's become a liability instead of an asset. This could be a kidnaping; we don't know. It could turn into a hostage situation. In any case, it's something best left to people who know what they're doing. No offense."

"None taken," I said. "I think you're right." I turned to Kennerly, who had put a patient-but-skeptical look on his face. "It's going to take the resources of the law-enforcement network to track down a guy with a five- or six-hour head start. Assuming he had the good sense to split as quickly as possible after the event, Jennings could be three, four hundred miles away by now. In any direction. I'm pretty wonderful, but even I can't cover a four-hundred-mile radius by myself. There's only so much of me to go around."

"*If* he left town," Kennerly said—a trifle smugly, I thought—"any direction he might have chosen, he'd have run into terrible weather. The way I hear it, the whole Midwest is virtually shut down." So it was; I'd heard the same thing on the car radio on the drive out, but forgot it almost instantly since it didn't affect me. The snowstorm out west—the one that had delayed Castelar's flight last night—had traveled this way, bringing high winds and low visibility and up to twenty-four inches of snow in some places. By some meteorological miracle, it had changed course at the last instant, wreaking the rest of its havoc to the north of us, across the Dakotas and into Minnesota and Wisconsin.

Meanwhile, the rest of this part of the country was treated to the same paralyzingly cold winds we had been receiving, which was as bad as or even worse than the heavy precipitation. When the thermometer flirts with windchills of fifty and sixty below, a car can freeze up even while the motor is running. I had seen plenty of stalled vehicles dotting the highway between here and the city, cars that had been literally blown off the road, and semis whose diesel fuel had turned to jelly in the tank. Kennerly was right: Jennings wouldn't have gotten very far at all, even if he had been foolish enough to start out in the first place.

Banner was on the same wavelength. "Our best guess is that if he did try to rabbit, he'd get no more than fifty or sixty miles out of town. In all likelihood, he's still in the area. But that doesn't change anything. Finding him is still a job for the police."

"No argument here," Kennerly replied expansively. "But everything you've said supports my conviction that your first priority will be finding Jennings. That's as it should be. However, *my* first priority is finding Kate. Whether she's with Jennings, whether she went with him willingly, whether she knows her father has been murdered—it's all academic. I just don't want the search for Kate to take a back seat, and with all respect, it's *going* to as long as you're hunting a suspected murderer."

"Ever hear of the FBI? They've gotten pretty good at handling kidnapings over the years."

"I'm unconvinced this is a kidnaping, and wouldn't the FBI require some evidence of a crime? In any event, I'd rather spare the family the additional publicity, the additional stress, if it can be avoided. And I think it can."

Banner remained silent.

"That's why I want someone whose first—indeed, only—priority will be finding my client's daughter. My friend's daughter. If that overlaps the search for Jennings, if that runs parallel to the search for Jennings, then so be it. Just as long as it isn't *secondary* to the search for Jennings."

Kennerly paused for effect. As are all good trial lawyers, he was an actor at heart. His head swiveled slowly from me to Banner, then back. "What do you think, lad—are you up to it?"

Someday I'll learn, maybe. Not today, obviously, but someday. My responsibility had begun and ended yesterday. The job was complete. I found the girl, got her safely deposited in a hotel, and made my report. Selah. *Pax vobiscum.*

Happy trails. There was no need for me to feel obliged to become any further involved, to participate in a needle hunt in a haystack of uncertain dimension. Banner was right, this was a job for the law and its legendary long arm. Despite what the writers of television shows think, the police are better equipped to handle this sort of thing than is a solitary hero. No matter how rugged and handsome he may be.

But then, you can't get into the Private Eye Hall of Fame without tilting at an occasional windmill.

I told him I'd do it. "But later, I want to talk to you about your definition of easy money."

◦ • ◦

With that settled, Banner finally proceeded with her presentation. It had to do with time of death and angle of entry and caliber and deflection and the ongoing search for the slug. Little of it mattered to me. You can't run a ballistics check unless and until you have the murder weapon, and even then it's mainly a matter for lawyers to sweat over as they try to make or break a case. The cops were guessing the weapon was a .38, which is only about the most common handgun in the universe. And the time of death didn't have anything to do with what I was about; again, it's something that takes on significance when you get to court, and we were still a long way from that.

Not being real keen on police procedurals, I drifted a little during Banner's recitation. I tried again to imagine what a classy girl like Kate saw in an apparent creep like Jennings. I tried to imagine how and where I would begin my search. I tried to imagine how Kim Banner would look with her clothes off. Job-related stuff like that.

However, just to be polite and make it look like I was interested, I did ask one question: How come Castelar had lain out here undiscovered for several hours; why wasn't anyone in the house roused?

"That's not surprising," Banner said. "For one thing, look at how far away the house is from the road—six hundred feet if it's an inch. For another, these trees"—she swung an arm to indicate the gnarled old ones fronting the property—"would muffle the shot. So would the wind and the snow on the ground. Plus, it was very late and people were asleep, and there was only one shot. *Plus*, of the four bedrooms—"

"I think I get the picture . . ."

"—two, the son's and the youngest daughter's, are at the back of the house. Kate, of course, wasn't in hers, and Mrs. Castelar is evidently in the habit of taking sleeping pills at bedtime."

"Sorry I asked."

"You're welcome. We try to be complete. Now, if there's nothing else, I'd like to see if they've dug up that bullet. With the snow and the ice and these trees . . ."

There was nothing else, and Banner, moving carefully on the slippery surface, crossed the road to check on her people's progress. I watched her, the way she moved: purposeful, direct, even when she was fighting to keep her balance. That's not easy.

Then Kennerly took me by the elbow and nodded in the direction of the house. "Let's go in," he said quietly, and it was okay with me; I was about to send my feet a telegram to see if they were still around. We climbed over the dike that had prevented the cab driver from taking Castelar up to the house last night and tramped up the long unpaved driveway. It was shaped something like a hockey stick, running straight as a shot past the north side of the house, then curving lazily around back.

The house itself was a beauty—big and old and sturdy and white, whiter than the snow surrounding it. The sun was fully risen now, and a wisp of smoke was winding straight up from the house's tall red brick chimney and frost was glimmering in the windows and on the bare trees in the yard. The stuff of Currier and Ives or Norman Rockwell. Except for the Grim Reaper in the foreground.

The distance from the road to the house was about an eighth of a mile—a goodly distance by city standards, but not as far as it may sound if you're unaccustomed to walking more than ten feet to get your mail. Even at our leisurely pace, the trip took no more than four minutes. It was made in silence.

We followed the driveway around to the back of the house, where it widened and ran up to a newish-looking three-car garage about fifteen feet off the back porch. Quite a distance farther back, at the very edge of the yard where it met the field beyond, stood a large weather-beaten barn that must also have held a vehicle of some sort: Tracks both automotive and human crisscrossed the snowy expanse between the barn and the driveway. A smaller shed stood forlornly to the south of the barn, overshadowed by a tall old blue-gray grain silo.

Kennerly held open the porch door for me and I stepped in. The flooring was of thick wooden planks that bumped and rumbled hollowly but solidly beneath our feet. Snow boots, shovels, pavement salt, and other seasonal paraphernalia were stacked near the door to the house, alongside an old porch glider that had been covered for the winter. Kennerly didn't knock but went straight in. I followed.

The kitchen was large and modern and, most important, warm. The ceiling stretched up a good ten or twelve feet—none of this modern seven-and-a-half-foot nonsense, where even a guy of my average height feels he has to duck. The room was well lined with cupboards and cabinets and all the latest conveniences, while in the center stood an island containing the range and a dining counter. Umpty million copper-bottomed pots and pans hung suspended overhead. A tired-looking black spaniel in one corner looked up at us when we came through the door, decided we weren't whom he wanted to see, and, with a canine sigh, again rested his chin on the edge of his wicker bed.

I was scratching the dog behind his ears when the kid came in.

This would be Vince, I said to myself, Kate's younger brother—though not much younger. I knew he was a senior at UNO, so that must have made him twenty-one or twenty-two to Kate's twenty-three. He was tall and skinny and blond, clean-shaven and baby-faced, with hair trimmed close on the sides and back but puffed into a fluffy pompadour on top. He wore a gray V-neck sweater with no shirt, faded jeans with tapered legs, and battered penny loafers with no socks. He tore into the room like a pack of hounds was after him, but the only one in sight was the mourning one groaning gently under my fingers.

"What's going on?" Vince Castelar demanded of Kennerly.

The lawyer peeled off his heavy blue overcoat, hung it on a solid peg near the door, and went to work deliberately on the iced-up zippers of his overshoes. "How's your mother, Vince?" he asked quietly but insistently.

Something in his tone or manner upset the kid. He didn't say anything, but a hot flush splattered his cheeks, the way it will with blonds of a certain complexion, and his eyes were murderous when he said, "Fine. She's upstairs. Bruhn gave her something." Bruhn was the family doctor, called in by Kennerly. "What's going on out there?"

Kennerly was done with one boot and having at the second one. "The police are gathering information, Vince, looking for evidence. That's all. Same as before."

"God damn it," he said with the precision of someone

for whom cursing has not yet become commonplace. "I told you they're wasting their time here. They should be out looking for that bastard Jennings. He's killed my father"—his voice went tight but it didn't break—"and now he's got Kate. They should be looking for him instead of playing in the snow. Did you tell them that?"

Kennerly straightened up and ran a hand through thinning hair flattened by his hat. "Not in so many words," he told Vince. "For one thing, finding Jennings isn't enough; they also have to find evidence to convict him, if he did it—"

"*If?!*"—

"—*if* he did it, and playing in the snow, as you put it, might just turn up some of that evidence. The bullet, for instance. For another—"

"Listen, he did it all right, I—"

"—what you see out there is not the entire police force, although it may look like it. While these people are doing their jobs here, other people—OPD, the state patrol, sheriff's departments in all the adjacent counties—are doing *their* jobs. And that includes keeping an eye open for Walt Jennings. All right?"

It wasn't, but the youngster couldn't think of anything to say about it. So he rolled a narrow shoulder at me. "Who's this?"

I had something wise to say to him, but I reminded myself that his old man was murdered only a few hours ago and kept it to myself. Kennerly patiently filled him in. "He's the private investigator who found Kate yesterday. I've asked him to look for her again."

"Well, then, what's he hanging around here for?" I wondered how they liked Vince's singleness of purpose down at the business school. "If Kate was *here* we wouldn't need him, would we? Tell him to go find Jennings, then he'll have found Kate, too."

"Tell him yourself," I said. I don't like being talked around, and it was becoming obvious that this pup wasn't traumatized or grief-stricken. He was just a jerk.

"Fine." He at me. "Why don't you get the hell out of here and go do the job you're being paid to do."

"That's better. Now shut up and mind your own business."

Before he could open his mouth, another voice said, "I think that's a good idea, too."

I looked up, through the archway to the dining room, to the foot of an enclosed staircase that ended in a far corner of that room, near pocket doors that separated it from the living room at the front of the house. Leaning heavily against the woodwork was a middle-aged woman. Her dark hair rose dramatically from a widow's peak high on her forehead, darted back behind her head, and reemerged on her shoulders. She wore little make-up—a light lipstick that looked recently applied, and perhaps a little something around the eyes; I wasn't certain—and her skin was pale, almost luminescent, in contrast with her black hair and the chocolate-brown robe she had wrapped tightly around her.

Emily Castelar was what mystery writers invariably describe as a "handsome" woman. She was not beautiful, although she may have been once. Now she was fighting the battle of the bulges and sags. She was losing, too, which I suppose is inevitable. The skin around her eyes was loose and puffy, although it was not inconceivable that she had been crying recently, and the flesh along and under her squarish jaw was following the letter of the law of gravity. The robe billowed noticeably at her waistline.

"You're supposed to be resting, Mom," said Vince, turning toward her.

"I'm fine," she said with a casual wave of her hand. Unfortunately it was the hand she had braced herself against the wall with, and when she took it away she pitched to the right and banged her shoulder against the other wall.

Vince was to her instantly, helping her to a chair at the dining table. "I'm fine, I'm fine," she repeated. "It's the shock, I suppose . . ." That and a handful of tranquilizers, I thought. Uncharitable, I know. But Kate had told me her mother swallowed downers like candy on even a typical day, and this wasn't a typical day, not for any household.

Making solicitous, consoling noises, Kennerly crossed the parquet floor. "Vince is right, Emily; you should be upstairs resting."

She ignored him and inspected me. I stood in the arch, where the linoleum met the parquet, feeling vaguely uncomfortable, not knowing what to do with my hands except hold my hat in them. Don't get to go up an' work in de big house much.

"I apologize for my son's rudeness," Emily said precisely, primly, as if her tongue had turned to wood but she'd be damned if anybody knew it. "I gather you're the private detective, Mr. . . ."

"Nebraska." It was Kennerly. "He's the one who found Kate for us yesterday, Emily," he said, as if he were talking to a child, and a slightly stupid one at that. "He's going to do that for us again now."

"He's going to try," I amended, stepping forward. "It doesn't mean much, Mrs. Castelar, but I'm very sorry." She took my hand, which was still cold from the great outdoors; hers was colder still. I looked into her face. The grayish eyes were shiny with tears, but behind the moist film they were dull and not quite focused. Her lips formed the words "Thank you"; there was no volume behind them. Then her eyes drifted away from me and toward the tall windows in the wall opposite her. She seemed intent on studying a small bird perched on a feeder hanging from a barren tree. Raymond Chandler could have told you what kind of bird, and what kind of tree, too; to me it was just a bird and a tree. After maybe twenty seconds it was just a tree, because the bird flew off. Simultaneously Emily Castelar looked around the room like someone just roused from a trance.

"Where's Kate?" she said to no one in particular in a voice composed of equal parts confusion and alarm.

I glanced at Kennerly but he didn't return the favor. His eyes were for Emily, and the creases in his brow seemed deeper than before. He leaned over her and took one of her pale, chilly hands between both of his. "Emily." She looked at him. "We don't know where Kate is. She's run away, remember? And Mr. Nebra—"

"I know that," she said impatiently, dragging her hand from Kennerly's grip. "I meant Amy. Where's Amy?"

This time Kennerly did glance my way, relief written all over his face in bold headline type. Whatever other problems she may have had, at least Emily Castelar's little red choo-choo was still on the track.

Vince said Amy was still in the living room, and Emily insisted on seeing her. After some lackluster protestation, Kennerly and the boy helped her to her feet and guided her through the pocket doors. The dog and I followed.

Like all of the house that I had seen so far, the room was like a spread from *Country Living*, complete with dark wood floor, great oblong rugs, high-backed furniture, brick fireplace, and burgundy-and-cream wallpaper above eight-inch baseboards. I wondered if you had to take oxygen up with you if you were going to paint the ceiling, which was crossed with heavy black beams.

At first I thought the room was empty; then I saw the young barefoot girl in plaid flannel pajamas, curled in a plush wing-backed chair and staring into the cold fireplace. Amy, the thirteen-year-old. She gave no sign of having noticed us enter the room. Emily Castelar moved stiffly to her daughter's side and, gracelessly, knelt near the chair. "Amy? . . ."

Nothing. Not a flicker. Her eyes were locked on the empty hearth the way a kid her age is supposed to stare at MTV.

"No change at all?" It was Kennerly, sotto voce, to Vince.

The boy was shaking his blond head very slowly, his eyes on his mother and sister, his face unreadable. "This is just exactly how I found her when I came down to see what was wrong with the dog. I don't think she's even moved." I knew from Banner's briefing that the spaniel had roused Amy to let him out on a pre-dawn mission. The dog took forever to come back, so Amy pulled coat and boots from the pile in the kitchen and went to investigate. She soon found what had captured the dog's attention. Then she came back to the house, planted herself in this chair, and evidently had been this way ever since, withdrawn and uncommunicative. After a while the spaniel, who was still outside, woke Vince with his barking. It was he—Vince—who called Kennerly, and Kennerly who called the authorities.

I imagined that Amy was quiet and solitary under the best of circumstances; she looked like that sort of girl. She was thin and pale and dark-haired, rather like her mother in complexion if not build. Her eyes, too, were dark, and liquid, and sad. Emily spoke to her in low, quiet words that I couldn't hear. Amy gave not the slightest indication that she knew anyone else was in the room, the house, the world.

Emily stood, relying on the back of the chair for support. She looked at us as if expecting suggestions. None of us had any, and silence hung in that rustic room like crepe, unrelieved by so much as the tick of a clock.

Through the small frost-painted panes of the front window I saw the last of the cops, still at it. It was like watching television: How could the scene out there have anything to do with the scene in here? Except in that Jack Castelar was not the only victim here, merely the most obvious.

My eyes were drawn, as if magnetically, back to the girl. We might as well have been dust motes dancing in the sun that spilled in from the dining room for all the attention she paid us, and yet in that moment she was undeniably the center of all our individual universes.

It meant nothing to her. She gazed into that dead fireplace as if it were a crystal ball, as if she were staring down her future.

The future, I could have told her, never blinks first.

Chapter Five

The sun was blinding and the sky was blue and Kate's maroon Cutlass was still in the lot of the restaurant on Grover near Seventy-second.

I sat behind the wheel of my car and swore unenthusiastically. There was no way in hell the car could have been anyplace else but where it was—but I can dream, can't I? If the car had by some miracle gone missing, it might have meant that Kennerly's pipe dream had come true, that Kate simply and coincidentally had disappeared on her own. That it was where she had left it yesterday meant only one thing: She had left with someone else.

And Kim Banner was right: Walt Jennings topped the list.

Narrowing the field to a mere hundred questions or so. Had Kate gone willingly? Before or after the murder? If after, did she know her father was dead? If before, where was she when it happened? Where did they go after the murder? And, most important, was Kate alive or dead?

This was fun.

I threw the Chevy into gear, drove out onto Grover and into the lot of the hotel next door.

The management had already been softened up by Kennerly, who had, of course, called hours earlier trying to find

Kate, so I didn't have to do much ice-breaking. In fact, the assistant manager, a tall, good-looking black woman, was as helpful as could be—which, unfortunately, wasn't very. She could tell me when Kate Castelar checked in, which I already knew. She could tell me that no calls were placed from the room, which still left the pay phones in the lobby, lounge, and restaurants. She could tell me that nothing had been sent up from room service, which was useless trivia.

She could not tell me whether anyone had been to see Kate, although no one had asked for her at the desk. She could not tell me whether Kate had received any telephone calls in her room, but none had gone through the switchboard. She could not tell me when Kate had left, but the bed had not been slept in.

Mainly because it seemed to be the thing to do, I asked to see the room. It was, of course, a waste of time, since the room had long since been made up, the management having had no reason not to. But I took the key and went up and tried to look detectively.

The room was like any modern hotel room anywhere in the world. I think they're all stamped from a single die. It was as tidy as a church social, and if any Clews had been waiting to jump out at me from behind a door, they were long gone now. Still, I looked through the dresser and the night tables and the closet, and even tossed a glance under the double bed. Zip.

I wandered down a narrow corridor until I found the housekeeper, a short, skinny Laotian woman with a stolid face but lively eyes. We went through the routine; she had already been quizzed by the assistant manager, so the answers were fresh in her mind. As far as she could remember, the bedspread was mussed like someone had sat on it but it had not been turned down. A bar of soap, a washcloth, and a face towel had been used in the bathroom, but no bath towel; and the wastebaskets were empty except for the soap wrapper. Since Kate's having scrawled a cryptic message on the wrapper was about as likely as my being named Miss Teenage America, I did not ask to see where they dumped the garbage.

I gave the woman five bucks, took the room key back to the front desk, and left the hotel.

Business was good over at Perkins, and I realized with some surprise that it was getting on toward nine-thirty. Breakfast. I hadn't had any. That didn't bother me much; what did were the first dull throbs of caffeine withdrawal.

I climbed into the car to get out of the wind, took off my hat, and rubbed my forehead. That never helps, but it gives a guy something to do.

Well, what next? Kate's mother and brother had provided the names of a couple of her college friends. I could toddle over to the campus, nose around, ask a few questions, and hope for divine intervention. A distressing amount of detective work is like that—groping around for a light switch—but the assignment was daunting enough already without my leaping headlong into it before laying a little mental groundwork first. That meant making some preliminary assumptions; they would determine the course of the investigation.

First assumption: Kate was alive. If she wasn't, the endeavor was *really* pointless. But my second assumption was that Jennings had taken her with him, and it would make no sense for him to do so only to kill her. If he was going to kill her—for whatever reason—he'd have let her lie where she dropped, as he did Castelar. No, he had taken her with him to be his good-luck charm if the cops cornered him.

The third assumption was that they were still in the environs. Our typically horrendous winter weather made that one easy to swallow.

All right, so they had had to go to ground. Where? Four possibilities suggested themselves: a place known to Jennings; a place known to Kate; a place known to them both; or the first likely-looking place they encountered. The first of these, I figured, would be a hideout Jennings had established for just such an emergency. The second was more likely a place of solitude, a private thinking post where Kate was in the habit of going to be alone. The third could have been a spot where the two met in secret to plight their troth, whatever the hell a troth is. The fourth—well, if they'd simply jumped down the first available hole, there was no way I could try to get a trace on it, so it wasn't even worth considering.

That left me three perfectly good, logical angles to follow, provided me a place to get started, and gave me a rough idea how to organize my time. I didn't know if it would come to anything, but at least my client was going to get something for his money: legwork.

◦ • ◦

The Jennings place didn't look much better in today's cold sunlight than it had under yesterday's ominous overcast. Or maybe it was just my having gotten up on the wrong side of the bed and at the wrong hour of the day. I parked where I had yesterday; where Kate's car had been there was now another dark late-model sedan. It had no markings on it, but it might as well have had POLICE in chartreuse neon lettering in the back window. You can almost always pick out an unmarked police car, just as you can almost always spot a cop in mufti. The aura, I guess.

I knew OPD had been to see the Jennings woman, of course, but I didn't figure they'd still be going at her—or going at her again so soon. This threw a spanner into the works of my carefully thought-out approach, since cops are not notoriously fond of civilian audiences breathing down their necks while they're trying to work. Hell. I got out of the car and crossed the street. Odds were, they'd just toss me out of there, what with the beard and everything, but nothing ventured . . .

The door was opened by a short, broad plainclothesman with colorless eyes and hair so blond as to be almost white. He stood there like a cigar-store Indian, filling the door frame, but the house was so tiny that I could see pretty much everything in it even so. The door opened into a small square living room with threadbare powder-blue carpeting, smudged walls, and water-stained ceiling tiles. Straight back was an even smaller kitchen, in which Kim Banner sat at a Formica-topped table, talking to someone I couldn't see. Against the south wall of the living room were two closed doors; I assumed the nearer was the bedroom, the farther the bathroom.

I asked the white-haired cop if Detective Banner was there, knowing full well she was.

He looked back over his right shoulder. "Banner."

She looked up, saw me, and turned down the corners of her mouth. She said something I couldn't hear to the person I couldn't see, got up, and came over.

"Okay, Swanson," she said to the other cop. "Go look after the baby." He went. Then she said to me, "You don't waste any time, do you?"

"Neither do you."

"This?" She laughed humorlessly. "This is an exercise in futility. The detectives we sent over earlier didn't get anything useful out of her, but I thought maybe I'd have better luck myself."

"Have you?"

Banner shook her head. "Neither will you," she said cagily.

I shrugged. "I guess I'm like you. I have to find out for myself."

She considered it. I said, "Now or later. You can't shut me out indefinitely." Banner thought about it some more, then moved aside. I took a single step into the room and she grabbed my arm.

"My show." Soft but sincere. "You're an innocent by-stander. Right?"

"Right."

"You want to know anything, you ask me, okay?"

"Okay. Can I have a cup of coffee?"

She looked to see if I was being a wiseacre again, but for once I wasn't. "What with everything, I haven't had my usual hundred and twelve cups yet today, and I feel like I'm wearing a tam-o'-shanter made of concrete."

This time there was a little something in her laugh. "I know the feeling. We'll get you fixed up."

The other cop, Swanson, was leaning against a narrow range crammed into one corner of the kitchen. Seated at the cheap plastic-topped table on a cheap plastic-backed chair, her hands wrapped around a coffee mug, was a thin and hard-looking woman with hair the color of copper wire and, by the look of it, the same consistency. She wore old and comfortable-looking blue pajamas under a well-worn tar-tan robe tied sloppily at the waist, and sat with one bare foot tucked under her.

"More company," Banner said as we entered the room. The woman shrugged. "This," Banner told me, "is appar-ently Jennings's wife, Christina."

"What'cha mean, 'apparently'?" the woman demanded in a voice that went with the hair. "I'm his wife. I've been telling you that all morning."

"So you have," Banner said pleasantly. "It's just that our records don't show Jennings as having a wife; neither do the county's."

"Well, is that my fault? Things get lost, you know."

"They always give the happy couple a copy, too."

Christina Jennings, or whatever, looked back at her coffee mug. "I told you already, I can't find it right now," she said lamely.

Banner looked at me. I looked back. We were thinking the same thing: How many women in North America can't lay hands on their marriage certificates, given about five minutes' lead time?

"Well, never mind that," Banner said, handing me a mug from the drainboard on the counter next to the sink. I poured myself a cup. Four people in that room were about three and a half too many, so I tucked myself as best I could into a corner where the icebox partly blocked a narrow, streaked window that overlooked the back yard, and gulped hot, sludgy coffee. "That's not important right now," Banner was saying. "What is important is where your husband was between about midnight and two this morning." She left enough of a gap between "your" and "husband" to make the implication unmistakable, but beyond an if-looks-could-kill look, Christina refused to rise to the bait.

"I told you that, too, and the guys who were here before," she said, a trifle animatedly. "He was here, with me, all night."

"What were you doing?"

"We weren't doing anything. We were just at home, you know?"

"You must have been doing *something*." This from the other cop, Swanson.

"Well, of course we were doing *something*," Christina said exasperatedly. "You know, we were just, like, watching TV and stuff."

"What sort of stuff?" Banner.

The woman sighed deeply. "I don't know. The sort of stuff you do around the house at night. I did the dishes, swept the kitchen floor, called my mom . . ."

"Did you take out the garbage?" I asked.

She looked at me like I had just dropped from the heavens. Banner looked at me, too, but with a somewhat different expression.

"Can it, Nebraska," she said, so I canned it and poured another cup of whatever this was we were calling coffee while she went at Christina again. "You don't know where your marriage license is, you don't know where your husband is, you don't even know what you did last night. What *do* you know, Christina?"

"I know I'm getting pretty damn tired of you people not believing me—"

"Try telling us the truth and we'll try believing you." Swanson.

"I *am* telling you the truth."

"Then you must be some kind of stupid."

She went up like a bottle rocket. "I'm not stupid, you dirty motherfu——"

"Hey!" Banner yelled. "Knock it off. Sit down." Christina sat, sullenly, and rested her head against her folded arms. "This is no good; we aren't getting anywhere." Banner's hoarse voice was gentle. "Now, I know you're upset, and I'm sorry, but we need answers, Christina, and I don't think you're being straight with us. I don't want to have to take you downtown, but if you—"

She stopped because we had all simultaneously become aware of the heaving of Christina's slender shoulders and the soft, almost inaudible sound of her cry.

Banner looked at Swanson. He shrugged with Scandinavian impassivity. She looked back at Christina, who raised her head from the table to show us her red, streaming eyes. "He killed that man," she said, sobbing.

The cops traded looks again. Banner sat in the only other chair at the table. "Tell me about it," she urged softly. "From the beginning."

Christina took a minute or two to compose herself, then told it.

Walt Jennings had been home in the early evening, working on his favorite hobby: drinking cheap rye. And, as was typical when he drank cheap rye, he got increasingly unpleasant the more he drank. "He'd get mad at that banker, that Castelar," Christina told us. "Just furious. He'd say the man was responsible for everything that had gone wrong in his life since he came up here from Oklahoma, that Castelar had taken away his farm, what he'd worked and saved all his life to own, and that he was gonna—gonna kill him someday."

It was an old story, to Christina as much as to the rest of us, and she hadn't really paid that much attention to him, having heard it all before. Eventually Jennings ran out of booze, and that made him even madder. "At about eleven he put on his coat and I asked him where he was going at that hour, with the weather so crummy."

"What did he say?" Banner asked.

"He didn't say nothing, he just pushed me out of the way and went out."

"And that's the last you've seen of him?"

"I—I think maybe I should have a lawyer."

Swanson rolled his eyes and Banner sighed lightly. "Mrs. Jennings," she said, switching to the formal form of address and ridding her tone of any trace of sarcasm, "you can get one if you want one, but it's not you who's in trouble here. We're just trying to get an idea where your husband might have gone."

Christina narrowed her eyes and sniffed. "Isn't there some law about a wife not having to talk against her husband?"

Banner rubbed her temples. "That's right, but we're not in court."

"And you already told us he killed Castelar," Swanson reminded her.

"I was upset," Christina said haughtily, straightening in

her chair and facing him. But then she slouched again, put her elbow on the table and her chin in her hand. "Aw, what the fuck, I've probably said too much already.

"No, I saw Walt after that. For about two minutes. He came back here a few hours later. I don't know what time it was—I'd already gone to bed—but it was late, real late, 'cause I was up till almost one. I'm a pretty heavy sleeper, but Walt was tearing around here like to wake the dead."

"What was he doing?"

"Packing. He had this old green duffel from the army, and he was throwing stuff in it like there was no tomorrow—shirts and pants and underwear, and not folding them, either, just stuffing them in there like they were rags. And then—this is crazy—he came in here and started rummaging through the cupboards."

"He took food?"

She nodded. "Canned stuff, mostly, plus some candy bars and a box of Cheerios."

Jennings gave no explanation for his behavior, or any indication where he was heading. Christina asked him, but he ignored her. When she tried to get him to sit down and talk to her, he swung at her again, but missed. "He wasn't even looking, like the way you'd swing at a fly buzzing around you when you're trying to do something." She estimated he was here and gone within ten minutes at the most.

"And you have no idea what time this was?"

"Not really. When he left I sat down on the couch"—she nodded toward the living room—"and tried to figure out what was going on. I guess I fell asleep, 'cause that's where I was when the police—the other police—came this morning."

There was a brief intermission while Christina visited the bathroom, then Banner and Swanson backed her up and took her over the same ground again, looking for holes. I'd heard all I needed to hear, so I finished my cup, pulled on my parka, and stepped out the back door. No one protested. I stood on the ice-crusted cement stoop and looked at the footprints in the snow running from the door to two battered garbage cans in the far corner of the yard, and back.

They weren't particularly fascinating footprints, except they were broken and irregular, footprints made on hard, crusted snow, not soft new snow. I thought about that. It had last snowed three days ago—not counting the gravelly stuff spitting off and on yesterday—and it hadn't been all that cold in the meantime. Cold enough, sure, but not bitterly cold, because the skies had stayed overcast and that held in what warmth there was. The clouds blew out sometime in the small hours this morning, the hard, granulated snow quit entirely, and the wind came on with a vengeance, driving temperatures down to antarctic levels.

And crusting over old snow that had still been soft and moist where it lay untamped. Like in a person's back yard.

I went back to the garbage cans, following a path parallel to the footprints. The police wouldn't be able to do anything with them, but you try to be considerate. There were plenty of other prints, not only to and from the back door but also alongside the house, where the garbagemen would walk from the street, but these tracks were partly filled in and themselves crusted over, telling me they had been made some time before the temps dropped so sharply last night.

I yanked the lid off the nearest garbage can. It was full of garbage. I poked at the brown bags and newspapers, but they didn't look too interesting.

I yanked the lid off the second garbage can. More garbage. But half hidden beneath a white plastic bag was a dented three-pound Butternut coffee can with the orange plastic top in place. I fished out the can and peeled off the cold-stiffened lid.

The can held a dirty beige towel, wadded up.

The towel held a .38 Smith & Wesson Model 10.

Chapter Six

Kim Banner said, "What've you got there?"

I handed her the coffee can. "It followed me home, Mom; can I keep it?"

She held the can in her left hand, lifted out the dirty towel with her right, and shook it. The ends of the rag fell away and the revolver glinted darkly in her palm while she frowned at it like she didn't know how it got there. "What's this?"

"That's a gun, Detective," I said.

"Boy howdy, you sure are quick with those snappy comebacks."

"Us hard-boiled private eyes have a reputation to live up to." I shucked my parka and refilled the mug I'd left on top of the fridge. "But I wasn't trying to be wise when I asked about taking out the garbage." I explained about the footprints I had seen in the back yard and how they had to have been made after the snow froze over, sometime between, say, midnight and sunup.

"Well, aren't you clever," Banner murmured, lids drooping over her dark eyes.

"We aims to please, ma'am."

"My hero." She weighed the gun in her palm. "What do you know about this?" she asked Christina in a deceptively lazy fashion.

The redhead shrugged. "The yard's wide open; anyone could've stuck it in our trash cans."

"He says the tracks are new, and they run from here to the trash and back."

Christina gave this some thought. Then she sighed heavily and rolled her eyes. "All right. It's Walt's gun. I threw it away."

"When?"

"Last night, after Walt left. The first time, I mean. He talked lots about getting that banker, but this time—I don't know; this time I was scared he was going to go out and get good and drunk and maybe do something stupid."

"Like come back for his gun," Swanson prompted.

She nodded, head lowered.

Banner rewrapped the gun, put it back in the can, and worked the orange plastic lid back into place. I asked how long she thought the gun would stay fresh in the can and she said long enough to run ballistics tests—if "the boys" had ever found the bullet that went through Jack Castelar's brain. Then she put the can on the table and stood with both palms flat on either side of it, leaning over Christina Jennings. She studied the red-haired woman for a minute, maybe longer. Christina studied her coffee mug. The mug, I noticed, had my name on it, in white lettering against a red field. I must be more popular than I thought; just the other day I had seen a department-store counter full of toy footballs with my name on them. Come to think of it, they were red, too.

Banner let her head drop and she looked at me from under her right arm. "It doesn't work, does it?" she said.

I shook my head. "Still too warm last night. The snow wouldn't've been crusted over yet. The footprints would be all different. Smoother, better defined."

Christina made a face at me. "Okay, so maybe it was

later than I remember. I wasn't punching a time clock, you know."

"Yeah, it was later, all right," Swanson said. "Like *after* Jennings had already used the gun on Castelar."

Her metallic hair glinted as she spun around in her chair. "You don't know that," she said loudly.

He matched her volume. "You already told us he killed him."

"I didn't mean it," she yelled. "I mean, I was afraid he did. So that's why I tried to get rid of the gun."

"That's good." Banner's tone was heavy with sarcasm. "That's great. If the gun was lying around here, Jennings must not have used it to kill Castelar. Your getting rid of it would help him out a lot when he tried to prove his innocence."

Christina looked like she'd been hit between the eyes with a rubber mallet. "I didn't think of that," she said slowly.

"When?" I said. "When you threw the gun away last night—or just now, when you made up the story?"

She frowned and pursed her lips. "I don't—"

"You sure as hell *do* know what I mean." I tossed a glance under the table. "You need bigger feet to make prints like those outside—something more like a cop's."

Swanson started to protest but Banner cut him off. "Jennings threw that gun away when he came home to pack, didn't he?" she demanded of Christina.

The redhead looked up, first at me, then at Swanson, as if she expected one of us to break down and confess to it.

"*Didn't* he?"

She nodded. "That's what woke me up, hearing this back door slam when he came in from out back." She slumped back in her chair, which squeaked in response, and rubbed her eyes until they were red. "I didn't really think Walt was going to kill him. I mean, I heard it all before, you know? I just figured he was going down to one of the bars he hangs out at, or going to boff that other little bubblehead, so I just went to b——"

"Whoa, wait a minute, *what* other little bubblehead—Kate Castelar? You knew about her and Jennings?"

Christina made a noise that you might call a laugh. "Well, it ain't much of a secret, is it?"

Banner looked at me a little dazedly. "I guess not. Well, tell me about it."

Christina rolled her shoulders a little. "What's to tell? Walt's usually got a little piece on the side. He always has, as long as I've known him. Shit, I used to be it when he was living with this other broad—I mean, before him and me got married, you know?"

"You don't mind?" Banner was incredulous.

"Honey, I can tell you never met Walt Jennings. If he wasn't getting any on the side, he'd be all over me like fat on a pig, all the time. As it is I only get about three nights' sleep a week. No, I don't mind, as long as he keeps it kind of, you know, discreet. And he does. He thinks he's sneaking around behind my back."

"Well, how long's he been not sneaking around with Kate Castelar?"

"Oh . . ." She clicked her tongue against the roof of her mouth while she considered the question. "Six months, eight months. I don't know; they come and they go. It was still hot when this one started up, I'm pretty sure."

I said, "How'd they happen to get together anyway?"

She gave me a look. "I don't exactly keep records, you know. I suppose he met her in one of the bars he hangs out in. That seems to be where he meets most people. Come to think of it, he met *me* in a bar . . ."

"What bars? Where does he hang around, usually?"

"Excuse me," Banner said testily. I looked at her. "Innocent bystander, remember?"

"Well, don't you want to know too?"

She mussed her short blondish hair, then smoothed it out again. "Oh, all right." To Christina: "What places?"

"God, I don't know. They're just bars. You know, kind of cowboy bars, most of them, I suppose on account of the stockyards. There's one called the Cattleman he goes to a lot, I think. Another one called the Bottom Dollar. They're all off sort of that way"—she waved a bony hand—"off of L Street and around there."

It was hard to picture Kate in places like those names suggested. But, then, it was hard to picture her with someone like Jennings, too.

I said, "Did you see her when she was here yesterday?"

"I saw her, sure, the poor dumb kid, crying all over the place, pounding on the door, and yelling for Walt—but I didn't talk to her. No way do I need that kind of scene. No, I just pretended I wasn't home, and she finally went away."

"Gosh, I hope no one minds if I try and get us back on the subject here," Banner said impatiently. I shrugged. The other cop, Swanson, was watching us as if we were a not very interesting movie. Christina looked up expectantly. "You woke up when you heard him coming in the back door," Banner prompted.

"Oh, yeah. Well, that's it. I didn't know what he had been doing out there, and I guess I didn't even think twice about it, what with him running all over the place throwing things into that duffel bag. I forgot all about it until *he*"—I got the nod—"brought in that can."

I tried to look modest.

"I knew right away what was in it, and I knew Walt must've gone out there to hide it when he came home last night. And I knew why." She shook her head in disbelief. "I never thought he'd really go through with it."

Banner straightened herself up, stretched, and rubbed her lower back. "I guess that's it, Swanee, for now at least.

Mrs. Jennings, you'll have to get dressed now. We'd like you to come with us and give us a formal statement."

"Jesus H. Christ, what've I been doing all day?" she griped, but she got up, went through the living room and into the bedroom.

Banner made a noise and rolled her head a couple of times, working the muscles of her neck. "Better call the lab," she told Swanson, "and tell them we've got something for them if they've got something for us." He moved heavily, solidly, into the living room. "Well, I guess maybe it's a good thing I let you sit in after all," she told me, reaching past me for the coffeepot and emptying it into her mug. "Finding that gun's the closest thing to a break we've had, and you did a good job of helping get the straight story out of her."

"Her original story would have come apart like a crumb cake even without benefit of my staggering intellect. Then you'd've called in the Dead End Kids to tear the joint apart, and they'd've found the gun in no time; it was hardly well hidden."

"And he's modest, too. Any more like you at home, sailor?"

"I'm the last of my breed," I said casually. "Why, am I being propositioned?"

Her eyes were direct, open and smiling. "I have an unbreakable rule about keeping my professional and personal lives separate. I don't date cops."

"I'm not a cop."

"I know. And this case won't last forever."

"Even though it feels like it has already," I said, rubbing my neck.

"Well, then, maybe we'll see later."

"Maybe we will. I should tell you first—I'm sort of married."

"Sort of? That's a neat trick. What are you, another Walt Jennings—too much man for one woman?"

She laughed and I joined her. "Not quite. I—oh hell, it's a long story, and very complicated, and I'm not entirely sure I understand it myself. I suppose it's fair to say we're separated, and have been for a long time. We get back together every now and then—we're together now, in fact—but that only seems to underscore the fact that our differences can't be worked out."

"Sounds wonderful. I'm sorry, that was crass. I guess maybe I'm a little disappointed. I don't date married men."

"That's okay, neither do I. Cases aren't the only things that don't last forever, I'm afraid. I don't know where my situation is going, but it can't go on as it has been. I've known that for some time, I just haven't known what to do about it. I'm not sure I do yet. But—well, as you said, maybe we'll see later."

I grinned at her and she grinned back. "Maybe we will."

We were still grinning like idiots when Swanson reentered the room. I cut it out but Banner didn't care; she smiled up at him questioningly.

"They found the slug," Swanson reported. "It's pretty banged up—it was imbedded in a tree trunk, and they figure it must have ricocheted more than once to get there."

Banner raised her eyebrows. "Heavy sucker."

"Solid lead. Flat-nosed. And from a thirty-eight, all right." Banner looked up at me cheerily. I smiled back. "As for the trees on the other side of the road, where the killer hid: no good," Swanson continued. "Bartels says it's next to impossible to get decent footprints in snow anyhow, and this was all messed up and stuff besides."

"Figures." Banner was philosophical. "You know, if this character hadn't gone around shooting off his big mouth about killing Castelar, he could have probably gotten away with it pretty easily. The setup is perfect, just perfect—way out in the middle of nowhere, darker than the inside of a ripe olive, more than half a mile away from the nearest neighbor."

"You know what they say," I said. "There is no such thing as the perfect crime."

"Hah. You don't know my mechanic."

Christina emerged from the bedroom wearing gray slacks and a maroon sweatshirt over a white turtleneck. She had run a brush through her stiff red hair and put a little makeup on her face and she didn't look half bad—or wouldn't have, if she'd lost her ugly scowl.

"All right," she said shrilly, "let's get this over with." To me: "Unplug that pot, will you? Walt'd kill me if I let this place burn down."

"Lucky we have his gun," Swanson said, and steered her toward the front door.

Chapter Seven

Millar College is one of those peculiar little liberal arts institutions you'll encounter here and there on the Great Plains—or, as I notice they've been calling them in recent years, the Central Plains—springing up like sunflowers and, sometimes, vanishing just as quickly. Frequently they exist in remote, even isolated areas, and you wonder who on earth thought to put a college *here*, and who on earth attends it. Back when I was in college, lo, these many years ago, the consensus was that such schools existed for students who couldn't get into a *real* school, or were afraid of the competition, or both. You went to a place like Millar, the reasoning went, you got your 2.5 average, and then you left and got married or sold Dodges or something.

The analysis was a little shaky, but that didn't bother us then and it didn't bother me now. Kate Castelar, after all, seemed to fit the profile. From what I gathered, she had hardly been a scholastic ball of fire, having had to stick around a semester after she ordinarily would have graduated in order to rectify some deficiencies in her academic record. She had managed to escape with her B.A. at the end of the fall term, just before Christmas, so there were still kids around who knew her. In fact, her best friend and a boyfriend had another semester to go before they were turned loose on society. Kate's mother had given me their names and the assurance that they were very close to Kate, but I knew from experience that such assurances aren't always worth much. Even on through college, kids change friends at an astounding pace, and parents are typically hard-pressed to keep up. But then, it was a place to start—and what else did I have?

I parked illegally in a permit-only lot and, lowering my head against the wind, trudged up a hillock to the campus. A handful of fairly new buildings, a handful of fairly decent teachers, a handful of fairly conscious students—that was the norm for such schools, and by outward signs Millar was no different. It being only a few days into the spring semester (although a Midwestern January is hardly what you'd call springlike), I knew better than to waste my time in the library. I asked a kid where the student union was, and he pointed me toward a half-buried flat-roofed one-story rectangle slung between two taller sand-colored buildings that could only have been dorms. A dirty diagonal path to the union was tramped in the snow on the lawn, but I stuck to the sidewalk. Bad enough I was trespassing—having a twenty-year-old dislike of academic bureaucrats and no particular reason to expect any cooperation if I went through proper channels—I could at least keep off whatever grass may have been dormant under the snowcap.

Whoever Maureen L. Hathaway was, her Memorial Student Center was nearly deserted. That may have been because the one o'clock classes were in session, or it may just have been because the place was astonishingly unappealing. It was all linoleum and hard plastic chairs at wobbly round plastic-topped tables, cold harsh fluorescent lights, and pale green concrete-block walls—all steeped in the smell of old hamburger grease emanating from the ubiquitous snack bar at the opposite end. Hungry as I was, I was not yet so famished that I would actually consider eating there.

I asked a trio of girls at one of the tables if they knew

either Jo Richter or Tom Black, and, if so, where I might find them now. The girls knew them both—it was a tiny college; they probably knew everybody—debated the issue a bit, and decided that Jo had class this hour, but Tom was probably at his work-study job in the campus post office. They gave me directions; I thanked them and left. No one asked my name or business, the beard notwithstanding.

The post office was in the basement of the Ad Building, a fifty-year-old red brick number that was one of the few really academic-looking buildings on campus. The others could just as well have been part of a hospital complex or an office park. A set of well-worn marble stairs took me down to the basement, and once there, there was only one direction to go—along a wide, abbreviated, windowless hallway, one side of which was made up of scores of three-inch-square lockboxes, the other of standard institutional wall tiles.

At the end of the bank of mailboxes was a postal counter, but its steel rolling wall was down, locked. I continued down to a banged-up blond-wood door, the kind with the big metal plate at the bottom. One of those engraved plastic signs you see everywhere said EMPLOYEES ONLY, but the door stood a quarter of the way open and muted rock music leaked out. Culture Club, I think, but I don't keep up on the bands much. I never quite got over the Beatles breaking up, you know?

I put my head through the door and looked into the mail room. It was long and narrow and nearly filled with open gray canvas bags in wheeled aluminum-tube carts and similar bags, closed up tight, on the floor along the far wall. There was only one worker in the room, an athletic-looking boy with short dark hair and rather heavy features. He wore a dark blue sweater over a light blue turtleneck, jeans, and battered tennis shoes with Velcro strips in place of the laces. When I tapped on the door he glanced away from the boxes, into which he had been slipping letters, then back just as quickly.

"The window closes at noon," he recited as if it wasn't the first time. "You'll have to come back in the morning."

"Are you Tom Black?"

Again he looked, this time for a beat or two longer before he went back to the boxes. "Yeah. What about it?"

"I'd like to talk to you about Kate Castelar." I entered the room and pulled out my wallet.

He studied my I.D. for several seconds, and when he looked back at my face his voice was quieter, lower, and colder. "I heard about her dad. That's real terrible. But what's with Kate?"

He didn't need to have the whole sorry mess, so I didn't give it to him. I told him that Castelar's murder had been extraordinarily hard on Kate, that she had run away, and that I was looking for her. It was true enough, as far as it went. "I was hoping you, or someone else you can think of, would have any idea where Kate might go if she wanted to get away, be by herself, do some thinking."

"I don't think so," he said breezily, after mulling it over for perhaps as long as three seconds. "Sorry."

I said, "It might work better if you thought about it for a—"

"I don't have to think about it," he said testily, slamming a letter home. "I know what I don't know, and I don't know anything that would help you. Kate and I aren't real close."

"Oh yeah? Her mother seems to have the impression you and Kate *are* real close."

He shrugged elaborately without turning away from the boxes. "Yeah, well, Kate's mother kind of lives in her own world, you know?" He made a harsh sound and fired another letter into its pigeonhole. "Funny, isn't it? The mother's a space case and the son's a total asshole and both of the girls are pretty strange, so who gets killed? The old man, the only halfway normal one in the bunch. Funny."

"Yeah, it's a riot. You sure seem to have the family all scoped out—I mean, considering you're only a nodding acquaintance."

He threw his letters onto a narrow shelf that ran below the lowest row of mailboxes, turned toward me, and folded his arms tightly across his chest. "Okay. Kate and I did go together for a while. But we broke up. Last year, before summer break, and we haven't even spoken to each other since then. All right?"

"Why'd you break up?"

"None of your fucking business, is it?"

"I don't know. My fucking business right now is to find Kate, and you're not being very helpful. I'm sorry if she dumped you, but it happens. Don't let your ego get in the way here. You might not think so, but you could know something that proves helpful to me—to Kate." I swiped the gist of that last part of the speech from any number of private-eye novels. I've never known it to be true, but what the hell, it sounds impressive.

He glared at me for several seconds and I wondered if he was going to take a swing at me. If he did, I figured I'd just have to take it and leave; I didn't have any right to be on campus in the first place, much less leaving bruises on the student body. Assuming, of course, it would be me leaving the bruises.

As it was, it was all academic, so to speak, because when he unfolded his arms it was only to place his hands low on his hips, lean against the unsteady-looking shelf, and sigh heavily, resignedly. "All right. I'm sorry. It's just . . . Kate's kind of a sore subject with me, is all."

"No fooling."

He smiled ruefully. "Yeah. Well, anyhow, I sure haven't heard from Kate or anything, if that's what you're wondering. You know, if she needed a place to stay or something, she wouldn't call me, not in a million years. She'd probably call one of her girlfriends . . ."

"I don't think Kate probably would contact anybody; what I'm trying to find out, like I said, is whether she had any special, private place she used to go to, maybe that you and she used to go to."

"Well, there was this Pizza Hut out on the highway; you mean like that?"

I somehow doubted that Jennings and Kate were hiding from the law in a pizza parlor on Highway 36. "Not exactly," I said. "When I was in college, there was this storage room under the old gym, and I knew how to get into it. So sometimes in the evening I'd go down there, just for the solitude. Sometimes I'd bring a friend with me . . ." I hadn't thought of that in ages, and the recollection of it now caused a sudden keen stab of sadness. The "friend" had been Jen, and the hours spent huddled there with her seemed infinitely long ago, seemed to belong to somebody else's past, not mine; somebody who had a future ahead of him instead of a history behind him.

Tom was nodding gently, almost as if caught up in the same reverie. "I don't know," he said thoughtfully. "Usually we'd be, you know, together here, in my room. Or at her house, if her folks weren't around. Or—"

Suddenly he seemed unusually interested in the dull gray tiles beneath his feet.

"Or?"

He brought his eyes up without moving his head. "Well . . . there was this place we went to a few times, just before—before we broke up. In a way, I suppose it was part of the reason we called it off." Another great sigh. "See, Kate's folks have this other house besides the one they live in. I guess they bought another little farm near theirs a few years ago. They rent out the land and all the buildings except for this little three-room farmhouse that was there, and that's empty—well, except for some furniture and stuff that no one uses. None of the kids were supposed to go down there, but Kate got a copy made of the key one time and, well, like I said, we went there once or twice."

That was more like it. Surely the cops would have checked out all the buildings on Castelar's property as a matter of course, but it never hurt to follow up on these things. I made a note in the little wire-bound pad I carry to augment my criminally unreliable memory and asked Black if he could think of any other similar places Kate might have run to.

He shook his head, still studying the scuffed flooring. "No. I don't even know if she'd go there. We had a couple of really bad scenes there, some pretty big fights, stuff I don't like to think about, but—I don't know, maybe she doesn't care."

"You said the place contributed to you two calling it quits. What did you mean?"

He eyed me from under the ribbon of dark hair that slid toward his brow when his head was lowered. "Is it important?"

I shrugged. "In this business, you never know what's important until you've got all, or almost all, of the pieces together. It's like . . . don't you always do about twice as much research as you need for a term paper?"

Tom gave a snort of a laugh, accompanied by a half-smile and an uneasy shifting of his feet. "I suppose," he said resignedly. "Okay. Well, you know, Kate and I went together for about a year, and most of that time we were . . . sleeping together."

"No fooling. You know, I've heard that that happens on campus every once in a great while."

"Like I said, usually we'd be in my room here or Kate's room at home when no one was around. And that was all right, you know, that was cool. But after she got the idea of us sneaking over to the other place—well, then it started getting a little heavy for me."

"Heavy?"

"Yeah . . . Kate always got off on some shit that was a little, you know, kinky. Which was okay; I thought it was kind of exciting, too, kind of—to tie her up a little, maybe give her butt a couple of slaps, order her around—that kind of stuff. Nothing too serious, you know. Just playing around, doing something different every so often.

"But then she started to really get into it, and it started getting a little too bizarre for me. Especially after she got the key to that little house. In the dorm, you couldn't make too much noise because the walls are like tissue paper. And even at her house, you never really knew when someone was going to be coming home. Usually her brother, creeping around the joint like Boris Karloff or somebody. But in the other place, there was no one around for miles, usually, and no chance of anyone walking in. So she kind of went crazy, really got into these elaborate S and M scenes that were just too much for me. At least, as a steady diet." He made a small gesture with both hands. "Well, that's it, I guess. She wasn't interested in normal sex anymore, and she wanted me to be rougher and rougher with her—I mean, spanking her or whipping her with a belt until she cried and begged for forgiveness; real weird shit like that—and I just thought it was getting kind of sick. I wasn't her daddy and I told her that, and I told her that these feelings of worthlessness or guilt or misdirected anger or whatever they were were getting in the way of our relationship. She had a real negative self-image and it was getting worse, and I thought she should see someone about it. But when I'd tell her this she'd just laugh it off, tell me I was too straight, too uptight. We had a couple of big fights about it, and she said it was just a game, and that if I didn't want to play it with her she'd find someone who would. And I said that was a good idea. And she said she thought so too."

Again he made the gesture.

"That was back in May, just before the end of the term, and that was the last time I saw her. I mean, except around campus." Tom hadn't so much as glanced at me since he began his story; now he raised his head and looked at me directly, something like a challenge in his eyes and in his voice: "Does that help you any?"

I hadn't known how to react while he was telling it—I was glad that he hadn't seemed able to look me in the eye—and I didn't know how to react now. One of the really swell parts of this crappy business is that you can pick up so much fascinating trivia about people's private lives; you get these charming glimpses at the skeletons everybody has stashed in one closet or another; you get the intimate, inside story about others' secret selves, the little quirks and hang-ups that we'd prefer remain hidden from the world at large, and maybe even from ourselves. Sometimes the tidbits are useful, important, even vital to the matter at hand; more often, however, they are not, they are merely the noxious by-product of the investigator's excavations. Either way, you can't forecast it before you start digging. Either way, some damage will be done, if only to someone's self-esteem. Either way, a skeleton is awfully hard to hide again once it's been dug up.

And people ask me why I want out of this line of work.

I didn't have any answer for Tom Black and I didn't feel like trying to make one up. I said I was sorry if I'd made him uncomfortable, but I was sure he'd agree that the important thing was to find Kate. He didn't say anything, but he reclaimed his stack of mail so I figured the audience was at an end. I gave him one of my cards and urged him to call me if he thought of anything else, thanked him for his trouble, and retreated toward the door.

He stopped me as my hand touched the knob.

"Just for the record," he said quietly.

I turned to face him.

"*I* broke up with Kate. Not the other way around. Okay?"

"Okay." What the hell did I care?

° • °

Jo Richter, Kate's best friend, didn't have much more to offer; in fact, she didn't have as much to offer as Tom had, and I was slightly grateful for it. Tom's revelations had left me with a bad taste in my mouth and a sour feeling in my belly—although, let's be reasonable, either or both could have been due to the lousy coffee that had constituted my only meal thus far today—even if they gave me some insights into the nagging question of what a girl like Kate Castelar saw in a guy like Walt Jennings. If she was possessed of a growing sense of worthlessness or unspecified guilt, then she may have felt that consorting with someone of Jennings's character was just the sort of thing a rotten kid like her deserved. That Jennings had a professed loathing for Kate's father, whom she loved, would make it even worse—or better, from her point of view. Finding out that he had a wife, or at least a live-in lover, must have sent her into a masochistic seventh heaven. In fact, she had as good as told me that she was getting what she deserved.

Having proved to myself that I could churn out half-baked pop psychoanalysis just as well as Tom Black could—maybe even better, since I'd been at it longer—I went in search of the Richter girl and found her exiting her one o'clock class. She had another at two, which gave us ten minutes—about eight minutes more than I needed. Jo and the others in the clique hadn't seen much of Kate that last semester, because Kate had a new boyfriend—an "older guy," she told me, and I restrained the impulse to kick her in the shin. Kate didn't talk to them much about the boyfriend. At least not to Jo, a tallish, chubby girl who had dark hair worn high on her head and low on her neck and the sort of personality that would not encourage you to confide in her. Unless you simply were trying to avoid the expense of renting a billboard. It quickly became apparent that the Richter girl was going to be of no real help, and if Kate's confidante knew nothing useful, no one else was very likely to either.

The little hand of my watch was on the two and the big hand was sneaking up on the twelve. I was tired and hungry. Millar College seemed to have afforded all the education I was liable to get there. And the longer I stayed the more I risked attracting official attention, which I did not want. It had been a lot of years since I was called down to the dean's office; I didn't care for it back then, and I didn't see as how I'd like it any better now. So I thanked Jo Richter, quit the relative warmth of the Science Building, and allowed the stiff prairie wind to blow me back to the badly plowed lot my car was in.

On the windshield was a green ticket, trapped under the wiper and fluttering like a dying bird. It threatened the withholding of my grades until I coughed up for a fifteen-buck parking fine. Such documents may strike terror in the hearts of recalcitrant Millar frosh, but not the likes of I. It went into a ball and to the ice underfoot, where the wind immediately sent it scurrying off.

Less easily handled were a few alterations that had been made to the vehicle itself.

Someone had taken an intense dislike to the windshield and had hit at it three or four times with something small and hard and blunt. Maybe a pipe. Angry white spiderwebs spread themselves across the surface of the glass, radiating from small silvery hearts where the blows had fallen. I guessed that whoever was responsible had wanted to smash it in entirely, but you need something with heft and surface area—a brick, a sledge—to do a real number on safety glass.

Belatedly realizing this, my anonymous pal had taken another approach, touching up his handiwork with a little black paint flung creatively across the starred glass. Then, too bashful to put his name to the work, this automotive-minded Jackson Pollock had merely scrawled STOP across the hood with a half-dry brush or a wadded rag or something.

Stop what?

Ordinarily no one tells you to stop something unless you're *doing* something. And I wasn't doing anything. Or, at any rate, I didn't feel like I was accomplishing anything. If he did, then he was more easily impressed than I am—or perhaps he knew something I didn't, and something he didn't want me to know.

I didn't for an instant entertain the possibility that I was the hapless victim of random vandalism. For one thing, none of the cars parked nearby had been molested. For another, that faint but legible message on the hood was not along the lines of STOP KILLING WHALES or STOP THE ARMS RACE or STOP ABORTIONS HERE; it was definitely, specifically directed at your humble correspondent.

Stop.

Stop what?

God*damn*. Bad enough I didn't know what in hell I was doing, now I had some lunkhead telling me to cut it out. If I was on to something, I wished he'd've left me some sort of hint. It would have only been polite. I unlocked the car and climbed behind the wheel to get out of the wind, rubbed my dry, itchy eyes, and tried to make some sense of it. Could Tom Black have run out here and done it while I was hunting up Jo Richter? No, not enough time—even if he'd had the paint in his knapsack, even if some eerie supernatural power enabled him to pick out my car from an entire lotful—and besides, why should he have? He hadn't had to tell me as much as he did; he could have left it where it was when he first told me to go to blazes.

Who else, then? I thought back over this unnaturally long and still unfinished day. Whom could I have stirred up, whom might I have made nervous . . .? Well, whom had I met? Kennerly. Banner. Emily Castelar, Vince Castelar. Christina Jennings.

Christina Jennings.

The redesign of my car wasn't the work of a woman. Despite my best efforts, I'm still enough of a sexist to say that while a female hand might have flung the paint, the one that swung the pipe (or whatever) was attached to a man. But the general idea might have been hers. I was the one who found the gun that implicated her husband; maybe she was afraid I'd find something else. She could easily have lined up a friend, a relative, to follow me out here and try to scare me off the—

Nope, didn't wash. By the time I had decided to come out to Millar, Christina Jennings was safely wrapped in the loving arms of the Omaha Police Division. She would've had time to have lined up someone to follow me from her place all the way out here *before* Banner and Swanson took her downtown (as they say in the movies). When would she have had time? From the minute she first set eyes on me, she had been out of the company of the cops only when she was in her bedroom dressing for her date with the police stenographer. Even if she'd had an extension in the bedroom, Swanson had been on the living room phone almost the whole time.

Besides, why would Christina sic anyone on me? So I found the gun, so what? As I'd told Banner, someone would have come across the gun sooner or later, and probably sooner. And what good would it do Christina to try and scare me off the case? It wouldn't help Walt any. Even if I turned in my badge right now, went straight home, and cooked up some new excuse for not working on my novel, the cops would keep right on looking for Jennings until this ol' world was as cold and dead as the moon. And when you're talking cops, you're talking one whole *lot* of windshields.

Okay, not Christina. Who? Certainly not Kennerly. Banner? Nah; she was more the type who'd dump the paint over your head. Young Castelar? This morning he had been pissed because I *wasn't* out pounding the pavement. Emily Castelar? Riiiight.

Hell, this was the wrong approach. Whoever had made this mess couldn't have just up and decided to reach out and touch me, because even *I* hadn't known in advance I was coming out here.

That left two possibilities. One, someone here on campus had been busy. Which I doubted very much. The only candidate was Tom Black, and I'd already ruled him out.

So, behind door number two: Someone had been following me, perhaps all day, certainly at least since I'd left the Jennings place. Someone who had a vested interest in my search for Kate. Someone who was obviously quite distressed over the work that I was doing, the places I was going, the people I was talking to, the questions I was asking. Someone who felt strongly obliged to try to persuade me to change my ways.

And although I couldn't make any sense of it, although I tried to ignore it, one name kept popping up in my head like a cork in a rain barrel.

Walt Jennings.

Chapter Eight

It gave me a creepy feeling.

I caught myself checking out the parking lot, looking for suspicious characters, expecting to see a blue Ford pickup.

What I saw were blue hard-edged shadows, long and growing longer by the moment, reminding me that winter afternoons out here in the nation's breadbasket are short indeed. I estimated two, two and a half hours before darkness crept in, and I wanted to run one more errand and at least get started back to the city in that time. The idea of ripping around on unfamiliar country highways in the dead of night in the dead of winter didn't exactly set my heart a-thumpin'—especially since I wasn't going to have the luxury of an unimpaired view of the road.

There was nothing to do about the damage done by the blows to the glass, but if that had been my only problem, I think I still could have navigated well enough. The points of impact themselves were white and opaque, but there were only about four of them, each no bigger than a quarter, and they were clustered on the passenger side.

That must have been where the vandal had stood, because the worst of the paint was on that side, too, on the windshield, down the right fender, and onto the parking lot, where the droplets had eaten jagged black cavities in the snow.

I circled the car a few times, feeling sick and mad. The Chevy was old and beat up, and it probably wasn't worth as much as the paint splashed over it, but it was mine, it was a part of me, and even after I repaired the damage, it wouldn't be the same. If you've ever had your home broken into you'll know how I felt—vulnerable, exposed, slightly numb.

Since the damage hadn't gotten any better by the third circuit, I stopped, stripped off a glove, and gingerly touched the paint. It was dry, cold, and slick. I prodded it with a thumbnail, and again more forcefully. It peeled back, a little stubbornly—like the stuff you scrape off to reveal secret numbers on game cards from fast-food joints—but it peeled back.

Whatever kind of paint this was, it didn't adhere at all well to ice-cold glass.

I tackled it with an ice-scraper, which worked okay, but I soon discovered that once an edge was loosened the dried paint could be pulled away in long, uneven, brittle-rubbery strips. Between the peeling and the scraping and a few shots from the washer, I managed to remove the worst of it, except where it had bled into the threadlike cracks in the glass. The visibility situation was not what you'd call ideal, and the sun had sunk noticeably in the half hour or forty-five minutes I'd spent on clean-up detail, but by sitting tall in the saddle and relying heavily on the outboard mirrors, I figured I would be able to avoid calamity on the drive home.

But first things first.

I found the highway right where I had left it and traced it back toward Omaha until I found my exit. Instead of heading south, however, I looped a wide loop that put me into the northbound lanes, where I stayed for the next five miles or so. And there, where the highway intersected with a well-lighted franchise-dotted four-lane strip, sat the West Omaha State Bank and Trust.

The name had led me to expect a real bank building, of the old-fashioned variety—stone steps and white pillars and gold eagles on the peaked roof—but this was in fact a modern and new-looking building, indistinguishable from any suburban bank or S&L. It was a squat square box of red brick and smoked glass, sitting at an angle on the lot next to a Dairy Queen. At first I thought the lot was empty, and I wondered if the place was closed out of respect for Jack Castelar. But as I pulled off the street I spotted four cars parked behind the building, near the drive-through lane. Employee parking. I swung round the front of the building, put the car next to the handicap parking slot at the front doors, and stepped out onto the sand-sprinkled pavement. After a brief pause to moon over the violence inflicted on my poor old Chevy, I turned to the outer doors of the bank. A neatly lettered four-by-five card taped to the glass indicated that tomorrow was the day the place would close *in memoriam*. I guess they figured they should give their regulars a little notice.

The lobby was small and square. Not too surprising, that; so was the building. Three pale wooden desks were deployed at strategic locations near the south and east walls of the room. The latter of these walls was decorated with two so-so Western-motif paintings separated by a great wooden door bearing a plaque whose two lines of gold lettering said, respectively, J. A. CASTELAR and PRESIDENT. Directly across from me, on the north, was the tellers' counter, and beyond it the drive-up. The tellers, I noticed, made do with fake wood for their work station; Castelar's door was the real thing. Mounted on the west wall was a writing counter (also phony wood) and small pigeonholes filled with deposit/withdrawal slips and the other paraphernalia of banking, as well as three ball-point pens of such inestimable worth that they were anchored to the wall more solidly than the table was.

The bank was empty but for two tellers behind the

counter, a young gum-chewing woman in her early twenties and a middle-aged, sharp-featured woman with gray-salted hair. They were huddled over a blue vinyl binder stuffed fat with green-and-white computer printouts. I crossed the thin brown indoor/outdoor-type carpet and stood patiently at the counter. As far as the younger teller was concerned I wasn't there, but the older one looked up, stepped over to the window, and asked if she could help me. She didn't act as if she meant it, but she did ask and that's something.

I went through the introduction, the I.D. flip, the explanation, the whole bit. The teller, whose name tag said she was Donna Avery, seemed impressed, which is always gratifying. She turned her head, tucked her pointed chin against her right shoulder, and said, "Jan, do you know who this man is?"

"No," said Jan, not looking up.

"He's a *private detective*." She didn't have to whisper the last two words; I knew I was a private detective. "He's looking for Kate."

Jan, a tall, thin girl with short reddish hair, looked up and flashed a smile that went on and off like a neon sign. "Hi," she said, and then turned back to her work so quickly that for an instant I wondered whether she was greeting me or the binder.

Donna was more talkative. She put her elbows on the counter, leaned in conspiratorily, and asked in a just-between-us-girls way, "What *really* happened to Kate?"

Since I didn't know what she had heard or been told, I didn't know what she was after. What she got from me was the party line, the slightly abridged story I'd told everyone at Millar: Castelar's murder affected Kate deeply and she ran away. No one needed to know much more.

Clearly this wasn't the sort of tidbit Donna craved. She made a half-disgusted sound, straightened up, and said, "Yeah, that's what *he* says too."

"Who's this?"

Donna angled her head briefly toward the door to her right and said, with some distaste, "Mr. Castelar."

I nodded. Kennerly had told me that Jack's older brother, Charles, would be minding the store. That's why I was there now. Uncle Charlie being the only Castelar I hadn't met, I thought it wouldn't hurt to drop in, offer my condolences, see if he had any thoughts about the murder and his niece's disappearance, and, generally, size him up. My understanding was that he had not been overwhelmingly close to the kids, so I doubted very much that he'd be able to offer much. Still, a guy tries to cover all the bases.

"It was a real shock to all of us, I can tell you," Donna was saying. "First Jack, then Kate. . . . It's so hard to believe. Jack Castelar was such a great guy; who would want to hurt such a wonderful man?"

I started to say I didn't know, but she wasn't looking for a reply. "Well, of course, Jolly Charlie here"—another cant toward Castelar's door—"didn't hardly say anything. He doesn't have the time of day for the likes of us. He showed up this morning, said there had been an accident and his brother was killed. Then he holed up in the office—*Jack's* office, him not even cold in his grave—and started arranging the interviews."

Jack wasn't anywhere near his grave, much less in it, but I didn't share the thought. Instead I said, "Interviews?"

"For the interim manager."

I knuckled a burning eye. There are two types of people who make investigatory work so rewarding. The first type seems to think you already know the story; his replies to your queries are phrased accordingly, as if he believes all he has to do is jog your memory. The second type enjoys being in the spotlight, enjoys knowing something you don't know, and stingily apportions his answers like Scrooge parceling out the coal. Donna Avery belonged in the former category, I decided, which didn't make getting the story any easier.

"What interim manager?" I asked patiently. "I thought Castelar himself was going to be managing the bank now."

She shook her head. "If he was, there wouldn't be one of us left after today. The way he acts, you'd think he was *Prince* Charles." She chuckled in appreciation of her own cleverness. "Luckily, he hates banking as much as we hate— Well, anyhow, we figure he's looking for someone to run the place for him until Vince—Vince Castelar—gets out of college next summer."

That was news. "Vince? Isn't he a little young?"

Donna opened her mouth to answer, but stopped as the door to Castelar's office opened and a tall, pear-shaped, middle-aged man—sixtyish—stuck his carefully coiffed head through the six-inch opening. He frowned at one of the wooden desks outside the door, then looked up at Donna. "Where's Carol?"

"She had the afternoon off, Mr. Castelar, remember?"

The frown deepened. "No wonder she didn't pick up the intercom," he murmured, and made to withdraw again into the office. Donna thwarted him, calling out to him, and again the silvery head appeared, the frown now having taken on a distinctly impatient cast.

"Mr. Castelar, this gentleman is a private detective. He's looking for Kate, your niece."

He gave her a look. "Yes, Donna, I remember her." After a moment's hesitation, he stepped into the lobby, closed the door completely behind him, and crossed the seven or eight feet of carpet that separated us. Castelar had a curiously springy way of walking for a man his size and weight and age. It was as if his heels were coated with the stuff of Super Balls, and bounced up an inch or two after every step. It made his round face, pink under the silvery white of his hair, seem like the dot you followed on the old sing-along shows.

I showed him my I.D. and he ignored it, gazing down at me with heavily lidded eyes. "My sister-in-law told me she had hired a private detective on the advice of that shyster lawyer of hers, that Kennedy—"

"Kennerly."

The gray eyes widened a bare fraction of an inch, and I could see why Donna had called him Prince Charles. We did not like to be interrupted, or corrected. "Thank you," he said dryly. "I told her I thought this was a matter best left to the police. After all, what do we pay taxes for? But this . . . *lawyer* seems to think you're some kind of Sherlock Holmes. Are you?"

"Oh, I wouldn't say that." This wasn't false modesty, or any other kind; it's just that, as much as I love those old stories, I don't think Holmes could have detected his way out of his own bedroom if he had the blueprint. A kid with a 007 spy kit is a better detective.

"Then I wonder what motivates him. . . . Does he get some sort of kickback or rake-off from you in exchange for convincing the bereaved that they need your, ah, services?"

"Yeah, that's right; I give him twenty-five percent of my fee and it's almost enough for him to buy a paper and a cup of bad coffee."

Castelar smiled primly. He had a small, perpetually pucked, fishlike mouth, the corners of which now ascended minutely, leaving the rest of the placid face unaffected. "Funny," he said, meaning he didn't think so. "But I think it's a sinful waste of money anyway, and after I talk with Emily again tonight I'm sure she'll agree. Consequently"—he lifted one pink hand in a lazy backhand stroke—"you may as well prepare your brief or report or whatever you'd call it now, because I can virtually guarantee that by tomorrow morning you'll hear from Mr. Kennedy informing you that you'll have to find another widow to bilk." He turned away from the counter and bounced toward the office door.

"Kennerly," I repeated. "And until I hear from him, I intend to give full measure. Since the meter's running and all."

He paused.

"I'd like to ask you a couple of questions." I always feel vaguely silly saying that, but I've never come up with a better way of putting it.

He turned. "No," he said plainly. I started to ask why not, but he anticipated me "Because I can't think of anything you could ask me that would be any of your business. As I understand it, your job—your totally redundant and soon-to-be-ended job—is to look for Kate. Not to harass me as I try to ensure that this bank will continue to operate smoothly—and that my own business will not collapse while I'm distracted here." He completed another hand gesture, this one tight and choppy.

"What sort of line are you in?" I asked conversationally. "If there were a bank in my family, I'm pretty sure I'd be in the banking dodge."

Again the tight smile. "You prove my point. This is none of your business."

"You know, no matter how often I hear that, I never get tired of it."

"And I do not find you the least bit amusing."

"Really? I think you're a stitch. Funniest thing I've seen all week. A man less upset by his brother's murder than by being called away from his business because of it; a man less concerned with the whereabouts of his missing niece than with how much it's costing to look for her; a man less interested in what he can do to help find her than in getting back to the VIP cooling his heels in the fancy private office. That's funny, all right. Real funny."

His round and ruddy head swiveled a quarter of the way toward the door behind him, and his pursed lips protruded even farther. When he glanced at me the gray eyes looked even sleepier than before. "Persistent. And self-righteous, aren't you?"

"Maybe self-righteous," I said, although it wasn't so much that as not knowing when to keep my big mouth shut. "Definitely persistent," although it wasn't so much that as sheer pigheadedness. "I've been hired to look for Kate and I'm going to look for her, whether or not you approve, whether or not you think it's any of my business, whether or not you cooperate. But I'll tell you one thing: If I had a brother and my brother's daughter turned up missing the day after someone shot him through the head, by *God*, I'd be doing everything I could to find the kid instead of pissing and whining like a dowager recovering from an operation. And I'll tell you something else, too—no extra charge—if you had cooperated with me from the start instead of putting on a show for the hired help, I'd've been out of your hair ten minutes ago."

Castelar had stood motionless through my declamation. Now he moved. He opened his mouth and a clipped "Ah" emerged. Then he spread his arms, which made him look something like a fat blue pin-striped gull getting ready to fly, and said, "At last I see!—You think Kate is hiding *here* at the *bank!* Do you want to check the vault? The night depository? Perhaps a safe-deposit box?"

Was it something genetic, something attached to the Y chromosome, perhaps, that made Castelar males so relentlessly disagreeable? Was this the way the family handled grief? Or was Prince Charles, like his nephew, Vince, just a self-inflated clod? Legitimate questions, these, but asking them would gain me nothing, except perhaps forcible eviction, so I choked them back down, settling for a contemptuous look as I pushed off from the plastic counter, pulling my gloves from the parka's side pockets. "I'll let you get back to your important guest."

Castelar glanced yet again at the door while I concentrated on burning holes through him with my eyes, at the same time tugging on my gloves. He faced me again. No holes, but he did raise a hand and pluck once or twice at the lower of the pouting lips.

"You're right," he said suddenly. "I've been thoughtless—inexcusably thoughtless. I hope you understand, my brother's death has upset me enormously. We were very close. I still think this is something the police can and should handle, but of *course* I want to do anything I can to help find Kate. Please . . ." He gestured toward one of the wooden desks in a far corner of the room. Shrugging inwardly, I went and sat in one of the plush blue-and-chrome guest chairs while Castelar edged toward the door behind him. "Give me one minute to explain to this person and I'll be right with you," he said before disappearing into the office.

Maybe I should go into real estate, I thought glumly; all of a sudden I had become amazingly persuasive.

I scooted around in my seat and caught the eye of my friend Donna, who had retreated to a discreet point when Castelar and I started up. I shrugged. She pointed a forefinger to her ear and spun it—the finger—clockwise a few times.

She cut it out when Castelar zipped out of his office and over to the desk and, with a speed and fluid grace I would not have guessed him capable of, into the chair opposite me.

"Now then," he said briskly. "What can I tell you? I should say first that Kate and I have never been particularly close, and I doubt I'll be able to help you much. Not that there's animosity between us, but we are separated by the years and, perhaps because I have no children of my own,

I'm not especially good at relating to others'. Particularly not the girls. I get on pretty well with Vince, I always have. But Kate, and Amy . . ." He ended the sentence with an oral shrug.

His confession made my standard question about Kate and her hangouts redundant, but I asked it anyhow and got the expected answer: *I don't know.* Castelar pleaded ignorance concerning Kate's interests, attitudes, and associates. He knew about Walt Jennings, of course, because it concerned his brother and the bank, but as far as details went, he could provide nothing. He had been unaware of the blow-up between Kate and her mother the day before, and of Kate's subsequent disappearance. As for her most recent vanishing act, he knew—yes!—zilch.

Unhelpful as he was, I still stretched out the interview a bit longer; after having made such a big deal about his reluctance to hear my questions, I was damned if I was going to let those questions occupy only three or four minutes. "What happens to the bank now?" I asked blandly.

Castelar frowned. "What does that have to do with anything?"

I lifted my shoulders. "Nothing, I suppose, but it's frequently helpful to have the big picture, as they say, just to help keep things in perspective." Bullshit.

But he seemed to buy it, if not wholeheartedly. "As far as policy and management," he began slowly, "nothing happens. At least not immediately. I am hoping to find someone to manage in the short term, but his job will merely be to keep the operation on course and running smoothly."

"And in the long term?" Donna Avery had already given me that answer, but I could hardly believe what she had predicted.

It was true, however: "It had always been my brother's plan to bring Vince into the bank and, eventually, turn it over to him entirely. Vince was to start here next summer, and Jack was going to prepare him, groom him, over the next eight or ten years. By that time Jack would have been ready to retire and Vince would have been ready to take over for him." Castelar leaned back in the desk chair and it squealed mildly. "I don't see any reason to change the plan. Vince is eager to learn the ropes, he's bright and dedicated, and I don't think it'd take him any ten years to figure the place out. My plan is to get someone with experience to look after the place and teach Vince the job, and then turn it over to him in a year or two."

"That's a lot of responsibility for someone so young, isn't it?"

"Have you ever checked the ages of the directors of some of the multimillion-dollar computer companies? Age isn't the issue, ability is; and I think Vince will prove able. Besides, he won't be much younger than I was when I took over the place."

I looked at him questioningly and he smiled slyly, eyelids drooping, giving him a faintly Oriental look.

"That's right," he said sleepily. "When I was not much older than Vince, I, too, was heir apparent. As the eldest Castelar male—in fact, the eldest Castelar, my brother and I being the only two—I was the obvious choice, as far as the Major was concerned."

"The Major?"

Another small smile. "My uncle—great-uncle, actually—the founder of the bank. He was a lifelong bachelor, as I am, and very much determined to keep his corporate offspring in the family. Since my father died before the Major was ready to retire, I was appointed successor. I even served, for just over two years—the worst two years of my life. Finally I abdicated. I thought the Major was going to have an attack, but he adjusted, especially when Jack proved adept in financial matters. Jack did more with this bank than I ever could have. With this farm economy and all . . . and I think I see your next question coming. But after all these years I doubt I'd be competent to manage the place anymore, even if I wanted it. Which I do not. I'm all in favor of having a bank in the family, but I have no wish to be saddled with it."

"So Vince is the boy, just like that," I said wonderingly. Why couldn't my old man have left me a bank instead of a '59 Buick with bad springs?

Castelar made a deprecatory gesture. It, like all his gestures and other movements, had seemed peculiar, and now I realized why: His motions included only the part actually in motion, nothing more. When he smiled, his eyes remained unmoved. When he raised his hands, palms up, as now, the rest of his large body remained stationary. Like the robot gunslinger in a drug store.

"Technically," he said a little impatiently, "it has to be approved by the board. But inasmuch as Emily now holds some eighty percent of the voting shares—I assume Jack left all his shares to her—I doubt Vince will encounter much opposition."

Corporate annals are filled with cases of mothers and fathers squeezing out sons and daughters, and vice versa, but given what I knew about Emily Castelar, it didn't strike me as too likely she had killed her husband in order to take over the bank. "Who else sits on the board?"

He sighed—gently, but I still caught it—and thought about it a few seconds. I waited, dimly aware of a half-remembered tune falling softly from a speaker imbedded in the ceiling, trying to put a name to it. It was a pop-rock thing from the late sixties, but it had been sanitized and homogenized and Simonized, for all I know, until it was nothing but lilting strings and sexless horns, completely untainted by character or personality or, indeed, identity. Generic music. Before I could draw a bead on it, Castelar spoke again:

"Myself, of course." His face was distorted with the look of someone studying a hastily prepared mental list. "I still own a few shares, though I sold most of them last year . . ."

"What for?"

He looked up sharply. The man did not like to be interrupted. "I needed to raise some capital," he said primly.

"Business trouble? Incidentally, you didn't tell me what business you're in . . ."

The look grew long, evaluative. "Television, if you must know. I'm a partner in a UHF station in Papillion. And when you look into it, as you undoubtedly will, you'll find that the station is doing nicely. I needed money for personal reasons."

I raised my eyebrows and smiled expectantly.

Castelar sighed theatrically. "I don't see what it has to do with anything, but all right: I had some investments go bad and I needed cash immediately to cover them. Happy?"

"Why didn't you borrow the money?"

"*Obviously* I didn't want to."

"Well, surely the bank, this bank, would've loaned you the cash. Don't corporations always make low-interest money available to their top people? And what good is it having a bank in the family if you can't get money from it? . . ."

His pink face deepened perhaps a shade. "I didn't say I couldn't; I said I didn't want to. I preferred to liquidate some assets rather than go into debt at this time. It better fit my financial plans. All right?"

"It's okay with me. Who'd you sell to?"

"Jack bought most of them. I sold a few to one of my partners, and some to an uncle in Oregon, who already held a few. He's my mother's brother, not a Castelar, and Mother left him a handful of shares. Then we have three or four cousins in the South with token shares that the Major left in his will, and that accounts for the stock." He bent his mouth into a smirk but, again, the rest of his pink face remained steady, as if molded of smooth, shiny plastic. "Any good motives there?" he wondered with mild derision. He laughed brusquely. "None of us would stand to gain from my brother's death, if that's what you were thinking."

Was it? Probably, on some level. Mainly, however, I was just stirring the pot to see if anything interesting floated to the surface. Nothing had—nothing outside of Castelar's sudden change of heart, mind, strategy, whatever. His impatience was beginning to show again, but he had been just as nice as pie, as helpful as could be—in an unhelpful sort of way—a real prince.

I wondered why. I had spent most of my adult life poking into other people's business—for the army, for the paper, for anyone with the cash and a halfway decent reason. My suspicious nature had long since become second nature, and Castelar's about-face made me suspicious. Real suspicious. All kidding aside, I knew I wasn't such a swell salesman that I could get someone turned around 180 degrees inside of ten minutes. If I were, I'd've gotten out of this line ages ago and into something worthwhile, like getting girls.

Was it possible that I had nicked a nerve with my impassioned God-country-and-family speech? Yes . . . just. But to these jaded old eyes it looked like the attitude adjustment occurred when I alluded to the man, woman, or child waiting in the private office, and that piqued my curiosity. Was it someone who shouldn't have been there, someone Castelar feared I might begin wondering about if he kept up the big stall? Why? And, more to the point, who? Did he, she, or it have anything to do with my business, or was it a case of

Castelar playing around with somebody's wife? (Or husband; these "lifelong bachelors" . . .)

I could have jumped up, crossed the small room, and yanked open the door before Castelar could have stopped me. But it would have paid off only if I knew by sight whoever waited on the other side—not a likely possibility. Besides, that kind of stuff's for amateurs. We pros have more subtle—and more fun—ways to find out things like that.

So I just went on smiling emptily, as I had been since Castelar's last statement, and let the silence lengthen into the uncomfortable range until, finally, Castelar interrupted it. "Well, if that's it, then," he said, placing his palms flat on the desktop, preparing to launch himself to his feet, "I do have work to get back to . . ."

I stood, and so did he. I thanked him for his trouble and turned again toward the front door.

"By the way," he said as I reached it. "I meant what I said before. About your services not being needed, about talking to Emily about discharging you. While I'm at it, I think I'll try to convince her to get rid of your friend Kennerly too."

"Kennedy," I said, and pushed open the door.

Chapter Nine

The place was dark and empty. And hot. Jen has the charming habit of coming out of a bath soaking wet and stark-naked, and deciding that the apartment is cold. So she throws the little lever on the thermostat all the way to the right, dresses . . . and leaves. When I came through the door at about five-thirty, it was like walking into a clothes dryer. The needle on the thermostat hovered at around eighty-five. I don't much trust the accuracy of those things, but I trusted the senses that told me it was bloody warm in there. I nudged the plastic indicator down toward the seventy mark, deposited my winter wear in an easy chair that was seldom employed as anything other than a coat rack, and snaked a can of Falstaff out of the back of the fridge. It's my firm if unsupportable conviction that Falstaff doesn't taste as good since they closed the Omaha brewery, but it's still my drug of choice, out of habit, nostalgia, loyalty, parsimony—you call it. The top popped with a satisfyingly sharp *snak!* and I poured the contents into an oversized glass mug, letting the head rise to the very rim. Just like in the commercials.

Jen had accepted a dinner invitation from some friends, her note read, and she expected to be out late. I was more than slightly relieved, and more than slightly ashamed because of it, but I just wasn't in any kind of mood for whatever round we were now in. We had gone at it again yesterday afternoon and evening and on into the night, and made about as much headway as we had all the other times, all the other years. She accused me of being afraid of growing up, of going out and testing my mettle in the wide world. I accused her of being afraid of herself and obsessively seeking constant outside distraction to mask an emptiness at the very core of her life.

Like the song says, we both can't be wrong—so I must be right.

True, I was reluctant to leave Omaha for the bigger, glitzier metropolises—metropoli?—of the world. Omaha was home, was comfortable, and there's nothing wrong with comfort as long as it doesn't become stagnation. Jen equated this with a fear on my part of sinking in deeper and faster-moving waters, and I seemed unable to find the words to express my feelings and beliefs. Yes, I was afraid of failure—what sensible man isn't?—but not failure as in success-and-. I feared failing *myself*. I was afraid of running away, because I knew what an easy out that became. Christ, I had done enough of it in my time. Changing jobs. Changing careers. Changing directions. Looking for something. Hiding from something. I didn't know. All I knew, ultimately, was that I was stuck with *me* whether I lived in Omaha or London or Athens or Mudslide, Montana, and that I had better start dealing with that reality instead of subscribing to the attractive fantasy that the emptiness, the purposelessness, and the anger I felt were all due to external factors that I could easily elude, by flight.

That's why I had to stand my ground. Literally and figuratively. Perhaps at some future time, when I was certain, absolutely certain, I wouldn't be running away, I would leave this Paris of the Plains and lay siege to some other unsuspecting dot on the map. But not now, not just now.

A couple of telephone messages and a small stack of

mail rested near the phone. The calls didn't look too urgent, and neither did the mail. The usual assortment of bills, an invitation to subscribe to a magazine I'd never heard of, an offer to take advantage of mind-boggling savings on meat prices if I bought a quantity sufficient to feed a small nation, and the latest in a seemingly growing number of pamphlets, catalogues, and flyers from purveyors of surveillance equipment. I didn't need any parabolic microphones, voice-activated tape recorders, or bug-detectors—the most sophisticated piece of equipment I own is a little black suction-cup microphone that sticks against the earpiece of a telephone to make tape recordings of conversations, and I've never used it except when doing interviews for an article—but they're fun to look at, and it's flattering to think that someone somewhere believes I could be in the market for such things.

I threw away half of the mail and set aside the other half to look at later. Then I turned off the fluorescent doughnut over the sink and stood in the dark, savoring the coldness of the beer, thinking.

The drive home had been a bitch and a half. It was like driving with blinders on—or, more accurately, an eye patch—and making right turns was largely a matter of guesswork and good luck. But by keeping to the right-hand lanes, keeping a healthy distance between me and my fellow motorists, and keeping a close eye or two on the mirrors, I didn't feel like a menace; merely a threat.

What had seemed menacing was the dark blue Thunderbird that appeared to be dogging my trail almost to my front door. I noticed it, a few car lengths back, shortly after turning onto the Blair High Road. It was one of the new, scaled-down T-birds, and I was admiring its sporty lines. Then, probably because I was relying so heavily on the mirrors, I began to notice that the driver never let himself get too near, and neither did he let more than one car ever separate us.

He stayed with me down the High Road, down Military Avenue, down the Northwest Radial Highway.

When I turned off the Radial and onto Decatur, he continued straight down the highway. I drove partway up the Decatur hill, past my place, until I was certain the T-bird was out of sight. Then I backed down the hill and parked across the street from the building.

Paranoid, sure. If I had ever paid attention before, I'd've probably been amazed at the number of times other drivers' routes duplicated my own. And every road I took was a major artery in its area.

One little thing did gnaw at me, though: The Thunderbird's front license plate had been obscured by snow. But it hadn't really snowed for a few days now, not the wet, sticky stuff that would cling like that, that would hide a license plate below a bumper.

Beyond a certain point, paranoia becomes good sense.

License plates reminded me . . . I carried the phone into the living room, where cold silvery light filtered in from the street, and dialed as I fumbled through my parka's pockets in search of my notepad. I found it, flopped on the couch and, while I waited for the switchboard to connect me, wondered why we persist in "dialing" numbers on push-button phones.

A few years ago I did a small and discreet favor for a fellow in the DMV, and occasionally I call up to make him regret the if-I-can-ever-do-anything-for-you that he thought was his parting shot. I was hoping he hadn't yet left for the day—and I was in luck for once, though not by much, judging from his tone. And this was *before* he knew it was me. He didn't warm up much after he found out, and you'd've thought I had mortally wounded him when I told him I had four license plates to check out—one for each of the cars standing in the bank lot when I'd left. But he didn't say anything except that he'd have to call me back in a few minutes.

I didn't expect my business with Banner—to ask whether the farmhouse that Tom Black had told me about had in fact been checked out—would take more than a few minutes, so I got back the dial tone and called down to her station. I was right, it didn't take more than a minute. Banner wasn't in.

I left a message, set down the phone, lifted the *World-Herald* into a thin sliver of light from the street, and gave the front page the once-over.

The murder was the big story. No surprise there, though I always find it a little strange when the alleged lead story is overshadowed by a gigantic AP Wirephoto of kids playing in the snow in Bedford, Massachusetts, or some other real-life drama. To even things up, however, the Castelar piece was adorned with *two* photographs, one a standard personnel-file portrait of Castelar, the type of picture they run on the business page when someone gets promoted, the other a full-face mug shot of Walt Jennings. I realized with a kind of jolt that I hadn't even known what Jennings looked like. My job had been to find Kate, and although she was probably with Jennings, I had never thought to wonder about his appearance. He was good-looking enough, I suppose, in a slick kind of way. Or maybe that was the fault of the police photographer, whose handiwork it was on display. He had longish dark hair combed back—this is Jennings, not the photographer—close-trimmed long sideburns, and a smug look, as if he had won a lottery instead of a trip to the pokey.

I was too lazy to turn on a light and properly read the story, but I gathered that nothing had broken since noon. The paper said police indicated satisfaction with the investigation so far. It said law-enforcement agents throughout the five-state area were on alert, although local police felt that snowstorms in the surrounding territory—and moving into eastern Nebraska—had probably prevented Jennings's getting too far. It gave the number and description of Jennings's truck. It mentioned that the murder weapon had been recovered, but that the suspect should still be considered armed and dangerous.

There was no mention of a certain brilliant and dashingly handsome private investigator having turned up the gun.

The phone rang, and without preamble four names tumbled into my ear. I scribbled them into my notebook alongside the appropriate license numbers: Martin J. and Donna R. Avery; Janice A. Pinkowski; Charles B. Castelar; and the Greater Omaha Vending and Amusements Corporation, Inc.

The receiver went dead in my ear and I set the thing down, throwing the notebook next to it on the coffee table. That was that; Castelar's pal was someone who wanted a loan in order to keep a jukebox business afloat. Another mystery solved. On to the next job.

Which, I realized as I stood and the room made a sudden counterclockwise turn, had better be to break the fast I'd been keeping since last night's dinner.

Back in the kitchen, I filled the kettle and set it on a medium flame, then started butter melting in a skillet over very low heat. I stuck a cassette in my K-mart blue-light-special stereo, which I feared was getting ready to head for that big electronics store in the sky, entered the bathroom, stripped, and got under a shower as hot as I could tolerate. For a time I simply stood, face directed toward the spray, eyes closed tight, and let the water warm me, relax me, soothe me. Then I found shampoo, soap, razor, and took comfort in the mindlessly familiar activities of washing, rinsing, and shaving. The razor felt clean and good on my throat as I close-shaved slowly up to just below my jaw, feeling with the fingertips of my left hand where the new beard began, suppressing once again the impulse to keep going and get rid of the scruffy thing. But I'd let it go this long, and in a few days maybe it would be filled in enough that I could shape it up a bit around the mustache and make it look like a real beard. So I left it, shaved my throat, made a couple of passes across the back of my neck for good measure, rinsed off, and got out.

The kettle was at its pre-boil rumble and the butter was sizzling quietly when I came back from the bedroom in clean sweatshirt, jeans, and gym socks. I filled the infusion pot with hot water from the tap and set it aside; then I broke three eggs into a bowl, added milk and pepper, and whipped them into a froth with a table fork. I turned up the heat under the frying pan and dumped in the mixture.

When the kettle lid began rattling I emptied the coffeepot, spooned a generic "all-purpose grind" into it, and added boiling water. Then I slipped the plunger dingus over the top of the glass beaker, shoved it down to the bottom, and drew it slowly upward again to suspend the grounds and let the brew steep.

The eggs were kicking up a fuss. I punched holes in a couple of bubbles and let the unset goop run into the bottom of the pan. I don't know if Paul Bocuse would approve, but what the hell, it's fun. When it was about half-cooked I dropped three great blobs of peanut butter onto one end and folded the other over them.

The coffee was ready. I lowered the plunger again and it dragged the grounds to the bottom of the beaker.

I threw two slices of wheat bread into the toaster.

The omelette wanted to be flipped.

Spenser, eat your heart out.

° • °

The six o'clock newscasts were underway, but I guessed that the Castelar business had led off all three so I skipped them, turned down the stereo, and sat at the coffee table, eating by what light ricocheted in from the kitchen to augment the street lamps. Local news programs give me indigestion anyhow. One of my great unproven theories is that a television station could make a million bucks if it dropped out of this Action News/Eyewitness News/Big News/Newswatch/Newscenter nonsense and simply called the news what everyone calls the news—the news—but it was another of those things no one sought my opinion on. In any event, I doubted that even the combined might of KETV, KMTV, and WOWT had turned up anything new and exciting on the Castelar case since the newspaper had come off the press. And since none of them had interviewed me about my role in finding the murder weapon, screw 'em.

Actually, I was having second thoughts about that accomplishment. Or fifty-second thoughts. I don't like to make the mistake of thinking that anything that comes simply should be suspect—but *damn,* that had been simple. Even simple-minded. Sure, bad guys do lots of stupid things. It's not that they have the market cornered, it's just that their stupid things count more than ours usually do. However, the more I thought about this particular stupid thing, the unhappier I got. I've never had to get rid of a murder weapon, mainly because I've never murdered anyone except in my imagination, but I like to think I could come up with something better than throwing it away. In my own trash can, no less. I'd drop it down a sewer drain, toss it in a snowy ditch along the highway, hide it in somebody *else's* garbage—but not my own back yard with big fat footprints leading right up to it. Unless I hoped someone would find it.

Why would I hope that?

I wouldn't.

I took a sip of the coffee, congratulating myself on the fine brew I make, while part of my brain took the question I'd phrased, turned it around, looked at it this way and that, shook it up like a Lucite-encased snowstorm, and eventually set it aside.

Jennifer would have enjoyed this. She had more than once accused me of having a positive fetish for finding totals, for trying to get life to balance out on both sides like a chemical equation. She would have felt obliged to assert that I *liked* this kind of activity, despite my protestations to the contrary, that I truly enjoyed looking for *X* and figuring out where it fit into the mathematical sentence.

She was probably right. It was the connecting thread—the common denominator, if we haven't already overworked the arithmetic jargon—in my sundry vocational experiments. And this particular equation held enough anonymous *X*s and *Y*s and *Z*s floating around to keep a physicist happy for a year. I don't suppose I'd've collected many worry lines if I didn't get values assigned to all of them—unlike mathematicians, private detectives don't necessarily have to find *all* the answers, just the important ones—but one or two would be nice. Like, who had doctored my car, and why? Why was I being tailed, and by whom? And where, oh where were Walt Jennings and Kate Castelar hiding?

So that's three things; so sue me.

The latter question was still the most important, naturally; the others would probably fall into place once the big one was answered. I felt I had exhausted the Castelar angle, but that still left me Plan B, the Jennings approach. Perhaps *he* had some sort of private retreat or someplace he secretly rendezvoused with women or, not to put too fine a point on it, a hideout prepared for just such an exigency. If I frequented Jennings's haunts, maybe someone could provide me a lead. (That's detective talk.)

It would give me a whole new set of people to tell me to mind my own business.

And it was a good excuse to avoid the typewriter.

I went back to change clothes again. My bed, a couch that folds into a bed or a bed that folds into a couch (I haven't decided which), looked positively seductive, but the internal slave-driver told me there was no time for that now. *We'll be together again someday, old friend,* I thought as I freed up some floor space by turning it back into a couch. I had bought the thing a few months earlier because, when folded up, it left enough space in the room for a steel office desk (secretarial model) in addition to dresser and nightstand and other bedroom accoutrements, and that in turn gave me back my kitchen table. When folded down, it left so much carpeting showing that you'd need two, maybe three green stamps to cover it, but since I usually had my eyes closed then, I didn't mind.

I sat down and laced my boots. Then I stood and weighted my pockets with all the sundry impedimenta you just can't get along without, and paused momentarily at the desk.

The surface was largely covered with precise stacks of query packets—article proposals, photocopies of some of my work, two large gray envelopes (one for sending out, one for getting back), mailing and return-address labels—all neatly clipped together and waiting for one or two of their brothers to get ready so they could all go to the post office together. But at the far left corner was another pile, anchored by a dictionary: two manila folders, a fat one crammed with notes—some typed, most scribbled—and a thinner one holding forty or fifty sheets of cheap yellow paper, the uninspired beginnings of The Next Book.

I glanced at the notes. Yep, that was my handwriting, all right, but it felt like the words had been written by someone else. I recognized the plot, the characters, the scenes, but it was like reading the *TV Guide* recap of a movie you only dimly recall ever having seen. I hadn't touched the thing in more than a month now. I had been busy "conceptualizing," "brainstorming," "percolating"—which is to say, procrastinating. Why? Because writing is hard work—anyone who tells you otherwise is trying to fool you or himself—and the writer, like anyone involved in a creative pursuit, lives with the constant subliminal fear that *this is it*, that he's going to wake up tomorrow and find that the muse has up and moved to Taos, New Mexico, the creative juices have evaporated forever, and the literary license has been irrevocably revoked.

All those ideas, all those images, all those stories floating around in that gray void of the imagination—how to snare them, identify them, put them down on paper in some kind of intelligible, literate, entertaining fashion? And having done it once, how do you do it again? When I was writing The Book, I heard intermittent voices telling me that it was not as good as I thought, that it was in fact no good at all, that I would never complete a manuscript nearly ten times longer than my longest nonfiction piece, that even if I *did* I'd never place it, because I didn't have an agent or a track record or an uncle in the publishing business. (Actually, the voices telling me that last part were *real* voices, belonging to self-styled experts.) But that was okay. Demoralizing, yes, but okay. Because I had nothing to lose but my time and sleep. I had no reputation on the line; I had no reputation, period. I was just another slob who thought he could write a novel.

Now I was a slob who had written a novel, had had editors say complimentary things about it (while rejecting it, however), and had found a house willing to publish it. Now I had a reputation—albeit unfledged, and known to only the tiniest handful of people—and however insignificant it might be, it was what put its scrawny neck on the block now. If The Book had been stillborn, who would have known but me and a few anonymous editors in far-off New York? But now people in my little circle knew of my small literary triumph, and expected more. If The Next Book crashed and burned . . .

"Shit," I said to the desk as I threw the folder onto the stacks of queries. Was this tough? Was this heroic? Was this hard-boiled? Hammett was no quitter. Neither was Chandler or Macdonald. Was I?

Yes.

Or rather, I had been, for too long. I had already decided that I had to hang tough, stick to my guns, stand my ground, be true to my school, and like that. Which meant more than keeping the same old address. It meant I had to quit farting around and start actually doing what I was supposed to be doing, what I said I was doing. "Suit the action to the word, the word to the action," wrote the bard; he ought to know.

But it was probably also Shakespeare who coined the phrase "Easier said than done."

I put out the light and and left.

Chapter Ten

Christina Jennings might have been waiting for me. She had tidied the place up, put on soft music and softer lighting, and answered the door wearing a green dress and an expectant look. The look melted as soon as she saw me, so I guess I wasn't her Mystery Date. I wondered who was. A picture flashed through my brain, the picture of Jennings walking into the house and me wrestling him to the ground and forcing him to tell me where Kate was and finding her and being a big hero. I didn't see where I could get rich in the bargain, but it was a nice dream even if it vanished as quickly as it appeared. To be hanging around the house, Jennings would have had to be an even bigger fool than current events made him out to be. And Christina's dress was not of the honey-I'm-home variety. It showed a lot of her left leg and all of her back, and left little of the rest of her to the imagination. The shade of green was almost right for her penny-colored hair, and the net effect was pretty stunning, in a blowsy sort of way. I decided Walt wasn't the only one in the family who occasionally worked the midnight shift.

Christina pulled a sour face and turned away as soon as she recognized me, but she didn't slam the door on my foot, so I followed her into the tiny house.

"Guys like you never let up, do they." She snared a pack of Winstons and a throwaway lighter from a low, square coffee table.

I closed the door on the cold. "You mean there are other guys like me?"

She lighted the cigarette, threw the pack and the lighter on the table, and turned back to me. "What do you want now? I told the cops everything I know—about three times already."

"Yeah, but which version? Seems to me the story changed once or twice when I was here before." I wondered how she knew I wasn't a cop; I didn't think Banner had introduced me that morning.

"I already told the cops that, too. I was trying to cover up for Walt, you know, but I could see I was making a mess of it, so I gave it up and told the truth." Her look was direct. "I guess I'm not a very good liar." She made it sound like a challenge. What was I supposed to say? *Aw, don't be so hard on yourself. I bet you're not a bad liar at all?*

"Uh-huh," I said.

"Then screw you," she said heatedly. "You don't like it, talk to the cops. They believe me."

"They told you that?"

She said nothing. She walked back toward me—the tired little room was so small that this required only a couple of steps—and I thought maybe she planned to scratch out my eyes or something equally dramatic, but she was heading for the narrow window next to the door. She parted the faded old curtains, raised the yellowed roller shade behind them, and opened the window several inches. "Stuffy in here," she said, blowing smoke at me.

It wasn't particularly. I moved away from the window and leaned against the door in the stance they teach you at hard-boiled school. "I'll be gone in a minute," I assured her. "I can see you're expecting company."

If I had anticipated a profound response to this display of detective skill—an impassioned denial, a bawling confession—I didn't get it. One tottered on the brink, I think, when Christina parted her pale-painted lips as if to gainsay my assertion; but she caught it, and herself, turned her unpronounced words into an absent, meaningless smile, and drew once more on the cigarette. The gesture, as it finally emerged, was neutral, implying neither admission nor denial. She exhaled the smoke and let the smile expand. "Don't worry about it," she said calmly.

Christina moved away from me again, slowly. She straightened an electric clock on top of a television on a cart, turned off the record player—the music had already stopped—then clicked the three-way floor lamp up to its highest setting. That brought her over to a well-worn armchair. She dropped herself into it and crossed her legs. The green material slid back a good distance and showed a lot of skin. What the books call showgirl's legs, I thought idly, though I wasn't exactly sure how they were different from anyone else's legs. I guess it depends on whether sequined nylons would feel at home on them. They would have on those legs. Or gams; do we hard-boiled types say *gams* anymore?

I glanced up and felt stupid when I saw her looking at me looking at her legs. Smooth move. She smiled again and sent smoke toward the ceiling, and somehow caused her dress to fall away even more. When she looked at me her eyes were steady and amused. "Is that what you came for," she scoffed, "to stare at my legs?"

"We like to check out all the angles. Curves, too. But legs are just a hobby and I'm working now. I really just wanted to talk. Let's talk about cars first."

"Cars?" She laughed brassily. "Sure. Then do you want to talk about girls, or sports?"

"Or about girls who are sports? No, cars is cool. Let's start with mine."

Her mouth remained twisted mockingly, but her eyes were serious and her voice level. "All right. Fine. Tell me about your car."

"It's a ten-year-old red Chevy Impala badly in need of a new lower ball joint. As of today it also needs a paint job and a new windshield, because someone took an intense dislike to it in a parking lot this afternoon." I watched her face while I gave her the capsule review. Her expression changed not at all, except perhaps for the smile growing fixed as she grew bored with my rendition.

"That's too bad," she said when I wound down. "Vandals are all over, I guess."

"This wasn't vandals. Not in the usual sense. Someone was sending me a message."

She took a final drag on the cigarette and smashed it to death in an amber ashtray she had balanced on the chair's threadbare arm. The ashtray had pale lettering in the bottom but I couldn't read it from that angle. When she was sure the cigarette was a goner, Christina said, "What, you think I did it?"

"I confess the thought crossed my mind—"

"Yeah, that's right," she said blisteringly. "On the way down to the police station I asked the cops to stop by your place so I could mess up your wheels a little. The white-haired guy even pried the lid off the paint for me."

"—but I quickly gave it up. The time-frame was all wrong. And I couldn't figure out what your motivation would be."

"Yeah, me neither."

"But Jennings, that's another story."

"Walt?" she spat. "You're crazy. What'd he do a thing like that for?"

I shrugged. "Maybe I'm scaring him. The detective said modestly. Maybe I'm getting too close for comfort. His comfort."

She made a spitting, puffing kind of laugh. "Close to what?"

"To him. The way the cops figure it, the weather all around us was and is too crummy for travel. That means Jennings and the Castelar girl are probably around here somewhere. I've been trying to figure out where *somewhere* is."

"And you figure you're getting warm, so Walt trashed your car."

"That's about the strength of it."

"Why didn't he mess up *you?* I mean, he already killed a guy; what's he got to lose?"

"Not enough time. From what I gather, it took forever and a weekend for him to work up to killing Castelar, and look what Castelar did to him. The way I look at it, I'm safe from physical injury for the next four or five years." I said it breezily, but she had a point.

"Well, maybe," she said dubiously. "That's the sort of stunt that Walt used to pull—chicken stuff, kinda, like thumbing your nose at someone when they're not looking. If someone'd jump his space in a parking lot—you know?—Walt'd never confront him, but when we'd go by the other guy's car he'd put a long gash in the paint with his keys. But that was before. I don't think he'd risk getting caught doing bullshit stuff like that now. If he thought you were breathing down his neck, he'd maybe come out and make sure you knocked it off, but he wouldn't risk it just to fuck up your car." As she spoke she shook her head with conviction. "Nah, if he's hid good, he's going to make sure he *stays* hid."

"Hid where, do you think?"

Christina leaned forward to shake another cigarette from the red pack on the low table. I didn't get to see any cleavage because the front of the dress reached all the way to her throat, so I had to settle for the legs, which were still there. She stuck the cigarette between her lips and said, "I thought I already told you that. The cops, too."

"Yes, you mentioned a couple of bars."

"Yeah?" she said expectantly.

"Well, I'd like some details, please."

"I don't have any details. I told you guys everything I know. The Cattleman and the Bottom Dollar; those are two of the places I heard him talk about once or twice. The only two I can remember."

"All right—but he must go *someplace* besides bars."

"If he isn't in a bar, he's with a girl," Christina said, and her eyes were green and direct. "If he isn't with a girl, he's here with me." I waited for her to add "A woman," but she spared me that.

I said, "That doesn't leave him much time for a job."

"He doesn't get much work in the winter. Since he lost the farm, he sort of works wherever and whenever he can. Construction, farm, yard—stockyard, I mean."

I said I knew and asked where he went when he was with other women. Not very delicately put, I know, but since Christina didn't seem much concerned about it why should I have been?

"How should I know? I never asked him. I figured they went to the girl's place or they got a room somewhere. They could do it in the back of the pickup, for all I care."

"The modern couple, eh?"

"What do you mean?"

"Well, I mean, Mama doesn't mind Daddy's girlfriends and Dad doesn't mind Mom's boyfriends. Very democratic."

The eyes went cagey on me. "What makes you think I've got a boyfriend?"

I widened my eyes. "A girlfriend, then? We're more modern than I thought!"

She spat smoke at me. "You have a dirty mind."

"'Suspicious' is the word. You don't get all dolled up like that to do the laundry, do you?" She smiled perfunctorily. "I didn't think so. Is he anyone I know?"

Her mouth opened so as to show only the lower teeth, the way the women on "Dallas" do when they're trying to look sexy, and her topmost leg dangled languidly. "He? Maybe you're right, maybe it is a girl. Would that turn you on?"

"I don't know; maybe I should stick around and see."

She waved the cigarette expansively. "Have a chair. Have a drink. Stay as long as you like."

Then the business with the window shade *had* been to signal someone to stay away, and I could stick around and let him—or, let's be liberal, her—do drive-bys until dawn. But what would be the gain? I pushed away from the door and straightened up. "No, thanks. I guess I'm getting conservative in my old age."

She shrugged. "Suit yourself." She made no move toward rising.

I turned and put my hand on the doorknob, then stopped. "Just one thing," I said. "How'd you know I was private?"

Christina smirked. "What's the matter, don't'cha like anyone else doing detective work? Well, for one thing, I saw that car of yours. That's no cop car. So I asked those other two and they told me."

"The direct approach," I said. "I'll have to try that one sometime." I dallied at the door a moment. It didn't look like Christina was going to really come on to me—obviously no devotee of private-eye novels, she, or she'd have known what was expected of her—so I thanked her for the loan of the hall and left.

◦ • ◦

I sat out in the car for thirty minutes, burning gas, running the heater, listening to the radio, watching the stars in the clear indigo sky. I was parked half a block down and across the street from the Jennings place, and I kept my headlights off and my foot away from the brake pedal while I studied the house in my outside driving mirror. The roller shade had come down almost immediately after I left. The living room curtains parted a couple of times as Christina peered out into the inky night, but no one showed. One car, a banged-up Malibu wagon, drifted lazily down the street, but not so lazily that you got the idea the driver was checking things out. Eventually the car vanished into the night, never to return.

Finally I got bored and cramped, and the relentless output of the car heater was putting me to sleep. Whomever Christina had been expecting, whomever she had tried to warn off didn't seem likely to happen by in my lifetime. And it probably didn't have anything to do with my business anyhow. It's ridiculous to believe that the only people who like to keep their private life private are people who have something to hide. Me, I get a big charge about keeping trivia mysterious. It drives my friends crazy.

I cracked open a window, put on the headlights, popped the car into gear, and slid off into the night.

Chapter Eleven

They were not the sort of places you'd take a date after the movies. They were dingy and cramped, hot and smoky and noisy, filled with hard, emaciated, sideburned cowboys in checked shirts with fake-pearl snaps on the pockets; with hard, garish, bewigged women crammed into blue jeans a size too small; with hard, unsmiling, big-bellied bartenders unversed in the art of crafting exotic drinks but able to expel unruly drunks the way you'd flick away a housefly, and after you've visited the first two or three, the thrill begins to get a little frayed around the edges.

I had gotten used to being stared at. It was understandable. After all, I wasn't up to the dress code. I wasn't wearing—I didn't even own—cowboy hat, cowboy boots, and one of those Western-cut fur-trimmed winter coats like McCloud always wore. I didn't have a wallet chained to my belt. I didn't walk like I had a bad case of jock itch. Worst of all, I didn't have a familiar face, and while these were neighborhood bars, it was not in the "Howdy, neighbor" sense, but rather in the "You're not from the neighborhood" sense. Strangers are a strange sight there. "Cheers" it ain't.

Consequently, the responses I got in the first three I visited—the Cattleman, which Christina had mentioned, plus the Broken Bow and the Crow Bar, which were practically next door and seemed to be of the same ilk—ranged from dead silence to know-nothingness to unmasked hostility. Oh, a few people had been willing to talk; you'll always find a couple of talkers, even if they're inviting you to go to hell with every other sentence. But no one really had anything to say. Some figured Jennings had done it, some figured the cops had it in for him. Some said Jennings had been right there in the bar last night, some said he hadn't been around in weeks. Some wanted to be bought a drink before they'd talk, and I soon discovered that that wasn't as economical as it seemed. Cash you can grab back if they bullshit you; you can't get beer back into the bottle.

There was no reason to expect the reception or the results to be any better in any of the other joints lining the streets, but sometimes you just go through the motions.

So I went through four cowboy bars in something less than three hours, starting with the Cattleman and working my way through the neighborhood, and by eleven I was pushing open the painted-over glass door of the other name Christina had given me, the Bottom Dollar.

It was a long, narrow, high-ceilinged place with all the charm and personality of a monk's cell, and not much better populated. Perhaps a dozen people, I guessed as I sized up the room. The building had presumably seen better days, but they were far beyond living memory now. The hardwood floor was badly scarred, its finish worn almost completely away. The wainscoting was scuffed and warped, and the wallpaper above it was faded and torn, discolored by decades' worth of cigarette smoke, stained by the dried remains of airborne liquor.

To the right of the room as you entered was the bar. It too was real wood, and it too had been badly abused. The foot- and elbow-rails may have been brass in a previous life; now they seemed to have transmogrified into some new and unknown metal roughly the color of strong tea. Behind the bar was a yellowed mirror, one of those moving-picture clocks advertising Hamm's beer, and an impressive array of liquor bottles. The bottles' tax stamps were still intact. I'd've bet it had been absolute ages since anyone in the Bottom Dollar had ordered a daiquiri or a Mai Tai or a Tequila Sunrise or anything sexier than a boilermaker. I toyed with the idea of breaking the monotony, but the bartender didn't look like the type who'd know how to make a really good King Alphonse. Or who'd like to learn.

He went well with the bar, though, because he had seen some rough stuff too. He was a short guy, shorter than me, but broad enough for two. He had very short hair the color of metal filings and a shapeless nose that had been broken—hell, smashed—more than once and a lined, stony face. His little finger (he had only one) was as big as a thumb. His thumbs were as broad as shovel handles. His hands—okay, you get the idea. Once upon a time he had probably been built like a chopping wedge; now he was well into his fifties and the beer and whiskies had caught up with him, settling in around his gut, bulging over the top of his grimy apron. A Bruno if there ever was one, I told myself as I wandered over to the near corner of the bar.

I leaned against it and watched him at the farther end engaged in quiet discussion with a younger man. The younger man had greasy blond hair and a prominent Adam's apple and something hidden under the hand he had cupped on the bar. Bruno's hands lay placidly on either side of the other man's. But for only a few seconds. Then Bruno's hand moved as the other man pulled his toward himself and the bartender's hand ended up where the other's had been, covering whatever the customer had been concealing. A pretty fair piece of legerdemain, it was, with neither of the men ever looking anyplace but in the other's face during the exchange. Then the younger man left the bar and approached a door set in an outcropping of the wall that ran behind the bar. The door was marked PRIVATE but that didn't bother our hero. He pulled it open and gave me a glimpse of narrow wooden stairs leading up. Then the door was closed and Bruno, or whatever his name was, was moving down toward me. His left hand now in his pocket, I noticed.

He looked at me, saying nothing. I opened my wallet. He looked down at it, moving only his eyes, then back at me.

"Yeah?" he said. Impressed as hell. They always are.

"I'm looking for someone."

"Yeah?" he reiterated. He went back up the bar, toward a pair of upright rails between which stood a girl with an empty round tray. She said something to him and he grabbed three longnecks from under the bar, one-handed, and pried the caps from them with easy, economical grace. He used a bottle opener, but he probably wouldn't have had to. The girl left with her tray, but Bruno stayed where he was, leaning against the back counter, arms folded, studiously scrutinizing the brittle paper on the wall ten feet across from him.

All right.

I pushed off and moved to the back of the room, eventually coming to a vacant four-top from which I could see the whole place. The table was plastic on a single wobbly support; the chairs were torn vinyl and pitted chrome. I selected the one that seemed most likely to stand the strain and sat and studied the waitress as she flirted with a couple of cowboys who were with a very drunk woman whose platinum hair was piled nine inches on top of her head. One of the men—the one who had his hand high on the drunk woman's thigh—said something to the waitress, who looked surprised, laughed, and batted him lightly on the shoulder before taking the empties and moving away. The other cowboy made a halfhearted grab at her as she walked by, but she slapped his hand away playfully and sidestepped out of his reach with practiced skill.

Then she was at my table, the smile still in place, the giggle still rising up in her throat when she asked what it'd be.

"Coffee." I might have said milk from the look she gave me, but she shrugged and began to head back to the bar. "Just a second," I added, and she turned back to me expectantly. "Old Walt Jennings been in here lately?"

The smile stayed, but it changed somehow, became less genuine. One dark brow inched away from her eye. "I don't have time to talk," she said. "I'm working now."

"I won't keep you. I just owe Walt some money is all, and I been trying to find him so's I can pay it back. You know old Walt, don't you?" The spaghetti-Western speech pattern came naturally after the first couple of bars.

She studied me for a minute, her expression unchanging. She was a pretty girl—pretty, not gorgeous—twenty-three, twenty-five, with long wavy dark hair and looks that may have been Greek. She wore a Western shirt with the topmost buttons undone, well-worn brown cords, and cowboy boots. Not the sawed-off Dale Evans type, but full-fledged boots, elaborately tooled, reaching almost to her knees. The legs of the cords were stuffed into the tops.

"Sure I know him," she said at last. "He's a regular."

I grinned. "Up or down?"

Her smile remained intact and her tongue came to join it, running quickly along the cutting edge of her small teeth. "Maybe both," she said, and the giggle bubbled up on the end of it before she turned again and left. That didn't tell me what was going down on the second floor. Girls or a game, I figured. Maybe both.

She and Bruno were exchanging words. He looked over at me once, caught me looking at them, and quickly turned his attention back to the wallpaper. Maybe he was thinking of redecorating. The girl came back with a heavy white, or once-white, mug centered in her cork-lined tray. The smile was gone, replaced by a tight, troubled scowl, and she didn't meet my eyes as she set the coffee in front of me. I grabbed her wrist lightly and she froze.

"What's the problem?" I said.

"No problem, if you let go of me right now." Her voice was even, but with a nervous underpinning.

I didn't budge. "Look, I don't want to create any heat for you. As the bartender probably told you, I'm a private investigator. I'm trying to get a line on Walt Jennings."

She yanked her wrist away. "You didn't expect to find him in here downing beers when every cop in town's looking for him, did you," she said acidly.

"I don't know that I expect to find him at all. Mainly I hope to find someone who knows him well enough to tell me where he might have holed up."

She looked at me. "No one around here's going to tell you that, mister. Even if they knew. You understand? That's not how they're put together."

"All right. Tell me this: When was the last time Jennings was in here? Who knows," I added quickly; "you might help fix an alibi for him." That not-quite-hidden gun at the Jennings place had been bothering me more and more all evening. My thoughts were still random and unfocused enough that I was reluctant to come right out and say the word, but I was thinking of something along the lines of what you'd put around a picture of the wife and kids.

Her eyes went skeptical. "That's right, the cops are always looking for ways to help guys like Walt Jennings get out of a jam."

"I told you, I'm a private cop. I don't even care about Jennings so much, just someone who might be with him. What's your name, anyway?"

"Lauren," she said hesitantly.

"Okay, then, Lauren, here's what I can tell you." I took a pull from the mug. What can be better than coffee that's sat and cooked all day on a hot plate? I set it aside. "The cops think Jennings killed a man last night—"

"I know that already."

"—and then went into hiding because the weather's been too bad to get out of town. Now, maybe he did it and maybe he didn't; I don't care. What I care about is another person who's probably with him. That's my job, finding the other person. I'll leave Jennings to the cops. Okay?"

Lauren stuck out one hip and rested the edge of the round tray against it. "Yeah," she said uninterestedly. "Well, look, he was in here last night and he was alone. That's all I know." She turned away.

"What time last night?"

When she turned again, her dark eyes were pleading. "C'mon, mister, you're gonna get me in trouble. I'm supposed to be working—"

"Early? Late?"

She sighed heavily. "Early. I come on at eight and he was already here."

"How long did he stay after you came on?"

The burly bartender had come from behind the bar and toward us with lumbering steps. Lauren threw him a glance over her shoulder. "That's all I can say," she whispered quickly and moved toward a booth a few feet farther on, wiping down the table with her damp rag. The boards under me shook as Bruno pounded past, grabbed Lauren just above her left elbow, and jerked her around, shoving his face into hers. He was trying to be quiet, but he didn't have the temperament or the voice box for it. I missed the first couple of syllables but "keep your goddamn mouth shut" came through loud and clear.

"He's not a cop," she whispered back. "He asked about Jennings. I just told him he was here last night. That's no secret, is it?"

"Stupid cunt," he said, pushing her away as he spat the last word. He grabbed the rag from her violently. "Gimme that," he growled, "and go upstairs. The Fat Lady'll want to talk to you."

A shadow crossed Lauren's face, but she went away quickly enough. Probably glad to get away from the old bruiser. I watched her go toward the door that led upstairs. From my angle I couldn't actually see the door—it was set in the narrow end of the outcropping that enclosed the staircase, facing the front of the room—but there was no place else for her to have gone but through it.

I stood, and the bartender was at my elbow. "What do you need, buddy?" he wondered in a voice that made it sound like he thought what I needed was an ice pick in my spine.

I matched his expressionless expression and made my voice go flat and rough. "Where's she gone?" I said. Tough. Hard-boiled. That's me. Someone who's played fast and loose with Mafioso—Mafiosi?—and lived to tell about it. Small-time toughs like you don't cut no ice with the likes of me, brother. So shove off. Put an egg in your shoe and—

"Nothing to do with you, buddy." Bruno was obviously ignorant of my accomplishments.

"Doesn't look like it to me. Looks to me like I was right in the middle of it."

"Well, it's between her and the boss now. Understand? So why don't you just head on home or someplace."

Coming from him, it sounded like a fine suggestion. I threw a dollar on the table and walked away.

But, of course, I took a detour as I came up even with the end of the bar. And, of course, he anticipated me.

When I thought back on it later I realized there had been a buzz among the Bottom Dollar's few patrons, but it was Bruno's quick and heavy footfalls on the floorboards that told me I wasn't going to get through the stairway door before he was on me. Realizing this I began to turn, and was able to sidestep enough to avoid being flattened like a bug against the wall near the door. I had some of the wind knocked out of me, but Bruno had it worse, because he had expected to have me as a cushion between him and the wall when he smashed headlong into it. It shook him enough that I was able to dance away, out into the room. No way did I want to be confined to that corner, my back against the wall.

He turned heavily and stopped, half-crouched, arms bent away from his body, hands knotted into fists the size of telephones. His expression was still as vacant as the moon, but his face had gone pink from the exertion.

I didn't want to get into a slugfest with him. Sometimes these big burly guys aren't as tough as they seem—they never had to become tough, because their size alone always intimidated people—but old Bruno here looked like he was the genuine article. Or had been. He was older and fatter and slower now, and the effort of pushing himself rapidly across six feet of floor had set his chest to heaving, but you'd still want to keep him at arm's length, or better.

Then he lunged for me, swinging his left like a sledge. I had seen it coming about twenty-four hours earlier, however, and was easily able to feint a duck under it, pulling back at the last instant. His right fist sailed through the air where I should have been, pulling him off-balance. Then I stepped back in. And made a very bad mistake.

I committed the unpardonable sin of assuming a fat man was a soft man, slammed my left into his belly with almost enough force to dent the frosting on a chocolate éclair, and realized with sick horror that Bruno wore his nice thick pad of hard fat over a nice thick pad of hard muscle. My punch had about as much effect as a baby's kiss, and gave him time to regain his balance. Now he showed me how it should have been done, sending his left into my stomach so hard that my knees buckled and the picture went gray and fuzzy around the edges. By some miracle I got an arm up before his right crashed home. My left arm went numb from the shoulder down, but I didn't mind that so much; it was supposed to have been my head. A roundhouse like that would surely have knocked me cold, and any blow strong enough to put you out carries the threat of at least some brain damage. This, in my book, is something to be avoided.

Luckily there was a table behind me, so I could lie down for a second or two and rest up. I heard glass shatter as the bottles that had been on the table ended up on the floor, to somebody's evident amusement. I turned my head to one side and saw, as if through a piece of gauze, the drunken woman who had been with the two cowboys. She was still with them, in fact, and one of them had it in mind to help me to my feet but I didn't want to get up yet. I started to tell him as much, but then Bruno was approaching rapidly again.

It was only instinct that caused me to raise one knee protectively as he hurtled down at me, but then a golden shaft of light cut through the fog closing in and illuminated a particle of reason.

I straightened my leg like a piston and let Bruno carry his momentum square into it. The heel of my boot sank into his gut where it ballooned over the small apron. I saw his mouth drop open and his face go the color of fresh plums just before the table went over and me with it.

There seemed to be a lot of beer on the floor, and I seemed to be lying in it. I turned over, got up on my hands and knees, got one foot on the floor under me, and paused while my stomach argued with my head over whether I should pass out or throw up. They couldn't reach an accord, so I put my weight on the foot and stood, carefully. Nothing broken, as near as I could tell, except for some beer bottles, and I hadn't even been cut by the pieces of brown glass around me. My left shoulder throbbed and my guts felt like someone had tried to rip them out through my navel, but I imagined I would survive. I straightened myself as best I could and looked around the room. My two cowboy friends were bent over Bruno, who lay sweating and groaning on the floor. The girlfriend had kept her seat, and was now locked into spasms of soundless laughter. I hoped she'd laugh herself sick. I guessed she had just enough beer in her to do it.

No one was paying much attention to me, and the few who had been staring went back to their own business when I met their eyes. Don't tread on me, boy. There's more where that came from and I'll be happy to show it to you just as soon as I'm off the critical list.

Trying not to lurch too badly, I covered the five or six feet to the door with the store-bought PRIVATE sign nailed to it, tugged it open, and hauled myself up the stairs, hoping tonight was not the night the rickety handrail came away from the wall.

◦ • ◦

The stairway was long and narrow and steep; getting up it took some doing. But, oddly, when I reached the top I found I felt better. A little light-headed, along with all the other symptoms, but I no longer felt I was going to black out at any moment.

The old and bowed stairs ended at a three-foot-square landing with blank walls to the front and the right. To the left a narrow hallway went back the other direction, toward the front of the building. The hall was lighted by a single bare bulb, and broken by four closed doors along the wall opposite the staircase.

I looked back down the stairs. The door was shut, as I had left it. No way to secure it, however. If I'd had a wire coat hanger I could have looped it through the door handle and twisted it around a handrail brace, but somehow I had neglected to bring one along. Besides, Bruno didn't strike me as the type who'd agonize long over whether or not to smash down a door.

I moved down the dusty hall runner as quickly but as quietly as I could, pausing to listen at the first door. Nothing. From behind the second door came the squeak of mattress springs moving in an unmistakable rhythm. The door was locked. I thought I had been quiet in trying the knob, but a male voice—the blond man from downstairs?—gasped the protest that he still had time.

The third door. Nothing. I paused again, expecting at any moment to hear a ruckus from below, the hammering of several sets of angry feet on the stairs. I had put myself in a bad spot, cornered myself. There appeared to be only one way out, and that was back down the stairs and through the valley of the shadow of death. Perhaps now was a good time to be thinking of potential escape routes. Perhaps one or more of these rooms had a window leading to the outside . . .

I was about to open the door to the third room when I heard it. A muted *whack!* followed by a low moan, then several more blows in quick succession and a louder, longer moan. I felt clammy sweat gather along my spine, and it seemed to take my legs a little while to get the idea that I wanted to go check it out.

The noise had come from behind the fourth door, the last one at the end of the hall. I put my ear against the wood panel, but could hear nothing but the murmur of voices and a quivering, snuffling sound.

When the next *whack!* came, it sounded like a rifle going off in a small room. I was through the door before I fully realized I had made the decision to enter.

The room was tiny and dingy and stuffy—right in line with what I had seen of the rest of the building. The floor was warped and beat-up, the walls were cracked and peeling, the ceiling was water-stained and buckling. There were two windows, I noted subconsciously; one at what was the front of the building, overlooking the street, the other on the wall opposite the door. Both were closed. A radiator under the second window puffed out an oppressive amount of heat and made quite a fuss about it.

Sweating in the heat, behind an ancient wooden desk planted in the middle of the room, sat a woman. A fat woman—monstrously fat. She looked up quickly as I flung open the door, and the hard, sharp eyes sunk deep in the folds of her fleshy face glinted angrily in the pale fluorescent light. Standing next to the desk was the girl, Lauren. She had her hands extended, palms up. The Fat Lady had her chair swiveled around toward the edge of the desk and had reached across to grab Lauren's wrists in her flabby left hand. In her right she held a heavy steel ruler, which she was preparing to bring down once more across the girl's outstretched palms.

Lauren's head was back; she swayed unsteadily in the dim light from the desk lamp and a dull croaking moan escaped her parted lips. She was pale, and it wasn't a trick of the bluish lighting: The Fat Lady's face was flushed and shining.

"Who the fuck are you?" the Fat Lady demanded in a voice that had had too much cigarette smoke and cheap whiskey washed over it.

I ignored it, took two steps across the floor, grabbed the upraised ruler out of her hand and flung it backhanded across the room. I had sort of been aiming for the glass—it would have been a nice effect—but since the radiator produced a gratifying clang when the ruler collided with it, I was satisfied enough. I didn't see the point of answering her question; my name would have meant nothing to her—I'm not Zorro or Captain America or anybody—and I would rather have shoved her out the window than talk to her. If I could have gotten her crammed through the window, that is. I treated her to a minute's worth of a stare that was meant to be hot and contemptuous. Then I turned to the girl.

"Are you all right?"

She nodded dazedly.

The Fat Lady had let go her wrists; I now grabbed them and held her hands to the cool light. The skin was unbroken, but the palms were red and swollen. Lauren moaned again.

"Go run some cold water over them," I said. "Then go home." She looked at the Fat Lady and the great loathsome slug nodded. The girl moved unsteadily toward the door.

"Wait a minute," the Fat Lady rasped when Lauren reached for the knob. Lauren stopped and looked back toward the desk. The Fat Lady angled her several chins toward the opposite corner. "Pick it up."

Lauren glanced at me and then turned her eyes toward the floor, crossed the room, bent, found the ruler, and brought it to the desk.

"All right," the Fat Lady said when the girl had set the ruler in front of her. "Get out of here."

When the door clicked shut the Fat Lady turned on me. "Where do you get off busting into people's offices an——"

"Shut up," I said. "Let's get some light in here." I turned toward the wall switch near the door, illuminated the bulb in the overhead bowl, and turned back to the Fat Lady. I liked her better with the lights out, because then I could only imagine what a disgusting creature she was. Her hair was gray and wild and oily. Her make-up consisted of a lopsided smear of red across a mouth that looked like it belonged on a Muppet. The exposed skin of her face and forearms was rough and flabby, as if it had been stretched out of shape. She was not merely fat, she was bloated. Next to her, Nero Wolfe would look like the Thin Man—and I don't mean William Powell.

Equally ugly was the black automatic resting on some papers on the desktop, not three inches from her right hand. Maybe it had been there all along, maybe she had silently removed it from a drawer when I turned away to put on the lights. It was all academic now.

"Sit down," the Fat Lady suggested. It sounded like a fine idea.

Chapter Twelve

Give the devil her due: She didn't wave the thing around or point it at me or threaten me with it in any way. She didn't touch it, or so much as allude to its presence. It could have been a paperweight for all the attention she called to it. But it wasn't.

I sat on a couch—the sprung and tattered centerpiece of an old sectional—shoved against the wall opposite her desk and started to put my right ankle on my left knee, casual-like. It made my poor, abused gut ache. So I started to spread my arms across the back of the couch, but that hurt worse. I settled for sitting forward, hands planted on knees.

The Fat Lady opened the desk's center drawer, pulled out a pack of Pall Malls, and slammed it against the desktop half a dozen times to tamp down the tobacco. Then she yanked the plastic tab around the top of the wrapper, ripped open the foil, and liberated a cigarette, which she stuck in a corner of her maw while she rummaged in the drawer for a match. She found a tattered folder, lighted the cigarette, and threw the spent match on the floor.

"An old joint like this could go up in a minute," I said.

She shrugged, and the folds of flab on her jowls rolled. "I got insurance." She stood up—the effect was negligible, since she wasn't much taller standing than sitting—and waddled around the side of the desk. She wore a shapeless black shroud that spread tight across her chest, stomach, and backside. Her white legs stuck out below the hem of the dress; they too were shapeless—rather, they were the shape of an umbrella stand. The legs ran straight from the knees into plain black unheeled shoes, the tops of which cut into the flesh where her ankles should have been.

The Fat Lady propped herself against the edge of the desk, resting her folded arms against the colossal shelf of her bosom. She smiled down at me. At least I *think* it was a smile; it could have been her dinner making a return engagement. "Let's start this again," she said in what she probably thought was a gentle voice.

Before she could continue there was a racket in the hallway outside. Her face took on a sour look that wasn't too far removed from the smile. The door burst open and in came Bruno, looking a little ashen, I noted smugly. Other than that, he wore his only expression: none. He looked at the Fat Lady standing there smoking her cigarette, looked at me sitting there watching her, looked back at the Fat Lady. "Thought you might need help," he said tonelessly.

"Oh yeah? What for? To protect my virtue?" She laughed sarcastically and told him to get out. He got. "Stumblebum," the Fat Lady said, but I noticed she waited until his footsteps had gone far down the hall before she said it.

"I wouldn't want to go against him too often," I said measuredly. "He's slow and he doesn't have much wind, but if he connects it's lights out."

She eyed me appraisingly. "He used to be pretty good," she said after a long drag on the gasper. "Never a contender or anything, but he was okay."

"Heavy?"

"Middle, back then. Twenty-five, thirty years ago. But he was the same then as now. Never learned how to move. He could drop anybody with a single punch, but the dancers, they could always wear him out."

It was to cry, except my gut hurt too much.

"But you ain't here to talk about Edgar."

Edgar? Nah. Bruno. Bruno was a much better choice.

"No. I'm a private inve——"

"Yeah, yeah." She waved her hand and sent cigarette ashes fluttering across my pants legs. "Me, I'm Ella Fitzgerald." I pulled out the wallet, opened it to the right leaf, and handed it across. The Fat Lady hadn't been the least concerned as I reached for it. It so happened that I wasn't carrying—I'm not a big fan of guns—but she didn't know that. Evidently she didn't much fancy anyone's chances of shooting his way out of her place.

"Nebraska!" she hooted as she let the wallet close itself. "Pretty funny name, ain't it?"

"Could be worse. They could call me the Fat Lady."

Her face solidified into a grotesque parody of mirth. She sucked the cigarette down to the halfway point and exhaled the smoke into my face. "Yeah, you're stupid enough to be a private cop." She tossed the wallet at me and I caught it against my belly, which was a mistake. I must have gone two shades whiter, but the Fat Lady didn't comment on it. "That piece of paper doesn't give you the right to come in here bustin' heads and butting into other people's private business," she was saying as I tried to get my breath back. "Lauren says you're nosing around, asking about Walt Jennings. Says you say you're looking for him but you *ain't* looking for him. What kind of bullshit's that?"

I couldn't see what lying would gain me, and I couldn't be sure how much of what little I'd told Lauren she'd told the Fat Lady. All of it, probably, what with the ruler trick and all. "I've been hired to find someone who may be with Jennings. That's about it. Seen him lately?"

Again, it might have been a smile. "How do I know who your someone is?" she wondered, purposely opaque.

Play the idiot game. "Not someone. Jennings."

She said nothing.

"Lauren told me he was in last night."

"Lauren talks too much. We're gonna have to work on that."

"You mean 'work over,' don't you?"

The Fat Lady lifted the ruler from the desk and it glinted in the yellowish light from overhead. It was a solid-looking thing, bronze-colored and festooned with advertising. "You talking about this little fella? Stings a little, I suppose—but that's the point. We got certain rules for running this business, and every so often someone has to get reminded of them."

"Wouldn't it be a lot more efficient to just toast their tootsies in an electric skillet? You'd burn a few kilowatts, but you wouldn't work up such a sweat."

She shrugged. "The door was unlocked. I didn't nail her shoes to the floor. If she'd'a walked out, I wouldn't've tried to stop her. But she didn't." Again the shrug. "Her choice."

"Uh-huh. What have you got her on?"

The Fat Lady laughed a mirthless caw, pushed away from the edge of the desk with some effort, and rolled back around to her side of the desk. "You're guessing," she spat before lowering herself with a *whooof!* onto the flattened cushion of her swivel chair. The chair was the armless type favored by typists. She probably couldn't have wedged herself into an ordinary desk chair.

She was right, of course; I was guessing. But it was a good guess, as her attitude proved. It wouldn't be the first time someone had given away the razor in order to sell razor blades, only in this case the freebie was probably heroin; and, given Lauren's looks, the Fat Lady was almost certainly more interested in putting her to work in one of the upstairs rooms than in selling her more horse. Lauren couldn't have been hooked too badly—she didn't look or act it—but badly enough that she'd rather suffer the ruler than withdrawal.

Yes, it's great being a private detective; you get to meet such interesting people.

"So I'm guessing," I said. "What about Jennings?"

"What about him?"

"Was he in here last night?"

The last half of the cigarette vanished in one long drag. She used the fag end to light a second one, then threw the butt on the floor and squashed it underfoot. When the Fat Lady squashes something, it stays squashed.

"Could be." Smoke leaked out of her nostrils. "I didn't get downstairs much last night. Too much business up here." The maybe-smile reappeared.

"You strike me as the sort of person who keeps a pretty sharp eye on everything going on."

"Oh yeah?"

"I understand Jennings is something of a regular here."

"Oh yeah?"

I stifled the impulse to say *Yeah!* and see if I could turn it into a contest. "Does he usually come alone?"

She looked at me evenly, cigarette hanging out of her mouth, arms folded across her breasts, a faint particle of amusement playing around the porcine eyes. "I suppose," she said at length.

"Does he ever come in with anyone else, a woman—say, his wife?"

Again she cawed. "Walt Jennings never had no wife."

"Really? There's a woman going around who says she is."

"And I'm Ella Fitzgerald," she repeated. I guess that's what passed as wit around there. At least she didn't say "Oh yeah?" again.

"Why would she say she was if she wasn't?"

She took the cigarette from between her lips and studied the hot end of it. "Must be love. How the hell should I know? This Christina chick's pretty cra——" She clapped her mouth shut and narrowed her eyes.

"—zy," I supplied. "You know her."

"I seen her."

"In here?" A halfhearted nod. "With Jennings?"

She made a noise. "You bet," she said sarcastically. "Anyway, who gives a shit? I'm only interested in what you're doing tearing up my place."

"I told you: I want to find someone who's probably with Jennings. That means I should find Jennings. His wife—or whoever—said he hangs out here. I'm hoping somebody here might know where he'd've gone to ground."

"They might. Doesn't mean they'd tell you, though."

"I get that impression. The thing is, what if Jennings didn't do it, didn't kill the man everyone says he killed?"

"What if?" She replaced the cigarette but she didn't smoke it; it just hung there.

"The word I get is that Jennings was here last night, in the early evening. If he was still here when Castelar was busy being killed, or here so late that he couldn't have gotten out there in time to do it, then anyone who could step forward and say so would be doing Jennings a favor, not ratting on him. If nobody does, they'll probably end up hanging it on him. And hanging him."

She took the Pall Mall from her red mouth and leaned forward. "You're not getting the picture." She paused to spit a fleck of tobacco from her tongue. "Nobody's interested in giving Jennings an alibi. I sure as shit ain't. He's an okay guy, I guess, and he's a pretty good customer, but he ain't my boyfriend. The way I look at it is, I don't like people nosing around in my business, so I don't go nosing around in theirs. That way there's never no hard feelings, right? If Walt Jennings was here playing bridge with me at the exact minute they say this other guy got his, I still wouldn't tell you. I wouldn't tell anybody. I wouldn't say yes and I wouldn't say no; I wouldn't say nothing. Not because I want them to burn him or anything, but because it's nobody's goddamn business. You get me?"

"Like a dose of clap. That sounded like a farewell address."

"So take the hint, why don't'cha."

Pain and nausea rolled through me as I stood, but I made myself straighten up and look down at her. The private-eye code called for me to say something contemptuous or foreboding or wise-ass at this point. But I couldn't think of anything good. So, rather lamely, I said, "I've been thrown out of rural banks, two-bit bars, and private homes today, and I keep hearing variations on the same theme—*butt out*. That's all right. People can slam doors on me all over the place. It doesn't mean I'm going to go away; it just means I have to find a different way in." For good measure, I added my best withering sneer but she didn't wither much. I guess she wasn't such a delicate flower after all. She regarded me dispassionately, and I had the uncomfortable sensation that she was some grotesquely overfed frog deciding whether it was worth the effort to snag a passing fly: me.

I shook it and, unable to recall any appropriately caustic parting shots from the many detective novels I've read, was turning toward the door when the old girl made up her mind about whatever she had been inwardly debating. She lifted a pudgy paw. "Hang on a second," she wheezed.

The Fat Lady pirouetted—not a pretty sight, believe

me—and found a small scratch pad among the clutter of her desktop. "You know CB?"

"I know it." I didn't think anyone called Council Bluffs "CB" anymore—that seemed to have peaked out in the late seventies—and when I say I knew it, I knew it as well as most Omahans know the city across the river, which isn't very. I don't have much occasion to go over to CB, and I don't know many people who do. The traffic pretty much comes this direction.

"Okay. Kinda the other side of their downtown, right?"

"Right."

She ripped off the sheet she'd been scribbling on with a chewed-up stick pen and handed it to me. It bore a childish line map drawn in blotchy blue ink. "You go on a while and all of a sudden things start to get kind of scuzzy. The neighborhood gets real bad, nothing but winos and hookers and pushers and stuff. Then, sort of set back on a little hill, you see this place." She bobbed her head at the map. "Big old four-story house, square, beige stucco, sitting off by itself kind of. You can't miss it. About a hundred years ago it belonged to a railroad tycoon or something. Then the area got built up and they turned it into apartments. Then it was a hotel. Now it's just cheap rent for winos and vagrants. It's a good place to lay low for a night or two, because the cops don't worry much about the bums who live there."

My heart throbbed in my ears. "Jennings is holed up here?"

She made her face go blank. "I don't know. I don't know him and I don't know that place and I don't know you."

That robbed a little energy from the surge of excitement pulsing through me, but I still could have shouted out loud. This was not exactly the mental picture I had been lugging around all day—I had been thinking more in terms of a deserted warehouse, the kind that Batman always gets to infiltrate—but this was the closest thing to a break I had encountered so far. I could have kissed the fat old thing, except I'd forgotten the iodine. Instead I nodded, folded the scrap of paper, and opened the door. Then I paused. "Tell me," I said, "why the sudden change of heart?"

Again the piggy eyes were shiny and inscrutable. The Fat Lady turned, maneuvered her bulk around to the business side of the desk, and reacquainted her voluminous backside with the mashed cushion of her chair. She threw the memo pad onto the desktop, Bogarted the Pall Mall, and fixed her eyes on a point somewhere beyond my right ear. "I don't ever want to see you in here again," she said, as if it were an explanation.

Banished. Expelled. Thrown out into the night, where there will be wailing and gnashing of teeth. A fate too horrible to contemplate.

I shrugged. "Okay."

◦ • ◦

Going down the stairs wasn't too bad, but I still allowed myself a moment or two and wiped the clammy sweat from my face before I pulled open the door and entered the barroom.

Business had picked up in the time I'd been upstairs. The furniture had been righted and the glass and beer had been swept up and no one but Edgar—the hell with that: Bruno—gave me a second or even a first glance as I tried not to limp toward the front door.

Bruno's gaze followed me out onto the street. There was no telling what, if anything, was behind it.

Snow was falling, softly but seriously, wet, cottony flakes. The girl, Lauren, was sitting in a lighted bus shelter halfway down the block.

I stepped through the open dorway and stood under the small heater in the ceiling. Strangely enough, it was working, but it wasn't enough to overcome the cold sweeping through the transparent plastic walls of the shelter.

Lauren ignored me at first, the way you always ignore people in situations like this, then she became aware of my staring at her and, timidly, glanced up. "Oh, it's you."

"No argument here. You okay?"

"Yeah. Thanks." She went back to studying the bus-route map mounted under a filthy plastic pane opposite her.

"What's she got you on?"

The eyes flickered my direction. "Nothing."

"Uh-huh. You let her beat you like you were a schoolkid because it's fun, right? What do you get on your birthday—birch rods soaked in vinegar?" A picture of Kate Castelar, and an echo of what her ex-boyfriend had told me about her, flashed through my mind.

Lauren's eyes flashed, and they were moist. "Shut up," she hissed. "It's none of your business. You don't know anything about it."

"I know enough. I know what goes on upstairs. I know how it works. First the shit's just a little fringe benefit. It's all in the brochure: group health, pension plan, paid vacation, hot and cold running heroin. All free. But expenses keep rising, you know, and then all of a sudden the employee's expected to kick in. However, the job doesn't pay that well and you don't have the money to support the habit, so the Fat Lady graciously allows you to work it off. Upstairs. On your back."

Lauren was crying now, her head down, her gloved hands clutching her bag, the shoulders of her red jacket shaking. Mr. Wonderful, that's me; spreading cheer and goodwill everywhere I go. "It's not like—that," she snuffled. "No one's ever asked me to—do anything . . ."

"That's because you haven't been on the stuff long enough. And when you have been, she won't have to ask. You'll be on your knees begging her to let you do anything to get it—"

"Shut up!" she bawled. "You don't know anything about it, so just shut up!"

"I can help you, Lauren. I want to help you. I can get you into a program . . ." I didn't know if I could or not, but it's what they always say on TV. I suppose I could have; ultimately it didn't matter, because the girl suddenly jumped up and pushed past me.

"Lau——"

"Leave me alone, dammit." She lashed out at me, hitting me in the arm, and stumbled out of the shelter and on up the dark street. "Just leave me alone," she yelled.

I stood in the plastic cubicle and watched her disappear into the night. The snow kept coming down, gently; there was no wind. After a minute or so the overhead heater switched itself off. I left and walked slowly up the street, in the other direction.

◦ • ◦

I sat in my car and studied a real map and thought. I had almost begun to believe that I was developing quite the silver tongue. I mean, first Charlie Castelar had crumbled before my relentless logic, then the Fat Lady had melted like a box of chocolates left on top of the refrigerator. But my little exchange with Lauren put me back in touch with reality, or what passes for reality in my line, and set me to wondering again about the first two episodes.

I was slightly more comfortable with the Fat Lady's suddenly seeing the light than I had been with Uncle Charlie's unexpected conversion. That the Fat Lady was involved in all kinds of unsavory endeavors was obvious; she therefore had a legitimate interest—although "legitimate" isn't the correct word—in seeing that people didn't go prying into her affairs.

It didn't necessarily mean she really was handing me Walt Jennings on a platter, just that she wouldn't hesitate to if it served her purposes.

The defroster was running warm and I had a pretty good idea of how to get where I was going, so with some swearing I got the map folded and put away, slipped the car into drive, and threaded my way up to the expressway, across 80 and up 29 and around the northern part of Council Bluffs, around the top curve of Iowa where, following the path of the Missouri, it bulges like a backward B into Nebraska. I made good time; traffic was light, because of the hour, because of the weather. The snow must have come on duty some time ago, by the way it had piled up. I'd've rather it had been seventy degrees and sunny, but this was surely an improvement over the dry, gritty, pissy stuff we'd had the past two or three days, and the sub-subarctic winds that had come with it. This kind of snow made driving more difficult—it was slippery, and the moisture it contained softened the packed snow underneath it—but it was a change, at least, and I welcomed the marginally warmer temperatures that came with it.

As spotty and vague as they had been, the Fat Lady's directions proved reasonably easy to follow. I got lost only once, and half an hour, forty-five minutes later my headlights were illuminating the big square building, seated atop a broad bluff above what once had been a business district but was now a neighborhood of boarded-up storefronts and crumbling façades and smashed windows. The streets were littered with garbage and broken bottles. Only a few souls risked the elements and the neighborhood after dark; more than one of the few I saw slept huddled in doorways.

The placement of streetlights had become less regular. The night was black and moonless; snowflakes seemed to jump out of nowhere and into the glare of my headlights. I sighted my destination before I could figure out how to get to it; eventually I pulled around behind the abandoned stores and found an unpaved road leading up the bluff. The road was unplowed, had been all winter by the looks of it, and I fretted over the sound of deep snow dragging against the undercarriage of the car—not the sort of neighborhood I care to spend the night in—and for perhaps the hundred thousandth time thought that a guy who doesn't have better sense than to live in this part of the world should at least have the sense to get a Blazer or a Bronco or some similar vehicle for his winter driving. In one of those four-wheel-drive monsters you could drive up the side of a ten-thousand-foot-high mountain of snow, let alone an eighteen-inch drift.

The road soon put me out onto the clear bluff where the house sat, and ended abruptly just beyond the house. No other building stood up here, not even one as badly careworn as the old house. Many years ago, I imagined, the seclusion of the place was indicative of exclusivity, of the social and financial status of its owner. It must have had a remarkable view. Today, however, the view was of bleak, lifeless, undesirable property, and the solitude seemed to indicate only neglect, decline, a figurative as well as literal end of the road.

I braked and gazed up at the place. It stared back vacantly, like a skull. A little tremor, a *frisson* of excitement, anxiety, anticipation, slid like an ice cube down my spine. I told myself this couldn't possibly be it, there was no chance in a million of finding Jennings or Kate or both behind that dingy stucco façade. Nebraska's Theory of Diminished Expectations: Anticipate nothing, and you'll never be disappointed.

Yeah, well, it's a swell theory.

A few battered old cars rested at the side of the road; mine felt right at home among them. A few more hollowed shells and decaying remnants littered the surrounding lots, resting among the tall ice-encrusted weeds thrusting upward through the snow, collecting thick coats of silver and white over equally thick coats of rust.

I got out and looked around. It was the wide-open spaces, sort of, and yet the indigo sky seemed very close, as if it might crash in on me without warning. Against it the building stood forebodingly, and the flecks of snow dancing about it now seemed threatening, not picturesque. The cold night air was neither crisp nor bracing; it was a lifeless cold, the bitter chill of death.

"Got to stop staying up for those late horror shows," I breathed on a halfhearted chuckle of self-derision. I shivered into the fur lining of my parka and trooped up the unshoveled walk to the unshoveled steps to a sagging porch.

The building was not entirely dark; a dim yellow light burned behind the grimy drapery on the large leaded-glass window in the front door. I waited uncertainly a minute, then tried the heavy old door. It was unlocked. I went in.

It was easy to imagine how the house had once been. The door opened onto a large, high-ceilinged room that had, in another life, been a spacious and elegant entrance hall. I could imagine it with polished hardwood on the floor and gleaming wainscoting on the wall. I couldn't *easily* imagine this, but I could imagine it. Now, however, the room was given over to a scarred and stained desk-and-pigeonhole arrangement that had the look of being rescued from some ancient and long-vacant hotel mere seconds before the wrecking ball descended. The flooring was dull and cracked linoleum; the walls, woodwork, fixtures, and all, had been very badly painted very long ago in some color I would not hazard a guess at. The ceiling bore the evidence of leaking pipes.

I removed my hat, shook off the snow that had collected on it, and took a deep breath. Not too bad; I'd been in worse, in places that reeked of old sweat, of stale wine and putrefied food and sewage, of vomit and urine and other things not worth dwelling on. Here there was only the smell of stale smoke, of dust, and the mustiness of forgotten humanity.

The room was deserted.

I poked my head through the open archway to the left of the entry and into the darkened space that had once been the living room and, behind it, the dining room. The two rooms were now filled with old chairs and benches of the sort you used to see in bus depots—I always wondered what had become of them—attentively facing an old black-and-white console TV at the far end. The set was on but the volume was down; the seats were empty except for one bench occupied by an old man sprawled in soundless slumber.

I turned at the sound of footsteps on the once-grand stairs behind the front desk. An emaciated old black man with nappy white hair and a day's worth of stubble hobbled slowly down the stairs, his hand—which looked like it had been carved from teak—tight on the wooden banisters. "Yeah," he said without inflection when he'd come down far enough to catch sight of me.

"I'm a private investigator. I'm looking for someone who might be staying here; he'd've most likely checked in last night or this morning, early."

"No fooling? A private investigator?"

I looked at him. He wasn't being smart. "No fooling," I said, and showed him my I.D. He took it and looked at it and admired it as if it were a picture of my grandkids.

"Huh." He handed it back. "I don't remember there ever being a private investigator in here before," he said reminiscently, lines of concentration joining the permanent creases in his dark face. "And I've been here since '54. June. Some cops, and lots of people from the county, but no private investigator." He put the accent on the *in*. "You say you're looking for someone . . ."

I nodded, and reached around for the newspaper I'd noticed on the high desk's work counter. I folded it away from the sports pages back to page one and held it out to the old man with my thumb on Jennings's mug shots. "Him. Like I said, he'd've just showed up last night or today."

He carefully extracted a pair of glasses from one of the two front pockets on his old plaid shirt and positioned them on his flat nose. The glasses were an old-fashioned style, black plastic that turned transparent below the frames and halfway back on the bows. One of the bows was held in place with electrician's tape that partly obscured a dirty lens.

He peered closely at the newsprint. "I saw this," he said ruminatively, "I saw it on the ten o'clock news on the *tee* vee. Real strange thing, in't it? But this man—Walter Jennings—no, sir, never seen him."

"You're sure, Mr.—"

"Boyd, Howard Boyd. But everyone calls me Pete."

I looked at him. "Why?"

He screwed up his face again. "I don't know. If I ever did know, I've forgotten. But everyone does."

"Uh-huh. Well—Pete—are you sure? Maybe he checked in when someone else was watching the desk."

Pete Boyd laughed briefly. It was curiously high-pitched, compared to his speaking voice. "There is no someone else. I'm the general manager, desk clerk, bookkeeper, bellhop, and janitor, too. But you're welcome to check." He went around the desk and lifted a scratched and dented recipe box onto the writing counter. I doubted seriously that Jennings would have used his real name, but I gamely opened the box and riffled through the dog-eared cards anyway.

I stopped and looked up at him. "Pete, according to this, no one's checked in for more than a month."

Boyd nodded cheerfully. "I could of told you that."

"Then why didn't you?"

"You'd of wanted to look anyway," he said, and he was probably right. "You know, son, we don't get a lot of the tourist trade here."

I forced a smile and handed back the file box. "Tell me, Pete, when you do have people checking in, what do they do if you're not around?"

Again the laugh. "I'm always around."

"You must sleep sometime . . ."

"Well, then, that's what this is for." He pressed a cracked plastic doorbell bolted to the desktop near my elbow. Far away a buzzer sounded.

I said, "Then this front door's always unlocked?"

"Pret' much always. Nothing here to steal."

"But someone could come in while you were asleep, take a key from a box, and get a room without registering or waking you."

He rubbed his whiskery chin. "I s'pose. A'course, I'd find out come Tuesday, when they bring their sheets and towels down for clean ones—if I din't notice them comin' and goin' before then. I'm good with faces, I am, and I think I'd know someone who din't belong here."

"This one"—I tapped the newspaper—"wouldn't be coming or going much, and when he did he'd want to make sure no one saw him. Plus, he may have someone with him, a girl, a young woman."

Pete found this amusing in the extreme. He bent way over and laughed at the worn linoleum behind his work station. "I'm sorry, mister," he managed to get out when he was about through. He removed his glasses and wiped at one eye with a grayish handkerchief. "But no woman ever stays here, no young one, at least." He returned the glasses to their pocket and leaned his bony elbows on the lower counter. "Look, son, I think you're confused. You think this is a hotel.

Well, it isn't. I mean, it *is* and it isn't. Mainly it's just a place for tired old men—old, or old before their time—to come when there's no place else to go. If they got a couple of bucks, they can stay upstairs in a room. When they run out of bucks, I let them sleep down here for a while." He shrugged. "That's it. Nobody comes here 'cause they want to. Anyone told you otherwise, they were putting you on."

I was beginning to suspect that was the awful truth, but I wasn't ready to admit it. Instead I said, "Mind if I look around anyway?"

"Shee-it," Boyd breathed without malice and he pushed himself upright and came around the desk. "Come on."

I followed him up the old steps and down the short halls on the top two floors. Once they had no doubt held sitting rooms and spacious bedrooms; now they had been subdivided into smaller, much smaller units; the few that had been left a reasonable size because the placement of doorways or stairs made subdivision impossible were crammed with narrow old beds or thin mattresses on the floors.

Boyd knew the registry by heart. At the door of each occupied room he'd murmur the name of the tenant, half to himself, half for my benefit. He refused to use his master key on any of these doors. "You don't need to look inside," he said irritatedly after my third or fourth request. "I know who's in there and it ain't the fellow you want." But he was perfectly willing to let me into any and all of the several rooms that were supposed to be vacant. Each of them was, and obviously so.

Finally there was no place to go but back downstairs, me feeling foolish, him looking amused.

"Sorry you didn't find your man, son." His voice was gentle but at the same time mirthful. "I knew you was wastin' your time, but . . ."

"I get paid for it; I'm sorry to have wasted *your* time.

Let me reimburse you a little . . ." I reached into my pants pocket and came out with a ten, which I proffered.

He looked at it, looked at me. In his dark old head Boyd's eyes were liquid, bright and shining, like a kid's on Christmas morning. He spoke slowly, in a low conspiratorial rumble. "If it's all the same to you, son—I'd rather have me a smoke."

I smiled. He didn't mean he'd rather have a Lucky. Either way, he was out of luck. "Fresh out," I said. "Hamilton's it."

"Well, then, okay." The bill disappeared into his shirt.

Chapter Thirteen

So now the question, I reflected as I stood on the old house's front port, was whether the Fat Lady had *deliberately* sent me on this fool's errand.

I tended to think so—I mean, look at the sort of woman we were talking about—but what would she have gained by having me run out here looking for wild geese? I was already heading out her door when she decided to give me the info, so it wasn't that she was trying to get rid of me. If she was worried about being soiled with the dust my search for Jennings would raise, this certainly wasn't going to placate me. If this was supposed to have been a setup, if guns were supposed to have been waiting for me in one of the dingy, dirty upstairs rooms, it hadn't come off very well—luckily for me, since the possibility only now popped into my pointy little head.

No, I decided; the Fat Lady had wanted me to stay the hell out of her business and, after my award-winning performance in her office, figured that the best way to ensure that was to cooperate a little. Maybe she really thought Jennings might have been here; it was certainly a good place to go if you wanted to be forgotten. Or maybe she was just the type who thinks it's funny to give rubber bones to starving dogs.

I could have asked the Fat Lady, but if she wasn't leveling with me before, why would she now? Besides, she had made it more than clear that she didn't value my friendship or appreciate my company, and I was in no shape for another go-round with Bruno.

Plus it was very late and I was very tired, the snow was coming down even more heavily, and it seemed that the best thing I could do for Kate right now was to go home and catch about ten hours' worth of safe and restful sleep, sleep, sleep.

Gee, maybe I *was* becoming irresistibly persuasive in my old age; I sure didn't put up much of a struggle against my own sales pitch.

I crossed the road to the car, worked my way back to up I-29, followed it west and south to 480, crossed over into Nebraska, and inched along the waxy freeway suspended above Omaha's downtown. I was almost getting used to having only half a windshield.

I was not yet to Creighton University, beyond which the freeway curved north and vanished into my neighborhood, when I became aware of a car in the center lane, driving in the blind spot behind my left shoulder—a moronic thing to do even when road conditions are good. But then, I've known for years that I'm the only one in town who knows how to drive properly. I slowed down to fifty, and so did he. I took my foot off the gas and let her drop to forty-five, which brought the other car up alongside me.

A dark blue Thunderbird, long and shiny, with dark, frosted windows.

I got a very bad feeling in my belly and it didn't have a thing to do with my injuries.

A glance at the side mirror confirmed my suspicion that the T-bird's front plate was snow-packed, as its rear plate had been that afternoon. Very thorough.

I took my foot off the accelerator again, just as the T-bird swerved into my lane slightly. From reflex, I jerked the wheel and sent the car onto the narrow shoulder six inches or so, avoiding the collision. My car bounced and bumped in the frozen-melted-frozen snow at the side of the road, but I fought the wheel and kept from smashing into the concrete wall at roadside—or, worse, *through* the wall and down to the streets below. I couldn't see what I was doing, naturally, because that was the side of the windshield made virtually opaque by starry cracks and traces of black paint, and I didn't want to oversteer to the left and end up in the other guy's front seat, but I managed to wrestle the machine back onto the highway and into the inside lane.

The T-bird had dropped back a few yards. Now it surged forward again. Apparently he—or she, or they: I could see absolutely nothing through the smoked glass—was finished sightseeing and now interested in activity.

I hit the gas and nudged the needle back to fifty-five, but the Thunderbird matched it easily. I didn't stand much chance of outrunning a powerful car like that, even if I'd been inclined to risk it on that tricky pavement.

He swerved again and this time I was a bit too slow on the uptake. The side of his wraparound front bumper struck my fender with a metallic *thunk*, and my right front tire detoured off the road again.

We had come up on the south side of the Creighton law school.

I hit the brake. Started to slide. Scraped against the dull gray concrete wall and skidded away, onto the road. Let up on the pedal and spun the wheel a couple of times to match the changing angles of the skid. Risked a very shallow sigh of relief as I saw the spaghetti junction up ahead, where 480 split itself into who knew how many lanes traveling every which way. If I could fake him out there, get him going the wrong way . . .

My relief was short-lived. The Thunderbird hit me again—or maybe I hit him—and that did it. My nose moved toward the wall. I stood on the brake. The rear of the car swung right and collided, even as I had collected myself to let up on the brake and wind the wheel into the spin. That's what saved me. The car twisted left, out into the middle traffic lane, and I played the wheel as the machine swished back and forth on that road like the pendulum on a grandfather clock. The car three-sixtied once and tried for another but couldn't make it. It ended up crosswise on the freeway, the headlights pointed north, the single remaining taillight south.

I slammed the car into park before it stopped rocking, hit the glove-box catch, yanked out the canvas pouch, and shook out the .38. This time there was no hesitation, no indecision.

I levered myself out of the passenger-side door so as to keep the Chevy between me and the T-bird, my miscellaneous aches and pains having miraculously vanished. I went automatically into the Weaver position—both arms extended, left hand supporting the right hand holding the gun—then crouched near the back tire and braced my arms against the trunk.

The Thunderbird was stopped in the center lane forty, fifty feet on. I waited perhaps a minute. He didn't get out, he didn't back up; and I sure as hell wasn't coming out from behind my shield. Finally he got bored. I saw the brake lights go out and a plume of white smoke burp from the tail pipe, then an oatmealy snow erupted behind the back tires and he fishtailed on up the freeway, leaving me groping for a suitable metaphor for the incident.

I stood and eased the hammer home and surveyed the damage.

The right side of the car was a mess, but what the hell—compared to the afternoon's carnage it was nothing, a BB ding following a bazooka strike. The car needed repainting anyhow, and I had other things on my mind. Like why had the T-bird followed me this afternoon? Why had its mission now become more than a simple shadow job? Did it have anything to do with the vandalism to my poor old abused Chevy? Did it have anything to do with my visit to the Fat Lady's and the merry chase she had sent me on?

Above all, who was behind it?

If I somehow conjured up the answer to that one, I figured, the others should fall into place; and I had a good shot at it. The fluffy wet snow and the warmer temperatures had conspired to denude someone's carefully concealed rear license plate during the bumps and grinds of our little demolition derby.

I found my notepad and jotted the number while it still figured prominently in my short-term memory.

Shoving the gun into my coat pocket, I took a hike around the Chevy, decided a dead taillight was nothing to a man who'd been driving around all day without a windshield, and decided to get the hell out of there before a Good Samaritan—or a cop—stopped. I was having enough trouble believing what I had just been through without having to try and sell someone else on it. This sort of stuff happens all the time in books and movies, but not in real life. Not in *my* real life, anyway.

But as they say, there's always a first time.

I slid behind the wheel, slipped the gun from the zippered pocket of my parka, and returned it to its hidey-hole. I got the Chevy turned around, took the curve around the west side of the campus, and headed north to Hamilton Street, four blocks from Decatur. I drove very carefully and very thoughtfully, my head filled with green T-birds and license plates and fat women and anonymous messages scrawled on car hoods. And the image of a young pretty girl named Kate Castelar. The picture went with the other components the way bowling shoes go with a wedding dress.

I found a place to park on Decatur and gazed up at my second-floor apartment. Pitch-black. Jen was still out; if she had come home and gone to bed, she'd've left on the light over the stove. She always did.

Have you ever wanted something badly, almost desperately, and yet known with complete certainty that you'll never have it? That's how it was with me and Jen. Under the heartsickness I felt because I knew she would soon be gone was the duller but deeper pain of knowing there was no resolution, that our situation could never be any other way as long as we were who we were. And if we were anyone else, would we feel the same about each other?

It was much too late and I was much too cold to work that one out. I locked up the car and headed up the icy steel-and-concrete stairs to my apartment, dreaming of dreaming, of renewing my acquaintance with my pillow, of knitting up the ravell'd sleave of care, or at least sticking a safety pin in it. But the telephone was making noise as I opened the door. According to my wristwatch it was 1:20. I had been on the go for over twenty hours and I wasn't sure I had the energy to lie down. Correction: I think I had just enough juice left to smash Mr. Bell's invention into about nine hundred and ninety-nine thousand bits of plastic and wire. The only thing stopping me was that the phone now belonged to *me*.

I watched the thing for a little while, but it didn't look like it was going to knock it off any time soon. After I had satisfied myself that mental telepathy doesn't work—not with machines, at any rate—I sighed and shrugged off my parka. One of these days I'll learn to let ringing phones lie. But not tonight, obviously.

I lifted it and spoke to Mike Kennerly.

"Finally," he breathed harshly over the wire, which is a hell of a greeting at any hour of the day. My internal disk drive started whirring, trying to locate an appropriate rejoinder, but before it could, Kennerly's voice rushed on excitedly: "I want you to get over here right away. I'm at the Castelars'. Vince spotted Walt Jennings here not an hour ago."

Chapter Fourteen

Someone in the past fifteen hours had removed the blockage from the end of the long driveway. I pulled in and followed it as it curved around and ballooned out behind the house.

Every light in the place was on, and if that's an exaggeration it's a small one. I shut off the engine and looked at my wristwatch. Two thirty-seven A.M. That's the one that comes in the middle of the night.

I got out of the car just as the back door opened and three figures silhouetted against yellow light from the kitchen stepped onto the enclosed porch. I could hear the old spaniel yap; he thought he was going for a walk. I stood near the car from the sheriff's department, my hands crammed into the furry pockets of my parka, and waited for the three to cover the twenty feet between the house and the cars parked behind it.

They stepped into the grayish light of the yard lamp mounted high on a pole near the point where the drive began its southward curve. Kennerly, Vince Castelar, and Knut, the sheriff's man and my erstwhile dancing partner from nine hundred million years ago, or perhaps it was just this morning. Knut was doing the talking. He was giving sage advice on keeping doors and windows locked, but he quit when he drew close enough to make out my features.

He offered me a smirking grin, or perhaps it was a grinning smirk.

"You just keep turning up like a bad penny, don't you." His voice was as flat as the farmland surrounding us. He carried his enormous flashlight, though it was extinguished, and as he spoke he brought the business end of it up in a lazy arc that ended in the palm of his left hand, where he slapped it a few times. A Freudian analyst could have made something of him and his big black lamp.

"Always invited," I answered noncomittally. I didn't feel the need to strain my little gray cells, as Hercule Poirot calls them, to concoct an alienating wisecrack. The guy already didn't like me. Besides, maybe he thought he was just being clever. "You keep pretty long hours yourself, don't you?"

"Night shift. Twelve hours. Eight to eight."

"That puts you right in the middle of all the excitement then," I said, for want of anything better. I moved my eyes toward Vince. "At least, I hear there's been some excitement."

The boy's blond head bobbed in the semilight, but it was Kennerly who spoke. "Like I told you on the phone, Jennings was here, prowling around the place, not two hours ago."

I looked at my watch. Ever notice how you do that whenever someone mentions a time, even if you've checked, as I had, only a minute earlier? "Say—twelve-thirty?"

"Closer to twelve," the boy said. "I was in my room, studying. Mom and Amy were both asleep."

"The doctor gave Emily something to help her sleep," Kennerly supplied.

"Well, I thought I heard something at the front of the house," Vince resumed. "I went and looked in on my mom and my sister, but they were both sound asleep."

"And then the dog started acting peculiar," Kennerly

interjected. I looked at him. His eyes were alight and he was having trouble standing still. He was as hopped up on excitement as the kid was. I smiled at him. "You were here too, then?"

Only a little of the wind left his sails. "The dog?" I said to Vince.

He nodded. "He's been acting weird all day, you know, but then he started sort of whining and shifting around kind of, real restless. I asked him if he had to go out and he got all excited. Then I heard the noise again, sort of a thump against the front of the house. I went into Kate's room and looked down from the window. I could just see someone messing around in the bushes by my dad's study window."

"Jennings?" I said.

"Maybe," Knut said, and Vince was quick to jump on it.

"Maybe, shit!" His voice rose and thinned with the emotion of it. "What do I have to do to get people to take me seriously?" He turned back to me. "I ran down the stairs, turned on the outside lights, and ran out onto the front steps. He looked up, just for a second, but it was him all right. Jennings. I saw him clearly."

"Then what?"

"What do you mean, 'then what'? Then he ran off."

"Ran? On foot? Which direction?"

"South." He pointed.

"Did you chase him?"

"I wasn't exactly dressed for it," he said sarcastically. "I was in my robe and slippers. And—" He looked at Knut, who was looking at me. "Well, he might have had a gun."

"What about the dog? I don't mean did the dog have a gun, I mean did the dog chase him?"

Vince shook his head. "I wouldn't let him. Same reason—I didn't want him to get shot either."

"You made a great target, standing out there on the steps with the light behind you," Knut said derisively.

The kid looked down and hunched his shoulders in the thick pea coat he wore. "I told you, I didn't think of that then."

I said to Knut, "It seems funny that he'd run off to the south. You'd think he'd have his car on the road right out front, which is—what, west?"

"It seems funny he'd come back here at all," Knut said with a significant glance toward Vince, who ignored it. "But if he did—"

"It was him," Vince insisted.

"—he probably parked down the road a ways so no one'd hear him coming up to the house. Why he'd come up to the house in the first place—why he wouldn'ta' stayed hid till the weather broke and he could make a run for it—that's what I don't get."

"I told you *that*, too," Vince said exasperatedly. "He killed my dad, he probably killed my sister, and now he's going to finish off the rest of us, too."

"Now, Vince—" Kennerly began.

"Then why didn't he just go ahead and do it last night when you were all asleep and he didn't have the cops looking for him?" Knut countered, not doing a very good job of keeping the annoyance out of his voice. He snatched off his cap and shook away the snow that had accumulated on it. "Naw, I tell you, kid, someone was here, all right—the tracks in the snow outside the window prove that—but Jennings? I doubt it."

"I *saw* h——"

"I assume," I cut in, since Vince and the deputy had been down that road once or twice already, "that there were footprints in the snow in front of the house."

"Yes, there were footprints in the snow in front of the

house," Knut said mockingly. "The snow was all tramped down under the window; so what?"

"I don't mean under the window. I mean footprints leading to and away from the house, to and from where Jennings—or whoever—left his car."

Knut's head was bobbing like a toy dog's in a rear window before I was halfway through. "We followed them. We may not be big-city cops out here, but we're not stupid. They went off through the trees south of the yard, then cut across the corner of the field on the other side, and on to the road. The road's covered with tracks from cars and trucks and other equipment running up and down all day, so that's no help." He shoved the cap back over his close-trimmed hair. "The way I figure it, someone read about Castel— Mr. Castelar's murder, or heard about it on TV. They thought this'd be a good time to bust in and see what they could get away with."

He looked at me with challenge in his eyes. Maybe I'm getting old or maybe I was just tired, but it didn't seem worth the effort to rise to the bait.

Knut sneered triumphantly and hoisted himself up on his toes half an inch or so. "Well, if you *gentlemen* don't have any more questions—" We gentlemen glanced at one another. None of us was in a big hurry to keep him around. "All right, then. I'm freezing my tail off." He walked around the front of his car to the driver's side, stopped, and pointed the end of his flashlight at Vince. "Remember what I said about keeping them doors locked."

"They *were* locked," Vince said in the singsong of someone who knows he's not being heeded.

"Yeah. Well." He opened the door and threw his cap onto the seat. For the first time he seemed to notice my Chevy parked next to his patrol car. He looked it over then looked at me. "This your car?"

There were only three cars parked behind the house, and only three of us, including Knut, who didn't live there. But I let it slide. "Yep," is all I said. Yes, I must be getting old.

"State law says the driver must have an unobstructed view of the road. I could ticket you for driving a car that's in this condition."

Well, maybe not that old. "When did you *see* me driving it?"

He gave me that squinty Dirty Harry look again, slammed the gigantic flashlight through a leather loop on his overloaded belt, and got into the car, making sure we all heard him slam the door.

"Why do you do things like that?" Kennerly wondered mildly when the car door had shut.

"Everybody needs a hobby." Knut backed out from between my car and Kennerly's, swung around in a wide curve that nearly brought him into contact with the fat pole the yard light was rigged to, then roared off down the driveway churning snow and gravel. His tires didn't squeal; tires don't squeal on unpaved roads, except on television. But I was surprised he didn't turn on the siren.

We turned almost simultaneously toward the house. Three minds with but a single thought: thawing out.

We were in the soft warmth of the kitchen, struggling with boots and coats and the dog, who was glad to see us, before I asked if Banner had been notified. Kennerly threw his coat over a peg and said, "I took care of that before I came out. Rather, I called the station and spoke to the night commander, since Banner was off duty. He didn't think it was necessary to bother her at home, since Vince had already called the sheriff. The sheriff's department is to automatically notify OPD if they turn up anything pertinent to the homicide investigation." His eyes strayed toward Vince, who was patting the dog and talking to it the way you talk to a dog. "But it doesn't look like they did."

Vince looked up, his lips twisted into a sardonic imitation of a smile. "What you mean is they didn't believe me." He stood and faced me. "Knut said I was so worked up that I'd've said my own mother was Jennings if I didn't get a good look at her. Do you believe that?"

"Sure," I said. "It sounds like his sort of original thinking."

"And I did get a good look at him," he insisted. "Look, come here—"

I followed him through the kitchen, through the dining room, and into the living room, Kennerly dogging my trail, the dog dogging his. Vince led us to the front door. He yanked it open and the cold muscled into the room; then he bumped open the frosted-up storm door and stepped onto the small concrete stoop.

"Look!"

Reluctantly, I stuck my head out and looked where he pointed. The lamp fastened to the house next to the door was illuminated, and in its light I could clearly see the mashed-down snow near the bushes at the window in the southwest corner of the house. And I could see tracks to and from the mess, running diagonally across the yard. It was easy to tell which were coming and which were going: a person's heel nearly always leaves a scuff just before his foot makes the actual snowprint.

"Very nice." I retreated into the house.

Vince closed the doors and doused the outdoor light. "Do you see? There was plenty of light for me to see him clearly when he looked up."

"Vince," Kennerly said, "we don't doubt you." He looked at me. "Do we?"

I scratched at my beard. The skin under it was dry and

itchy. I looked at the dog and said, "Obviously someone was out there. No question. Vince thinks it was Jennings—"

"I know it was—"

"—and since he's the only one who saw him, outside of Fido here, we'll have to assume it was him. But Knut asked a good question, as much as I hate to admit it: How come?"

The Castelar boy clenched his fists in impotent rage. "Have I lost my voice, or has everyone else gone deaf? It's obvious—as I keep saying. He came to finish off the rest of us."

"Why?"

He really did lose his voice, for perhaps as much as half a minute, while he stared at me as if I'd just slid down the chimney like good Saint Nick. "Why?" he finally managed. "Because he hates us."

"That'd be a good way of demonstrating it."

The kid had a rejoinder but the dog interrupted it. He emitted a low growl, then set off toward the kitchen door in a quick, albeit floppy, trot. A car's lights stroked the living room drapes and we heard the crunch of frozen gravel on the north side of the house.

"Someone's here," Vince said unnecessarily.

By the time we got there, the back door was opening and the dog was prancing around, happier than I was to see Vince's uncle.

Charlie Castelar ignored the dog, ignored me and Kennerly, and said to Vince, breathlessly, "Are you all right? Is everybody all right? I was out—I got here as soon as I could . . ."

"Everybody's fine. I didn't mean to upset you. I just left the message on your machine because . . . I don't know, because I thought you should know, I guess."

I looked at my watch again; and, again, I don't know why. "Out kind of late for a school night, aren't we?"

He seemed to notice me for the first time, and displeasure dominated his features. "I don't feel I have to answer to you." He shucked his topcoat with quick, sharp movements and, seeing that the wall pegs were loaded, draped it over the butcher-block-topped island in the center of the room. Glancing superciliously at me and Kennerly in turn, he said, ponderously, "Obviously I couldn't convince my sister-in-law to get rid of the two of you. Fine. It's her money, and her life. But stay out of *my* life." He looked at me under lowered eyelids. "I think I was more than cooperative this afternoon. But don't press me."

Then he turned to his nephew. "Now what exactly is going on?"

So we got to hear it again, from the top, and Vince managed to wrap it up mere seconds before I collapsed under the weight of boredom. Castelar voiced the eternal question—why would Jennings come back here?—and before the kid could launch into his theory again, Kennerly butted in:

"What about Knut's thought, that it could be someone, a burglar, thinking he could take advantage of the situation here?"

I made a face. "Yeah . . . but I doubt that your common garden-variety burglar would come all the way out here unless he was very sure of some kind of extraordinary haul—you don't have, like, lots of silver or stamp collections or artwork lying around here, do you?"

"Dad used to collect pennies, but I don't think they're worth anything."

"Not enough, probably. And any burglar who was connected enough to unload stuff like that—in other words, a pro, not a kid raising money for his next fix—would also be savvy enough to thoroughly case the place before he started messing around with the carpentry. He'd *definitely* make a circuit of the house. And when he saw the light in Vince's room he'd pack up and go home. That's why they're properly called burglars and not robbers."

"So it *was* Jennings."

"Could be."

Kennerly said, "Do you think he'll come back? Maybe even yet tonight?"

"How should I know what I think? He hasn't done a damn thing yet that's made any sense; who knows what he'll try next? I might be willing to make a guess on his coming back if I could dream up any reasonable motive for his coming around here in the first place."

"Jesus Christ," Vince said animatedly, his eyes growing wet, his cheeks dotted with red. "I keep telling you why he came here—why doesn't anyone take me seriously?"

"Maybe you could try cutting out the whining," I said angrily. "Stop acting like a spoiled kid who thinks he's not getting enough attention and start pretending you're an adult. You might pick up the habit."

"Here, now—" Charles Castelar said hotly.

The kid looked as if he wanted to deck me, or try to, but he merely stood there, glaring balefully at me, his teeth grinding, his fists again knotted at his sides. I reminded myself that his old man had been killed only twenty-four hours earlier; that entitled him to more slack than I was cutting him. I said, gently, "I apologize. That was out of line. It's late, we're all tired, and we're all *very* keyed up and worried about Kate."

The anger went out of him like air out of a balloon. "I used to worry about Kate all the time," he said forlornly. "Now I don't think I need to anymore." His voice was empty, hollow. Something in it made my scalp crawl. Vince looked at Kennerly, his uncle, me in succession. "Well, if he hasn't killed her, then where is she?"

"Very good question," Castelar murmured. Then, regarding me smugly: "Perhaps you'd like to field that one, Mister Private Investigator."

Kennerly jumped in with characteristic optimism: "I think it means she's uninvolved after all. I think she's gone into hiding on her own—perhaps she's afraid of Jennings, perhaps he made some sort of threat against her, too—"

"Perhaps, perhaps, perhaps," I said irritably. "We have lots of good guesses but we don't *know* anything. Except that if Jennings is still lurking around, there's a much better chance of his getting caught. And then, presumably, we'll find out about Kate. However, I don't think that's going to be tonight. Not that there's much of tonight left anymore. And since these twenty-hour days get to be a bit much on someone of my advanced years, I think I'm going to run on home and put in a little sacktime before tomorrow's festivities."

"Just a minute," Kennerly said hastily as I turned toward the door. "I want you to stay here tonight. In case he comes back."

"What good will that do? Vince can call the cops just as well as I can."

"Besides, this day has been real hard on my mom and Amy; I don't think we should disrupt things even more."

"It's an unnecessary precaution and an unnecessary expense," Castelar proclaimed vigorously. "I think it's criminal the way you two are . . . *feeding* on a grieving, confused widow. Do you stay up nights trying to come up with new ways to pad your billings?"

"I get paid by the day," I shrugged, rapidly coming to the conclusion that if Castelar didn't like the idea, it must be good.

"And I get paid to act in Emily Castelar's best interests," Kennerly said solidly. He turned to Vince. "I think protecting her life qualifies."

"I can look after her."

"And what if something happened to you? What if Jennings had been armed tonight and had shot you when you went outside? Where would that have left your mother? She's so doped up on tranquilizers that she hardly stirred when the deputies were tramping up and down the yard with flashlights and floodlights—how would she defend herself? And Amy—what about Amy?"

"Oh, this is ridiculous," Castelar said, leaving the room in an angrier version of that curiously bouncy walk of his. A moment later we heard the rustle of a newspaper in the living room.

Kennerly looked up at me. By the fire in his eye I could see that there was very little use in arguing with him. Besides, he did have a point, a good one. So when he asked me if I had a gun, I told him there was one in the car; when he told me to go get it, I went.

Chapter Fifteen

The place to be was on the ground floor, in the study, since that's where the action had taken place earlier. Vince fixed me up with a sleeping bag and a pillow on the leatherette couch. The study, which was at the end of the short hallway that ran parallel to the stairs from the dining room, had probably been a bedroom once upon a time—the single closet suggested it—but now it was a small comfortable office, with a desk and a file cabinet, the couch and a coffee table, and three custom-made bookcases side-by-side on the south wall. These held more photos and nicknacks than books, as well as a bar set and a pair of partly filled decanters, a stereo receiver, and a small color television. Castelar had lacked only the outdoorsy scenes on the walls, maybe a couple of Terry Redlin prints, to give it that country-squire look.

The kid had rounded up a toothbrush that he was fairly certain had never been used; I held it under the hot tap for a good long time before I let it anywhere near my mouth. When I padded back across the hall to my bedroom pro tem Vince was arranging a heavy mug and an insulated carafe of coffee on the low table near the couch.

We had debated about whether I wanted anything to eat or drink—I taking the position that I did not, Vince handling the opposition. Finally we had compromised on the coffee. Once Kennerly had finished thoroughly beating him about the head and neck with the idea, Vince had accepted my spending the night and set about playing the good host, largely, I assumed, because his mother was, shall we say, indisposed.

"How's your mother holding up?" I asked as it popped into my head.

Vince poured off a cup and positioned it next to the white plastic pot. "Pretty good, I guess. She's still real upset, of course, but I think it's going to be all right. She sort of moped around all day, kind of confused, and then she went to bed at around eight. I looked in on her a few times and she seemed to be resting."

Out like a light, more like it, based on the impression I'd gotten from both Kennerly and Kate. "How about Amy?"

He was unzipping the sleeping bag, throwing the top part over the back of the couch, smoothing the half that lay on the seat. It was a plush green thing with red flannel lining, a camper's sleeping bag. You could survive nuclear winter in there. "She's doing a lot better. That psychiatrist came by this morning and they did a marathon like all day. I guess you've got to jump on these things right away. Anyhow, she was pretty encouraging—the doctor—and she says Amy's already showing good response. It's true, you can see she's coming around; she's not totally vegged out like this morning. So they can probably treat her at home at first, then later in the doctor's office. That way they don't have to screw up her life any more than it already has been."

I took the mug from the table and sipped tentatively. Lousy. I was getting used to bad coffee, but this was the worst so far. "Your uncle left without saying good-bye."

Vince finished fussing with the bag and perched on the couch's big round arm. "He said good-bye to me," he said through a grin. "He waited until you were in the bathroom. You know he called here tonight in an uproar. Like he said, he wanted Mom to fire you and Kennerly. But she won't."

Imagine my relief. "How'd your uncle get along with your father?"

He shrugged. "Okay, I guess. I mean, they weren't best friends or anything, I don't think, but they got along okay as far as I know."

"Your uncle told me he recently sold a lot of his shares in the bank."

Vince nodded.

"Why'd he do that, do you suppose?"

"I suppose he needed money. Or maybe he thought he could make a better investment."

"He said he needed the cash to cover a bad investment. But if he did, couldn't he have gotten it from the bank?"

"Sure. If that's what he really needed it for, Dad'd've fixed it. But if it was for something else . . ." The grin returned. "Charlie entertains a lot, I guess you'd say. He likes women an awful lot. And he never does things halfway or settles for second best. If it was just a question of living it up too much, Dad wouldn't've been in a real big hurry to bail him out."

Interesting. "Your uncle plans to turn the bank over to you pretty soon now."

The grin broadened. "Like it was up to him," he said pleasantly. "It's up to the board, and my mom *is* the board, pretty much. In fact, the reason Charlie's at the bank now is because I asked him to step in. Acting for my mother, of course. The last thing on her mind today was the bank, but I knew that business had to go on as usual. So I asked Charlie to take up the slack for a while. He wasn't thrilled, but he knows I'm right: You can let anybody manage the place, but you have to have a member of the family setting policy, and he's the only one to do it until I can step in."

"You seem pretty confident."

"I'd better be. There's no one else. Charlie won't do it,

not permanently. My mother certainly can't. And Amy's a little young."

"What about Kate?"

He gave me a long look that went through me and left marks on the wall beyond. "If we ever get Kate back . . . well, she can't even balance her checkbook."

It hung there a minute or more and I forced down some more bitter coffee. I was going to have to do something about the quantities I was pouring into me lately. Caffeine overdose is an occupational risk in my line—both of my lines, the writing and the gumshoeing. Occasionally I'll get concerned and trim back my number of cups, or pots, per day, and my palate responds in an appealing fashion. But when I let the average creep back up, I'll drink any brown water you set before me. I may bitch, but I'll drink it.

Tonight I didn't even bitch. It wouldn't've been polite. I drank some more and wished it would do something about the dull, leaden ache behind my eyes. I suspected sleep would be the surest cure.

A framed photograph of the entire family, dog included, stood on one of the bookshelves. From the looks of the kids, I gathered it had been taken two or three years ago in the magazine-spread living room. I traced a finger across the glass, over the image of Kate, standing alongside Jack.

"Your father planned to bring you into the business slowly, in stages. What did you think of that?" I turned leisurely from the picture.

Vince shrugged. "I didn't see why he wanted to go so slow. I was ready for real responsibility, and I knew I could learn the job in a couple years, not seven or eight, or eight or ten—the estimate kept changing. Besides, he'd've still been around, as chairman and probably CEO. He could've let me run the day-to-day."

"Sounds like you had it all figured out."

He smiled. "I've known since I was twelve years old that it's what I wanted to do."

I nodded and ambled aimlessly around the room. Stopped at the window—it was still snowing, but far less persistently—inspected a brass drake on the desk, gave the globe the inevitable spin. "Did you and your dad disagree a lot, Vince?"

"Yeah, we did," he answered without hesitation. I looked up from Mali. Vince was still perched on the arm, his feet on the edge of the coffee table, his arms, folded, resting on his knees. "The police know this; everybody does; it's no secret. We fought all the time. The generation gap or something." He smiled perfunctorily and so did I, wondering how long it'd been since I'd heard the term. The last time I had, I think the word *groovy* occurred in the same sentence.

"Dad . . . he had trouble taking me seriously. I don't know why. Maybe he was used to telling people what to do and them doing it. Maybe I was a threat to him. Maybe he just thought I was stupid." There was no humor in his faint smile, only pain.

More time passed before he resumed. "Anyway, he never let me have any real responsibility, never let me take the initiative on anything, never . . . never took me seriously." He looked up from the globe beneath my fingers; his eyes had fastened on it, unfocused, as he spoke. "So, yeah, we fought a lot. Or I should say *I* fought; he wouldn't even take *that* seriously, usually."

"What about Kate?"

"I never fought with Kate."

"I mean, did she and your dad fight?"

"Never seriously. You know—maybe he didn't like the people she was hanging around with, or he thought she was spending too much money, or her grades were lousy—that kind of stuff. Until she started going out with Jennings last summer, that is. Then they fought a lot. But even then it was usually Mom who'd get bent out of shape, and Dad would be the one to smooth things out, almost ending up taking Kate's side."

"Why do you suppose she went out with him?"

"Who, Jennings? Wish to hell I knew. I never could figure her and her boyfriends; she could sure pick the dorks."

So thought Kate, I recalled. I shrugged. "I don't know; I met her old boyfriend, Tom Black, today—he seemed pretty nice."

"He's an asshole."

"Guess I was mistaken, then. How'd they ever get together—Kate and Jennings, that is? I wouldn't guess their circles'd overlap."

"Well, she sort of knew him from the neighborhood, you know. We all did. You'd see him in town, usually going into a bar, back before he lost the farm. Then last summer I guess she ran into him down in the city, bar-hopping with some friends of hers."

"Did she ever talk to you about him, or any of her male friends?"

He shook his head and returned his eyes to the globe.

"Oh, I had the impression that you two were—are—very close."

"We were," he said without looking up. "We are. I—sometimes she'd tell me. I didn't want to hear about it, but sometimes she'd tell me because she knew it bugged me. You know?" He looked at me. "Like the way a kid will do something just because he knows it ticks you off? It didn't mean anything. Kate and I loved each other, we really did. And anyway, she was making it all up."

After talking with Tom Black, I wasn't so sure. "Why did it bother you so much?"

"Why wouldn't it?" he said with some heat. "It was such

a waste. She had money and status, looks, brains—if she'd've used them—but she was wasting her time with jerks and losers." He laughed. "I sound like Dad. But it's true. I'd try and talk to her about it, try to make her see that she was cheating herself, but she'd only laugh. That's when she'd tell me these . . . stories."

"Stories."

He nodded desolately. "She liked to pretend she was kind of fast, you know? Not promiscuous, just . . ."

"Adventurous?"

His eyes went white-hot. "Who told you that? That son of a bitch Tom Black—did he? 'Cause if he did, then he's a goddamn li——"

"Take it easy, kid, you'll burst a blood vessel. And after all, you're telling me the same thing, aren't you?"

"No, I'm not." His temperature had come down, but what's a few hundred degrees from white-hot? "I'm telling you it was just a put-on, an act, sort of a game between me and Kate. A tease, that's all. When I'd rag her about seeing Jennings she'd needle me, make up stuff about what they did, about what she let him do, disgusting things, really sick . . ." Vince's eyes had wandered away from me; now they returned. "You know, she probably fed Black the same bullshit, or told someone she knew would tell him. And he's such a jerk, he probably believed it." He shook his head. "That girl, she sure knows how to pick creeps."

I recalled Kate complaining that her mother objected to everyone she dated, and wondered if Vince didn't take after Mom's side of the family in that respect. I didn't wonder for long, however. The day was fast catching up to me, and Vince could see it. He apologized for keeping me up, urged me to sack in as long as I wanted, and all but salaamed out of the room. Strange kid, I thought as I sat and emptied my pockets onto the coffee table. Baring his teeth at you one minute, snuggling up to you the next. I had a dog like that once, years ago. Had to have him put down.

The light hurt my eyes, so I put it out and Brailled my way across the room to the desk in the far corner. I lifted the receiver, heard the dial tone, and called my place. After it had rung a dozen times I hung up.

It was true that Jen slept like one dead, but I was certain she wasn't asleep. Not on Decatur Street, at least.

Well, why not? What we had going for us hardly fit any working definition of a marriage, or any definition of a working marriage. Nor could I claim to have kept unswervingly to the straight and narrow. I knew that she had spent time with other men, slept with other men, in every corner of the world; why should I be upset if she was doing it here?

Why indeed.

I had poured myself another cup of coffee—don't ask me why—and I stood with it at the window. It was an old-fashioned window, tall and wide, and its many small panes had each collected frost in the same corners, just like in the paintings. There was still no moon, but in the diffused light from the yard lamp behind the house, the snow that blanketed the long expanse of lawn was a soft, soft blue; the trees that hid the road were black and stark, except where velvet-looking puffs collected in crooks and on branches.

Dancing silver in the night air, large, porous flakes whirled and collided soundlessly and fell to earth. It was a Christmas-card scene, far removed from the winter wonderland of travelers' advisories and highway fatalities, of heart attacks and broken bones, of kidnaping and vandalism and sudden death in the night.

Kate wasn't dead. Like Vince—judging by my conversation with him—I had been having trouble deciding whether Kate belonged in the present tense or the past tense in my own thoughts, even though I had necessarily operated under the assumption that she lived. Now the knowledge came into my mind with sudden, solid certainty, in one of those quantum jumps of logic that force you to go back and try to find the path that brought you to your conclusion. In this case, I couldn't. I didn't have any "proof," any more than I'd had that morning. It was sheer intuition that jelled the proposition into certainty in my mind. It hinged mainly on the absence of the corpse, of any trace whatsoever, as if she had stepped through the looking glass. Again I asked myself why a killer would make the effort to conceal one and not the other. You can swing only once, no matter how many corpses you leave littering the landscape.

The idea that Jennings had come back tonight to polish off the rest of the clan fell apart like cheap shoes, too, when you thought about it. Jennings's beef had been with *Jack*, not the whole famn damily. And it was true that Jennings could have taken care of everybody and the dog last night after doing in Castelar. Or before, while awaiting his arrival from the airport.

All right, then, assuming Vince was neither mistaken in his identification nor hallucinating, why was Jennings skulking around tonight?

To see Kate.

I rested my head against a windowpane. The cold glass was soothing on my slightly feverish forehead. I lifted the window a fraction of an inch, for the room seemed stuffy and warm.

It made sense. Some. It explained a few things. Kate's disappearance had been kept out of the news; if Jennings had not abducted her, then he'd have no reason to expect her to be anyplace other than home sweet home. With every cop in the lower forty-eight looking for him, naturally he'd have to come furtively, under cover of dark, to meet with Kate and tell her—tell her what? *Gee whiz, kid, sorry I offed your old man; no hard feelings, I hope.*

Not too likely. Try again: *Gee whiz, kid, everyone says I offed your old man, but I didn't.*

But if he hadn't, who had? And where, oh where was Kate?

Good work, amigo, you've managed to bring the thing around full circle and give yourself a five-alarm headache in the process.

I lowered the window and meandered back to the couch.

Well, maybe Kennerly was right: Kate kidnaped herself. Maybe she feared for her own safety and went into hiding. But wouldn't she go to the police? Wouldn't she at least get word back to her family?

I sat with my feet on the coffee table and a hand on my throbbing gut. To say the least, it had been one hell of a day. Only *one* day? It felt more like three. And no wonder: This case, if "case" was the word for this abysmal mess, was really three separate but entangled cases: the murder, the missing person, and the manhunt. (Every writer knows, when in doubt, alliterate.) It was interesting to note the order in which those three sprang to mind, because Kate and her thin-air act was indeed at the center of everything, although all the overlapping pieces threatened to obscure her image.

Where was she?

Or was Vince right? Had Jennings killed her, either before or after killing Castelar, for some reason that I couldn't imagine? And had he now come back to finish the job, to wipe out the rest of the family and simultaneously, in his mind, wipe the slate clean?

Even so the question still remained: *Where was she?* . . .

Sometime, somehow, I got the half-empty cup repositioned on the coffee table. I must have, because that's where it was six hours later when I woke from a short, fitful, and not at all refreshing slumber.

Chapter Sixteen

She was small and slender and fine-featured, with long straight chestnut-colored hair that she wore gathered at the back of her neck. Her eyes were large and very, very blue, her mouth was small and very, very pink. She wore a smart gray suit, a red blouse with a floppy bow tie, and a countenance equally startled and amused as I stumbled into the dining room.

Who could blame her? I had awoken, if in fact I had, feeling like yesterday's breakfast warmed over. My head pounded, my gut ached, my eyes stung, and my mouth felt like some joker had carpeted it while I slept. After spending several minutes in the downstairs half-bath trying to comb my hair into shape, or at least get it to stick out symmetrically, I had given up and stuck my head under the spigot, letting cool water pour over the back of my head for a good long time. It made me feel a little more human, but with my slicked hair and my patchy beard I looked like I should've been selling hot watches at the airport. To make matters worse, my clothes looked like they had been slept in. They had.

I padded in on stockinged feet, half-smiled sheepishly, and pushed on through to the kitchen where—huzzah!—coffee awaited. The dog tap-tapped over, his tail flapping in such wide arcs that it thumped against his sides on the end of each wag. I patted him absently, then stood looking out the window over the sink, slurping hot coffee. The morning was gray, a little foggy, and the large barn at the edge of the yard was just a whitish smear against the dust-colored sky. A light but consistent snow fell at an angle that indicated a slight north wind.

I watched it vacuously for a few minutes until I felt the caffeine collide with my brain; then I topped off my mug and went back to the dining room. The woman looked up again from the leather portfolio she was studying. "Good morning," I said, but it came out more like *gr mrg,* so I cleared my throat and tried again.

"Good morning," she answered, with emphasis on the second word. She spoke with the barest trace of an accent that I could not identify on the strength of two words. I indicated the chair nearest her and she nodded in invitation.

I sat, drank, smiled. At least, it was a smile from my side of my face; no telling what it looked like from hers. "You'll have to forgive me," I said. "I'm useless until I've had my first pot of coffee."

"You and everybody else around here; they're all sleeping late today." Was the accent Scandinavian? "The aftereffects of yesterday, I suppose . . . although you look more like you were at a big party that I wasn't invited to." She smiled and her eyes glittered like blue diamonds.

"We had some excitement around here, but I don't know that you'd call it a party. Incidentally"—I extended a paw—"my name's Nebraska. I'm your friendly neighborhood private detective."

She laughed. "That would have been my last guess." She took my hand. "I'm your friendly neighborhood headshrinker. Koosje Van der Beek." She pronounced the first name the way some of my East Coast acquaintances pronounce "kosher"—*KO-shuh*—and the last name to rhyme with "heck."

"Van der Beek," I repeated. "Sounds Dutch."

Koosje nodded. "Nebraska," she said. "Sounds . . . Nebraskan. Are live-in private detectives the new status symbol, like aerobics instructors who make house calls?"

I smiled into my cup. "Do I look like a status symbol to you? No, I've been hired to look for Kate, the oldest daughter. But apparently Walt Jennings, the suspected perp—private-eye talk—was skulking around here last night, so I was moonlighting as a bodyguard." I frowned. "By the way, how did *you* get in?"

"Amy came down and let me in, *after* I had pounded on the back door until my knuckles were raw. Didn't you hear me?"

"No."

"No one else did, either. Didn't you even hear the dog barking?"

"Not a thing. Some bodyguard. Well, then I guess Amy *is* much improved; yesterday you could have driven a Panzer division through here and she wouldn't've so much as glanced up."

Koosje nodded gravely and guided a spoon in narrow ovals through the pale surface of her café au lait. "The key is to begin intensive treatment immediately. It's fortunate that Dr. Bruhn, the family physician, knew that. A lot of people, including a lot of professionals, still believe that a troubled child will 'snap out of it.' The rising suicide rate among adolescents, and pre-adolescents, says otherwise."

"Will Amy be all right?"

She sipped contemplatively. "I *think* so." Her words were measured, guarded. "The thing is, her father's death is only part of Amy's problem. I'm convinced of that. My guess is she's been seriously bothered by something for some time, perhaps something not even related to the murder. That event merely—well, you could say it was the last straw. Her troubles overwhelmed her, and she withdrew into herself. Now, yesterday we were able to break through that to an extent, to overcome somewhat the huge shock of her father's death. What we need to do now is go further, find out what *really* is upsetting her, and work on that. Otherwise I can almost guarantee a regression, perhaps a severe one, in no more than six months."

"Makes my job sound like a snap by comparison. Listen: Last night Vince was concerned that my presence here would upset Amy further. Do you think that's so? Should I make a run for it before she comes down?"

Her eyes went past my head toward the stairs behind me. "We're about to find out," she said calmly.

Amy emerged from the staircase, wearing blue jeans and a lemon turtleneck and the same infinitely sad expression as yesterday, and stopped dead in her tracks when she saw me. The dog bounded over floppily to say good morning, but the girl ignored him. Koosje greeted her brightly and asked if she remembered me. Amy nodded emptily as I sat there smiling until my ears hurt. "Why don't you get something to eat," Koosje said in that same chipper voice, "and then we can get started." The girl said nothing, but she moved past us and into the kitchen—giving me wide berth, or so I thought—and soon we heard the opening of cupboards and the fridge.

I looked at Koosje, who shrugged expressionlessly.

Amy returned presently with a bowl of cornflakes and a glass of orange drink. She said nothing, but her eyes were locked on me as she went around behind Koosje and sat opposite me at the big wooden table. I tried another smile, to no apparent effect. Damn this ratty beard.

After a few silent moments Koosje said, "Are you having any luck with your job? I wouldn't even know where to begin looking."

I glanced at the kid. It didn't seem to me that we should be talking about this in front of her—but then, I wasn't the doctor. "Mainly I've been nosing around, talking to people who knew Kate or Jennings, hoping to get some idea of where they might have gone to ground—the assumption being that the hideous weather in any direction you'd care to go has effectively trapped them in the immediate area. I thought I was on to something last night, but it dead-ended on me."

Abruptly Amy said, "Are you a policeman?"

I looked at Koosje. Her face was blank. I turned back to Amy. "No, I'm a private detective. Your mom hired me to find Kate."

Amy went back to work on the cereal. I polished off my coffee and was about to ask Koosje if she wanted more when Amy again spoke: "Do you have a gun?"

This time Koosje raised one delicate eyebrow a fraction of an inch.

"I own a couple, but I'm not wearing one now. I usually don't. I don't like them very much."

"Have you ever shot anyone?"

"Yes . . ."

"Did they die?"

I always have to think about that one, because of Viet Nam. Somehow, those deaths aren't supposed to count, like self-defense isn't supposed to count, but they do. It was a long time ago and it was on the other side of the world and sometimes it seemed as if it had happened to somebody else instead of me, but it still counted. Every one of them counted, even the ones I'll never know about.

"Some did," I hedged.

"My dad was shot," Amy said quietly, solemnly. "He died."

"I know, honey. That's why I don't like guns."

A single tear slipped down her long face. She wiped it away with the edge of her hand.

"Ready to go to work now?" Koosje asked. Amy nodded without looking up. "All right, why don't you run down to the family room and I'll be along in a minute. Okay?" Another nod. She stood and took her dishes into the kitchen, moving somnolently; a little later we heard three pairs of feet—Amy's and the spaniel's—on the basement stairs.

"How'd I do, coach?"

Koosje fastened the brass catch on her portfolio. "She had questions and you answered them. The questions indicate that she's preoccupied with her father's death—which is natural. She's trying to come to terms with a violent and senseless act. The answers were the only ones you could give. Generally speaking, it's less risky in these cases to tell the truth than to lie. We're into honesty here. I have to help Amy become honest with herself and her feelings, and it's hard to be straight with yourself when no one else will be straight with you."

I opened my mouth and made the phone ring. Koosje stood. "I don't think anyone else is up yet." She moved briskly into the kitchen. I followed with both of our coffee cups and busied myself with them as Koosje lifted the receiver and identified herself. There was a pause, and then she turned toward me. "For you." She slipped a hand over the mouthpiece and stage-whispered, "It's a woman—with a very sexy low voice."

"I told her never to call me here," I said, trading coffee for the phone. Banner was on the other end of the line. She sounded a light-year away; I guessed she was patched through from a car. "How did you find me?"

"Hey, Marlowe, you're not the only detective in town, y'know. I've been calling your place since eight; finally the light went on and I called your Kennerly. Say, your friend there's got a pretty sexy voice."

I watched Koosje dribbling milk into her coffee. "The feeling seems to be mutual. Would you like me to introduce you?"

"Maybe some other lifetime," Banner said coolly. "Right

now I want to get together for a little council of war, talk about this and that, whether you've made any headway, whether we've made any headway, that sort of stuff. I'm at the Jennings place."

"Can't it wait? I feel like death itself, I slept—badly—in my clothes, and I could use a shower and a bite to eat first. What are you doing at the Jenningses'?"

"Working," she said slowly. "Let's just say you're not the only one who feels like death this morning."

◦ • ◦

I was just as glad not to have breakfasted. By the time I arrived, just over an hour later, the body was gone, but the condition of the house was all my imagination needed to work up a fairly graphic sketch. To put it succinctly, the dingy little place was an abattoir. The slaughter had begun in the tiny bedroom, with the killer then following his fleeing victim into the living room, where the grisly job was finished. Blood had dyed the tatty blue carpet deep purple, almost black. Furniture was turned over and smashed. Splatters of gobbets of things that didn't bear thinking about decorated the walls and furniture and drapery.

Oddly, what horrified me most was the bloodstained doorknob and the dark vertical streaks on the door and wall, trailing down to the baseboards.

I thought of Christina Jennings the way she had looked last night, talking about Jennings, engaging in flirtatious badinage about her mysterious date, flashing her legs at me. And then I thought of her as she must have looked later last night, slashed, mutilated, dying . . . groping for the doorknob in a desperate and futile attempt to attract help. The thought made my stomach pitch.

"She didn't make it," Banner's hoarse voice said from behind me. I turned. She stood in the doorway between the wreck of the living room and the minuscule kitchen at the back of the house. "She bled to death." She nodded at the white tape outline in the middle of the purple-black patch.

I picked my way through the debris that used to be the living room and came close enough to catch a whiff of Sucrets. "I didn't see you when I came in." The front door had been barricaded by yellow plastic ribbons promising the ancient and terrible curse of the Omaha Police Division upon him who dared enter here. I had been admitted, by a uniformed officer, through the back.

"Ah, but I saw you." She widened her eyes melodramatically. "I was calling in some stuff. From the car." She hefted the phone and the severed line dangled limply.

"I've never had the guts to do that," I said distractedly. "Judging by the looks of the room, I suppose Christina . . ."

"To ribbons," Banner confirmed quietly. "Even if there had been a passerby to help her—and that's doubtful; the coroner set the time of death at between eleven P.M. and two this morning, give or take—they don't think she'd've made it to the hospital."

"Good Christ. Was she raped?"

Banner shoved her hands deep into the pockets of her overcoat and eyed the room not-quite dispassionately. "The post-mortem will tell. I doubt it, though. The setup's wrong. The way I see it, she was in there, in bed, with the guy. He had the knife, and he may have hoped to get it over with quickly: There was a deep wound in the stomach that appears to have been inflicted first. The rest, the slashes came later, when she tried to get away." She paused. "Let's get the hell out of here."

I followed her out the back door. She simply stood for a moment, hands in pockets, staring out over the back yard. The snow had completely filled in the tracks from yesterday. If the precipitation had come a day sooner, the garbageman would have gotten the murder weapon, not us. Like the song says, what a difference a day makes.

"Sorry," Banner said suddenly. "You'd think by now I'd be used to this kind of scene." She began to walk, and I followed her along the narrow path leading around to the front of the house, where any number of cops, some in blues, most in plain clothes, went about their chores with quiet, routinized efficacy.

"I don't think anyone ever really gets used to it. Different people develop different ways of handling it, that's all, and some are better than others at closing it off or redirecting it. That's how it was in the army, at any rate."

"Did you see combat?"

"Some. Not like a lot of guys. I spent the majority of my hitch in Military Intelligence—how's that for an oxymoron?"

"And I was guessing you were Lithuanian."

"An oxymoron is a self-contradiction—you know, military intelligence, voluntary compliance, business ethics."

"Oh, that's right; I bet you author types know all sorts of big words. Tell me, how does a private investigator come to be a writer?"

I shrugged. "Same way anyone else does, I suppose; same way anybody comes to be anything: You just do it. In my case, the wonder is more how come it took me so *long*. I think I always knew it's what I wanted. Other stuff just kept getting in the way. And speaking of other stuff . . . That's what we writers call a transition."

"Oh yeah? Well, now, where was I? Okay—she was naked when we found her, her clothes were neatly folded in the bedroom, and there are no signs of forced entry, so we assume her assailant was a lover."

"Some lover. I've heard of post-coital depression, but this is too much. Do you have any possible motive or—dare I say it—a suspect?"

The back walk came around the south side of the house and curved to link up with the walk from the front door to the street. We were by now nearly to the curb. "Yeah-h,"

Banner said guardedly as we stopped at the end of the sidewalk. She shifted the throat lozenge in her mouth. "But we haven't got all the bugs ironed out yet. We've got the murder weapon—managed it without you this time, Sherlock—a very large and very wicked-looking hunting knife that the killer thoughtfully left in the bathroom. Where, I should add, he apparently took a nice hot shower after he finished the job. The knife is Jennings's. His initials are burned into the handle, and we found a toolbox in the front closet that contained a leather sheath the knife fits. Could Jennings have come back and killed Christina last night? Possibly. Motive? Well, maybe he thought Christina had been more help to us than she really had been. Or to you." She looked at me slyly. "How did she seem when you were here last night?"

I laughed. "You are a detective after all. What gave me away?"

"Your ever-vigilant police force. A patrol car spotted your car and called in the license number."

"Wait a minute, if you had the place under surveillance, then how'd the killer—"

"Who said anything about surveillance? We stepped up patrols in this area, sure, but twenty-four-hour surveillance costs *beaucoup* bucks, and we couldn't justify the expenditure. No one expected Jennings'd come back here."

"Well, it's no secret; I *was* here last night—in the early evening, this was. And Christina seemed just fine, perfectly relaxed, not like a woman who expects to get killed. What she was expecting was company, probably masculine company; I mean, she was really dolled up. But I couldn't imagine it being Jennings. I still can't. His hanging around here would be even stupider than his hanging around the Castelars'. He'd be putting himself at risk fo——"

"Wait a minute: What do you mean, hanging around Castelars'?"

I looked down into her face and saw genuine perplexity. "That business out there last night." No change in her expression. "Vince. Thinking he saw Jennings. Last night. Out there. Hello?"

"Nobody told me anything about this."

"Didn't Knut call you?"

"No, the son of a bitch," she said, grinding what was left of her Sucrets into fine granules between her molars. "Damn it."

"Well, he didn't appear to be buying into Vince's story wholeheartedly. Maybe he decided it wasn't worth the bother . . ."

"That's not *his* decision," Banner rasped fiercely. "It's his job to report it; it's *my* job to decide whether it's worth the bother. Damn him. I'm going to have to have a chat with the sheriff this morning. Anyway, what *did* go on last night?"

I showed her some exciting scenes from last week's episode and she absorbed them without comment. "Who knows," I said when I'd finished the recap, "maybe killing Castelar set him off—like a dog getting his first taste of blood. Maybe he killed Castelar and killed Kate and got frustrated when he couldn't kill the rest of the family so he came over here and killed Christina. It's crazy, all right—but then, so was our lad Charlie Starkweather."

Banner smiled indulgently. "Before you get carried away completely, consider this; it's one of the unironed bugs I told you about." She paused and blew a frosty sigh—of weariness, frustration, resignation, something—into the cold gray midmorning. "I got a call from the Iowa state cops this morning. Seems they found Jennings's truck. Stuck in a drift on I-29 just north of Sioux City. A deputy reported it abandoned at about eleven-thirty last night."

Chapter Seventeen

It's an easy trip: You simply get on I-29, just across the river from beautiful downtown Omaha, and head north. That's it. It's not the most scenic drive in the world, but it does take you directly and almost effortlessly into Sioux City, Iowa, hard by the banks of the Missouri River.

Problem is, it gets you there after about ninety minutes—meaning it would be tough for Jennings to have killed Christina in Omaha between ten P.M. and two A.M. and abandoned his truck north of Sioux City in time to have been discovered there by eleven-thirty.

Unless he did it the other way around. "He *could* have decided that the weather had improved enough for him and Kate to make a run for it," I said dubiously, the tone of my voice matching the look on Banner's face as she leaned against the unmarked car at curbside. "Maybe for Canada. He got stuck, so he turned around and came back. He could've hitched a ride on the southbound lane or stolen a car—you wouldn't expect a murderer to shrink from grand theft auto—and gotten back here in time to kill Christina, if he was of a mind to."

"Uh-huh." Her voice, her posture, her whole attitude said she didn't think it too likely. "And what about his surprise cameo appearance at the Castelars'? Say he killed Christina at eleven on the dot. Give him fifteen or twenty minutes to get himself cleaned up and everything. He doesn't leave here until eleven-twenty or eleven-thirty, and it's a good hour's drive to the Castelar place. He can't make it there by midnight."

"Unless he drives like a maniac."

She squinted at me. "He's trying to *avoid* the cops, remember? All he needs is to be picked up on a traffic violation. In a stolen car, no less."

A uniform appeared with a clipboard, which he handed to Banner. I waited while she signed several forms. My head hurt and my gut hurt and I didn't want to have to think, much less speak, so I didn't mind the interruption. The uniform told Banner that the back door had been sealed and she told him there was no reason for everyone to hang around any longer. He set off for one of the patrol cars left on the street. The cruiser was one of the older ones that OPD was phasing out. The old models—white sedans with blue markings, like the new ones—had a friendly OPD slogan pasted to the front doors: YOUR SAFETY IS OUR CONCERN. This one, however, had been through the wash once too often, and part of the decal had torn away. As far as this cop was concerned, then, OUR SAFETY IS OUR CONCERN. Tough town.

"What if you run it the other way?" I said wearily when the cop had left. "Jennings ditches the truck near Sioux City, we know not when. He secures transportation back to the Big O in time to stage a midnight reconnaissance of the Castelar place, and is scared off by Vince and the mutt. He returns to the city and, unhappy about his evening being ruined, kills Christina."

"You have a real gift for invention, Marlowe. I can't wait to read this book of yours; it must be a masterpiece of imagination gone wild. Okay, say he gets scared away from the Castelars' at twelve-fifteen, twelve-twenty, somewhere in there. Give him an hour or so to get back to town. One-thirty."

"Giving him half an hour to shove Christina off the mortal coil before the deadline. No pun."

"Except Christina hit the sack with her killer first. That eats up your half-hour. And then some."

I shrugged. "Maybe Jennings has no staying power."

"Maybe Vince Castelar's mixed up on the time."

"He certainly seems definite."

"Come on, Nebraska, you've worked with witnesses to this or that over the years. You know how unreliable people's memories can be."

"Some people's memories. I look at what we have, it seems to bring us to the conclusion that Walt Jennings could not have killed Christina."

She looked at the sky in a speculative way. "Well, if you have any other nominees, now's the time. Meanwhile, nothing changes for me. The APB stands, the local investigation continues, and the beat goes on."

"'The beat goes on?' You're dating yourself."

"At least somebody is." She pulled a throat lozenge from her coat pocket and went to work on the foil wrapper. "Personally, I think Jennings did kill her, but I can't figure out the timing, so give him the benefit of the doubt on that one. But with Castelar . . . hell, everything points to Jennings. He had the motive and the means, he's unaccounted for at the time of the killing, he came home behaving very peculiarly *after* Castelar was killed, he hid a gun that turned out to be the murder weapon, and then he packed and split."

"So said Christina."

"And look what happened to her. I know there are lots of problems with the time-frame, but I say Jennings felt she had stabbed him in the back—bad choice of words—and repaid her in kind. God*damn* it!" She had been fumbling with the lozenge wrapper and getting nowhere. Now she grabbed the fingers of one glove in her teeth and yanked it off so she could get a nail under one corner of the foil. "Damn sadists. Next time I'm getting the kind you just pop off the little card." She tossed the thing into her mouth and jammed her hand back into the glove.

"But don't you think everything's just too pat, that everything points *too* directly at Jennings? I mean, the gun was hidden so badly, and the knife wasn't hidden at all."

"What're you saying, a frame?"

"Big enough to put around *The Last Supper*. Not that you'd put a frame around a fresco . . ."

"Again, I'll give you the benefit on Christina," Banner said. "She could've been killed by someone else, like a jealous lover, who heard all about Jennings on TV and figured one more killing wouldn't make any difference to *him*. It's a real stretch. Lover boy—whoever he might be, why ever he'd want Christina dead—would have to plan it out literally overnight. He'd have to know where Jennings kept his hunting stuff, he'd have to invent some reason for going into that closet and getting the knife, then he'd have to sneak it into the bedroom to use when Christina was most defenseless." She shrugged. "It could be"—she pushed herself away from the side of the car and walked around the front of it to the driver's side—"but the trouble is, I work for this crazy bunch that sort of expects me to stick with what-is and leave could-be out of it." She pulled open the car door. "Hop in; I don't think this cold air is doing my throat much good."

I opened the door on my side and slid in. Banner started the engine and shoved the temperature and fan controls to their highest settings. I looked out the window at the forlorn house, gray against a gray sky. "Not quite forty-eight hours ago I was sitting in almost exactly this spot with Kate

Castelar. No one had been murdered, no one had gone missing, no one was . . . out there, somewhere . . . It seems like a lifetime ago. Someone else's lifetime."

Banner looked into my face and rested a gloved hand on my arm. "We'll find her. She's with Jennings and we'll find Jennings."

"I don't know. Jennings killing Christina—I can't make it work. I think he took off, taking Kate. The weather got vicious. So they ditched the truck and went for a walk in a blizzard . . .

"You know, several years ago there was a nasty snowstorm here. The kind that comes from nowhere and dumps thirty-six inches in an hour. This place I was working at closed up at noon, the weather was so bad. The streets were clogged, so I left my car in the lot and hoofed it. It was only about a mile. But the snow was up past my knees, and by the time I got to my street I was so exhausted that all I wanted to do was lie down and rest. For just a minute. This was in broad daylight, I knew where I was going, and I could see my building right there in front of me. So I kept walking. But Jennings and Kate, they'd be out at night, in unfamiliar territory, and who knows how far from shelter. What if they stopped to rest for 'just a minute'? You're forever reading about some poor slob found frozen to death a hundred feet from his own front door because he couldn't see where he was going and had to rest for just a minute."

"Hey." Her face, and her voice, had gone earnest. "We don't know positively that it's the right truck—"

"But the license—"

"Screw-ups happen. In the dark, in a blizzard, a rookie up on the highway might've read the plate wrong. Hell, anyone might've. Besides, he'd mainly be interested in seeing whether anyone was still in the pickup. No one was. Maybe someone saw them go off the road and picked them up.

Maybe someone happened by a few minutes later. Maybe it wasn't even them in the truck—Jennings'd know we'd be looking for it, maybe he sold it to someone. I don't know. I do know that we *will* find them. As soon as the weather lifts, the state and county cops up there are going to be all over the place, checking all the homes and businesses and farm buildings, covering all the bases. If they're there, they're not going anyplace.

"But the thing is, they're not there, they're *here*. Christina was killed by the same man who killed Castelar—different MO, but it only makes sense—and I can't see Jennings running up and down the highway all night. No, Iowa's got the wrong truck, or Jennings got rid of it, or something. He's been here all along, and Kate's with him, and we'll find them."

"You're guessing, Kim." It was the first time I had called her by her first name, or even thought of her by it. It sounded funny.

"So sue me."

I had a better idea. I'd seen enough movies to know what the dashing young adventurer is supposed to do at a time like this, and it didn't have anything to do with lawsuits.

The kiss was deep and sweet, albeit Sucrets-laced—and brief. "Awright, break it up, break it up," Banner growled as she pushed me away and straightened up behind the steering wheel. "I told you before, I don't mix business and pleasure. Usually." She glanced at me and then out her window. "Jesus Christ, is that your car? What happened to it?"

"No, that's *my* car," I said. "Like it? I'm hoping to start a fashion trend." The defroster had developed a squeak that went through my head like a nail, so I reached forward and lowered the fan lever a notch or two. "Actually, I have the distinct feeling that someone wants me to go back to my typewriter and leave this case alone. You can't see it very well from this angle, but my remodeler painted STOP on the hood after dumping the better part of the can on the windshield—*after* he realized he wasn't getting anywhere smashing it in."

"Good Lord. Any idea who?"

"Once upon a time I had half-thought Christina, but it didn't work right then and it certainly doesn't make sense in light of recent developments. I don't mean just the murder; I was buzzed once or twice yesterday by person or persons unknown in a new blue Thunderbird. Which reminds me: Do you know anything about a charming creature called the Fat Lady?"

Banner nodded. "We know the Fat Lady real well. I forget her real name. It might just as well *be* the Fat Lady, because that's what everyone calls her. She used to be a fairly well-connected madam back in the fifties, but then the political winds shifted and she took a nosedive. Now she's just another hustler looking to make a buck, and she's spread out all over the map."

"Literally as well as figuratively."

"She's still got a few girls—strictly down-scale—and she's into drugs, numbers, sharking, liquor, guns. That makes her sound like public-enemy number one, but we're talking a couple of girls, a couple of guns. You can own stock in a hundred companies, but if you only own one share of each . . ." She ended the sentence with a shrug. "Every so often she oversteps the line, or one of her girls propositions an undercover cop, and we haul them all in. Nothing ever sticks. Not that anyone tries real hard; the Fat Lady's hardly worth worrying about. Why are you?"

"I'm not worried; just interested. One of Jennings's haunts is run by the Fat Lady. I was there last night and had a spectacularly bizarre evening. First one of the hired hands beat up on me, then the *grande dame* herself pulled a gun on me, refused to answer any questions of any variety about Jennings, and made it clear that my smiling face was unwelcome on her property. But *then* she gave me a lead to follow up. It was a dead end—but was it an *intentional* dead end?"

"Sure it was."

"Oh. Thanks for clearing that up for me."

"She was trying to get rid of you. Did she send the T-bird?"

I shook my head. "I was being tailed before I ever even heard of her, or she of me. Same with the new paint job on my car. And it doesn't make sense, the Fat Lady sending me on a merry chase just to get rid of me; I was literally on the way out when she suddenly changed her mind and started talking."

"She was funnin' you, brother," Banner said with conviction. "A woman like the Fat Lady turns helpful for one of two reasons: to make a buck or to save her butt. What's the story on this supposed hideout?"

I told her about the old ramshackle transients' hotel and gave her rough directions to it. She made a few notations in her book and pledged to ask about it down at the station.

"And on the subject of hideouts," I said, "I meant to ask you about a second, disused farmhouse on the Castelar property. I understand Kate had a key to it."

"Yeah, the sheriff checked it out first thing yesterday, as soon as we learned that she was missing again. It was locked up tight; no sign of anyone having been in for ages. Why? Were you thinking maybe she and Jennings were hiding out there?"

"Too much to hope for, I know. But I once spent not quite four days looking for a runaway who turned up in the basement. He slept in a storage room under the stairs during the day and sneaked up for food at night. It could have gone on forever except Ma wondered where all the milk was disappearing to."

"Well, I can ask the sheriff to take another look at it when I call to bitch about Knut." She added it to her list. "Anything else?"

I looked at her a long time, and finally she glanced up. "Just one more thing," I said, and leaned close. She brought her notepad up between us and batted me lightly on the nose with it.

"Ixnay, Nebraska." Her voice was soft and hoarse. "Like I said before, maybe later."

I sighed theatrically and popped open the car door. "It's been like this ever since I left Krypton," I said, and stepped out into the snow.

Chapter Eighteen

I found a pay phone in a 7-11 and called my friend in the DMV; he was, as usual, purely delighted to help me out by running the Thunderbird's license-plate number through the department's computer files. This required only a few minutes, and I held the line until his dulcet voice again serenaded my ears.

"How much longer is this blackmail going to go on, Nebraska?" he demanded in tones both hushed and outraged.

"Blackmail is such an unpleasant word. I prefer to think of it as doing a favor for a friend who did you a favor."

"That was years ago."

"It was a big favor."

"Well . . ." He seemed to be running out of steam. "How many little favors does it take to pay off a big favor?"

"Beats me. Tell you what: I'll let you know when we get there, okay? Now: Who owns the T-bird?"

"It's registered to the Greater Omaha Vending and Amusements Corporation. You know, it's funny," he added musingly, "that's a real familiar-sounding name to me . . ."

"No fooling," I said, and returned the gray plastic receiver to its stainless-steel hook. It was a real familiar-sounding name to me too. Until yesterday I had never even heard of the Greater Omaha Vending and Amusements Corporation; now it seemed that every time I turned around I was looking at a car registered to it. Or being run off the road by one.

I got the address out of the phone book, filled up the Chevy, and went downtown.

The bells of St. Mary Magdalene were calling the faithful to the church's special no-frills Mass—a quick hymnless, musicless, sermonless service tailored to office workers' lunch-hour constraints—as I coasted up to the curb across the street from the vending-machine company. This section of the downtown district, home of missions and pawn shops and liquor stores and whitewashed windows, had been untouched by renovation and rehabilitation. The old two- and three-story red brick buildings were dingy, decrepit. Many bore the faded and ancient traces of advertisements for long-deceased businesses on otherwise blank façades. Many more were crumbling, gutted, vacant. They had been empty for years. They would remain empty for a few more years, and then they would be regenerated. Inevitably. Before the decade was out, the few struggling businesses that remained here because rents were cheap would be forced to close up or move on because suddenly the neighborhood had become the trendy new place to live or work, and they couldn't touch the rents any longer. You read it here first.

The building I was interested in was an old brick number that sat on the northwest corner, a narrow and deep two-story. I imagined it was once a retail store, perhaps a grocery, and the proprietor lived upstairs. The front of the building featured a huge old plate-glass window next to a disintegrating wooden door that had been painted dark green a very long time ago. The second floor featured a pair of tall skinny windows half-shielded by yellowed shades, no curtains. The east side, the side facing the cross street, was blank except for the gaping hole of a loading bay that had obviously been added not that many years ago to facilitate the comings and goings of heavy, bulky vending machines.

I got out of the car, crossed the street, and wandered nonchalantly up the sidewalk. There were no trucks or other vehicles in the tiny lot adjacent to the loading platform, but the building was backed by an alley that bisected the block. One car was parked in the alley, the Diplomat that had sat in the lot of the West Omaha State Bank and Trust yesterday afternoon.

I doubled back, hopped the three or four steps at the side of the loading dock, and stuck my head into the bay, a big, cold, unadorned space of stained concrete floor and bare walls against which sat a number of vending machines of various types, ages, and states of disrepair. At the far end of the space was a small enclosed room constructed of drywall and plate glass. The foreman's office. But it, like the rest of the bay, was dark and deserted.

"Lunchtime," I said aloud.

I crossed the concrete floor—or maybe it was cement; who can keep the two straight?—and listened to the flat echo of my footfalls. No one came running. I took a vague diagonal path toward a gray steel door set in the same wall as the enclosed office, about ten feet down, expecting interference and encountering none.

The door opened to a blank wall, recently and cheaply constructed, badly painted in a brown-and-beige two-tone. The wall served to create a short corridor. At the very end was a grimy, battered door labeled REST ROOM: next to that, in the longer wall, was a doorless opening. That put me in the front room with the big plate window, a room that had the look of a secretary or receptionist's space: steel desk with built-in typewriter-stand, three four-drawer filing cabinets, and the type of metal cabinet that invariably contains office supplies. All in the standard purple-gray of office furniture.

On the desktop sat a green four-button rotary phone. One of the buttons blinked rapidly in its holding pattern. I know how annoying it is to be left on hold forever. So I keyed the line and cut the connection.

At the back of the small room was yet another door, a modern hollow-core wooden door, which was closed. There was no sign or label on the door.

I opened it quietly.

A middle-aged man with a middle-aged gut and grizzled hair sat on a vinyl-backed chair behind a metal desk somewhat larger than that in the outer office. It was only right; this office was bigger, too. A long, laser-carved wooden plaque resting on the desk read FRANK KIRBY, and I assumed it was he who was currently pawing through the desk's file drawer. He didn't notice me as I took in the room—the desk set, a guest chair, two two-drawer filing cabinets supporting a wooden plank piled with binders and papers, a year-at-a-glance calendar pinned to the back wall near another wooden door that led I knew not where. Perhaps into the office in the loading bay. Two potted plants, one I could identify as an ivy of some sort, one that was unfamiliar to me, struggled for life in the airless, windowless room. They were losing.

He had his phone off the hook, the receiver weighting a small stack of forms on the desktop. I reached over and picked it up. Only then did Kirby, who had been bent at the waist with his head nearly in the drawer, notice me. He gasped, startled, and reflexively pushed away from the desk. The chair wheeled back and crashed into the makeshift table behind him. The binders wobbled and a few poorly balanced sheets of paper fluttered to the floor.

Kirby was a large man, perhaps once athletic, now gone to pot. Probably the only exercise he got was stabbing the buttons on his television remote control. Even *I* have to get up off my duff and walk over to the thing. His gray hair was neatly and expensively styled; its gentle wave, whether owing to nature or artifice, was as smooth and even as a corrugated roof. His features were long and sharp, above a developing jowliness, and at the moment very surprised.

"Who the hell are you? What are you doing?" he spluttered.

I seated the receiver in its cradle. "I happen to know they hung up," I said, trying to sound cool and self-assured. It wasn't too tough: Kirby's response had been most gratifying. "That gives us some time to talk." I deposited my hat on a corner of the desk, unzipped my parka, and slipped my hands in its pockets. Then I thrust the corner of the left pocket toward Kirby, who had been inching one hand along the edge of the desktop and toward the center drawer. "Unless you're reaching for a pack of Juicy Fruit, I'd stop right there." I growled it as hard-boiled-sounding as possible. If nothing else, last night's scene with the Fat Lady had taught me firearm safety—*viz.*, how to make myself safe from firearms. I stepped around the side of the desk, opened the drawer with my right hand, and lifted out the automatic resting there.

"My, my." I weighed the weapon in my palm. "Who'd've guessed the jukebox business could be so rough. And a .45, no less." I slipped it into my right pocket. "It'll look swell in the trophy case."

"You son of a bitch," Kirby spat. "I'm gonna have your badge for this, you bastard. I got an injunction protects me from harassment."

"Accent on the first syllable, Frank, *har*assment, as in police harassment, as in what your injunction protects you from. I *assume*—if you could get one that protects you from general everyday harassment, we'd all be lined up at the courthouse. The problem is, I'm not the cops; I'm just Joe

Citizen, and so your injunction means about as much to me as the rules of the road mean to whoever's been piloting your shiny blue T-bird around town lately. Namely, nothing."

His bloodshot eyes widened slightly at the mention of the car and I tried not to smile. I hadn't done anything like this in months, and it was fun. So I was a show-off, so what? I had made bigger shots than Frank Kirby stand still and listen to me rant and rave, not necessarily in that order, and had lived to tell the tale. The ice I was on now was a good deal thicker than that on which I had skated around with the Mob last summer. Pleasanter all the way around. If Kirby didn't think so, well, tough.

I leaned against a wall and braced one heel against the edge of Kirby's desk, keeping both hands crammed deep into my pockets. "Up until about half an hour ago, Frank, I was at a total loss to understand where that T-bird came from, how it fit into the picture, why it was tailing me yesterday evening, and why it tried to run me off the freeway last night. I'm still in the dark, to be honest, but now that I know that it's registered to the same company as a car parked in the lot of the West Omaha State Bank yesterday"—the red-rimmed eyes narrowed—"I know who can lift from me the veil of confusion, cause the scales to fall from mine eyes and the clear white light of understanding to shine forth. Are you with me, Frank?"

"I—"

"Speak up, son, belt it out. The dialogue's beginning to drag, the audience is getting restless, and I'm tired of carrying the conversational ball."

"I—there's a mistake here. Some kind of mistake. Got to be . . ."

"Well, that's not a very good start, but maybe you'll improve."

The phone rang and Kirby's hand went for it automatically. "Tut-tut," I said, waggling my left hand in its pocket. He stopped. The phone kept ringing. He looked at it, looked at me.

"This is my business here, you're wrecking my business," he whined. I could understand his discomfort; from what I could see, the coin-op business was lousy. I hoped Kirby had socked some away during the video-game craze. But I didn't hope that hard.

"Tough cookies," I said. "They'll call back. Probably."

Kirby made a grab for the phone but I guessed from the way his eyes had been shifting that he was going to try something, and I whipped his automatic out of my right pocket and into his face. He had the phone to his ear and was bawling into the mouthpiece, yelling for the police. Unfortunately, the call was coming in on a line whose button was not depressed. Kirby was talking to a dial tone. By the time he realized the problem and poked the lighted stud, the caller had hung up.

"That'll be about enough of that," I said through gritted teeth. "I think the picture'd be a lot prettier if you just sat there with your hands neatly folded on the desktop, fingers interlaced." I moved the gun marginally. "Today would be nice."

"You know," Kirby said ruminatively, his eyes cast down at the gun, his tongue darting out to moisten his lower lip, "I was just thinking I didn't put the clip back in that gun last time I cleaned it."

I hefted it without moving it out of line with his considerable gut. "Really? Feels nice and heavy to me. Shall we try it?"

He said nothing.

"Well, okay, maybe later. For now, let's get back to issues and answers. I want to know what you were doing at that bank yesterday. I want to know why you had me followed after I left there. I want to know why your guys buzzed me off the road. And I want to know now." Tough as nails, that's me. I had started this tête-à-tête with a psychological advantage, but the element of surprise is an unstable one with a short half-life, and I could feel it decaying even now. Kirby was coming to suspect that I wasn't going to shoot him—excuse me; *drill* him, us tough guys never just shoot anyone—so if I was going to get anything out of him I had to get it fast, before the suspicion solidified into certainty. And before any personnel breezed back from lunch. Thus the Alan Ladd act.

Kirby had folded his hands as I had instructed, perhaps because I had decided to leave the gun in sight, in order to help him remember it was around; now he separated his palms and angled his thumbs back in a constrained shrug. "Like I said, it's a mistake. In my line of work, Mr. Nebraska, a fellow encounters a surprising number of slow payers. When a guy owes you a substantial amount of money, it's a good idea from time to time to remind him that you're still waiting. D'you see what I mean?"

"Um."

"Good. So I guess there must have been some sort of a mix-up is all, and some of my employees got you confused with one of the slow payers I had asked them to follow up on. Probably transposed a digit on the license plate or something and came up with your car completely by mistake."

"Uh-huh. What we have here is a failure to communicate."

"Exactly."

"No, no—*you* and *I* have a failure to communicate. See, your fairy tale is ridiculous. I don't for a second believe you give your enforcers a license-plate number and have them comb the city trying to find it. Besides, if I'm a wrong number, how do you know my name? Also you're forgetting that I made your car in that bank lot yesterday. When I was in the lobby with Castelar, you were killing time in the inner office, no? You had plenty of time to get on the horn and call your minions. Maybe they were hovering around the neighborhood, maybe they picked me up en route back to the city. I don't much care about that. What I care about is—I can't think of any other way to put it—*how come?*"

He looked at me for a long time. "Okay," he sighed at length. "You seem like a pretty straight guy to me. I'm gonna be straight with you."

I braced myself. There are a few prefaces that always start the little internal alarm system a-clangin'. One is *Don't get me wrong;* another is *I'm glad you asked that question;* and another is *I'm going to be completely honest with you.* Whenever you hear a variation of one of those, look out.

Kirby leaned forward, resting his weight on his elbows and forearms. "Like I said, this business of mine, it's something else. And some of my competitors can be kind of . . . well, it pays to never turn your back on them, if you know what I mean. Now, I'm completely on the up-and-up—don't get me wrong—but some of these other guys, they have important contacts, right? Connections. Friends with last names that sound like some kind of pasta dish. You know?"

"Go on."

"Well, so that's how come I had to get my injunction. Because these guys spread a lot of money around police headquarters, and the next thing you know I got cops coming in here every other day, hassling me and my men, tearing the place apart, stopping trucks on their way to make deliveries. Bad for business, very bad. So my lawyer gets this injunction and then things cool down for a couple of months. But I know the kind of people I'm dealing with, see, and so I'm keeping my eyes open for their next move." He widened his eyes as if to demonstrate.

Kirby leaned back again, his folded hands still on the desktop, and raised his shoulders. "So here I am at the bank yesterday, my banker's been killed, I'm in the middle of trying to renegotiate a loan the guy I'm talking with doesn't know anything about, and then he tells me there's a private eye hanging around the place asking all sorts of questions. Well, naturally I get concerned. Okay, paranoid; I don't mind admitting it. I'm thinking, who knows, maybe they killed my banker so's to delay my loan because without it I'm down the tubes. Maybe this private-eye guy's supposed to throw a scare into the new banker—Castelar's brother—so he'll jerk me around and I won't get my money or something. Who knows, right? So I get on the phone, and the rest you figured already. I tell a couple of my employees to follow you and see what you're up to."

"All right, maybe that explains yesterday afternoon. What changed the program between then and last night when they tried to scramble me?"

"Oh no," he protested strongly. "No, no. I'm really glad you asked me that, because that was a mistake. You gotta believe me, that *was* a mistake. I didn't say anything about roughing anybody up. They must've misunderstood me or got carried away or something. I'm really sorry about that. I'm gonna have a long talk with them—"

The tone of his voice changed on the last mouthful of words and I wheeled in the direction his eyes had shifted. Too late. One of the very lads we had been discussing had edged open the door that I had come through. Now, as I turned, he took two long strides into the room and chopped me expertly on my right wrist bone. My hand and arm turned to Cream of Wheat, so I decided to set down the gun. On the floor. The lad casually stooped to scoop it up and pocket it as the door on the opposite wall opened and a tall, narrow-shouldered man in a bad hairpiece slunk into the room.

I should have anticipated it. As the great Chandler himself said, "When in doubt, have two guys come through the door with guns." My two guys didn't have guns—they weren't brandishing them, anyhow—but the intent was the same.

Kirby got to his feet. "Where've you two been? I thought this jerk was—"

"He still might," I interrupted. "Aren't we forgetting something?" I waved my left pocket in small circles.

The two men looked at Kirby, who was looking at me. The one who had knocked the gun from my still-lifeless right hand was edging his fingers ever so slowly toward the jacket pocket in which he had deposited my—rather, Kirby's—gun. I told him to cut it out and he did.

"He's bluffing," Kirby decided while this went on. "I never saw any gun except mine."

The hired hands each took a tentative step toward me. I stepped back against the wall.

And then I did a really stupid thing.

I shot a big hole in the pocket of my arctic parka.

Dramatic, yes, but dumb. I should have had the gun out and ready long before I needed it. I needed it now, obviously, but I didn't particularly want the hammer to catch on a corner of the pocket, as it very well might have if I'd tried yanking it out suddenly. So . . . good-bye, parka.

Still, it was almost worth it. Everybody froze in place and Kirby paled visibly. I glanced down at the torn and burned corner of my coat, at the jagged hole in the opposite wall near the baseboard, at the three other men in the room.

"Put 'em up," I drawled. Always wanted to say that.

They put 'em up, and I herded the two newcomers over

behind the desk, next to Kirby—*after* belatedly withdrawing the revolver from its pocket. The coat was already ruined, of course, but I'm not terribly proficient with my left hand—my right was still too numb to be of much use—and I didn't need the extra encumbrance now that the odds had changed. I wanted more freedom to maneuver my way out of there. Things were fairly even at the moment, thanks to my smoking gun, but they had the home-court advantage and it looked like the folks on the payroll were returning from lunch. The private-eye code forbade me from just rabbiting out of there, which is what I felt like doing, and required at least a mildly stylish exit. Certainly something a little more noteworthy than my departure from the Fat Lady's joint last night had been.

So I smiled benevolently at the assembly. "Winken, Blinken, and Nod," I said, largely because I thought it sounded like something the Saint would say. "It's good to have you all together, cousins, because then I'll have to say this only once: Leave me alone. Do you copy? Leave. Me. Alone. Stay out of my way, stay out of my hair, stay off my tail. Or the next time I come calling, Frank, it's not your wall I'll be putting a bullet through. Okay? And just so there's no misunderstanding—your competitors aren't the only ones who have big friends. *Capisce?*" That last part was pure malarkey, of course, but what did Kirby know? He'd thought I was bluffing about the gun.

I trailed my eyes from one face to the next. Cool, that's me. Jack Kerouac, James Dean, Elvis Presley—they didn't know from nothing, coolwise, compared to noble, heroic, and positively subzero *moi*.

I picked up my hat and arranged it precisely on my head. I slid out the door like the Shadow, closed it slowly, and then ran like mad through the reception area and out the door to the street. But coolly, of course. There was no sign of pursuit, no sign of anything, as I hurried up the block and across the street to my waiting car, jumped in, fired her up, and fishtailed away from the curb.

Geez, maybe they bought the cockamamie story.

° • °

I tooled around enough to convince myself that I hadn't picked up a tail, then headed on home. Jen would be there—presumably—and in case I hadn't made as big an impression as I hoped on the Greater Omaha Vending and Amusements Corporation, I thought it might be better for her to be elsewhere.

I needn't have worried. When I came through the front door, the first thing I saw were two suitcases in the middle of the room. And they weren't mine.

There's no point in going into a lot of detail. It was as I had predicted. No, not predicted: *known*. We'd played this scene so many times before that it was now a bit like "predicting" the ending of *Casablanca* or *Gone With the Wind* or any other movie you've seen eighteen hundred times.

In our little drama, only Jen's destination changed. This time it was Los Angeles. I thought she'd had "done" LA just a year or two earlier, but I abstained from commenting. At this juncture there was no point in sparking an argument. Everything that could be said had been said, everything that could be regretted had been regretted, every feeling that could be hurt had been hurt. We were left with no anger, no recriminations; only a kind of muted, stupefied sorrow.

She was flying out in a couple of hours with a friend of hers from college, a girlfriend.

Oh.

If I wanted to come with her I was more than welcome.

If she wanted to stay here with me she'd be more than welcome.

There was nothing for her here.

There was nothing for me there.

And so on.

I took off my ruined parka and balled it up and threw it into the uncomfortable armchair, then I perched on the back of the couch and watched her as she moved around the cramped, tiny apartment, gathering up the odds and ends she had missed, cramming them into this or that corner of this or that suitcase, inevitably having to sit on them in order to close and lock them.

Damn it, she was beautiful. And she was here, I could reach out and stroke her hair, her back, her breasts, and she would respond. But in a few minutes a hack would be laying on his horn outside, and when that happened it would be as if Jen and I were separated by the Iron Curtain, as if we lived on different planets, as if we had each existed at different points in history.

A car horn sounded downstairs.

Jen had already pulled on her tall leather boots and stowed her shoes in a gigantic shoulder bag. Now she pulled on her long coat and draped her scarf loosely around its collar, shouldered the bag and her purse, and lifted the two small cases in each hand. I didn't offer to help.

She looked at me and I looked at her, and neither of us spoke. It had all been said. Eventually the taxi brayed again and Jen smiled wanly, snuffled, and turned toward the door.

I moved over to the sliding glass doors and looked down one story to the street. The driver helped her load her bags into the trunk. Then she got into the back seat and he got into the front seat and they drove up the Decatur Street hill.

The taxi was an orange Happy Cab. How's that for irony?

Chapter Nineteen

I lay on the couch and looked out the glass at a gray flannel sky that couldn't quite work up the enthusiasm to snow. I could relate. Slowly the sky grew grayer and grayer, beginning the color of dust and deepening to ashes and finally charcoal. Ultimately it turned black. That was fine with me.

Chapter Twenty

So I allowed myself a good wallow in self-sympathy, alternately excoriating myself for being a total washout at everything and damning Jennifer for being such an unstable little airhead. I lacked the strength and the will to peel myself off the sofa until nearly six. I did, at one point, reach over and grab my parka to use as a blanket when the room grew chilly, and that maneuver depleted what small reserve of energy I had had. I mightn't have gotten up even then, but someone was rapping on my storm door. I could have pretended I wasn't home. I *felt* like I wasn't home, or anywhere, for that matter. But it was probably just the papergirl, and even a good-for-nothing loser like me hates to make a kid drag herself out a second time in the cold and dark.

I forced myself up off my back, my sore, cold muscles cooperating not at all, let the coat slide to the floor, and staggered toward the incessant rapping. I hit the wall switch next to the door and squinted against the floor lamp that came on. I pulled open the wooden door.

It wasn't the paper carrier, unless the old one had sold her route. It was my former sparring partner, Bruno, wearing an old and much-abused overcoat, a black watch cap pulled down over his ears, and, as usual, no expression.

I wondered mildly if he had come for a rematch, to even the score. I didn't much give a damn if he had.

He opened the aluminum door and poked his head into the room, glancing around impassively. Finally his eyes settled on me. "She wants to see you."

"Who?" I said stupidly.

Bruno closed his eyes momentarily. It was as near as I had seen him come to displaying an expression. "The Fat Lady," he said patiently. "At the bar. Midnight."

"I'm not doing anything," I said, turning for my coat. "Let's go now."

His arm came through the opening in the doorway and his hand closed around my bicep and tightened like a blood-pressure cuff, the glove's empty little finger daintily extended. "Midnight," he reiterated. "At the bar."

Bruno's arrival energized me materially. The blood again circulated through my brain. The muscles, albeit still sore and stiff, seemed game. This could be a trick, I thought, a trap. But to what end? I had been effectively trapped last night, and she had let me waltz out of the dive. I recalled what Banner had said about women like the Fat Lady, that they did what they did only to make a buck or save their butt. Which would this be? I wondered.

"Midnight," I told Bruno. "At the bar."

He nodded solidly, once, closed the storm door, and plodded along the concrete walkway to the stairs. The whole building seemed to vibrate under his footsteps.

I closed the wooden inner door, set the deadbolt, and kicked into place the towel that allegedly blocked the draft from the threshold. What was the old girl's game? You get into the habit of seeking out the ulterior motive. Sometimes there isn't one. But not so often that you lose the habit. I wondered why, less than twenty-four hours after inviting me to stay the hell out of her gin mill, the Fat Lady was now inviting me back. What was in it for her—or what did she *think* was? Above all, what in hell did it have to do with anything?

Well, I could lean against the door and pose questions to myself all night; the more profitable course was to go and see what the Great One had to say for herself. That gave me—I glanced at my wristwatch—not quite six hours to bump off. Terrific. Maybe I'd go stick my head in the oven for a while. It was an electric oven, so the gesture would be largely symbolic, but it was indicative of the way I felt.

The oven hadn't been cleaned in ages, however, so I went and stuck my head under the shower instead. Hot water and steam washed away some, not all, of the leaden feeling I'd had behind my eyes all day, of the thick cottoniness of my tongue. I hoped I wasn't coming down with something. I didn't think I was. Maybe it was the goofy weather—highs and lows and warm fronts and cold fronts and all that other stuff. I've never paid much attention to such things, I couldn't tell you what happens when the barometer goes which direction, but I'm nevertheless a mild believer in their having an effect on our health and emotions. On the other hand, it could just be a good excuse for what is commonly referred to as laziness.

After a time, when the room became so charged with steam that breathing was difficult, I shut off the water and stepped out of the tub. As I toweled off, I noticed that Jen had forgotten a small vial of cologne on the toilet tank. I lifted it to my nose and inhaled. I didn't know the name of it, but it was Jen, all right.

I let the bottle drop from my fingers into the wicker basket next to the sink.

° • °

The shower had helped, but not enough. I thought of making a pot of coffee, but it seemed like too much work. I opened a can of Falstaff and stood with it in my hand and my head in the icebox, trying to come up with a palatable-sounding menu and not having much luck. I checked out a couple of plastic containers and made a little game of guessing at what the contents had originally been. That was good for ten minutes. I flipped through the TV listings from last Sunday's paper. There was a movie on Channel 7, but it was described as "heartwarming," and two things I steadfastly avoid are "heartwarming" drama and "outrageous" comedy. I thought about going over to the Castelars'—I supposed I was still on bodyguard duty—but I didn't feel like it. I went back to my bedroom/office, folded up the convertible bed, and sat at my desk, staring at the typewriter like I'd never seen one before. Finally I decided that I didn't care much for the company I was keeping tonight and that I should do something about it.

The Omaha directory did not list an overwhelming number of Koosje Van der Beeks—one, to be specific—so I was pretty sure I had the right one. I copied the number onto a small scratch pad near the phone, a strange habit that I can't seem to break, then pulled another beer from the refrigerator.

It seemed distasteful to be calling one woman because I missed another. Dishonest, somehow. Not that I wouldn't have wanted to call Koosje in any case, but the timing was unfortunate. I wouldn't want her to think I turned to her only because I couldn't do any better. I wouldn't want *me* to think that either . . .

Shit, we had enough unspecified guilt and mealy self-analysis going on here to keep a seminary full of Jesuits going for six months. Pick up the damn phone and call the woman. She's probably got other plans already.

Koosje answered on the second ring and I identified myself.

"Of course I remember you," she said in her barely accented voice. "How many private detectives do you think I meet in a day?"

"Well, I know it's late notice and everything, but I was standing here staring at an empty icebox and I got to thinking that if you didn't have other plans, maybe I could buy you dinner. Or something." Is this guy smooth or what?

"Not a chance," she said airily, and laughed. "I'm about to put my dinner into the oven. Do you like eggplant?"

I don't, much, but I said I did and she told me where she lived—a fairly new apartment complex off Grant Street near Seventy-second. I told her I could be there in twenty minutes and she said give her at least half an hour to get the kitchen and herself cleaned up.

I zipped down the hall the way the Juice zips through airports, shucked my sweats, and climbed into something spiffier: lined navy chinos, lamb's-wool burgundy V-neck, and my battered old corduroy sport coat. Then I tossed a few things into a canvas gym bag that had never seen the inside of a gym, overnight-type things: socks and shorts, a gray polo shirt, my shaving kit, and Boorstin's *The Discoverers,* which I was doggedly working through despite its being about a hundred thousand pages of four-point type, twelve hundred lines to the page. It did, at least, add heft to the bag.

Fifteen minutes after hanging up the phone I was in line at the drive-up window of a liquor store I frequent down on Saddle Creek Road, swearing at a fat slob in a green Le Car who seemed to be laying in a six-month beer supply. Twenty-five minutes after that, Koosje was opening the door of her apartment to me, at the end of a short hall on the top floor of one of three four-story buildings with rustic woody façades.

Her long dark hair was loose now; it fell about her shoulders in lustrous ribbons. She wore very little make-up, a pale lipstick, and an aqua sweater-dress that ended just above the knee. A wide brass bracelet was her only jewelry.

I handed her the bagged bottle. "As far as I'm concerned, there are three types of wine: red, white, and pink. I couldn't decide which shade went with eggplant."

She pulled the bottle from the sack. "So you got *black*?"

"Very funny." I slipped out of my parka. "It's champagne. Well, not real champagne with a capital 'Cham,' but a Spanish sparkling wine that is very dry, light, fruity, and well-balanced, excellent for any occasion. See, it says so right there."

Koosje was studying the gold-and-black label. "Freixenet," she read. "Now how would you pronounce that? I suppose the *X* sounds like an *H* if it's Spanish. . . . So what *is* the occasion? What are we celebrating?"

I shrugged. "Nothing, necessarily. Or anything you like. Beginnings. Conclusions. The new moon. The old neighborhood. You call it."

She eyed me appraisingly. "Beginnings and conclusions, then. Is it cold enough to open now, or shall we wait?"

"It should be cold; I held it out the window on the way over."

"Then why don't you open it and I'll hang up your—" I handed over my parka. "—coat. What happened to this pocket?"

I was peeling the rubberized foil from the neck of the bottle. "Hmm? Oh—I forgot to take my gun out of it before I shot a hole in a wall this morning. Silly."

She gave me a distinctly worried look before hanging the coat in a narrow closet and sliding the door closed. "You're joking."

"I never joke. Just kidding."

We were by then wandering out of the tiny foyer and into the apartment itself—a spacious but not opulent living room that segued into a nice dining area, beyond which was a reasonably large kitchen. Koosje found a pair of fluted glasses, the right kind for champagne, and I unbound the stopper and eased it out of the neck of the bottle. It came away into my hand with a deep, hollow *ploonk!*

Koosje said, "I appreciate your not shooting a hole in my wall."

I poured alternately from one glass to the other, letting the bubbles rise and subside, and said, "My *deah* girl, one simply does *not* let a champers cork fly across the room like a misguided missile; the explosion absolutely *destroys* those precious little bubbles."

"I had no idea I was in the presence of a connoisseur," she deadpanned as I handed her a glass.

"I hope you found it inspirin', because it's the sum total of my knowledge, oenologically speaking, and I try never to miss an opportunity to show it off." I raised my glass. "Well, here's to crime."

She lifted hers. "To beginnings and conclusions," she corrected.

Chapter Twenty-One

• • • • • •

The dinner was ready so we went straight to it, Koosje pouring a dry red wine—"beloved zinfandel," she called it—after we had finished our first glass of champagne. We chitted and chatted, weaving in and out and to and fro in the awkward oral mating dance that human beings insist on performing. Eventually the meal was finished, and we carried the remainder of the Freixenet to the living room. It was dark and warm there, illuminated only by the range light angling in softly from the kitchen, and a handful of candles that Koosje lit, gliding quickly and silently through the room.

She stood holding her dead match and smiled down at me where I sat on the overstuffed sofa. "Shall I light the fire?" she asked.

I looked around the room, airy, simply decorated. "Where? In an ashtray?"

The smile broadened. "Not exactly." She stepped over to a Scandinavian-looking wall unit across from the sofa and folded open a cabinet. Behind the doors were a television set and, on a second shelf beneath it, a small, streamlined VCR. Koosje started both machines, found a tape from among a row of plastic boxes elsewhere in the unit, and eased the black cassette into the front of the machine. A violent snowstorm took over the TV screen, replaced after a few seconds with the image of a large fireplace, blazing away.

"Astounding," I said. "And more plot than most television programs, too."

"Someone gave it to me about a year ago. It plays for an hour, but I've only looked at it for five minutes or so. The problem is, you can't have a fire going and watch television at the same time." She made an adjustment to the color, then came and sat beside me on the couch. It was made of some corduroyish material, and there seemed too much of it for the amount of stuffing in the cushings. The result was that you didn't so much sit on it as sink into it. And so we did.

Then again there was a distinct, and distinctly familiar, awkwardness. Koosje reached for her fluted glass, resting on the coffee table at our knees, but I put a hand on her wrist and stopped her, pulled her toward me, and kissed her, first lightly, experimentally, then with increased boldness. It ended and she lay back against the cushions, the barest innuendo of a smile at her pale lips. I picked up her glass and offered it to her "Champagne?"

She took it, tasted it, and rested the smooth rim against her lower lip. "What made you call me tonight?"

"I don't know, Doctor. Could it be that I was attracted to you this morning and I wanted to get to know you better?"

"Mm. Could be. Is it?"

Time for a smooth line, boy; don't want to say it was because of another love gone wrong, as the songs have it. Time for a nice white little half- or one-quarter-truth to spare her feelings and save the night. I looked into the video hearth, looked back at Koosje. Ah, what the hell. Like they say, honesty is one of the better policies. "Partly," I confessed. "The other part is I've got this on-again off-again marriage that is off again, for good, I think, and I didn't want to be alone. Hell of a note for a first date, isn't it?"

She shrugged delicately. "Loneliness isn't the worst reason for men and women to get together, so long as it's not the only reason. I just had the feeling you were distracted, and I wondered if there was anything I could do."

"There is. You're doing it." I kissed her. "You're very perceptive."

"I'm a good shrink," she said easily. "Well—*pretty* good."

"Amy?"

She leaned forward and placed her glass on the table, tracing her fingers along its stem. "Mm," she repeated. It was a habit of hers, I had noticed during dinner, that half purr, half growl originating deep in her throat and meaning yes, or no, or nothing at all. Now, evidently, it meant yes. She released the fluted glass and reclined. "She won't let me in." Frustration tightened her voice, emphasizing her faint Dutch accent. "She holds back. She lets me come so close"—she held her left thumb and forefinger an inch apart—"and then she pulls away again, into herself."

I said, "It's been only a couple of days. Based on what I saw yesterday morning, you've made fantastic progress. Give it time."

She said, "I feel there is no time; I feel as if I have her suspended between two worlds and if I don't move quickly to pull her firmly and completely into our world, then I lose her to . . . *her* world. The world you saw her in yesterday morning."

"Jesus," I breathed into my glass.

"Mm. Oh, I shouldn't make it sound so dramatic. There will be ups and downs, there *will* be setbacks, and, you're right, these things take time. But these two sessions have been extremely intensive, and we've covered so much ground . . . It's frustrating, so *damned* frustrating, to feel that Amy is teetering on the brink of allowing me to know what really is troubling her—and only when I know can I truly begin to help her—but is always catching herself and pulling back at the very last instant. I want to give her the confidence to let herself go over the edge, to know that I won't let her fall. I want to begin treating the real problem, and I want to do it quickly. Until then, we're just dog-paddling."

"What is the real problem, do you think?"

She sat forward and again toyed with her glass. "I haven't the vaguest idea," she said bitterly. "Oh, that's not true; I have the *vaguest* idea. To keep it in layman's terms—"

"Bless you."

"—her father's death has triggered in Amy a monumental guilt reaction. Why, I don't know exactly. You know, sometimes a person will feel responsible for the death of a loved one—they feel that if they had been there they could have prevented it, for instance; or even that they caused it because they had felt anger toward that person after a recent argument. But I don't think that's what we have here. Amy doesn't blame herself for her father's death—not to any significant extent—but I do think there was some unfinished business between them, the weight of which is now squarely on Amy's shoulders, dragging her down. If only I knew *what* . . ."

"What about Emily, or Vince? Can they help you out?"

The corners of her mouth angled downward. "They're more in the dark than I am. Mrs. Castelar, as I am sure you've noticed, lives her life in a haze of alcohol and tranquilizers. Amy—any of the children—could turn the place into a dance hall and she wouldn't notice. Would you believe she had no idea of what went on out there last night? She slept right through it. And Vince—Vince isn't much less self-obsessed, I'm afraid."

"He strikes me as being very concerned about Kate."

"I'm sure he is; it doesn't do Amy much good. But I wish Kate *were* around; it seems that she and Amy were thick as thieves. Kate and her father occupy Amy's thoughts. Obviously, the father can't help; but perhaps Kate would be able to provide a clue, if she were found."

"We workin' on it." I looked at my watch. "In fact, in four short hours I have another date, this one with an interesting thing called the Fat Lady—not much to look at, but a lousy personality—who will, I hope, have something for me in the way of finding Walt Jennings."

We fell silent then and sat closely, gazing into the television set. It flickered and crackled at us for perhaps half a minute or longer; then Koosje abruptly asked, "Are you staying there again tonight?"

My mind had wandered, down the obvious path—whether Koosje could be wrong, and Amy was feeling responsible for her father's death because she *was* responsible—but I gave it up rather quickly. It didn't explain Kate, it didn't explain Jennings, it didn't explain Christina, or the Fat Lady, or Frank Kirby's bullyboys in the blue T-bird, or the vandalism to my car, or . . .

"Castelars'?" I said, quickly tracing my mental steps to where they'd left the main road. "I suppose so. I haven't been too good about touching base with Kennerly today—as you put it, I've been distracted—but I assume that until I hear otherwise I'm still on baby-sitting detail, and I packed accordingly. Why? Does it upset Amy to have a stranger around?"

Koosje shook her head and her dark hair shone in the glow of our electronic fireplace. "On the contrary, she seemed to respond to you very well this morning. I took her approaching you to be a positive sign. She seems to trust you, she seems to be comfortable with you. Maybe you can make her feel secure enough to lower her defenses just enough . . ."

"I wouldn't know what to say or do—"

"I don't mean you should say or do anything; just being around may have an effect, if only a small one."

"Oh, well, hell, that's easy; I've been around all my life." I slipped my hand across her stomach and we kissed again, more thoroughly than before. Then she held me very tightly.

"What are you thinking about?" I said after a while.

"Amy, of course. Why it had to be she who found her father yesterday. Why things like this always happen to the ones least equipped to deal with them." She adjusted herself so that her dark head, still resting against my shoulder, was angled toward my face. Her blue eyes were earnest; the set of her small mouth was serious. "What is it about some people that makes them victims? Is it true what they say, that some people send out the wrong vibrations or have the wrong aura or something? Why does life zero in on some and let others glide through unscathed?"

"I don't think life is that selective," I said, and in that moment it was coming from very deep within. "I think it's a more of a scattergun, hitting whoever it happens to hit. We're all potential victims, potential targets; some of us perhaps do get hit more often than others, some of us like to think so, and some of us just recover more quickly. But we're all on the line. Probably the best thing you can do is simply keep going and hope you don't get hit."

"Moving targets," Koosje said drearily. "What kind of way is that to live?"

"The only way, maybe. On the brighter side, life is equally blind when it comes to doling out euphoria. At any given moment it's a fifty-fifty chance, pain or pleasure . . ."

Her lips were on mine, and as the kiss lasted, the embrace grew warmer, even feverish. I slid my hand slowly up her side, along her ribs, over one small breast. She did not withdraw; she responded, pushing against my hand, my mouth, pushing me back onto and into the plush couch. I trailed my fingers down the smooth back of her sweater dress and then up beneath it where it had ridden high on her hips. The skin of her bare legs was warm and smooth; so too was her small, round behind as I fondled it, gently at first but with increasing force.

Her pelvis had been working against mine; now it stopped and she pushed back away from me, straddling me, balancing on her haunches. She reached and found the hem of her dress, wound it up and over her head, and dropped it on the carpet next to the couch. I raised my hands to the white straps on her shoulders, but she stopped me, took my wrists, and gently pulled me up off the couch as she rose and stepped back.

She stood before me in the flickering light of the "fire" and slowly shed the rest of her clothing; then, naked but for her high-heeled shoes and the brass bracelet she wore, she slowly undressed me, starting with my jacket and working down to my shirt, my belt, eventually everything. When she had set aside the last article she remained on her knees, her breath soft on my belly, her moist tongue slowly tracing downward, her warm mouth engulfing me.

And then she was moving away again, lowering herself slowly to the floor, gently pulling me down with her, onto her, into her. We stayed like that awhile. I began a rhythm, but she stopped me, so we simply lay for a time. I kissed her, kissed her eyes, her throat, the pink distended tips of her small rounded breasts. I nipped at them delicately with my eyeteeth and she moaned. I dragged my whiskery chin across them and she gasped; her hips began to undulate, slowly, then more definitely.

And then, just as quickly as it had begun, it ended.

There was no lack of willingness on my part, certainly no lack of desire, but a sudden and complete lack of means that no amount of activity or positive thinking could remedy. Eventually I took myself off of her and lay back on the soft yet scratchy carpeting. "Sorry," I said curtly. "Not enough starch in the old diet, maybe."

She moved to rest her head against my chest, her left arm below my rib cage. "Don't apologize. I know how hard you've been working, how badly you want to find Kate, how worried you are for her safety. I know that you haven't been getting much sleep. And I think I know that you're very unhappy about your domestic life."

I tugged at her long hair to make her look into my face. "Think you're smart, huh?"

"I told you, I'm a good therapist. *So* good, in fact . . ." She pulled her head away from my hand and again took up her tracings down my chest, down my stomach, which fluttered involuntarily under her tongue. Then in one easy, graceful move, she brought her right leg over my right shoulder, her knees planted firmly on either side of me.

At some point the video fire went out, and the only sound was of the tape automatically rewinding itself.

Chapter Twenty-Two

Her hair was still damp from the shower as I stroked along the back of her neck, feeling the silkiness of her hair and the smoothness of her skin. I stood close behind her, my face in her hair, my hands reaching around to massage her breasts.

She elbowed me in the stomach, lightly, playfully. "You made me lose count," she complained facetiously.

"Four," I said.

She looked over her shoulder at me, the teaspoon poised in her hand. "Really?"

I shrugged. "Close enough. Four is a good number. Forty percent is good; I use forty percent a lot. Also thirds—thirds are better than halves or quarters. People ask how the new book's coming along, I tell them I'm about a third done." I had, of course, wowed her during dinner with tales of my literary exploits.

"Psychologically speaking," Koosje said seriously, "you're nuts." She poured four more portions into the filter and poured through the boiling water. We watched it drip. "It looks awfully dark," she said critically. "I think I was up to six."

"What's the difference, the way you water it down with milk? Can you water something down with milk? Anyhow, I always thought they took their coffee black and very strong in Scandinavia."

"Holland isn't Scandinavia. And this isn't Holland." She turned and rested her back against the counter, linking her hands behind me. "When I was a little girl and I wanted to drink coffee because it was a grown-up thing to do, my father would give me, oh, about a thimbleful in a cup of milk. I just never got used to drinking it much stronger."

As she spoke I had slipped my hands slowly down her back; now I brought them up under the hem of the flannel nightshirt she wore and cupped her derrière. She gave me a look and her blue eyes were sly. "You don't have time for any more of that; you have another date, remember?" I looked over her shoulder at the clock on the stove. It was not quite ten-thirty. I sighed and returned my hands to the middle of her back, holding her closely.

"You're right. You should throw me out in about an hour. Maybe sooner; I may have scraping to do downstairs. Besides, it was just an idle threat, as you well know."

Koosje pushed away from me. "Will you cut it out? There's nothing to apologize for; even if there were, you've already done it. So stop punishing yourself. You don't hear me complaining, do you?" She paused at the avocado-colored refrigerator and smiled gently over her shoulder. "I have nothing to complain about." She opened the refrigerator and I admired the movement of muscle in the backs of her legs as she retrieved a gallon of milk. After our slow, warm, candlelit shower I had dressed again but Koosje had, as they say, slipped into something more comfortable: a soft, thigh-length nightshirt in a red Stewart plaid, with great billowy sleeves that she rolled back to her elbows. Contact lenses had come out before the shower—not too romantic, that, but what's a girl to do?—and were now replaced by a pair of large-lensed designer eyeglasses. Sophia Loren, I guessed by the small gold-plated initials on the bows. Unless, of course, Shari Lewis had begun a designer-eyeware line. The Lamb Chop Collection.

Koosje turned to hand me a filled cup. "What are you staring at?" she asked with mock sternness.

"Your glasses," I admitted. "They make you look very studious, very scholarly."

"They make me look like Mickey Mouse, but without them I'm like Mister Magoo, tripping over little things like shoes, steps, cars . . ." I watched her dilute her coffee. "And contacts are only good so long; then they start to feel like they're made out of wood."

"Luckily, red's your color."

"Charmer." She kissed me lightly and I followed her back into the living room, where we again took up our station on the couch. "Want me to start the fire again?"

"Nah, give the playback heads a rest. I've seen those things advertised—video fireplaces, video aquariums, I forget what all else—but I never thought anyone'd go out and spend real money on them."

"Nobody does. That is, nobody buys them for himself; it's one of those things that get bought only as gifts for somebody else. That's how I got mine; do you think I'd be crazy enough to spend money on something like that? Well? Do you? All right, that's it, get out!"

I laughed and kissed her briefly and copped a glance at my wristwatch. She saw me. "I wish you didn't have to leave."

"Me too. But I'd have to go anyway, even if I weren't seeing the Fat Lady, and spend the night at the Castelars', for what it's worth. I just hope this isn't another dry well. These midnight capers get to be enervating in a big way—especially when there are better ways for a guy to spend his time." I put my arms around her and breathed the fresh, berryish scent of her hair.

We were silent like that a few moments, then Koosje said, "Where do you think Kate is now?"

It was a question I had considered—a lot—and even

though I gave it a few seconds before answering, I could produce only the same result as always: "I don't know. I wish I did, believe me. There's so much going on that I can't get a handle on, and yet I have the distinct feeling that none of it pertains to what I'm after—finding the girl. I get buzzed by two sleazoids working for a guy who thinks I'm bringing the heat on him because I was at Castelar's bank asking questions about Kate the same day *he* was there arranging a loan. I get sent on a merry romp across the countryside because some old cow's got a fat finger in every mud pie in town and she doesn't want me poking into *her* business. I get my car redecorated by I-don't-know-whom for I-don't-know-why. Not to mention a baker's dozen of mind-your-own-businesses and get-out-and-stay-outs. All of which would be far more tolerable if they were germaine to my inquiry. But I'm going around asking question *A*, and people are getting their underwear in a wad because they're afraid I'll find out about *X*, *Y*, and *Z*—none of which is of any interest to me at all. I'm to the point where, if Jennings walked through that door right now, all I'd want to do is ask him about Kate. I don't care if he killed Castelar, I don't care if he killed Christina, I don't care if he wants to kill the rest of the clan and the entire Vienna Boys Choir on top of it. I just want the girl."

Koosje sat up and held me at arm's length, her hands resting lightly on my chest. "What happened to truth, justice, and the American way?"

"You have me confused with Superman, but that's okay; it happens all the time." I drank some coffee. "That sort of stuff's for the cops and the courts, mainly the courts. The private investigator's job is to perform the task he was hired to do, in this case, finding a missing girl. Period. As it happens, that task is running parallel to the search for a suspected killer—all the other junk that's going on must relate to *that* undertaking in some obscure fashion, I figure—but

I'm trying like mad to remember it's secondary. If my efforts help bring a killer to trial, great. If not, too bad. I'm not a seeker of justice, whatever it may be; I'm just a guy trying to do my job."

Koosje had again rested her warm body against me. "I think you like to pretend that," she said, "but I also think you're a good deal more compassionate than you let on."

I shrugged. "Maybe. Compassion's in the job description, I guess. You don't hire a private detective unless you've got problems, serious problems. Compassion helps."

"How did someone like you ever become a private detective?"

"What do you mean, 'someone like me'?" I laughed. "PIs aren't all craggy-faced guys in aloha shirts or mustachioed millionaires with time and money to burn. In fact, I daresay very few of them are. Some of them have wives and kids and second mortgages, potbellies and no hair, thick glasses and backyard barbecue pits. And they get into the dodge the same way I did: circumstance. I never went to school with anyone who wanted to become a private detective. Most start out doing something else, usually in the public sector, and go private for any number of reasons. In my case, I was mainly sick of office politics, of idiotic and pointless gamesmanship, of blind by-the-bookery, of incompetence so deeply entrenched so high up that it might as well be on the organizational chart. Me, I don't always know what I'm doing either, but I've never made the mistake of thinking that it's a virtue, or that the situation can't or shouldn't be changed. Geez, what got me going? Anyhow, that's the main reason I didn't go back into newspapering after I got out of the army, and the main reason I didn't stay in the army, and the main reason I eventually ended up freelance. End of report."

"Well, you're much better suited to being a writer. That

beard makes you look literary"—she stroked it lightly—"or it *will*, someday—not at all detectivey. In fact, I don't think you're a detective at all; I think it's just a line you use to impress women. I searched you *very* thoroughly and you're not carrying a gun."

"Packing," I corrected, "us hard-boiled private-eye types always 'pack' guns. And it's been years since I felt I needed one on a date. I prefer to use my animal magnetism to force women to do what I want."

"Mm. What do you *pack*, then, a snub-nosed .38? A Colt .45?"

"You don't want to know about that sort of stuff."

"Of course I do," she persisted. "I've never met a real-live private eye. What do you pack? A Beretta. A Walther PPK. A Luger. A—"

"I own two guns," I sighed, "both revolvers, .38s; one I usually keep in the car, the other at home. I'm not a fan of snub-noses or, in general, anything with a barrel shorter than three inches. They're less accurate, especially for someone like me who doesn't put in a lot of range time. I like the four-inch police revolver with fixed sights. I used to own an automatic, but I traded it in for the second revolver because, by and large, I like them better. I think they're safer, especially the single-action revolver, which is what I keep in the house. Having to pull back the hammer means having to think about what you're doing. My coffee's getting cold." I reached for it.

After a momentary silence, Koosje said, "I didn't mean to upset you."

"I'm not upset. I just—well, in the first place, I don't think of myself as a PI anymore, not primarily. If we had met at a party and you asked me what I did, I would have said I was a writer. As we got to know one another I'd've told you that I am licensed by the state to conduct private investigations and to carry a firearm and all that good stuff, but I would have automatically put that part of my life into the past tense because, mainly, that's where it belongs, in the past."

"Does it? Does it really? I mean, look at how we *did* happen to meet: Because you are involved in an investigation. No, let me finish. I know you said that you originally got involved partly as a favor to your friend Kennerly and partly because you needed the money. I can understand that. But what about the last case? And the one before that? And the one before *that?* Do you see what I'm getting at? You say you've closed the door on that part of your life, and yet really it's standing open a good six or eight inches."

I swallowed some coffee. "So what are you saying? That I should turn in my badge and ride out of Dodge?"

"I'm not saying that you *should* do anything; I just think maybe you'd be better off in the long run—happier—if you were honest with yourself, particularly about something as fundamental as your vocation. Personally, I don't understand why you can't pursue both careers; you do already; why not simply conduct yourself accordingly? Introduce yourself as a private investigator *and* a writer—or the other way around. The world's full of writers who are also teachers, lawyers, doctors, accountants . . ."

"Even cops. That's true; very few writers support themselves on words alone. But some do, and I think a person owes it to himself to believe that he can be one of the few, the proud, the Mar—— no, wait a minute, that's not right." She smiled indulgently. I cleared my throat. "I admit I'm holding the PI thing as my ace in the hole. What I ought to do is give it up—*really* give it up—and really give the writing life a fair chance. So far I've just been too chicken to completely close the door, as you say."

"Is it that, or are you unconvinced that you want to

close the door? I believe that if we truly want to do something, become something, change something, we will. It may not be easy, we may need lots and lots of help and support, but if it's something we really crave, we'll get it. And if we don't, if we're more in love with the *idea* of it, then we won't." She had been cradling her coffee in the palm of one hand; now she set down the cup. "That's a horrible oversimplification," she said with a shrug, "but so what? I'm off duty."

She smiled up at me tentatively and I grinned back. "You see," I said, shaking a finger of admonition, "this is why I don't like guns: They get people into trouble. They *are* trouble, usually more trouble than they're worth, and that's why they're not really a big part of the trade—contrary to what the direct-mail houses seem to believe. Every other day I'm getting an offer to subscribe to *Shoot to Kill* or *Urban Paranoia Quarterly* or some similarly bloodthirsty publication. But I've known veteran investigators who've never fired a gun in the field, and some who never even owned a gun. Stop looking at me like that; I know I'm changing the subject. Okay, what you say makes sense. I thought I had everything figured out, and I'd make my jump when the time was right. Maybe that was just an excuse, because the time's never right. I don't know. In any case, I think I should sleep on it—not that sleep is something I see in my very near future." I took another look at my watch. "Time for me to hit that trail, lady." I stood and retrieved my sport coat from the floor. Koosje remained on the couch, looking up at me speculatively.

"Will you have a gun when you go tonight?"

"Again with the guns? Doesn't modern psychology have something to say about that?" I slipped into the jacket. "I don't know. I'm feeling pretty paranoid these days, and it came in handy this morning. On the other hand, I didn't have one last night and I got out relatively intact. Like I said, guns are trouble. You start waving one around and then the other guy thinks that's pretty neat and he starts waving *his* around and in short order you have got a grade-A mess. I guess I'll decide when I get there."

Koosje stood and came to me and we just stood, holding each other, for a long moment. "Will I see you again?" she asked at last.

"Probably in the morning, at the Castelars'."

She went to the front closet, collected my parka, and helped me into it. When I turned toward her, her eyes were on the ruined pocket. They turned to my face. "Be careful," she said very quietly.

We kissed, and she hid behind the door as she held it open for me. I slipped into the hallway, squinting at its relative brightness. The coast was clear. I turned back toward the door and glimpsed her face, shoulder, and bare left leg. "See you tomorrow."

"Be careful," she repeated, and the door closed.

It had snowed again during the past few hours, overspill from one or another of the various storms and fronts and low- and high-pressure cells percolating all around us, but the night was still and warm. Relatively. My car was covered by a thick quilt of white. I brushed it from the windows and lamps while the engine warmed, and thought. Not about anything in particular; I simply let the thoughts come, let the random associations wash over me as they would. It had been a long, long time since I had felt so comfortable with a woman so quickly. It had been a long, long time since I had met a woman like Koosje. If I probed my feelings the way you would probe a sensitive tooth, I could still locate the pain, the ache of longing that I felt—and, I supposed, always would feel—for Jennifer. The emotion that I felt now—infatuation, love, whatever—didn't take away the pain, but it masked it somewhat, dulled it, the way a few drinks will handle a toothache.

For now, that would be enough. More than enough. And later . . . well, later I could worry about later.

I got into the car and drove.

Chapter Twenty-Three

"Upstairs."

"Nice to see you again, too," I said. Bruno, of course, reacted in no way whatsoever. I shook and brushed and stamped snow from me, and surveyed the barroom, crammed to the rafters with armchair cowboys and their women, stinking of smoke and beer and sweat. Another fun night at the Bottom Dollar. I crammed my hat in a pocket, unzipped my parka, and moved along the bar.

Things looked innocent enough down here; upstairs, though . . . I had spent a long minute in the car debating the merits and demerits of coming in armed. And decided against it. If this was a setup—and I couldn't make sense of that possibility—a single gun wasn't going to make much difference against however much accumulated firepower might be waiting. And while the go-down-fighting bit sounds real swell, I'd personally rather not go down at all. When you carry a gun, you make people nervous; when the other guy's got a gun too, you really don't *want* him to be nervous.

I pulled open the wooden door and climbed the stairs.

Silence. Well, no, not silence—the gang downstairs was far too raucous for a few floorboards to mute them very much. Let's say I heard no noises that originated on the second floor, even though I stood at the top of the stairs and listened for a good while.

Onward, hero.

As I had done last night, I paused at each door I passed in the narrow corridor, cocking my head, listening, waiting. No muffled sounds, no sounds of any variety came from behind the door panels. No hushed voices, no tinny AM radio music, no screech and scrape of bedsprings. A slow night. Or someone had rented the whole hall.

Bruno hadn't said so, but it was reasonable to assume that "upstairs" meant the old gal's office. I knocked my knuckles perfunctorily against the cheap wood and opened the door.

The first thing I noticed was the gun—us ace detectives observe little things like that right off—bigger than some foreign cars. Or so it looked, at least; even a palm-sized .22 looks like an antiaircraft gun when it's pointed at you.

The second thing I noticed was that the gun did not repose in the delicate mitt of the Fat Lady, but rather in the brown and bony hand of a rangy and mangy-looking cowboy seated behind the Fat Lady's desk. I forced my eyes away from the gun and up to his face, which appeared sallow, drawn. Maybe that was owing to the bluish light of the desk lamp, which provided only the barest illumination for the small, hot room—enough light, however, to see that it was Walt Jennings on the other end of the big-ass revolver.

I slowly lifted my hands up and away from my body, noticing that they trembled slightly, noticing that my stomach had dropped to my knees and my knees were turning to pancake batter. Still, I think I did a creditable job of keeping my voice steady and only three or four octaves higher than usual when I said, "I'm clean."

"You're late," Jennings said in a slightly tremulous tenor that did all kinds of swell things for my masculine ego but very little for my overall sense of well-being. Like I said, when it's the other guy holding the gun you want him to be calm and collected, so cool that penguins follow him home.

"The snow slowed me down. I didn't leave enough time . . . It really snowed a lot, and it's still coming down . . . I haven't heard any weather reports, though . . ." I stopped. I was babbling. Babbling's bad for the image.

"Get in here and close the door," Jennings yipped. I did, elbowing it shut, keeping my hands in plain sight. "Put your hands on the desk." He came around, keeping the unblued gun directed somewhat unsteadily at my midsection. The thought of grabbing the gun while Jennings undertook his clumsy pat-down flitted briefly and aimlessly across my mind, like a firefly on a summer night. Crazy ideas like that will occasionally take hold of me—ramming the son of a bitch who cuts me off on the freeway, planting a big wet kiss on a checkout girl, taking ukelele lessons, that type thing. Usually I lie down and wait for the feeling to pass. That being impractical at the moment, I settled for standing stock-still, trembling notwithstanding, and letting Jennings have his way with me. What I may lack in swashbucklery I make up for in sanity, sometimes.

The frisk was badly done. I could have had an entire set of steak knives taped to my shins; he didn't pat any lower than my knees. I suspect Jennings conducted it because "Miami Vice" made him think he should. "Okay," he said uncertainly when he thought he was done, stepping back a pace toward the door. "You sit over there." He swung the gun toward the battered one-third couch crammed against the wall across from the desk. It was the second time in five minutes I could have taken the popgun away from him. I could have shot out my right arm and knocked the lamp from the desk, dropped and hit Jennings low, grabbed the thing out of his hand, shoved it into his sweaty face, and demanded some answers.

I went and sat on the couch. Save it for the typewriter, I thought.

He should have told me to sit on my hands or clasp

them behind my head or keep them in my pockets or something else designed to prevent me from making the kind of quick moves he kept giving me openings for. But he didn't, and I didn't believe it was my job to tell him. So I crossed my arms and crossed my ankles and looked at him. He backed around behind the desk and sat in the Fat Lady's armless chair, resting his right fist on the desktop and keeping the silvery gun extended toward me as if it were a crucifix and I Count Dracula.

"Okay," he repeated. "What do you want?"

I raised my eyebrows, though I suppose the effect was lost in the semidarkness, and nodded toward the gun. "That makes it your party." Swiped that line right out of *The Thin Man*.

Jennings didn't notice. He sort of looked down at his fist as if he'd forgotten what was in it, swallowed—his Adam's apple bobbed like a buoy—and looked back at me. It was hard to square this nervous little man with the mug shot the *World-Herald* had printed. That man had been smug, smirky; this man was anything but. And it was harder than ever to picture Kate Castelar with him, but I'd worked that one over so much already that it was turning to mush.

"Yeah," he said rather dreamily. "Well—well, I hear you've been poking around, asking questions about me, looking for me." He tried to sound defiant.

"Me and everybody else in the five-state area, as the TV weather guys call it. You're not having the Fat Lady set up conferences with all of them, are you; that'd take forever. Incidentally, where is the old darlin'?"

"What do you care?"

"I don't, a lot. It's just that she organized this little soiree and I wonder why she isn't in attendance."

"This wasn't her idea; it was mine. I had to twist her arm plenty to get her to go along with it. But . . . well, me and the Fat Lady, we do each other favors every so often, and I reminded her of some of them, and she let me go ahead and set the thing up. *After* she got herself about a million miles away. But look, who cares about her?"

"You're right." My confidence was increasing in proportion to my fast-growing conviction that every passing minute diminished the likelihood of Jennings's using that gun. "There are other fish in the sea. The world's full of women. Let's talk about another one: Kate Castelar."

Jennings looked at me blankly. "Yeah?"

"What do you mean, 'Yeah'? Where *is* she?"

"What do you mean, 'Where is she?' How do *I* know? Home, I suppose." He looked at me closely. "Isn't she?"

"'Suddenly he felt very cold,'" I said measuredly, trying to size up Jennings, trying to decide if his perplexity was genuine or a good act. I flipped a mental coin. It came up tails: a good act. So I turned it over real quick when no one was looking, because experience, intuition, all the little gut instincts told me that Jennings *was* in the dark. Kate's absence had been kept from the press; the cops were keeping mum; and, at the family's—which is to say, Kennerly's—insistence, the FBI had not been summoned. Only a handful of people knew, some people I'd talked to, some people the cops had talked to, and anyone *they* had talked to; it was very possible that Jennings wasn't among them. Not just possible; logical, too: I couldn't make sense of his nocturnal visit to the Castelar house unless I assumed he was trying to communicate with Kate, something he wasn't apt to do if he had killed her or kidnaped her. Unless he had a *real* bad memory.

"All right," I said, "let's take it back to episode one. On the day Jack Castelar was killed, sometime between about four in the afternoon and the discovery of the body twelve or thirteen hours later, Kate disappeared. Thin air, not a trace, twinkling of an eye. Like that." I watched Jennings closely as I spoke. He looked surprised—the frown erased itself and was replaced by a certain wide-eyedness—but he didn't drop his jaw, jump to his feet, and yell "*What??!!*" or ham it up in any other way that might make you think he was pulling your leg. "The working assumption," I added, "is that she disappeared with you. And that it wasn't her idea."

° • °

Jennings slumped against the back of the secretarial chair and his arms fell to his sides. The gun was now out of sight. Not, however, out of mind; you'd have to *be* out of your mind to forget a thing like that. Jennings stared emptily at the desktop for maybe thirty seconds, then inhaled deeply and breathed it out with an "Ah, fuck . . ."

"I know what you mean. I gather your story is that you didn't snatch Kate, that in fact you didn't even know she was missing until I told you about it."

He looked at me without lifting his head. There was nothing in his eyes, nothing that was written in a language I could read, at any rate. "It isn't my story," he said behind another sigh. "It's the truth. I didn't do *anything*. They said you were spooking around, asking about me and some broad. I figured they meant Christina. And then when I heard on the tube this morning that she'd been killed and they were blaming me for that too, I decided maybe I should have a talk with you. The Fat Lady, she said you acted like maybe you weren't dead sure I killed Castelar." His mouth twitched mildly. "Which makes you about the only one in town, except me."

I stroked the velvety whiskers on either side of my mouth with thumb and forefinger. "Right now I'm not dead sure that Wednesday follows Tuesday. If you're as innocent as the Easter bunny, why don't you go to the cops? Why tell me?"

"The cops." His shoulders jumped but the laugh was inaudible. "There's a great idea. They'd listen to me real careful, write it all down, and then throw me in the can for like ever. I'm not stupid. I know how they figure it, how whoever killed Castelar figured it. I shot my big fat mouth off all over town, saying I was gonna get that son of a bitch someday. Big talk. I didn't think no one was listening. But somebody was." The mouth moved again, this time into a thin bitter line.

"Who?"

He gave me a pitying look. "How the fuck should I know? Someone else who hated the bloodsucking bastard but didn't go running off about it like me."

"All right, but what about Christina? Did you kill her?"

His eyes hardened. "No. But I could have. That dirty little gold-digging cunt sold me out. She could've alibied me, you know. But she didn't."

"You mean you *were* home that night sitting in front of the fire with a good book?"

"There ain't no fireplace in that dump," he said obtusely. "And I didn't say I was home, I said Christina could've *said* I was. I went out at about nine because I was supposed to meet Kate in this bar way out on Maple where we always meet. I waited for about an hour and she didn't show. I didn't think anything of it because sometimes that happens, she can't get away or something."

"Didn't you try calling her?"

He wagged his head. "Like I said, man, it happens. And I'm not real popular over there, you know, so I don't even bother to call most of the time. It's not like they'd give her a message if she don't happen to answer the phone herself."

"Then how do you communicate? Kate didn't know about Christina until the day before yesterday, so she must never have called your place. Unless you're luckier than you deser——"

"Kate found out about Christina? Fuck, man. I was hoping to get rid of Christina before she— Hey, cut it out, you know what I mean: get rid of her like break it off and kick her out." He rubbed his left temple. "Shit, that's the end of that. Too bad, too; that Kate is into some really wild stuff, man. Kinky. You know, sometimes she wants me to take this big bel——"

"Terrific. We're getting off-track here. You were waiting for Kate . . ."

He nodded. "Yeah. So, anyhow, about eleven, eleven-thirty, I split and came down here. I had a few drinks, smoked a little grass, and then some of us came upstairs and shot some craps until, shit, I don't know, four, five in the morning. I was pretty wasted by then, so I crashed here. 'Bout noon Edgar comes up and tells me Castelar's dead and the cops think I done it. Edgar, he's the bartender."

I said I thought perhaps I had noticed him.

"Well, I couldn't go home; I was afraid to call in case the cops could trace it. And then later on someone told me about what Christina told the cops, and I knew I was really fucked. So I stayed lost, figured I'd hang out until the weather got better, then split for Mexico."

"Mexico? Not Canada?"

"Canada? You kidding? Snow's for shit, man; I gotta get back someplace warm."

"The Iowa cops say they found your truck in a snowdrift up by Sioux City."

Jennings smiled—rather, he smirked, and he finally looked like the Jennings in the newspaper picture. "Not my truck, man. This is something I thought of once, thought it'd come in real handy if I had to split town or something. First thing I did, I hid the truck real good, then I took the plates off it, then I went around, you know, parking lots and places until I found a truck like mine. All the guys who work at the packing houses and stuff, they all drive pickups, so it didn't take too long."

"And then you switched the plates."

He half raised his arms in a shrug and I caught a brief glimpse of the gun in his right hand. "I figure a guy could buy a little time that way. Pretty smart, huh?"

"You've got the better mousetrap there, all right. But flash on this, Young Edison: If you were here with a bunch of other people shooting craps all night, then you've got what we in the trade call an alibi."

He grunted. "I got shit. I don't even know the names of half the guys. The other half are going to say they weren't here, on account of the craps, on account of the dope, on account of the girls. Get it?"

"What about the Fat Lady?"

"*Especially* the Fat Lady. Besides, the cops are gonna believe her any better'n they'd believe me? With Christina's bullshit about me coming home and hiding my gun and going out again? Be funny."

"You know about that, huh? Well, why did your wife lie?"

He snorted. "Course I know. And she ain't my wife. I mean, she wasn't. Not even what'cha call common-law. She liked to pretend she was, is all. Crazy broad. But a great ass." He shook his head gently, reminiscing. Sentimental fool. "Anyhow, I don't know what she was up to. I figure maybe she found out who really killed the old guy, told him she'd screw up my alibi for the right price. Hell, she'd've sawed off her own head for the right price. And the guy, he probably figured out real fast that she was the type who'd be squeezing his balls for the rest of his life, so he finished her and made it look like it was me again."

Close enough, I figured, though Christina had to have been in on it from the start in order for her to have had the murder weapon for us to find the very next morning. "Listen, was Christina seeing anybody on the side?"

"I think so, yeah. I'm not exactly sure, because I was spending a lot of time myself with Kate, but I'm pretty sure. Sometimes I'd come home real late and she'd have perfume on, or her face would be all done up, and it's a long time since she did that kind of stuff for me. That was okay, though. Like I said, I'd been wanting to split from her for a while, but I was kind of afraid she was calling herself Christina Jennings and telling everyone she was my wife because she figured on some sort of palimony deal, you know, and I was thinking she couldn't pull anything like that if she had another boyfriend. Why? You think that—holy shit, you think that Christina and her boyfriend killed Castelar?"

"Well, somebody sure did. That's the one constant, the one inalterable fact that I have to cling to these days. And somebody killed Christina, too, probably the same somebody. You're the number-one choice for that honor, as you well know. But there are still a lot of threads dangling."

"Like what?"

"Well, like someone roughed up my car pretty badly yesterday afternoon; wasn't you by any odd chance, was it?"

"Hey, I never even *heard* of you until last night."

"Yeah, well, there's one of the threads then. Another is why the Fat Lady sent me halfway across the Great Plains last night looking for you when she knew you were here. Another is why a joker named Kirby sent a small delegation to run me off the road. Another—"

"Oh, well, I can explain *that*. See, Kirby's been hiding me—"

"You know Kirby?"

"No, he's a total stranger helping me stay out of the can.

Of *course* I know him. I kind of do odd jobs for him once in a while." I was pretty sure he didn't mean fixing squeaky doors and patching ceiling cracks. "The Fat Lady knew that Kirby was already nervous about you because you'd been over asking questions at the bank when he was there. So she gave you that bum steer so's to give her time to call Kirby and ask him what they should do. That's when Kirby sent the guys out again—they knew where you'd gone, so it was easy for them to pick up your trail—only this time they weren't supposed to just tail you. They were supposed to lean on you."

"They gave it a good shot," I said charitably. "But what does the Fat Lady have to do with Kirby? And where do you come in?"

"God, where've you been living?" Jennings sighed. "Okay. Now, you know that Kirby's the biggest independent in the area, right?"

When the question is phrased like that, I always agree.

"Okay, Kirby's the Fat Lady's supplier. Her and all the other kind of small-fry, the guys too little for the Eye-ties to piss around with." He grinned malicously. "This Castelar thing's got Kirby sweating bullets, man, and you didn't help any. He's got the cops ragging him on the left and the Mob lickin' their chops on the right and sooner or later one or the other of 'em's gonna gobble him up like a plate of eggs."

I was only half listening; the greater portion of my mind was occupied with a game of fill-in-the-blanks, the blanks being those left after my meeting with Kirby that afternoon. Jennings's information clarified matters enormously, and certainly made more sense than the cock-and-bull stories Kirby had tried to feed me. I'm not quite so naive as to have accepted even part of Kirby's self-portrait as an honest businessman plagued by dishonest and underhanded competitors, but I figured he was just a small-time crooked coin-op vendor, not a pharmacist. And certainly not one of the size Jennings indicated. But it added up: Kirby's jumpiness, his assumption that I was a cop and his mention of the court order protecting him from police harassment, and the fact that he seemed to have plenty of money even though his vending-machine business looked about as vital as roller disco. Yes, it computed nicely; what didn't was the way Kirby kept turning up at odd points in the sequence of events. Coincidence? They happen. Kirby had every reason to be high-strung, especially since he was harboring a man wanted for questioning in connection with a murder investigation. (Don't you just love that kind of talk?) Maybe that part of Kirby's yarn had been on the level—he got spooked when I turned up at the bank when he was there, so he pinned the tail on me. An almost-innocent bystander. Maybe . . .

I said, "You're staying with Kirby? What'd he tell his family, you're the long-lost cousin he never knew he had from Yakima?"

Jennings pulled a face. "I'm not like in his guest room, man. He lined up someplace for me last night is all. Besides, he doesn't have any family. His old lady kicked the bucket a few years ago and his kid's in college someplace."

"Well, he's got his bully patrol to keep him warm."

"I heard he had a pretty hot piece stashed away for himself someplace, but I don't think that's on anymore. Well, who gives a shit about the old fart anyway? He booted me out when you came on, man; some pal." He gave a short, grim laugh. "I was thinking of feeding him to the cops, but I figured, what the fuck, right? Tomorrow the roads should be open, and I'm heading south while the cops are all looking for me north of here. So why make trouble? 'Sides, I may need Kirby to do me another favor someday. The Fat Lady, too." He smirked. He had all the angles figured, boy; just ask him, he'd tell you. He was one tough cookie, he was one smart bird. The kind of bird they'll occasionally find in the Muddy Mo come early spring, swimming under the last of the winter ice.

At the moment, however, I was more concerned about my closest relative: me. I had grown gradually uneasier about Jennings's sharing his plans for the immediate future. It suggested that perhaps he felt *I* was not going to have much of one, and therefore it was safe to unburden himself upon me. My unease was not quelled any when he brought his gun back into sight and aimed it lazily at my chest, which tightened in response.

I waited. He waited. The room was hot but the sweat pooling in the middle of my back was cold, clammy. Fuzzy noises from the bar downstairs, noises that had served as background music to our discussion here, seemed to grow louder though no more distinct than before, and melded with the sound of blood thudding in my ears. The seconds clipped along, tripped over one another, piled up, turned into minutes. Or maybe just *a* minute; time flies when you're having fun, and I wasn't.

Finally I cracked under the strain, forced my eyes from the gun and into Jennings's smarmy face, cleared my throat gently, and said, "So what's the point? Why tell me all this? Why risk it?"

He considered it briefly. "Because I didn't do it, man," he finally said bluntly. "None of it. I didn't kill Castelar, I didn't kill Christina, and I didn't do whatever's been done to Kate. But I can't prove it, and no one's gonna believe me. Except maybe you, if the Fat Lady reads you right. And if there's one guy keeping an open mind, well, maybe it'll make a difference how things shake out, you know? Wouldn't do Kate any harm either. She ain't with me; she's gotta be *someplace*. And, shit, maybe while the cops are all busy looking for me, you'll nail the *right* son of a bitch, get your picture in the paper, huh? Anyhow"—he stood abruptly—"I don't plan to stick around and find out. Wouldn't do me any good if you found the bastard the day after they hung me."

"Hanged," I corrected absently. "Pictures are hung, people are hanged. And no one's been hanged in this state since I don't know when."

"Yeah, well, then maybe they're overdue for one." He came around the desk and sidled toward the door, keeping the gun on me just the way he'd seen it done on TV. "Fifteen minutes," he said when he had reached back and touched the doorknob with his left hand. "I'm gonna tell Edgar that you can walk out of here fifteen minutes after I leave. You try to leave sooner than that—well, Edgar won't let you."

I could well imagine.

The door opened. When it closed again, Jennings was gone.

I sat in the dark and concentrated on unclenching every muscle in my body.

Chapter Twenty-Four

Kirby's house was a nice but not stupendous brick number in a nice but not stupendous block only a couple of miles west of my own home sweet hovel. The neighborhood was of wide, lazily curving streets, of parkways decorated by big old maples that shaded the charming houses on hot summer afternoons, of tall and narrow two-stories with white siding or red brick or, sometimes, both.

It only went to show the difference a mile or three can make.

I drove slowly down the boulevard until I found the address I'd memorized out of a phone book. The number corresponded to a high-roofed house set well back from the pavement in the middle of the block. From what I could see, it, like the rest of the neighborhood, was dark. Gosh, and it was barely two o'clock. Bunch of short-hitters.

When I reached the end of the block I pulled a U-turn in the intersection, dousing my headlights as I did so, and coasted up against the curb on the opposite side, toward the end of the block but well away from the pale light of an old-fashioned globe-topped street lamp.

I killed the engine and waited, listening. I don't know what I expect to hear when I do that, but I always listen for it nonetheless. As usual, I didn't hear it. So I got out of the car and crossed the street.

I cut diagonally across the yard of the last house on the block and slipped between it and the house next to it. Kirby's house was the fourth one from that end of the block—I had counted—and only one fenced yard lay between. One too many, my aching gut told me, but there were no alternatives. I waded through the shin-deep new snow that blanketed the scenery, hopped two sides of the chain-link with a minimum of swearing and scant appreciation for the absence of barbs along the top, and stumbled into Kirby's back yard. Winded, I leaned against the rear wall of his attached garage and watched my breath swirl whitely and vanish into the blue-black atmosphere until my pulse returned to normal. Vapor condensed and froze on my scant beard and mustache. I pawed at it with a gloved hand, but fast decided that the only sure cure was to get indoors.

No trick, ordinarily. Most American houses are only slightly harder to get into without keys than with. If you don't care how much noise you make, it's even easier. But I cared. Not so much because I was afraid of disturbing Kirby's beauty sleep as I was that he was jumpy enough to have invited one or both of his pals for a slumber party. And as everyone knows, you don't sleep at a slumber party. That's why I had been cute with the car's headlights, why I had broken my neck coming in the back way, why I stayed close to the house and out of line with the windows as I carefully, quietly cased the joint.

It was nothing unusual, as houses go. Front door; side door into the garage; sliding-glass doors from the walk-out basement to, probably, a patio now buried under eighteen inches of snow; a similar arrangement above it, with the doors opening onto a redwood deck.

Welcome to middle-class middle America, I thought glumly. If only *I* had become a pusher like Mom wanted . . .

The only item of interest was a small gold-foil decal

pasted to the permanent window on the aluminum outer door in front. The decal was in the shape of a shield, over which were printed the words: THIS HOME PROTECTED BY AMERICAN STANDARD SECURITY SYSTEMS. I smiled to myself in the darkness. There was no such animal, at least not in these parts. The sticker was a phony. They're supposed to scare away burglars. I imagine they do have some utility: The sight of one may paralyze a professional with laughter and render him helpless until the cops arrive. Beyond that, all they really do is let the cognoscenti know that the place is *not* wired.

It was quickly obvious that the basement doors were my best bet, because they were located away from the sleeping and living quarters of the house and because sliding doors typically offer little challenge. These were no exception. They were standard-issue aluminum-frame Webster doors. On the right, as you stood in the yard, was an outer screen door, which had no lock, and an inner double-pane glass door, which did. The doors slid to the left, sandwiching the stationary panes on that side. I slowly slid the screen out of the way and threw my flashlight beam on the glass door's lock.

No surprises there, either. Recessed in the door frame, I knew, was a steel hook. When you pushed up a latch set in the frame on the inside, the hook caught a notch in a nub of steel set in the outermost frame, which was bolted to the wall right and left, floor and ceiling. On my side of the door there was no latch, only a tiny depression about the size and depth of a dime, with a small keyhole in the center of it. When you turned the key the hook would unhook and the latch would unlatch and the lock would unlock. I had no key, of course, but a great thinker like me doesn't allow himself to get hung up on petty details.

I put out the light and stuck it in my back pants pocket,

while from the parka I pulled my impromptu do-it-yourself burglarly kit: a handful of tools and a roll of duct tape from the ever-growing emergency-repair box in the trunk of my old Chevy. With the care of a surgeon contemplating the first incision, I selected a plastic-handled screwdriver with a long and narrow blade. The rest of the equipment went back into my pockets, which bulged like Captain Kangaroo's.

I bent over and inspected the keyhole again, as if it were going to change. It didn't, but that was okay. I'm not much of a locksmith, but this wasn't much of a lock.

The blade of the screwdriver angled easily enough into the top part of the lazy S shape of the keyhole. I gave it a little twist to the right, slowly and gently at first, then more persistently, until the curve had flattened out enough to allow me to push the blade in farther until it met resistance about an eighth of an inch later. I pushed. Nothing. I pushed harder. More nothing. I braced my feet, grabbed the handle of the screwdriver with both hands, and leaned against it with all my weight while wiggling it slightly. Suddenly there was a sharp metallic *snap* and I stumbled forward as the lock mechanism gave, catching myself before I thumped into the glass.

It was to catburglary what rape is to romance, but it produced the desired result. I gripped the handle of the screwdriver with the pliers and, again using both hands, turned the blade slowly in the ruined lock. There was another, much duller sound from within the frame; when I tried the door, it slid back easily in its floor track.

I stepped through and closed the door after me, returned the tools to my pockets, and filled my hands with the flashlight and my revolver.

Apparently I was in some kind of large, long rec room. A Ping-Pong table—no, a pool table, I decided—stood immediately before me perhaps three feet. Beyond that I could make out the vacant, greenish stare of a television screen. As my eyes adjusted further to the darkness I could pick out the dark outlines of furniture, crouched in the gloom like big jungle animals, and an open stairwell at the far end of the room. I moved toward it slowly, gingerly, and risked a quick flash of the beam. The stairs were carpeted, which was a break.

The stairway door opened into a roomy eat-in kitchen partially walled off from the dining area, which in turn was not partitioned from the living room beyond it. The redwood deck was off the dining room; cold, pale light stabbed through a gap in the drapery over the sliding doors.

I started across the linoleum, then froze at the sound of footsteps upstairs. I heard running water, as the novelists so delicately put it, and the creak and tick and hiss of the house's plumbing. I relaxed marginally, then tensed again as I heard the footsteps on the front stairs, coming down into the living room.

If Kirby was staying here alone, then Sleepless here would be the great man himself. I wouldn't even have to coax him out of the arms of Morpheus with my .38. If, on the other hand, he had a baby-sitter or two on the premises . . . Well, I'd known that was a likelihood, one that I'd have to deal with.

I ducked behind the chairs of a large round table in a corner of the kitchen and held my breath while the footsteps continued down the stairs, through the living room, and into the dining room. He—I didn't know who; all I could see was a silhouette—quickly crossed the carpeted dining area to a large china cabinet against the far wall. Sleepless went up on tiptoes reaching for a squat, long, deep box atop it. I squinted through the posts of a chair back. He appeared to reach around the back of the box and grope for something, but when he turned away from the wall a second later, I was certain his hands were empty.

Ultrasonic alarm, I thought sickly. The place wasn't wired, but the box threw an invisible "net" across the room. A net that I had been but a fraction of a minute from wandering into. Thirty or sixty seconds later—thirty, judging by Sleepless's fleetness of foot—and it would have been goodbye eardrums, hello trouble.

A little shaken, I returned my attention to my unknowing savior. He had padded into the kitchen on stockinged feet and now yanked open the refrigerator door. I blinked against the sudden brightness as he tried to make a selection. He was one of the T-bird boys, all right, the bigger of the two, the one who had relieved me of Kirby's gun that afternoon. He was fully dressed—slacks and dress shirt—and the glossy tan leather of his shoulder holster glinted softly in the refrigerator light. The man was on duty, obviously; his twin was either upstairs sleeping or would be reporting for duty later. Either way, it was probably a good tactical move to get Sleepless out of the way now. Besides, what choice did I have?

I started to come out from around the table, the idea being that I'd slide up silently like the fog rolling in and get the drop on the guy while he had his head in the fridge. However, he made up his mind too quickly and turned away from the icebox with a couple of plastic containers that he deposited on the edge of the table. I became as motionless as the chairs I still half-hid behind. Sleepless didn't notice me in the darkness. He turned back to the icebox, grabbed a paper milk carton, and kneed shut the door. Then he flipped a wall switch and a fluorescent tube over the sink kicked into life.

I dived between two chairs and under the table.

Sleepless hunted through cupboards until he located a

glass, through drawers until he found a fork. He filled the glass, left the carton on the counter, and came over to the table with the milk in one hand and the fork in another. He hooked a foot around a chair leg and slid it away from the table.

I came out with the chair, the bore of my gun three inches from his groin. Sleepless gasped and jumped—a splash of milk dampened my sleeve—then froze.

"Gently, gently," I murmured. "Slowly and quietly." I smiled up at him. "Or you become Sam Spayed." I chuckled silently, deep in my throat. Good one, boy; who cares if the gender's wrong?

° • °

The rest was fairly simple: I disencumbered him a bit and tucked his automatic into my waistband, the parka's one undamaged pocket being stuffed to the breaking point. I signaled for him to set the glass and fork on the counter and secured his wrists with the duct tape I hadn't needed for the break-in. Finally I sliced off a long strip and wrapped it around his head, covering his mouth.

"Do not open till Xmas," I breathed, prodding him into the chair he'd selected for himself. When he was seated I leaned in close. "Kirby's upstairs?"

He nodded, after a brief hesitation.

"Anyone else?"

He wagged his head. No hesitation whatsoever.

I took my left thumb and forefinger and pinched his nostrils. After a few seconds Sleepless started spluttering, and since I didn't want him waking up the whole house, I let go.

"Positive?"

He nodded vigorously.

I taped his ankles to the front legs of the chair, put out the sink light, and slipped into the dining area, where I reset the alarm. Then I hotfooted it through the living room and up the front stairs.

The stairs doubled back on themselves at a wide landing, then climbed on up to a short and narrow hallway. I made out four doors—three bedrooms and a bath, I guessed. The first door I came to was slightly ajar, and a soft yellow light spilled out through the gap. I inched open the door. The room was empty. A tiny lamp on a nightstand produced the amber glare; the spread on the twin bed was rumpled and two pillows were propped against the headboard. An open magazine lay on the bed. A folded blanket was draped over the room's only window. This, then, had been the command post—until the hum of the refrigerator had had to be answered.

I swung closed the door and edged down the hallway. The bathroom and the other bedroom were empty, black. That left me the master bedroom.

This door was closed but not completely. I pushed at it with the fingertips of my left hand and it gave easily. The room was dark and in the darkness someone breathed deeply, the slight trace of a snore on the intake. I moved toward the sound while working the flashlight from my back pocket. Flashlights, guns, screwdrivers, pliers, tape, Boy Scout knife—I was not traveling light this evening. I got the thing out and scanned it across Kirby's sleeping form, fast, too fast to disturb the beautiful dreamer but not so fast that it failed to show the black automatic on the table at bedside. I put away the light and picked up the gun—one more for the collection—and, for want of anyplace to put it, kept it in my left hand. Two-Gun Kid.

I stepped back a pace and hit the wall switch with an elbow. The glass bowl in the ceiling sparked and lit the room and I said loudly, "Rise and shine, Francis," and Kirby made a loud noise and jumped as if his bed were on fire and made a grab for the little gun that wasn't there.

He sat bolt upright, chest heaving, mouth gaping, eyes bulging, forehead glistening—very dramatic. I smiled. "Good day, sunshine; can I get you a cup of hemlock?" It sounded like something Simon Templar would say, which is why I said it.

"You again," he managed eventually.

"Still."

"Jesus Christ, what're you trying to do to me? Gimme a heart attack?" He rubbed his flabby chest even as the light of understanding began to flicker dimly in his brain. "Hey, wait a minute—how'd you get in here—how'd you get past Novitt?"

"I have the ability to cloud men's minds so they cannot see me. You know, like the Shadow. Now if only I could get it to work on women . . ."

"Aw, come on, Nebraska, I already told you everything I know . . ." He started to get out of bed and I leveled my six-shooters at him.

"Just stay comfortable, friend, and so will I. I don't figure you for a great repository of knowledge, Frank, but I doubt you've told me *everything* you know. Like, for instance, you omitted the little fact that the Greater Omaha Vending and Amusements Corporation is actually little more than a front for your real trade in controlled substances. And you forgot to tell me that the local Knights of the Black Hand are real interested in that business, and may be looking to buy you out. Though not with money. And somehow you neglected to mention that you not only knew Walt Jennings, but that he'd been your bag man; and not only had he been your bag man, you were hiding him from the cops, who were and are sort of interested in talking to him about the murder of Jack Castelar—your full-service banker. Very forgetful there, Frank; you've got to start taking that lecithin."

I leaned against a tall dresser near the door. There are a few occasions in every detective story where the square-jawed, even-toothed, clear-eyed hero gets to stand around appreciating the music of his own voice. This was one of them. And as long as I had a captive audience—albeit a decidedly twitchy one, in Kirby's case—I was going to enjoy it.

"So," I said expansively, "I asked myself, in very much these words: What in hell is going on around here? And I think I've got a line on it, Frank, though maybe you can help out by filling in one or two minor gaps."

I frowned in rumination. "Our story begins," I declaimed, "with the murder of a reasonably prominent small banker, Jack Castelar. Everyone is quick to suspect a penny-ante hustler, one Walt Jennings, who is known to have hated Castelar and who is among the missing, his whereabouts unaccounted for at the time in question. So far, we're on solid ground.

"It's soon discovered that the banker's daughter, Kate, has vanished, too—we know not when, we know not where, we know not why. Once again, everyone blames Jennings, and once again that's not unreasonable. He and Kate were lovers; Kate was through with him, but these things are not always reciprocal. Maybe he thought he could change her mind if he took her on the lam with him; maybe she was just insurance.

"That's the synopsis. Oh, sure, a lot of other stuff clouds up the picture, stuff that may or may not have anything to do with the main event—and you know, Frank, that's a big problem with mystery stories. Too many of 'em assume that nothing happens that doesn't have some bearing to some extent on The Case—and that just ain't so. Life goes on, the world keeps on a-turning, and *things happen*. Separating the pertinent from the impertinent, that's the tricky part."

I paused, for effect. "I had a problem for a while with *you* in that regard," I resumed slowly while Kirby gulped and swallowed and swabbed his moist forehead with his pajama sleeve for perhaps the ninety-ninth time. "I was quite sure you hadn't just fallen off the turnip truck—I guessed that at the very least your vending-machine business wasn't completely on the up-and-up—but as far as involvement in the Castelar thing . . ." I shrugged. "I had a lot of doubt, and what could I do but give you the benefit of it?"

"Now hold on—" Kirby squawked.

"Shut up," I barked. "This is the monologue. When we get to audience-participation time I'll let you know."

He closed his mouth with an audible click and sat back heavily against the headboard.

"Thank you. Now where was I? Oh yeah, benefit of the doubt. That pretty much expired this evening, during a little midnight special with none other than the elusive Mr. Jennings himself."

"Hey, I don't know what that son of a bitch tol——"

"The only items of interest to *you* that that son of a bitch told me are, number one, that he had nothing to do with either murder or the disappearance—a claim I tend to believe because there's no good reason for him to risk coming above ground to lie to me, especially when it's the lie you'd expect him to tell—and, number two, that you, Frank Kirby, are the biggest independent drug supplier in the state, you modest son of a gun, you.

"So that leaves us with a double-murderer-slash-kidnaper still at large, and no neat hospital corners at the edges of the case. You can come up with people who may have wanted to kill Castelar—relatives who'll benefit from his death, other foreclosure victims, business rivals, all kinds of stuff that the cops are checking into—but why would any of them have kidnaped Kate? And if they had some unknown reason for killing the father *and* kidnaping the daughter, why kill Christina? What did she have to do with anything? See, the connections are incomplete; once you eliminate Jennings, none of the rest of the dramatis personae seems to meet the prerequisite, that link to all three of the victims."

All four, I corrected myself silently, *if you include Amy.*

"Except, perhaps, you."

He looked at me, but that was about it.

I let my eyes travel the room. It was smallish, but warm and comfortable. On the tall dresser I leaned against was a collection of framed photographs. The largest was a portrait of Kirby and a striking white-haired woman I took to be the late Mrs. K. Near it was the same woman, but with dark hair, and a small girl. Beyond it, the same girl, years later, in high-school cap and gown. One man's family. You don't think of guys like Kirby living in middle-class neighborhoods, cooking burgers on the grill, going to father-daughter breakfasts at the local junior high. You think of them as chiselers and cheats, pushers and murderers and kidnapers—all-around fiends, twenty-four hours a day. But we all have our various hats, our masks, our personas. Office buildings are loaded with guys who must be quick about stabbing their colleagues in the back because they're late for choir practice down at the church.

I turned away from the pictures. "When I found out about your pharmaceutical sideline, I got to thinking that it would bring a lot of cash rolling in, and in that regard the vending-machine angle was inspired, because *it* means a heavy cash flow, too, a legitimate one. If a guy was to salt the clean money with a little of the dirty, cook the books slightly, and live fairly modestly—well, who'd be any the wiser?

"But that works only as long as the sideline stays small and the front stays big. If the amount of dirty money begins to far exceed the amount of clean, then you have a problem. Because the IRS, the Organized Crime Unit, the district attorney—all kinds of people, really—are going to start wondering. Meanwhile it's only getting harder and harder to handle the money that's coming in hand over fist. The stuff just keeps piling up. And it's all dirty. Sooner or later, you've got to get it laundered."

Kirby didn't treat me to any sort of histrionics. I wouldn't have minded a tearful confession or a vituperative denial or even a maniacal laugh and the sneering revelation that Kate was trapped in his secret laboratory, where in exactly three minutes a pre-set timer would release a deadly copperhead to come chomp her on the ankle, heh-heh-heh. But Kirby would have none of it. He swallowed, with difficulty, I thought, and again dragged his sleeve across his brow, but said nothing.

"The way I figure it," I said, "Jack Castelar was running a little dry-cleaning service—for cash customers only. What sort of percentage do they take around these parts, Frank? Probably a lot more reasonable than down around Miami, I'd guess; fewer risks here. But there *are* risks, and the greater the money, the greater the danger. Especially for the banker. I imagine that Castelar wanted to up the percentage, and this made you unhappy. I imagine that you thought having his daughter on your side, in a manner of speaking, might make Castelar more receptive to your point of view. I imagine that something went wrong, Castelar got dead, and you had to begin negotiations all over again with the new administration. Luckily you still had an ace up your sleeve: Kate."

"That's crazy," Kirby said. Finally.

"I agree, Frank, but don't be so hard on yourself; who among us couldn't benefit from thirty minutes' couch time now and then? Besides, in some respects, it's pure genius. You knew that Jennings would be everyone's number-one choice to burn for both crimes. You arranged with Christina to queer any possible alibi—hell, I wouldn't be surprised if you were her secret admirer—but then she got nervous, or greedy, or both, and you decided, what the heck, what's another item on Jennings's tab? That puts you in the free-and-clear on a brace of murders and one kidnaping, boy, and still leaves you in the catbird seat vis-à-vis the West Omaha State Bank and Trust."

I pulled back the hammer on my gun.

"But it puts you in shit with me."

I had had ninety-nine and forty-four one-hundredths percent of Kirby's attention; now I got the other fifty-six one-hundredths. He tensed and fairly quivered, like a pointer in the field zeroing in on a fallen bird, and his thick hands had an unbreakable grip on the sheet covering his legs.

"Now wait—" he sputtered in a high whine.

I leveled the guns at him, feeling distinctly silly—what did I think I was doing; holding up the noon stage? Kirby, however, didn't see the humor in it, so I tried to mask any amusement I might have felt when I said: "I'm not interested. In any part of it. The drugs, the money, the cops, the Mob—I just plain don't care. I want to know only one thing: Where's the girl? Where's Kate? That's it. You tell me, we go get her, and it's farewell, my lovely; I'm out of your hair. You don't tell me"—I raised the guns fractionally, B-movie style—"and I put a dozen rounds into you."

He opened his mouth but nothing came out of it. Sweat glistened on his forehead and upper lip. The top edge of the sheet was stretched taut between his white fists.

I said, "*Now* it's time for you to talk, Frank," and punctuated the sentence with the twin guns.

Kirby coughed a little, dryly, and said chokingly, "You're wrong—you're all wrong—I didn't—I didn't kill anyone—"

"That's the wrong answer." I growled it. Yes, that's

right, I'm tough; stronger than dirt. "You looked awfully cherubic there when you were asleep, but I still didn't take you for an innocent babe-in-arms. I know you're up to your bushy little eyebrows in the business, so what say we just cut straight to the benediction, okay? I want to know where the girl is and I don't feel like waiting. Think fast, and talk fast—like your life depends on it. 'Cause it does."

A sort of a burbling whine came from his throat and a droplet of moisture blazed a trail down his right temple. "I—" he said, and I raised my eyebrows encouragingly. "I—okay, okay, you're right about the business, you're right about me, you're right about Castelar." It was like shaking a tree full of ripe fruit; the words couldn't tumble out of him fast enough, now that he was over his initial bashfulness. They trampled over each other in their mad rush to get out, and they and Kirby's face both wore a certain hysterical shading, but that didn't trouble me. Whatever it took.

"But the rest of it," he babbled, "you've got that all wrong, *I swear it*." His clenched fists trembled and the bedclothes waved like flags on Veterans Day. "I never killed Castelar. Things were going great, really great, they were working good for me and they were working good for him and we'd've been crazy to want to fuck it up. *Really*. I mean, I was *upset* when I heard he'd been killed, I was scared, 'cause I was sure that it was them fucking dagos that did it, you know, and that I was gonna be next." Foam flecked his bottom lip; he licked at it, quickly, and swallowed hard. "And you're right, I was at the bank talking to Castelar, the other Castelar, the brother, about keeping the arrangement going, but he didn't know anything about it and that made him nervous and I was afraid he was gonna do something stupid so *I* was nervous and then you came around asking questions." He took a breath. "And then I was scared you'd find out about me and Castelar if you kept snooping around.

So that's why I told Castelar to get rid of you and that's why I sent the guys after you but I called them off after you came in today and I was gonna leave you alone *I swear to God*. I've got enough problems already, especially if Castelar chickens out on me, I don't need a murder rap too, so I was gonna lay off you and I told Jennings he was on his own and I'm gonna turn the business over to the wops and just mind my own business *really* and I swear I didn't even know Castelar had a kid and I didn't know she'd disappeared and I swear—*I swear*—I don't know where she is or anything *you gotta believe me*."

I looked at him sourly. "That's real convincing and everything, what with all the swearing and what-not—"

"It's the *truth*." His voice broke on the last word. "You gotta believe me—" His eyes bulged with the effort, the strain of *willing* me to believe.

God*damn!* Had I overplayed it, underplayed it, botched the parlay? Had I failed to scare the man as deeply as he acted, to psych him out so thoroughly that he'd think I would actually kill him in cold blood? Or had I fucked up more royally, had I gotten it all, everything, completely, hopelessly, criminally bass-ackward?

"You *gotta*—" Kirby implored, straining forward, trembling violently, so violently as to appear to be in the throes of a seizure.

In my own way, in my own mind, I was just as desperate, just as panicky. If Kirby *was* culpable, and was an Academy Award contender, then what had my juvenile grandstanding cost? Now that he knew what I suspected, what would become of Kate? But if his fear was genuine—what then? Had I been taken in by Jennings and played for a sucker; had I been too quick to think the man wouldn't come forward only to lie?

Sweet Jesus, what was I *doing* here—what was I doing, *period*—what would I do next?

"You *gotta*—" Kirby repeated, and this time his voice quit on him before the second word was complete. His head dropped and his shoulders shook and suddenly the air in the room turned oaty, mealy, and Kirby looked up at me in his anguish, tears dampening his red and blotchy countenance; then he closed his eyes tightly and turned his face against the wooden headboard, which shook in time with the heaving of his shoulders.

I looked down at the sheet still gripped tightly between his hands and watched the spot of moisture over his lap rapidly grow in circumference.

"Christ . . ." I said dully through thick, numb lips as the iron in my fists suddenly grew too heavy to support. Nobody was that good an actor, I told myself. I felt ill, physically ill.

What did I do next? God in heaven, what did I do next?

Chapter Twenty-Five

• • • • • •

I went home. It seemed like the only thing to do.

I parked halfway up the block from my place, locked up, and trudged down the uncleared sidewalk past quiet, darkened houses. A few cars slid up and down the Radial, which my building faces, but otherwise the night was still in both senses of the word. Even the snow had quit, except for the occasional renegade flake parachuting to earth. A peaceful winter's night out here in the heartland. I felt none of that peace, however; just a dull, weary, wearying ache.

I paused in the cone of light that descended from the floodlamp on the north side of the building. The lamp illuminated the adjacent six-car lot, ostensibly for security. The lot currently held a seventh car, straddling the walk that I knew was hidden beneath the snow. The car was Kennerly's. He stepped out of it.

Half a dozen clever greetings jumped to mind, but I voiced none of them. Too much trouble. I stood at the corner of the building and waited as Kennerly, using his car and the one next to it as handrails, eased toward me.

"Well?" he wondered, a trifle breathlessly, when he reached me.

"You don't see her on my arm, do you?" I moved past

him, toward the open stairs at the front of the building. He followed.

"What happened? Did something go wrong?"

"Not something. Someone. Me." Our footsteps echoed dully on the icy stairs.

"I don't understand . . ."

I unlocked the front door and shouldered it open. "It's all very simple," I said, switching on a light and tearing off my coat. "I blew it. I fucked up. I went in and made my big fat grandstand play, only I was in the wrong stadium, or playing the wrong game, or up against a better opponent—I don't know."

I wadded the parka and slammed it into the armchair. Kennerly closed the door with a sigh, removed his own coat, and draped it over mine.

He joined me in the kitchenette, where I had pulled the jug of cheap bourbon from the short cupboards over the stove. I hoisted the bottle by its glass handle. "Drink?"

Kennerly for some reason looked at the square dark face of his gold watch. "Is it too early, for a drink, or too late? Ah, what the hell."

I took two tumblers from the draining rack next to the sink and dragged a tray of cubes from the freezer. "I should warn you, this is not the kind of stuff you're used to. It's aged forty-five seconds. The distillery doesn't dare put its name on the label. And it goes down fighting. But you get six bottles this size for about a buck-fifty, so . . ." I twisted the plastic tray, dropped ice into the glasses, and poured the liquor. The novelists always say *splashed* instead of *poured*, but this was definitely not a *splashed;* more of a *dumped*, in fact.

I handed Kennerly a glass, swirled the cubes in mine, and raised it. "Here's to heroics."

Kennerly tested his and made a face. "Are you going to

fill me in, or are we just going to stand around and get drunk?"

"We can sit, if you like." I returned to the living room and threw myself on the couch, resting my feet against the edge of the coffee table. "And I don't plan to get drunk. For one thing, I've got to get back to work in about"—I checked the time; it was just past three-thirty—"three hours, I suppose. For another, it wouldn't solve anything. And, most significant, swallow more than two or three of the house specials here, and it's terminal hangover." I took another slug, snared a cube with it, sucked on the ice, and watched Kennerly, propped against the wall where the kitchen met the living room, watching me.

I spit the cube back into the glass. "Okay. I went and did what I said I was going to." I had thought it might be a good idea to have someone know what kind of fool stunt I planned to pull, in case I didn't bring it off, and had decided that Kennerly deserved to have his sleep disturbed. After all, who'd gotten me into this? So when I stopped to look up Kirby's address after my audience with Walt Jennings, I called Kennerly and filled him in. He wasn't happy with my little scheme. He wanted to do things the right way, by the book—cops, judges, warrants, like that. I didn't want to wait. I had it figured out, had all the answers, had the master plan. The book was written for lesser mortals, not the likes of me, and what good would a search warrant do if Kirby had Kate stashed away someplace that no one knew about? It would only let him know that we were on to him, and give him time to make other arrangements. No, no cops. Just me: the solitary warrior, unfettered by such encumbrances as the Constitution, police procedure, and rules of evidence; the lightning raider, in and out like quicksilver—with the girl, if it worked.

"It didn't work. Either I put the formula together

wrong, or the theater lost a true artist when Kirby decided on the vending-machine dodge."

"Hell," Kennerly said bitterly, risking another mouthful of the cheap booze. He made less of a face this time. "Where does that leave us?"

"Give you a hint: We're up it without a paddle. If the fault is with my powers of ratiocination, if Kirby is as innocent as he acted, then we're no worse off than before, though certainly no better. If I was right, and Kirby simply outbluffed me . . . then we're well and truly screwed." I quickly sketched the picture for Kennerly, beginning with my meeting with Jennings and ending with Kirby's earnest, and damp, protestations of innocence.

"Perhaps it was Jennings who outbluffed you," Kennerly said quietly into his glass when I had finished.

"I don't think so. If the cops had grabbed him and he insisted he had been framed, I wouldn't believe it for a second. Neither would you; neither would the cops; neither would anybody. What else would he say? But the fact that he risked his neck to come above ground and tell me he was innocent makes me inclined to believe it. Because why should he bother? What *I* think hardly matters to him. I can't see what he could hope to gain."

"Time to escape, while everyone's barking down the wrong trail, that is, Kirby's trail."

"It wasn't Jennings who pointed me toward Kirby; that was my own bright idea. Jennings wasn't pushing any particular suspect. He was as much in the dark as I was. Am."

"I still say you should have called the police immediately. Which reminds me, I forgot to tell you earlier that Banner called my office, since she had been unable to locate you, and left word that the sheriff had followed up on 'the other place.' Does that mean anything to you?"

"Unfortunately, yes." I had almost forgotten about the

abandoned house Castelar owned. It was just as well; if I had remembered, I'd've been clinging to the hope that Kate was hiding there. This way it was not devastating, just disappointing; and not even all that disappointing, in the context of that night's overwhelming disappointments.

"Well, Banner's not going to be too happy when she finds out you and Jennings had a face-to-face and you didn't report it. I know, Jennings was armed, and he arranged a fifteen-minute lead for himself. You told me. But he might still have been in the area, even after fifteen minutes, and if you'd called OPD right away—"

"They'd've found nothing. Jennings is no genius, but he's shrewd. He's kept out of their hands this long, and I doubt he'd've come out into the open without a well-planned escape route lined up. Besides, I was—I *am*—more interested in Kate than Jennings."

"Well, I can't damn you for that, I guess." He took another sip. "You know, this stuff isn't too bad once it gets good and cold." I said nothing. "Well, if not Jennings and not Kirby, then who?"

"Damned if I know." I rubbed my eyes with my free hand. They were tired, dry and itchy, as they had been for days, and now the skin around them and the lids themselves were sore, chafed by my constant rubbing. I forced my hand away and scratched at my scraggly beard, watching particles of dry skin float down to my sweater. I brushed them away. "What do you think of Charles Castelar?"

"I don't, very often. Why?"

"I don't like him much. I don't trust him. I now know that his sudden cooperativeness yesterday was only at Kirby's insistence." I had told Kennerly about Castelar's abrupt about-face at the bank the day before. "What we saw last night, then, was the real Castelar again. And he's in an awful hurry to sweep me under the rug—and you too, for that matter. I got the definite impression he was pretty teed off because Emily ignored his advice to sack us."

"I did, too, but I still say you've got him wrong. I don't like him any better than you do, but I think I know him, or understand him, better. And he doesn't want to have anything to do with that bank. Trust me."

"You know what they say: When a lawyer says *trust me*, he means *fuck you*. Anyway, it might not be that he wants the bank. Maybe he needs money. I know that he recently sold off a fair amount of his shares in the bank because he needed cash. It seemed strange to me that he couldn't've arranged it through his brother in some other fashion; Vince tells me his uncle's a bit of a high roller, and that Jack mightn't've been in too large a hurry to loan him money if Charlie had just overindulged himself. Also, we know that Charlie was out late last night, while Christina was being killed."

"Lots of people were out last night while Christina was being killed," Kennerly countered. "We don't even know that he knew Christina, much less slept with her and killed her. What about Kate; why would he have kidnaped his own niece? And if it was money he wanted, why kill Jack *after* he cashed out his stock? If he'd've done it before, he'd now have more of a voice in the bank, and he probably could convince Emily to advance him the cash he wanted."

"Maybe he had some sort of beef with his brother," I persisted. "Maybe Kate found out what he'd done and he's keeping her under wraps until he figures out his next move. I don't know. All I know is that ol' Uncle Charlie's behaved peculiarly right down the line, and I don't think it'd hurt anything for me to check him out a little."

"You may be right," Kennerly said dubiously. "However—you don't need to bother."

I looked over but Kennerly refused to meet my eyes,

being more interested in some invisible spot on the carpeting.

"I see," I said slowly. "Time to call in the big guns."

"Enough time's gone by. We gave it a shot and it didn't work." At last he looked up. "It's nobody's fault."

It was my turn to look away, toward the drapes hiding the glass doors. "What does Banner think?"

"I haven't discussed it with her, or anyone. I wanted to tell you first; it's only fair. Anyhow, she's not going to object, I can guarantee you that. Remember, she thought we were a couple of idiots from the very beginning, wasting our time. In fact, as I recall, you did, too."

He was smiling. I imitated it. "Yeah, it's ironic: Yesterday morning I was full of reasons for your not putting me on the case; now I'm trying to think of one good reason you should let me continue with it." And not coming up with one, I could have added; there was no denying the fact that I had hardly set the world on fire this time.

"Well, that's it, then." He set his half-finished drink on the counter near him. "In the morning—at a more reasonable hour in the morning, I should say—I'll call Emily and tell her what we think. I'm sure she'll go along with it, but I have to run it by her first, of course. Then I'll call Banner and have her—"

"No, I'll do all that."

"Look, there's no need—"

"Yes, there is a need. I had this image in mind of my rolling up to the place with Kate beside me, returning her to the bosom of her loving family, accepting their accolades and eternal gratitude. The whole nine yards. Well, my bid for a hero's welcome has netted exactly zip. Worse, for all I know, it may have done more harm than good. I'm the one who botched it, I'm the one who should explain it. I planned to head on over there in a few hours anyhow; while I'm there

I'll tell them what you think we should do next. Don't worry, I'll sell the idea."

"I'm not worried about that; I just wish there was something I could say to convince you that you haven't 'botched' anything. It just didn't work out as we'd hoped."

"Thanks, Dad." I peeled myself off of the furniture. "Now, if you don't mind, I'm going to toss you out on your ear. I want to grab a couple of hours' shut-eye . . ." He went without protest. As he slipped into his cold-weather gear we talked about my getting my report to him, him getting my check to me, when we'd get together for lunch—bullshit like that. Finally I shut the door after him, set the deadbolt, and kicked the towel up against the bottom of the door.

I doused the lights and stretched out on the couch, but I didn't sleep. My brain was whirling like a Waring Blendor, getting nowhere fast. I was wrong when I told Kirby that he was the only one besides Jennings who met the three qualifications for the job of Chief Suspect, namely, knowing Jack Castelar, knowing Kate Castelar, *and* knowing Christina Jennings. I must have been. Eliminate Kirby as well as Jennings, and you're left with . . . whom?

Two possibilities: Someone known to us, one of the cast of characters running through this little drama, or someone unknown to us, a total cipher who had managed to keep himself or herself completely out of the picture thus far.

It had to be the former. For one thing, it was hard to imagine that someone with no discernible motive simply got the bug to knock off a pair of unrelated people and kidnap a girl while he was at it. For another, the conventions of the detective genre demand it. The desperate killer can't be some schlep who's unheard of until the last page. Not even Agatha Christie pulls such large rabbits out of her hats.

All right, then, who'd we have? Well, to entertain the

remote possibility that she removed herself from the proceedings, Kate; then Emily, Amy, Vince, and Uncle Charlie.

Uncle Charlie. There he was again.

Jennings had told me he thought Christina had been seeing someone on the side—not hard to believe, based on the way she had been gussied up last night when I stopped by. I had tried to put Frank Kirby into that space in the puzzle, since Jennings had also mentioned that Kirby had had a female friend. But Kirby, apparently, did not fit. So what if we tried Charles Castelar in that slot?

Obviously Charlie would know both Jack and Kate; he could have known Christina. It shouldn't be hard to check. Castelar was a bachelor; maybe he was looking for company one night and wound up with Christina. Or maybe he purposely sought her out, knowing she could help set up Jennings for what he had in mind. Either way, it shouldn't have been hard: The Fat Lady had given me to understand that anything in pants had at least an even chance of sampling Christina's wares.

He could pretend to be smitten by her red hair and shapely legs. Gams. Then, when Jennings was well and truly framed, exit Christina. Compared to fratricide, bimbocide's nothing.

Nuts, this was pointless. Sure, Charlie Castelar *could* have had a reason to want Jack Castelar dead; sure, he *could* have known Christina; sure, he *could* have bumped her off. But *did* he? Any number of people might have wanted Jack Castelar dead—dissatisfied customers, business rivals, even Emily or Vince or Amy or, yes, Uncle Charlie. Once you started digging, who could say what kinds of motives you'd turn up? But they all left you with the question of Kate: Why had she disappeared? If she knew who the killer was, why hadn't she been killed herself? If she had been killed, why had her murder been concealed while the others had not been?

No, something was still missing.

And finding it was no longer my responsibility.

I got up and carried my glass back into the kitchen, where I built another drink, this time *splashing* the liquor over the ice cubes and cutting it about fifty percent with flat generic lemon-lime that had been in the door of the fridge I didn't know how long. I stood leaning against the counter for a good long time, basking in the bluish rays of the fluorescent doughnut, thinking, thinking. And getting nowhere.

Eventually I turned off the light and wandered down the short hall to the bedroom. I turned the couch into a bed, but I didn't undress. I lounged on it for a while, leafing through magazines, finding nothing I cared to read. I picked up a Pronzini novel I'd begun before Jen dropped in and turned my routine inside-out. The book caused me to reflect on how detective writers are inordinately fond of anonymous narrators, perhaps because Hammett never named his operative for the Continental Detective Agency, but how the device really doesn't work over the long haul. Once you start capitalizing Continental Op or Nameless Detective, they stop being nameless.

Well, that was good for about eight minutes. I tossed the paperback aside and got up, wandered over to the desk, sat down, turned on the cheap lamp, and picked up some of the clutter. My notes on The Next Book. I didn't think much more of them now than I had earlier that evening. Yesterday evening, I reminded myself. I skimmed through them. There was a spelling error on the third sheet; I corrected it in blue felt-tip. I started to clean up some prose that was alarmingly awkward, even for rough notes, and soon saw that the single-spaced page was ruined. I took a new legal pad from a side drawer and began to write on it, first merely recopying the revised page, then, without even realizing it at first, taking off afresh from that point. Half a dozen pages later I saw what was happening.

The story line was going in a completely new direction from the one I'd previously sketched. It started from the same point and was heading for the same destination, but it was taking a new route to get there. This was not unusual. Back when I was just a pup, I thought there was but one way to tell a given story, long or short, fiction or nonfiction. You sat down and wrote *the* piece. But the more I wrote, the more acquainted I became with my craft, the more I came to understand that there is a virtually infinite number of ways to construct a story: different points of view, alternative approaches; various styles and tones, shadings and pacings—sometimes several within a single story. This knowledge is both good and bad. Good because it gives you range, breadth as well as depth, a choice of colors for your word-pictures; bad because you become uncomfortable with simply pounding it out like you did in the old days, you sacrifice speed for—you hope—the sake of surer, clearer prose.

After an hour or so I quit, reluctantly. I wasn't fooling myself: My writer's block, if there is such a thing, didn't disintegrate before the irresistible force of my astonishing self-discipline. It was largely my sense of frustration, defeat, impotence about the case I had been politely booted off of that propelled me back into The Next Book. There, on paper, I could indulge myself in the illusion that I have control, that events respond to me, not the other way around.

It's a pleasant-enough dream. But now it was time for an inoculation of reality, hard reality.

I set aside the pad, stood, stretched, and went to look out the small windows set high in the bedroom wall. Still dark. I consulted my watch: not quite six. Two hours until daylight, give or take a few minutes. There are times when I wish daylight would take the day off, when the night is calming, comforting, insulating. This was one of those times. But, as usual, there wasn't a damn thing I could do about it.

I shut off the desk lamp, stripped, showered, made coffee, dressed—all the usual up-and-at-'em stuff. At about seven I forced myself to go down to the car and get it headed in the direction of the Castelars'. Traffic was fairly heavy, thanks to the eight-to-five set. The DJ on WOW was painting a meteorological scene very much like yesterday's, but with the added treat of blizzardlike conditions in the afternoon or evening. Headlights flickered and flared against my damaged windshield, occasionally illuminating the webworks of cracks, charging them with light, making them look like jagged lightning bolts across a darkened summer sky.

The winter sky, meanwhile, had lightened almost imperceptibly. The day was on its way, like it or not.

I didn't.

Chapter Twenty-Six

Dawn must have been reading the paper before she came on duty: Her famous rosy fingers were tattletale gray when she showed up along about eight, almost simultaneous with my arrival at the big old farmhouse.

I pulled around back, got out of the car, and stood in the clean cold air, enjoying the silence of the flat, snow-blanketed landscape. An indifferent snow fell, had been falling intermittently for the last half-hour or so. That and the occasional breath of wind, toppling softened ice and snow from trees and buildings, were the only signs of movement. However, tire tracks up and down the driveway, and footprints and pawprints out back of the house, said there already had been some activity this A.M.

I'm not much of a wide-open-spaces type, but it was beautiful out here, no question about it, even on a gloomy, sunless day like today, even with the news I was bearing.

I headed up the cement stairs to the back porch. I had a key to the kitchen door, having lined it up yesterday morning in anticipation of coming in late last night, but I knocked a few times and waited several minutes before I used it.

The old spaniel greeted me, and I had to stop and stoop and pat him down sufficiently before he'd let me into the room and out of my winter wear. "Anybody home?" I called, even though somebody obviously was: I heard water running upstairs and saw that the coffee maker's orange light was illuminated. I wandered through the high-ceilinged kitchen and into the dining room just as Vince Castelar bounded down the stairs.

"Oh, it's you," he said, coming into the room. "I thought Mom had forgotten something."

"Up and off already? Where to, at this early hour?"

He continued through the dining room and into the kitchen. I followed, watched him take down a coffee cup, shook my head when he offered me one. "Charlie came by a little while ago to take her to the airport. Some of my dad's cousins from down south are getting in, I don't know, around nine, I think." He poured a cup and looked at me. "The funeral's tomorrow, you know."

I didn't know. I hadn't even thought about it, though I had been aware that burial had been delayed by the cops, by Kate's absence, by the weather. Evidently the M.E. felt he had learned all he was going to learn from the decedent; the relatives were winging in while there was a brief break in the weather; and Kate . . . Well, Kate was going to miss it.

Vince filled his cup and, leaning against the center island, faced me. "I thought you were going to stay here again last night," he said, a dash of recrimination seasoning his words. "I didn't stay up, because I have to go back to my classes this morning, but I didn't hear you come in—and, no offense, you don't look like you got much sleep."

"I didn't get any sleep; I was on the job. Crime waits for no man."

He laughed unamusedly. "Found Jennings yet?"

"Didn't have to. He found me."

Vince had been in the act of raising his cup to his lips; now he stopped and looked at me sharply. "What?"

I sighed. "When's your mother due back?"

"Not for two, three hours at least," he answered impatiently. "What do you mean, Jennings found you? You *saw* him?"

"Saw him, heard him, spoke with him. I would've asked to put my fingers in the wounds in his hands and feet and side, but it seemed presumptuous."

"And you let him go?" The boy was incredulous, and I didn't much blame him.

"I didn't have a lot of choice, Vince. He had me, as we in the business say, covered. However, if I didn't get my man, I did get some interesting information out of him."

"Yeah? What?" He was not impressed.

"Maybe I'll have a cup of that stuff after all," I said, stalling. The kid made no move to get it for me, so I helped myself while he looked on, irritated, disgusted, impatient. I took a white mug with black and red Scotties on the side, filled it, and gingerly tried the coffee.

"Well?"

"Did you make this coffee?"

He made an exasperated sound. "Yes," he spat. "Would you like breakfast, too? Come on, what did Jennings say?"

"He said he didn't kill your father. Or Christina. And he didn't know anything had happened to Kate until I told him. This is good coffee; do you grind your own beans?"

"And you *believed* him? Are you *crazy*? What would you expect him to say—that he was guilty?"

"I wouldn't expect him to say anything; I wouldn't expect him to show his face at all. If he was guilty, especially."

"If he was . . ." Words temporarily failed him. With his free hand he raked his fluffy blond hair into the disheveled pompadour he affected. "Jesus Christ," he finally breathed. "I don't believe you. You had him right there—you *had* him—and you let him just . . ." He shook his head, turned away from me, and gazed out the windows over the sink.

I said nothing, drank silently, waited.

Finally Vince spoke, without turning. "Aw, shit," he sighed. "I guess none of it matters anyway. I suppose it doesn't make any difference whether they ever catch Jennings. They'd put him in jail for a few years and then he'd be out, and Dad would still be dead. What's the difference?"

"Aren't we forgetting someone?"

He turned. "Kate?" he said sadly. "If she isn't dead already, she's as good as."

"That's a hell of an attitude," I said in sudden anger.

"Well, forgive me for being pessimistic." His voice was acid, his demeanor that of the other morning, when I first met him. "I guess I'm not as broad-minded as you, letting a killer go because he told you he didn't do it." Vince's face turned its splotchy red. Hot coffee spilled on his hand and wrist as his muscles quivered involuntarily in anger and frustration; he ignored it.

"Look—"

"Well, maybe it's better this way," he growled venomously. "I'd rather see her dead than—"

"Than what?" I found I was holding my breath.

He glared at me, turned, dumped his coffee into the sink, and wiped his hand violently on a checked dishtowel.

"*What*, Vince?"

He whirled as if he meant to throttle me; I may have drawn back instinctively, I don't know. Vince wadded the towel and threw it into the sink. "You know," he said angrily. "You've thought it, I've thought it—everyone has. That if Jennings didn't kidnap Kate, then she must've *wanted* to go with him. And that means she either didn't care what he'd done . . . or she helped him."

I talked, said the mindless, meaningless sorts of things the situation called for. Vince wasn't interested. He pulled the dishtowel from the sink and carefully folded it, smoothing it flat on the plastic countertop. "God, I wish she'd've listened to me," Vince said, but not to me, not to anybody. The heat was gone and his voice was hurtful, sorrowful. "I told her that sleeping with that son of a bitch was only making things worse, that sooner or later something bad was going to happen, real bad. But she only laughed." He seemed to recall that I existed, and cast me a glance over his right shoulder. "Dad too. I told you: He never listened. Never. I warned him, but he wouldn't take me seriously. He never worried about Jennings, but I knew something was going to happen, especially after Kate started seeing him. The tension around here . . . And the hell of it is, Kate didn't love Jennings, not really. I *know* she didn't. She couldn't have, not a pig like that."

"Then why'd she spend time with him?"

He closed his eyes. "Like I said before, I don't know. Maybe because he was different from the kind of guys she usually dated. You know. He was older, kind of rough, rough-edged. Maybe a girl would find that kind of guy exciting. I can understand that. But not *that guy*. Not Jennings." He opened his eyes. They shone with unshed tears. "Something was bound to happen. I kept telling them, something was bound to happen. But they never took me seriously. Never. Now he's dead." He wiped impatiently at his eyes. "And I meant what I said: I'd rather Kate be dead, too, than have anything to do with Dad's murder."

Neither of us had heard Amy come down the stairs and into the dining room, neither of us knew how long she had been standing there or how much she had heard. One thing was for certain: She had caught her brother's last few words, and she didn't care for them. I saw her—sensed her—out of the corner of my eye before I realized who or what she was, and jumped out of my skin and the way as she rocketed past.

She flew by me like she was on roller skates and lit into her brother like a Thai boxer, with fists and feet, pounding him, pummeling him, kicking him on his arms and chest and legs while he tried futilely to avoid the blows. Her screams were incoherent, incomprehensible. And loud: The hair on my arms quivered to attention; the spaniel tried to make himself very small in the far corner of the room.

I forced myself out of my paralysis of shock and grabbed Amy by her upper arms, peeling her off Vince. That was harder than it sounds: Though the girl was nothing but skin and bones, she was fighting like one possessed and I—foolishly—was worried about hurting her. Both of the kids were yelling now. I may have shouted a thing or two as well; it would have fit the mood. Finally I got her off him but she wanted more, and kicked and elbowed at me to try and get it. I crossed my arms above her small breasts and pulled her back against my chest, hard, giving her no room for leverage. "Stop it!" I yelled into her ear. "*Stop* it!"

Those well-chosen words calmed her, marginally. Her chest heaved and she still strained against me, but she was no longer the hellion. However, I didn't release her yet.

Vince was putting himself back together, touching scratches on his face and neck and examining his blood-dotted fingertips. "Goddamn," he breathed incredulously. "You drew blood, you little—"

He pulled back his arm and I pirouetted, dragging Amy, to put myself between them. "Enough of that," I said loudly, but Amy drowned me out:

"I don't care," she yelled. "You shouldn't have said that. Don't *ever* say that. Kate isn't dead. She *isn't*. And she didn't hurt Daddy. She loved him. She loved him better than any of us—" And with that the screams dissolved into sobs, loud, racking sobs that shook her slim, reedy body, and mine too.

I let her go.

Vince reached past me to touch her shoulder. "Jesus,

Amy," he began slowly, but she pulled away violently before he could speak further and ran through the dining room into the living room. The boy and I exchanged looks. I had no pearls of wisdom, and not enough breath to dispense them if I had.

"Shit." Vince snapped off a paper towel to dab at his face. The bloodshed was nothing—a paper cut produces more—but the welts on his face and throat were red and raw-looking. "I better go talk to her . . ."

I stopped him with a gesture. "Maybe you'd better not," I countered breathlessly. "I skipped my vitamins this morning and I'm not up for another workout like this." I gulped more air. "Why don't you go clean up a little. I'll talk to her."

He hesitated. "Well . . ." he said with a glance in the direction of the living room. "I should be getting down to school. I was sort of waiting for the doctor to show . . ."

"That's fine; I'll baby-sit till then. Go ahead."

He vacillated another instant or two, then went, through the kitchen and up the stairs. A moment later I heard water running through pipes in the ceiling. Only then did I follow Amy.

She was in the living room, in the oversized chair she had retreated to after finding her murdered father. Today, however, instead of staring mutely into the cold fireplace, she was crying softly, face hidden, forehead against her knees, hands wrapped around her long, long legs—she was nothing but legs, it seemed, and yet somehow she managed to fold them and fit them into the big chair with her.

I hesitated in the doorway, wondering if this picture was better or worse than the other day's. Better, I decided provisionally. But I was still uncertain how to proceed, how to keep from inadvertently doing her further injury. Just be around, Koosje had said. I shrugged mentally. That much I could manage, I figured.

So I came slowly into the warm, countrified room, and seated myself on a low bench near the hearth, facing Amy. She didn't seem to notice me but went on with her crying, her face still hidden. The scene called for me to offer her my handkerchief, but I didn't have one—not a clean one, at any rate. So I did nothing, said nothing, for a long while. Finally, however, I had to act: I reached across and covered the long, thin hands that were linked around her shins. The hands were freezing. I gripped them gently. "Amy . . ."

Her head came up. The sad eyes were infinitely more sorrowful now, red and streaming. "He shouldn't have said those things," she said, and sniffled.

"I know. So does Vince. He was just upset, you know, he didn't mean it. Everyone's real upset . . ." *Brilliant,* I thought, *absolutely stellar*.

"Kate isn't dead." She said it with conviction, gulping spasmodically for wind, wiping at her nose with a sleeve of her pink sweatshirt. "I *know* she isn't. And"—a snuffle and a wet hiccup—"she didn't have anything to do with the guy who killed my-my-my dad, either." She dragged the sleeve across her wet eyes and hiccupped several more times. "She wouldn't, ever—she *wouldn't*. Kate loved Daddy. She loved him a lot. More than I ever did . . ." She squeezed her eyes shut but the tears leaked out anyway and flowed down her long, smooth face. Her mouth twisted in a silent cry that again racked her body almost convulsively.

I got up off the stool and leaned over her, put my arms around her. Amy's slender arms wrapped around my back and held me tight, so tight I almost lost my balance. Her breath was hot against the side of my neck, her tears even more. "Come on, Amy, honey," I murmured into her dark hair, largely because I didn't know what else to say. How come when it really counts the *mots justes* vanish, the silver tongue tarnishes, the quick wit's shoelaces are tied together?

"I know that Kate's just fine, and I know you loved your dad a whole lot. I can tell by the way you're acting n——"

"Not e-enough," she sobbed. "Not like K-Kate did. I tried, I really tried, but I just c-c-couldn't—"

The blood was thundering in my brain now, making it difficult to hear or understand Amy even though she was speaking into my ear. A crazy sort of panic grabbed me by the nape of the neck, shook me a little, and rolled sweat down my back. I wished, hoped, prayed to hear the back door open and Koosje walk in *right now*—

She didn't. I heard nothing but the roaring in my ears and the sound of Amy's agony, seemingly miles and miles distant.

Gently, uncertainly, I pulled back enough to look into Amy's face. She wouldn't meet my eyes. I put a fist under her chin and raised her head, forced her to look at me. "Amy." I stopped, listened to the voices screaming in my brain, tried to shut them out. I swallowed and licked my lips, fearing—knowing, with gut-wrenching certainty—that anything I did at this point would be the wrong thing, one more wrong thing, one more miscalculation in a hideous morass of miscalculations, mistakes, misjudgments—

Koosje—damn it—*get* here—

"Amy," I repeated, my voice sounding curiously muffled and quiet compared to the shrillness of the internal voices. "Honey." I smoothed her long hair, still somewhat cool and damp from her morning shower. "This is really important. Okay? What do you mean when you say you tried? What do you mean when you say Kate loved your father better than you could? . . ."

The girl looked at me with a strange, eerie calm, and I was afraid that she was retreating, pulling back from me the way she pulled away from Koosje. Worse, I feared that I had forced a backlash, a regression, a flight to that other world

Koosje worried about losing her to. But apparently not. She sniffled and wiped her eyes again and spoke, very quietly, and I knew what she was going to say before she so much as opened her mouth:

"Kate used to sleep with him." She said it softly, slowly—as if she was trying to break it to me gently.

A missing piece clicked into place.

I could hardly hear Amy now over the pounding in my ears and the babble of voices in my brain. I suppose I didn't really need to hear any more, any of the slow, halting confession, of how, late at night, Amy would sometimes hear her father slip into Kate's room. How, even when Amy was much, much younger, she somehow knew what they were doing, knew that it wasn't right—but couldn't understand how it could be wrong if it was all right with her daddy. How she knew and feared that her turn would come someday. How it did, when she was eleven and the house was empty. How she tried to love him the way Kate did but couldn't, just couldn't. How her crying frightened him, drove him from the room. How he never loved her again after that, just Kate . . .

After a while I became aware that she had quit talking. I was looking straight at her but I hadn't seen her; now I came back to that room, and it was like coming out of a deep, drugged sleep. Amy was staring blankly into the fireplace again, and a shudder went through me. But I spoke her name and she looked at me with heavy-lidded eyes. "I should have tried harder," she said regretfully.

My throat was dry and constricted. I cleared it. "You didn't do anything wrong, honey. Do you understand me? You did nothing wrong." She smiled with ancient, infinite sadness, as if to say, *Poor man, you simply don't understand and you never will.*

I held one of her small hands between my own. "Are you okay?"

She nodded.

"All right. I have to go upstairs for a minute, okay? But I'll be here until Ko——until Dr. Van der Beek comes. All right?" Again she nodded sleepily.

I left her then, forced myself to walk slowly from the living room, then dashed up the carpeted stairs. They ended in a wide hallway whose walls were covered with framed photographs. One man's family, I thought bleakly as I flung open doors. Even in the best of homes . . .

The upper floor was vacant, no sign of Vince. As distracted as I was, I could hardly believe that he could have come downstairs and left without my hearing him.

The answer came in the master bedroom. Narrow French doors opened onto a small terrace on the south side of the house. From the terrace a long open-plank staircase, snow-covered, led to the ground. The snow had been disturbed.

"God*damn!*"

I tore out of the room and headed down the carpeted stairs to the dining room, jumping the last five or six in one of those foolhardy moves you wouldn't even think about if your brain were hitting on all the cylinders. I threw a glance into the living room: Amy seemed to be dozing in her wing-backed chair.

The dog thought this was the greatest thing since kibble. He was at my heels, he was in front of me, flopping around in the spaniel's loose-limbed way, whining with excitement as I tried to get my goddamn boots on. I wound the long ends of the laces around my ankles and tied them in front. It would do.

I stood to reach for my coat and, through the window over the kitchen sink, saw a heavy-coated figure moving across the yard, toward the large barn that stood in the distance, carrying a knapsack in his left hand.

I swore again and banged out the back door. The dog followed but I managed to trap him in the porch. He didn't like it much.

"Vince!" I yelled, starting toward him in an easy trot, already wishing I'd've spent the two seconds it would have taken to grab my parka. The snow fell freely now, and it was hard to see where the sky met the field farther on.

The walker paused, turned.

It was then I saw the long barrel of the rifle he toted in the crook of his right arm.

Chapter Twenty-Seven

I dived from the porch stairs, hit the ground, grateful for the cushion of the soft new snow, and rolled behind my Chevy, mainly for cover but also with a mind toward claiming the .38 in the glove box. For all I knew, Vince was merely taking the rifle to a gunsmith for repairs—but we nervous types tend to jump to conclusions, usually the unpleasantest one first.

I reached up for the door handle on the passenger side. Locked. Hell. I poked my head up just enough to peek through the window at the driver's-side door. Same deal. One of my few good habits was hitting the lock button with my elbow whenever I left the car. My insurance man had convinced me it was a good idea. I made a mental note to cancel with that agency if I ever got the chance. Of course, it wasn't his fault that my keys were in the pocket of my parka, in the house.

Crouching at the front tire, I tried to think. I could run back to the house and grab my keys. But I figured Vince was heading for the barn because he had a car or a truck there, and I didn't want to risk losing him. I had already blundered enough for one week.

So I stuck my head up over the fender and yelled again.

The boy was almost to the barn—he had double-timed it after my appearance, but the snow made it tough going. Now he stopped, dropped the backpack, and raised the gun. The swirling snow all but obscured the picture, but I could see that rifle clearly enough.

I fell back behind the car and waited for the report that didn't come.

The snow was too deep for a peek under the car, so I edged forward, my hands burning from the cold, and looked around the front bumper.

Vince was ducking through a side door of the barn.

I scrambled to my feet and toward the garage that stood to the south, ten or fifteen feet off the back of the house. Flattened against the rear wall. Waited a beat. Crouched near the foundation. Looked around the corner.

Nothing. Silence, except for my ragged, shivery breathing.

The back door of the garage was unlocked. I went in. It was warm here; an automatic gas heater mounted overhead purred softly. I hit the switch inside the door and two bare bulbs in the ceiling threw weak light on two cars, a small silver-gray Mercedes and a copper-and-tan New Yorker. The third stall, I guessed, was for the maroon Cutlass that the cops had impounded.

Besides the cars, the garage held bikes and toys, tires, tools, hoses, empty flower pots, a wheelbarrow, cardboard boxes, boards—the usual garagey junk. I was looking for some kind of weapon, a BB gun, a slingshot, but all I came up with was an old and heavy ax, suspended alongside other tools on nails driven into the wall studs.

Young Dan'l Boone, I thought, ripping the oiled-leather hood from the ax head.

After checking the cars—they were both unlocked, but the drivers had thoughtlessly neglected to leave the firing pins in place—I decided there was nothing to do but get on with it. I looked out through the grimy windows of one of the overhead doors and, seeing no activity in the direction of the barn, hoisted the door up.

The sound of the door's rollers in their metal tracks was echoed by a similar but louder noise from the barn. Its huge overhead door—the barn doors you've heard so much about apparently being a thing of the past—was slowly rolling up, mechanically.

I quit the garage and ran diagonally across the yard, half crouched and well aware of how ridiculous that position was: The area between the garage and the barn offered not so much as a tree stump for cover, and if Vince stepped out now and took aim, that was it. Unless I was quick enough to swat the bullet out of the air, like Wonder Woman, with the flat of the ax blade.

I hit the broad side of the barn, between the front corner of the building and the side door that Vince had entered through. The door-opener inside was still groaning and clattering; I thought and hoped it would be enough to cover the noise I made getting over here and the sound of the breathing I was now trying to get under control. When the most exercise you get is twelve-ounce curls . . .

The side door was ajar five or six inches. I bent low again and peeked in.

The barn was huge—what else would you expect of a barn?—dark, cold, and musty-smelling. It was also comparatively empty; Castelar hadn't farmed, he rented his land to others, and so he hadn't owned the massive combines, tractors, and what-not that such colossal buildings ordinarily house. The structure contained mainly—stuff. Odds and ends littered the far wall. High overhead, boards that had been placed across rafters supported cardboard boxes and wooden crates. On the dirt floor, at the far end of the barn, a thirties-era Buick rested on concrete blocks, half-covered by a dusty tarp.

Toward the front sat a Deere tractor, a smallish one, probably used for odd jobs and hauling. A riding mower, currently equipped for snow removal, was parked in front of it. Next to them stood a big rust-pitted blue-and-white Blazer.

The overhead door was literally overhead now; the rackety opener quit automatically. The Blazer's motor jumped in to fill the gap.

I was four feet from the passenger side. I bumped open the barn door, crossed the frozen dirt in two steps, and yanked open the car door with my left hand.

The rifle was propped against the seat. I reached for it, but Vince was quicker. He grabbed it and, immediately realizing he didn't have room to maneuver for a shot, swung it around and stabbed at me with the butt.

He caught me on the left side of my head, a glancing blow, but at the moment it felt like my ear had been torn off. My grip on the door frame dissolved, I lost my balance and slipped off the running board, collapsing into some litter piled against the wall of the barn.

Vince hit the gas and the Blazer roared out of the building.

I rolled against the wall in an effort to keep legs and other vital parts out of the way of the car's huge tires. Then I came up on one knee and gently probed the side of my head. My hand came away bloody and dirty. I figured I was lucky that my ears were cold-numbed, otherwise the pain might have been paralyzing. As it was, I merely felt like I could chew right through the barn wall.

I forced myself up and out the side door.

Vince was rounding the corner of the barn in a wide, half-skidding arc. He was giving it too much gas; all four wheels were spinning like mad, too fast for them to gain proper traction in the snow. The myth that you can't spin-out with four-wheel drive is just that: a myth.

I lurched forward, toward the machine. Vince saw me. It was reflected in his eyes. He grabbed for the rifle and I saw the barrel briefly above the dashboard, but what was he going to do with it, shoot out his own windshield? He must have asked himself the same question in the same instant, for the gun disappeared and he tramped on the accelerator again.

The big car—or truck, or whatever you want to call it—swung toward me. I half-jumped, half-slipped backward and fell flat into the thick, fluffy ground cover. No time to make snow angels, I thought wildly, fighting to my feet as the Blazer fishtailed past.

Vince had the thing more or less under control now. He played the wheel with the expertise you soon acquire driving in our Midwestern winters, and was getting the fishtailing smoothed out, getting the Blazer aimed fairly straight toward the long driveway, getting away. In the time it would take me to get inside, get my keys, and get going, I wouldn't even know which direction he'd chosen. The main highway was three miles north. And from there . . . anywhere.

Son of a bitch.

I grabbed the sweat-darkened handle of the old ax lying next to my outline in the snow. With no clear objective in mind I fell/ran toward the receding Blazer, the breath burning in my lungs, hands and feet and lungs throbbing from the cold, tears of pain and frustration running down my face and freezing in my beard. I felt like the kid in *Shane*.

The Blazer was into the curve where the drive fanned around the back of the house. He took it too quickly and the back end slid far to the right.

I was at the rear bumper.

A belch of blue exhaust choked me as Vince straightened the car and gave her the gas.

I pulled back the ax and, in a batter's swing, brought it down hard and fast. The blade bit into the right rear tire, just below the curve of the exhaust pipe.

The explosion of pressurized air that followed sent the ax rocketing backward, out of my grip. Luckily. Because I ducked to the left, cowering, covering my head, picturing a pretty graphic decapitation, while the Blazer growled and skidded and tilted to the right. Its momentum and the slight unevenness of the yard were enough to topple it onto the passenger side, its grille toward the house.

I pulled myself to my feet. It seemed to be all I was doing these days. My left leg must have gone on coffee break, but I managed to get over to the Blazer anyway and crawl up the undercarriage to the driver's-side door. I opened it.

Vince lay crumpled against the opposite door, bleeding, moaning and crying quietly. This is why you should always wear your seat belt. I reached past him and pulled the rifle out of the footwell near his head, then flung it—the rifle—backhanded across the yard as far as I could. Which was perhaps four feet. Then I reached back in and grabbed the ends of the short scarf dangling from inside his opened coat. I yanked on them and lifted his head four or five inches. He groaned and raised his hands limply.

"Where?" I croaked. There was blood in my mouth. I hadn't noticed before.

Vince groaned louder.

I released the scarf and his head fell against the door with a hollow *thump*. He groaned louder. I tugged on the knitting once more.

"*Where,*" I repeated, louder. Spit and blood jumped from my lips.

His eyes opened fractionally, closed again. He moved his mouth. "The—other place," he grunted raspingly.

I let go the scarf again and leaned back, raising my head, waiting out the dizziness and the nausea. I was kneeling on the back side window, my hands braced on the lower and upper door frames, my face toward the colorless sky. Snowflakes melted in my open mouth. Their coolness felt good.

The Blazer's engine had cut out, which is why I could hear the other car, turning into the driveway. I opened my eyes, squinted through the curtain of snow. The little red car drew nearer. *Koosje*, I thought stupidly. *What a morning to be late for work.*

I started the long climb down. It suddenly seemed like hard work. I'd've never made it if it weren't for gravity.

Chapter Twenty-Eight

In detective novels there almost invariably comes a point, usually along about Chapter Twenty-eight, where the tough-minded, square-jawed, hard-headed hero-for-hire explains to the benighted, befuddled flatfoots how he unraveled the complexities of the crime in question; how he deduced, logically and psychologically, the foul perpetrator's identity; and how he then tricked or trapped him into exposing himself, figuratively speaking.

There was no such scene in this little production. I had hardly been light-years ahead of the cops in my reasoning. And even after we had our man, even after Kate Castelar fingered him as her captor and told us how he had explained to her his scheme to kill their father and let Jennings take the fall, we could only guess at the number and depth of his motives. They were good guesses, a lot of them—most were proved out in the prosecutor's investigation, the hearing, and Vince's subsequent treatment—but they were still guesses. And for some reason, I had a hard time convincing the cops that I was just guessing right along with them, that I, unlike Philo Vance, had no secret inside line to the killer's psyche.

The sheriff and his men, who were waiting for me when I limped back from "the other place" with Kate, weren't too bad. They had plenty of questions, but this wasn't really their case and they were content to let it be so. The sheriff, a slow-moving, soft-spoken fellow about my height but with twenty pounds and as many years on me, seemed to think it was his responsibility merely to keep the motor ticking until OPD showed up; he questioned me halfheartedly while Bruhn, the family doctor, whom Koosje also had called while I was off being heroic, patched my ear and told me I may have cracked a rib.

The sheriff shook his head lethargically as I gingerly pulled my sweater down. "I've lived in this county my whole life, except for two years working for Uncle Sam, and nothing like this ever happened before," he said with mild reproach, as if it were my fault. "And I'll tell you something else." He leaned forward conspiratorially and the wooden dining chair beneath him creaked mildly. "We never used to have this kind of stuff—this child abuse, this incest, and stuff—when I was younger. You never heard a thing about it, now it's all you *do* hear." It struck me as the most fatheaded comment I'd heard in months—would a fifteenth-century European say the New World didn't exist before Columbus because he never heard anyone talk about it?—but I'd learned the hard way never to express such opinions to outstate sheriffs, especially when I'm in their counties.

I grunted noncommittally and said, "Don't you think you should move the party to someplace a little more secure?"

He leaned back in the chair. "He's fine up there. There's no fight left in him, and if there was, my men'd take care of it." Two strapping lads were keeping an eye on Vince in his bedroom; Koosje was off somewhere with Amy; Kate was asleep in her own bed, thanks to ol' Doc Bruhn, who seemed a little quick on the draw with the tranquilizers; and Mom, Uncle Charlie, and the southern contingent had yet to arrive. "Everything stays as is until OPD shows up and says otherwise."

I shrugged. It was nothing to me, and it was a hell of a lot more comfortable here than any county jail I'd ever seen. The coffee was better, too. I drank some and said, "Too bad our boy Knut missed all the fun and games."

The sheriff colored slightly. "He went off duty at eight. Besides, the only fun and games he'll be seeing for the next few weeks will be at a desk. He's on restricted assignment for not telling the Omaha police about the reported sighting of Jennings the other night. Dumb-ass jerk; I don't know what he was thinking."

"He was thinking he could collar Jennings himself and make 'The CBS Morning News.'" I chuckled sadistically. "The irony is, Jennings never was spooking around here, or anywhere. Vince concocted it—in part, I suppose, to make Jennings look even more culpable, to make everyone that much quicker to blame him for Christina's murder that same night." I winced inwardly as I explained it. I had been so sure of my theory about Jennings's hanging around that I never asked him if in fact he had been. If I had, it might have pointed me in the right direction that much sooner.

The sheriff opened his mouth but was interrupted by a racket on the back porch. Since I hurt everywhere, I let the old spaniel, who had been dozing under the dining table, take care of jumping up and trouncing over to say hello to the Omaha cops.

Kim Banner came through the kitchen in stockinged feet, still wearing her overcoat and cap, carrying a gigantic bag. The other detective, Swanson, the stout, pale one, was taking the time to hang up his coat and scarf. Neither of them fussed over the dog, so I called him over and scratched his floppy ears while he stood with his forepaws in my lap.

"Well, if it isn't Mr. Holmes of Baker Street," Banner murmured as she entered the dining room. She nodded at the sheriff, who had stood. "Another case solved, eh what?" She deposited the bag on the table, shucked her coat and hung it over a chair back, and rooted through the purse for a pair of low-heeled shoes.

"Now you see what comes of keeping pure thoughts."

"Uh-huh." She slipped on the shoes and looked at the sheriff. "What's the story?"

"The Castelar boy's upstairs. A couple of my deputies are watching him, but he's not going anywhere. He's pretty banged up, but he'll be all right. As for the rest"—he inclined his head toward me—"he can tell you better than I can."

Banner looked at me. Her face was serious, but her eyes were narrowed to half-moons. "Your time, boy. Tell our viewers all about how you cracked the case of the century. What was the big break?"

I raised my Scottie-dog mug. "The coffee."

One eyebrow went up and her mouth went down. Swanson, standing in the doorway between the kitchen and the dining room, made a noise.

"Seriously. I know it sounds insane, but the night I stayed here, the same night Christina was killed, as it happens, Vince made me a pot of coffee that was abysmal—thick, bitter, muddy, really awful. But the coffee he made this morning was fine. Great, in fact. Now, Columbo could build a whole case around that. Me, I'm a little slower. But I did get to thinking about how lousy I felt yesterday: logy, unfocused—dopey. I wondered if someone had doped me. The only one with the opportunity was Vince, and this place is lousy with downers. I sort of naturally wondered why he'd want to."

"To be sure you'd be out cold when he slipped out to murder Christina Jennings. Or whatever her real name is. Was."

"Very good, Watson. But wrong. I arrived here more than half an hour after the latest time the coroner thinks

Christina could have been killed. Vince already had dispatched Christina and hastened back here to make his phony report."

"But he made the report at midnight," Banner protested. "To kill Christina at eleven, shower and dress, and be here by twelve . . ."

"He'd have to move pretty fast. He did. But keep in mind, number one, that coroners' estimates of time of death are just that—estimates. That eleven-to-two figure could be off by ten minutes or more on either end. And number two, Vince claimed Jennings was here at around midnight, but he didn't actually phone the sheriff's office until . . ."

"Twelve twenty-two," the older man supplied.

I turned toward Banner and spread my hands. "If quizzed, he could say that maybe it was five or six minutes *after* midnight when he heard noises out front, then he checked on his mother and sister, investigated a little, and so on. The point is, he could have had something like ninety minutes between the time he knifed Christina and the time he called the sheriff. That's more than enough time."

Banner pursed her lips and raked a hand through her short blondish hair. "O . . . kay," she said speculatively. "And he killed her because she knew he had killed his own father and framed her husband, boyfriend, roommate, whatever you want to call him. She must have been in on it all along. And the cockeyed stories she kept telling us and taking back, they were to help us think Jennings was guilty, that she was lying to protect him." She wagged her head sadly. "Do I have to ask what was in it for her?"

"She was doing a big favor for someone who was going to wind up owning a bank. As Jennings himself said, Christina would've cut off her own head for the right price. Cutting off Jennings's would've been easie——"

"Wait a minute; what do you mean, 'Jennings himself said'—what have you forgotten to tell me?"

"Oh. Yeah." I cleared my throat and told her about my midnight rendezvous with Walt Jennings. I also told her about my subsequent meeting with Frank Kirby—I had to, because that was supposed to be the reason I didn't take time to call the cops as I should have—but I glossed over the details. Specifically, I omitted the parts about breaking in and tying people up and waving guns around.

As I spoke, Banner propped an elbow on the tabletop and rested her chin in her palm. When I finished she said, almost boredly, "You know, you're wide open to, oh gosh, a whole bunch of charges. I mean, it doesn't matter that Jennings is innocent. He was still wanted for suspicion, and you had an obligation to let us know that he had contacted you."

"A civic obligation, maybe, but not a legal one, I don't think. I couldn't have collared him myself." A slight lie, there; I think I could have taken him on any number of occasions, though getting out of the Bottom Dollar would've been another story. "And what good would it have done for me to call you, after he was long gone, and say he used to be there? It all zeroes out."

"And what about Kirby? You know, Narcotics has been working on him for a long time. If you've screwed that up . . ."

"Narcotics should kiss me: I may have quashed their dreams of seeing Kirby behind bars, but I have it on good authority that he is going to be retiring from business. I guess it's bad for his nerves or something."

She grunted. "Well . . . I hope you realize there are a lot of hard-asses who'd run you in just because."

"'Then I can merely say that I am most fortunate in my inquisitor,'" I misquoted from *The Benson Murder Case*. "Should I look forward to any trouble from the DA?"

"I doubt it. See, on top of everything, Jennings is dead."

"Holy shit," the sheriff said. It was his first commentary on the debriefing.

"You can say that again," Banner drawled. "We got it in the car on the way up from the city. The Kansas state cops stopped him for a minor violation—a dead headlight, or something equally stupid—near Lyndon, Kansas, wherever the hell that is, earlier this morning. Jennings rabbited. They chased him. He spun out on an icy patch and plowed into a light pole on the highway. Killed him dead, the poor bastard . . . All right, where are we at? I suppose the kid killed the old man because he wanted to run the bank; why'd he nab his own sister?"

"I think we're going to find out it's a whole lot more complicated than Vince just being peeved because Dad wanted to take his own sweet time turning the business over to him. There's that; there's a whole big father-son thing, with Vince feeling that Jack never took him seriously and wouldn't trust him with any real responsibility; and then there's the fact that, well, evidently, Castelar had an incestuous relationship with Kate, going back many years."

"Ho-ly shit," Banner said, flabbergasted, with a glance toward Swanson, who made no sign. Stoic.

"I agree," I said. "Even in the best families, huh? He tried to get something going with Amy a while back, but she got hysterical or something and it scared him off. Anyhow, I think you're going to find that all this—this stuff is kind of mixed up together in Vince's head and that it all, to one extent or another, figures into him doing what he did."

"Why do you figure he set up Jennings to take the rap?"

I emptied my mug. "I'm just guessing, but, in the first place, Jennings was the perfect target. He had the motive, he'd made frequent threats, he'd be the prime suspect even if you didn't try to frame him. With Christina's statement, he was practically in the chair. What I can't figure is where Vince and Christina linked up. My guess is that when he began concocting the plan, he poked around some into Jennings's life, turned up the fact of Christina's existence, and contrived to meet her. He'd know right off that her cooperation could be bought; she'd see the life of Reilly after the kid got his bank; and the rest, as they say, is hysterical."

"I don't suppose Christina found it too humorous when he slashed her to death."

"I don't suppose so either, but Vince could hardly be expected to let her live happily ever after. She'd soak him for the rest of his life."

"Plus, assuming Jennings was taken alive, Christina would have been put on the stand and grilled like a Porterhouse," Banner said meditatively. "You wouldn't want to gamble on whether or not she could take the heat. What's your second place?"

"Right. In the second place, Jennings was an appealing patsy because of his relationship with Kate. This morning, Kate told me something that Vince said to her the night he killed their father. She didn't understand it, but I think a headshrinker could have a lot of fun with it.

"That evening, fairly early, Vince called Kate at the hotel—it was no secret she was there—said he was going to the airport to meet Jack's flight and did she want to come along. She did; she wanted to talk to him. So he swung by for her, but, of course, he wasn't going to the airport. He told Kate what he had in mind, and she was, shall we say, unenthusiastic. Vince was prepared for that contingency with a pair of handcuffs and a bandanna to use as a gag. He subdued her and brought her back out here.

"But what he said to her was this: 'You'll come around.' Kate didn't get it, but I think what he was saying was, 'You'll come around to seeing that this is for your own good; I'm saving you from the old man, from Jennings, from yourself.' It's just a guess—you could talk to Koosje and get all the right lingo—but I know that Vince was extremely dismayed about Kate and Jennings. He felt that she was debasing herself, demeaning herself by being with him. And I think she was; I think it was purposeful. From what I hear, her sexual tastes had become kind of—well, out of the mainstream. Having your old man jumping you is bound to run all sorts of numbers on your sexual identity and emotional stability. Vince thought he was yanking her off the road to ruin. And he must have thought she'd see that sooner or later and all would be forgiven—after all, he couldn't've expected to keep her chained to a radiator in that other farmhouse forever."

"Yeah," Banner said, turning toward the sheriff. "How come your guys didn't find her there before, if they checked the place out?"

He cleared his throat but I spoke. "Don't take it out on him; she wasn't there. Vince situated her here, in the garage, in the back seat of Jack's Mercedes."

"Christ," said the sheriff. "She could've froze."

I shook my head. "The garage is heated. Odd as it sounds, Vince wouldn't've endangered her. Everything he did, or most of it, at any rate, was motivated by love. A distorted love, true, but love nevertheless.

"In fact, the reason he spiked my coffee—not that anyone seems too concerned about it—was to make sure I'd be sawing wood when he slipped out to check on Kate. She told me he did that several times a day and a couple of times at night ever since he locked her up over there. Which he did after he knew you'd inspected the place." I looked at Banner. "By the way, I thought you were double-checking that place for me."

She looked at the sheriff, who coughed gently. "We were going to get on that today."

"Yesterday would've been better for the girl," Banner upbraided.

I said nothing. It was true. But I was selfish enough to be glad to have played the hero after all, to have had the chance to charge up on my noble white steed—all right, my banged-up red Chevy—and rescue the fair damsel. Kate had been kept in the upstairs bedroom of the other house. The room was empty except for a flowered mattress and a thermostatically controlled electric heater, placed beyond her reach. She was handcuffed by the ankle to a radiator pipe, and only that foot and the top of her head was visible beneath the heavy unzipped sleeping bag she had wrapped around her—a bag identical to the one I'd borrowed the night before last.

When I woke her, when she identified me and the significance of my identity flooded into her mind, she cried. I held her. It was almost worth the cracked rib, the torn ear, the new set of bruises and abrasions on top of the old sore muscles, the lost sleep, the dashed expectations and accumulated frustration.

What am I saying? It was *definitely* worth it.

◦ • ◦

The morning faded into afternoon and the snow beyond the dining room windows continued. We agreed that Vince could've easily driven the Blazer over the blockage at the end of the driveway the night he killed his father, run the gun to the Jenningses' for us to find the next day, and masked his tire tracks with a little spadework. We decided his insistence that Jennings had killed Kate owed as much to his confused mental state as to his desire to stir up still more antipathy toward the fugitive. We disagreed about his plan for reintroducing Kate once she'd "come around": I said he must have had a scheme, a kidnaping story the born-again Kate would go along with, something to tell the cops. Banner was more of the mind that Vince was crazy and that was that. She speculated that Vince would eventually have had to kill Kate, too—perhaps even "for her own good"—once he realized that she never would see the light.

Eventually, when she got tired of hearing the same record over and over again, she kicked me loose and went to see about getting Vince transferred to a city facility. I got while the getting was good. The snowstorm hadn't let up any, and it was uncommonly dark for three in the afternoon.

The roads were becoming impossible and impassable by the time I arrived at Koosje's place not quite two and a half hours later. I breathed a sigh of relief as I burst into the lot and glided into what might have been a parking space. Every time I paused to clear freezing snow from my windshield wipers I wondered if I was going to be able to get moving again. Every time I began a turn I wondered where I might end up. Every time I stopped for a light I wondered if the numbskull behind me was going to be able to stop.

It's a winter wonderland, all right.

I locked the car, got my gym bag and a sack of supplies out of the trunk, and slogged through knee-deep drifts to Koosje's building.

"I was getting worried," she said when she shut her door behind me. "When we left the farm, you said you had one errand to run and then you were going to come here and get snowed in with me. I was beginning to think you decided to spend the night in a ditch instead."

"A couple of times it looked like it." I handed her the paper bag. "Provender. I found a liquor store that hadn't closed yet." I handed her the canvas bag. "My getting-snowed-in-kit. It pays to be prepared."

She took the things away and I peeled off my wet coat,

hat, and boots. The apartment was warm; it smelled wonderful. A Streisand record played softly. A fire glowed on the TV.

Koosje returned with a pair of glasses filled with beer. "This was your errand? You risked your life and a fantastic dinner for beer?"

"Not just beer, but Grölsch. You should like it; it comes from Holland. Anyhow, that was not the errand of which I spoke. I had to do something about the damage inflicted on my poor old car." I tasted the beer. It was grand—full, smooth, leaving a slight cereal flavor on the tongue.

"Couldn't a new windshield have waited? You've been driving blind for three days." She tried her beer and made a face. "Strong. Speaking of your car: You never explained to me why Vince smashed it up, and how he knew where it was to smash. Did he know you were going to the college?"

I shook my head and swallowed. "I didn't know myself until I went. But it wasn't Vince's handiwork on the car. About the only crime he didn't commit."

"Then—I don't get it."

"By process of elimination, Robin, and some educated guesswork, we come round to that unflinching public servant, G. Knut, sheriff's deputy."

She smiled and dropped herself next to me on the couch. "You're kidding."

"I told you: I never kid, unless I'm joking, and I'm not. It dawned on me this morning when the sheriff said Knut was in the doghouse. I had guessed that he had neglected to tell Banner about Vince's supposedly seeing Jennings because he wanted to make the arrest himself. That's why he pooh-poohed Vince's claim so adamantly, too. Meanwhile, I have this mental picture of him driving up and down the heartland all night, hoping to run down Jennings and get his picture in the *World-Herald*.

"Well, that was about as far as he could go toward keeping OPD out of 'his' case. But me . . . he already was unfond of me after our first encounter, and I'm sure he didn't want any competition from a private cop. So he made a forceful and very graphic suggestion that I abandon the case."

"He followed you." Koosje was delighted.

"He did. He was coming off duty just about the time I came on the scene, he went back to the station, changed, got his own car—a big red Dodge truck—and picked up my trail when I left the Castelars' sometime later. He must have followed me around all day, looking for an opportunity to do . . . something. He didn't have a clear-cut plan in mind; what he did had that spur-of-the-moment feel. He didn't have a hammer, so he tried to smash the windshield with that phallic symbol he totes around, that aluminum flashlight. The paint was some old stuff he had left over in the back of his truck." I drank beer.

"So your errand . . ."

"Oh, that. Well, it seemed to me only fair that Knut make good on the damages. So since I was in the neighborhood, and I doubted I'd ever get out that way again, I looked him up in town and stopped by to suggest he make restitution."

"And did he?"

"No. He laughed at me—and was I *relieved*. 'Cause I'd already slashed all four of his tires, plus the spare, in anticipation of his refusal."

"You—are—insane," Koosje laughed.

"He'll be heading for work in"—I studied my wristwatch—"oh, with this snow, maybe only another hour or so. And I figure, with the weather and everything, he should be able to get a service truck out there . . . oh, middle part of next week, say."

"Won't he be mad?"

"I hope so; that's the point."

She hid her eyes and shook her head and said, "Oh no" several times.

I emptied my glass and stood.

"If you need another one," Koosje said weakly, "take mine."

I took her glass. "What I really need is a shower." I looked down at her and wiggled my eyebrows. "I might need some help in there; I'm pretty banged up, you know."

"Sorry, you're on your own. I've got to keep an eye on the stove."

"Yeah, sure, a few hours later and everyone forgets you're a hero."

Koosje had one of those massaging shower heads; I stood under it quite a while. It was no substitute for a full night's sleep, but it was doing a creditable job of unkinking the knots and washing away the effects of the past few days. Vince Castelar would never stand trial, I knew, but that was no longer my concern. Let the cops, the lawyers, the shrinks, and the judges sweat that one. I was more worried about the girls, but Koosje had been hopeful—especially about Amy, now that we knew what had been at the root of her problem. I counted that as a victory; it was a hell of a lot more important in my book than a murder conviction.

I limped out of the shower, dried myself, wiped fog from Koosje's large plate-mirror, and looked at myself, distorted, in the watery glass. Not too much the worse for wear, externally, at least, and those scrapes and bruises would heal. Elsewhere, deeper, I could still probe and easily find the pain, that ache of longing, that would take a good deal more time to dissolve. But Koosje would help. A lot. And as for Kim Banner—well, I don't suppose either of us knew at that point. As we'd said all along, we'd wait and see.

It wasn't as if I'd given Koosje my private-eye fraternity pin or anything.

"Hell," I told my reflection. "When did I get so dynamite with women?"

It had no answer for me, so I shrugged off the question, lathered up with a bar of hand soap, found my razor, and began to shave. I moved slowly, carefully, from the base of my neck up my throat to the edge of my beard, back and up, back and up.

On my fourth pass my reflection and I exchanged glances. "What the hell," we said simultaneously; and I went ahead and got rid of the silly, scruffy thing.